For Stuart Watson

Jeff Buchanan was born in New Zealand. He works as an aid and development specialist in developing countries. For the past decade he has been based in Papua New Guinea with his partner. His children's fiction has been highly successful. *Sucking Feijoas* is his first novel for adults.

This revised and expanded edition published in 2001
by Gay Men's Press, PO Box 3220, Brighton BN2 5AU

Gay Men's Press is an imprint of Millivres Ltd,
part of the Millivres Prowler Group,
Worldwide House, 116-134 Bayham Street,
London NW1 0BA

www.gaymenspress.co.uk

First published 1998 by Tandem Press, 2 Rugby Road,
Birkenhead, North Shore City, New Zealand

World Copyright © 2001 Jeff Buchanan

Jeff Buchanan has asserted his right to be identified as the author of
this work in accordance with the Copyright, Designs and Patents Act 1988

A CIP Catalogue record of this book is available from the British Library

ISBN 1 902852 30 3

Distributed in Europe by Central Books
99 Wallis Road, London E9 5LN

Distibuted in North America by Consortium,
1045 Westgate Drive, St Paul, MN 55114-1065

Distributed in Australia by Bulldog Books,
P O Box 300, Beaconsfield, NSW 2014

Printed and bound in Finland by WS Bookwell

Sucking Feijoas

Jeff Buchanan

1 Just a kiss

'I wonder if there are Japanese queers,' George Crossett thought as he went into the Seaview Road toilet block. An ammoniac smell greeted him, its familiarity in his nostrils as keen as the apprehension over the last week with the threat of a Japanese invasion of New Zealand. He wondered briefly if Japanese queers would solicit in the same way as Allied servicemen did, but the thought was too traitorous, too revolting; a bandy-legged Jap who would smell of fish and salt. There was nothing in his imagination that allowed for a Jap to be attractive enough to have sex with. Uniform, power, masculinity; all his usual associations of lust had nothing in common with the enemy.

George did up his fly and surveyed the empty toilets, the grey walls, the row of cubicles, the broken sink and the ineffective light bulb. The taboo world where men like him gathered. Queers. Poofs. Nancies. This was the world where he felt secure. But it wasn't always that way. He remembered the young man who had spat in his face and the pimply youth who had demanded fifteen pounds. The ideal of security congealed and went sour in his head like the concept of humanity did in the minds of those New Plymouth people who had heard what the Japs did to women and children.

He left the dank toilets and entered the bright sunlit world. A fleecy cloud, odd in its aloneness, hovered in the distance. He crossed the shingle road and sauntered down to the gun emplacements that had just been concreted into permanence on the side of the hill overlooking the glinting Tasman Sea.

Out there were Japanese submarines, no doubt spying on him at this moment. He laughed at the thought that they would be the only people who were watching him cruising in his lunch hour, alone on the high cliff overlooking New Plymouth, a windswept port on the west coast of an island at the bottom of the South Pacific. New Plymouth, so remote, always so secure, suddenly taken by the shoulders and shaken by an awareness that war was about to blast its cosiness. He stood for a moment or two with his eyes closed, seeing himself repulsing the enemy, dead men littered about him, having to fight with all the glorious valour that he'd heard about from the ageing men who had fought at the Somme and Gallipoli: George Crossett battling the Japanese in his home town in 1942, a machine-gun gripped in his hands; the smell, the blood, the heroism.

'Goodness!' he exclaimed as an approaching American serviceman disturbed his reverie.

'Great day,' the man said. 'Surprise you, did I?' He gave a quick laugh.

'I…' George mumbled. He dropped his cap and as he bent to retrieve it, the other man scooped it up, touching George's hand as he did. They looked at each other in a half-crouching position, their faces close enough that had they puckered for a kiss, their lips would have brushed.

'The bunker's handy,' the American said, straightening himself and brushing his uniform. With a mixture of magnetism and physical pressure, he led George into the gun emplacement's dark opening, which smelled of fresh concrete and new secrets.

'But…' George uttered. Pinned against the wall as he was, he found the courage to dismiss danger at the prospect of sex with a uniformed American. It was like being in the toilets. When you got to a certain stage in the proceedings, the fact of danger made the hurry all the more exciting. He undid his trousers, fumbling first with his belt and then with his buttons, and then smiling with the sweet relief of his trousers falling. The American took a step back, excited by the sight of a man undressing. George turned, his heart bumping madly, so that the American could enter him all the more quickly, with rehearsed military efficiency.

'Nice ass,' the American said. He didn't pull down his trousers but stood there staring, so George turned to see what was happening. For a moment, he thought it was a set-up, that the man was about to flash a military card and put him under arrest for soliciting. Those much-whispered-about cases; solicited, humiliated, dishonourable discharge. But the man smiled, in his eyes a sweetness that George could hardly fathom.

'Kiss me,' the American said. 'I've never been kissed by a Kiwi.'

George wasn't used to tenderness from strangers. For a second or two he was transfixed.

'Come on,' the American urged. 'Just a kiss.'

They embraced, kissed and clung to each other.

'You have beautiful lips,' the American said. 'I didn't know that Kiwi men could be so passionate.'

Suddenly they heard footsteps coming up the path and the sound of voices, several men talking in an animated tone as they approached the gun emplacement. George hadn't pulled up his trousers. He looked with terror at his companion.

'This'll be the first to go into operation,' a thick voice said.

'The Japs'll bomb it. They're not stupid.'

'As soon as it's dry we'll camouflage.'

'How much room is there?'

A shadow appeared across the aperture where the guns would be placed, and under which the two men were crouching. George looked up and his eyes met those of Captain Smart. The two men stared at each other for several tortuous seconds, and George would remember forever the surprise, amusement and loathing in Smart's expression.

'The Americans reckon on four placements for each...' a very proper British voice said. Captain Smart retreated but then reappeared at the doorway, his back blocking what light entered through that small aperture. 'This concrete's still wet, gentlemen. The bastards mixed in too much water. Now let's have a look down there at number two position.'

The party of men moved away, the crunching gravel sounding in George's ears like the tintinnabulous effects of fear. He was just about to whisper, 'They've gone,' when the shadow again moved across the dim light in the gun emplacement, and Smart's voice hissed, 'You bastards move it as soon as you hear me whistle. Up the back way, through the gorse, so that you don't bump into the hierarchy parked outside the toilets.'

George felt frozen. The American's face was taut with apprehension. 'Be aware,' Smart snarled, 'that you'll pay for this, you filthy bastards.' This time there was no surprise or amusement in his eyes, only loathing.

*

George felt unsettled for several days after the incident in the gun emplacement. It was so easy to be stupid, to get caught. He stood at the front window of his house, which he shared with his elderly father, Albert. There was a view of Mount Egmont to the left of their section; its huge volcanic cone, bare of snow and tinged purple in the summer, reared above the trimmed privet hedges. His father was out in the garden tending to his roses, struggling to rear perfect blooms, applying some secret formula of skill and determination that George had never tried to understand. The Tasman Sea and the port were also visible - the scene was as peaceful as any citizen could require. The sea was a smooth teal lake behind the garden in full bloom. In the background the wireless hummed some inconsequential song about love and loss and fortitude. He felt nothing for the lyrics, a popular ditty that everyone was dancing to in the halls and cabarets filled with wartime revellers. It was music for the sort of place where you tossed a girl around and said sweet things in her ear as the violins and crooning melted the night. Sweet words in a girl's ear, the sea, the view, the fact that in those ships out there in the port there was so much life, so much happening, and yet in George there was the thick confusion of not belonging.

He went to his bedroom, lay down and slipped into a doze. He was wrenched from the middle of a frightening dream by the voice of his friend Desmond Potter.

'Wake up, George. Your old man was walking down to the shops, said to come in and find you.'

'Bloody nightmare about the Japs, the bastards.'

'Bloody nightmares all right, mate,' Des said. 'Looks like the Solomons for our division.' He was tall, his thick blond hair recently cropped by the military barber. 'Reckon you've got the right position being stuck here in charge of supplies.' He said it with such a voice as to indicate some malice at George's role as stores accountant, ordering the fruit, vegetables and dairy supplies for the troops.

'Don't bring that up again, Des,' George said. 'I'm the one who trained as an accountant. It's my line. Who'd feed you bastards if it weren't for me?'

Des sat next to him on the bed. He was in uniform, though he could have been in civvies, considering it was his furlough. But he no longer bothered. It was as if the only suitable outfit now was the one that proved what he dreaded: being shipped off to some hell-hole in the Pacific to get blown up by Japs.

'Des, I'll…' George searched for words.

'What? Not getting sentimental again, are we? All girlie?'

'I heard this morning that you were going.'

'So why didn't you visit me? Were you just going to stay in bed sulking?'

'You know why. I didn't want to speak to Sybil. Do I need to say it? Your boyfriend coming to see the man he buggers.'

'Sybil doesn't know about us. How could she?' Des said. It was a well-used line, no better than a refrain from a song now tired from habitual humming. He put his hand on George's leg and stroked it in a way that did not match his sarcasm.

'How could anyone be that dumb?' George asked. 'Anyway, how does she feel about you going? The silly bint.'

'Jesus, mate, the sooner you get a Jap bayonet up your bum, the better. Put you out of your bloody misery. Kiss me, you bastard. Come on, with your tongue.'

George complied, then asked, 'When do you go?'

'Six days, with the Americans.' Des was unbuttoning George's fly, slowly, intent on the fact that it was a soldier's outfit, and not satin and lace like Sybil's outfits.

'It's come to this,' George said. 'Like the day...'

'Don't say it.'

'...you told me you were going to marry Sybil.'

'I didn't have a family like yours, a father to protect me.'

George had stripped off. He ran his tongue across the light blond stubble on Des's face, then down his chest and across to his left nipple. 'You'll rot quite quickly in the tropics,' he whispered.

'You'll be up there soon enough. They need every man they've got.'

'They *do* need every man,' George thought. 'Even those they hate, like me. That's why Smart hasn't acted.' Again he saw the captain's eyes filled with loathing. 'Who'll order your cheese and cabbages?' he asked.

'They'll stick sheilas in that position. You wait.'

Albert Crossett had come back from the shops; they heard him banging pots and whistling in the kitchen as they played with each other.

'I'm going to miss this,' Des said. 'Sybil wouldn't have the slightest idea about companionship.'

Des fucking Sybil, that old vision, the one that made George squirm with hatred. Des with his mouth on her nipple, his cock pushing inside her. 'Blast it,' he said, propping himself up on the cushions with his arms crossed.

'What's wrong now?' Des asked.

'Of course,' he answered himself. 'What else? You want me to wash it in front of you each time? Boil it in chlorine?'

'You can wash off juices, but…' George said.

'There's a world war on and you're still carrying on about silly issues, George.'

'I want you,' George said. 'You say it's sentimental, but it's a fact.'

'Jesus, mate. You, me. Two men, it's…'

'You love me?' George asked.

'You know I do,' Des replied. I've never said that to Sybil.'

'That you love me?' George said sarcastically.

'What do I have to do to prove it? Okay, I made a mistake and got married, but it was because I had to.'

'Bugger,' George said, 'I hate being a fairy.'

'Except when there's a man in your crotch,' Des said.

'It's not fair, is it? It'll be Sybil who gets to grieve openly if you don't make it back, wail and all that, and all I'll have are a few bloody letters and some memories. I won't be able to say a thing to anyone.'

From the kitchen they heard the Zip boiling and the old man hoicking as he turned it off.

'Come back, Des, please,' George pleaded.

'You want me to?'

'God!'

'God won't help you, you fairy,' Des said. 'Or me. God doesn't like homosexuals. I'll have to make a pact with the devil if I want to return from the Solomons and marry a bloke.'

*

It was a wet wintry day in 1936. Albert Crossett and his son had returned from the funeral. George at the age of seventeen, standing in the living room wearing a black suit, with a black tie and armband. He looked about but couldn't move, his legs stuck to the carpet as if by glue, his head alive with the horrors of the last few weeks. The room still smelled of medicines and visits from old aunties and neighbours. He closed his eyes and wanted to go running out of the garden, deadened by winter, and rushing back to see Des, who, with his family, had waved goodbye at the cemetery and gone home.

'It's all over,' Albert said to his son. 'We're on our own now that Mum's gone, but she suffered and now...'

'Why did the minister have to say so much about God?'

'That's the way things are, son. Hypocrisy if you like, but remember that your mother had a belief in God. It was important to her.'

'I don't understand,' the boy said. 'That minister has only been in New Plymouth two weeks and he talked as if he had known her so well.'

'We'll have tea in the kitchen,' Albert said. 'Mrs Baker's baked us some scones,' he added.

'Mrs Baker baked the scones. Lucky she isn't a butcher!'

'Oh,'Albert said, 'it's a funny old life, isn't it?' He was pouring the tea when suddenly, as if he had just remembered something, he got up and walked across to the drawers in the kitchen cabinet. Rummaging about, he produced a packet of Capstan cigarettes.

'Mum hated you smoking,' George said.

'Have one,' his father said. 'Special occasion. Helps the nerves.'

The gust of a gale came swooping in off the flanks of Mount Egmont and bashed against the side of the house.

'Did Desmond say he was coming to visit you later?' Albert asked, drawing with obvious luxury on his cigarette.

'He said he would if his mother let him, but she reckoned it might be too much for me, I mean with Mum...'

'His parents don't know that you play with each other, do they?' Albert said.

The eyes of father and son met and locked for several seconds before the youth flushed, looked away and stammered, 'We... we play lots of games.'

'I'm not talking about football, George.'

'I...'

'It's all right. I know what you and Desmond do in the bedroom. I found your sheets with stains on them. I never told your mother of course, and I think you should avoid letting his parents into the secret.'

'But...'

'Life is difficult, and there are a number of things you need to know about it. I saw what was happening, but I've waited two years to talk about it because of your mother.'

George felt shame eat him like acid going through his body, a sensation travelling from his legs to his ears, like a vile liquid swilling around in him. Something had ended and he wasn't quite sure what.

'I don't like smoking,' he said. 'It makes me feel sick.'

'When I was in the army in the Great War – you've heard all the stories, the medals are in the top drawer.'

'I know, Dad...'

'In France it was. There was a man from Auckland in my division. I was only four years older than you are now, twenty-one. God, how they forced us off to that quagmire I'll never work out, but it changed a lot of us. I saw...'

He got up and went to the window so that he wouldn't have to look at his son. For a minute he didn't speak but stood there looking at the direction of the mountain and seeing only cloud and rain and the pohutukawa trees being thrashed by the gale. He leaned against the kitchen sink, his arms pushing against it, with his head lowered as tears flowed from his eyes.

'I loved your mother,' he said finally, blowing his nose on his handkerchief. 'Phyllis was everything to me. I've been thinking right throughout this illness, these two years, that I want to make her a memorial garden. She loved gardens, George. The two of us can do it if you'll help me.'

The night had come running in as if the absent sun had been dispensed with nothing more than a cursory wink. The howling wind was scratching at loose places in the corrugated-iron roof, those sounds and that feeling that preceded a storm, for which the Taranaki coast was famous.

'Well,' Albert sighed, 'I'd better get on with answering the sympathy cards.'

George lay in his bedroom listening to the wireless: the Prime Minister's views on the Depression, Hitler in Germany and the rise of Spanish fascism. It was an enormous world. The wind fused the ugliness and sadness he felt with the vastness of the experience. The huge wind, and the monstrous ocean, he saw them struggling with each other in an infinity of space and darkness, and the little Morse code signals he'd learned at Scouts kept going peep, peep, peep, uselessly against dark and evil. The sperm in his sheets on which he and Des had wiped themselves on so many occasions. The pungent smell. He'd thought of it as being thick and delicious, like slightly aged custard, but it now had another meaning. He got up and went into the living room, where his father sat playing patience. At the door he stood watching the weak fire licking a damp macrocarpa log, the purple flame insignificant, cheerless.

'Dad,' he said, 'I want you to finish what you were telling me about the man from Auckland.'

'I was upset, son, about your mother.'

'In France... what did you say about it?'

'Bring me the matches. They're on the kitchen table.'

As George handed his father the matchbox their eyes met.

'There isn't anything wrong... not in my estimation...' Albert faltered.

'With what?' George knew what, but he couldn't say it because he was seventeen and addressing his father.

'Many things happened in that war.' For a moment Albert fidgeted with his cigarette packet as if expecting to find within it something to help him through this moment, but then he replaced it on the table and smiled.

'There are some men who like women and some who don't. You're very young... Your flirtation with Desmond, I've watched it. It's very strong, but it might be something you grow out of. I was married to your mother, a wife...' They both looked at the ceiling as he paused. 'Basically, men who have strong feelings, sexual ones, for other men, are thought to be evil, sinners, misfits. They're called... do you know the names?'

'Queers,' his son said. Their eyes met again fleetingly. During two years of nursing a sick woman they had learned to say deep things with glances.

'I was in France when I met this man from Auckland. I was taken aback. It shouldn't have happened. I never thought about going with French whores because I was devoted to your mother. Well... well, about men. I mean... there were thoughts... but... but I met this man called Jack and we...'

'Like Des?'

'Yes, only we were both married. We were in our twenties, but yes...'

George suddenly felt very grown up. His mother had died two days ago and he had just been to her awkward and confusing funeral. Now his father was trying to tell him something important.

'In fact,' Albert continued, 'we would've stayed in Europe after the war if he, if Jack, hadn't drowned at Brighton Beach. It was a very strong friendship, many men had them.'

The ashtray was filled with cigarette butts and Albert got up to empty them in the fireplace. His cardigan looked shabby and sad.

'Look at me, George,' he said. 'It's like not believing in God. Most people do. You and I don't, but we keep that quiet. It's the same with this matter we're discussing. You must be very careful, because most people think it's an aberration for a man to love another man, and you'll get into enormous trouble if you flaunt it. And some men like that can't accept their own natures.'

'Jack?' George asked.

'Yes, Jack. He drank a bottle of whisky and then walked out into the sea because he couldn't stand the anguish of being a homosexual.'

*

'What did Sybil say about you coming out here with me?' George asked. The sea swelled languidly and slurped around the rocks, the seaweed slithering about, brown and black fronds thick and shining.

'She doesn't understand,' Des said.

'But why should she?' George replied. 'She's not my father. You weren't that lucky in marriage. Money, yes.' He looked at his lover, the rocks of Moturoa Island and the sun hard behind him. His blond hair was shaven into bristles that appeared iridescent in the light glinting from the heaving sea. George blinked, capturing the moment. His handsome boyfriend, the trials they'd been through and this snatched moment of happiness, the two of them together on an island. He passed Des the flask of whisky and indicated with a jut of his head and a smile that he should take a good swig of it. 'It's mad,' he said, 'that two men can't live together.'

'Mad? It's not mad. We're homosexuals, mate. Men can't.' Des tipped back the flask. 'Forget it.'

Two seagulls rose in perfect harmony, then swooped down and screeched a protest at the two intruders.

'Like the bloody Japs,' George said. 'Precision bombing.' He gulped the whisky, its strength taking him aback, and as he coughed he said, 'How the hell can we repel the Japs? They'll do the same here as they did in Nanking and Shanghai. They don't like white people any more than they do the Chinese.'

'That's why I'm going to the Solomons, mate,' Des said. 'So bastards like you can sleep safely in your beds in New Plymouth.' He picked his cap off the rock and slammed his fist into it fiercely, then threw it down again. 'The bloody thing is,' he continued, 'that fighting Nips is the only thing I've ever felt right about. It's cut and dried. No way out. It's not like this balancing act between you and Sybil.'

'When you get back,' George said, 'we'll get a farm together. No one will notice if we're farmers. Leave Sybil. Cut and dried.'

'Shut up,' Des said. 'The police will find out. Everyone will be suspicious. They'll cut and dry us all right, and you know it.' He stood up and raised his hands against the sun, staring back at New Plymouth and the mountain that rose up behind it. 'There's a dinghy on its way,' he said. 'I can't say goodbye to you in the same way I have to Sybil.'

'You shouldn't have married.'

'How many times do I have to say it... I couldn't stand the thought of everyone knowing. And sooner or later they'll get to you. Bachelors.' He laughed. 'Confirmed bachelors, only till you're thirty and then...'

'Money didn't enter into it, of course,' George said snidely. He realised that he had unintentionally cocked his head in that way Des said only queers did. He did it again, accentuating the movement. 'We could have lived together with my father as cover.'

'That's not true. We'd be caught for sure, and I don't want everyone knowing. It wasn't for the money, you know that. I just don't want to be one of them. A poofter. A queer.'

'So why did you call yourself a homosexual just now?' George asked, looking up and shading his eyes against the sun's glare.

'We both are, face facts. But I can get an erection with a woman and you can't.'

'Only because I never wanted to or never tried.'

'Then you try living here as a bachelor when you're older. Look at Jim McTuffety. Everyone laughs at him. What about James Marikovich? Laughing stock, and he tries to look normal.'

The approaching dinghy, with two figures, disappeared momentarily in the swell and then bobbed on the crest of a wave before it fell back again.

'But I don't look queer like McTuffety or Marikovich,' George said.

13

'You wouldn't knock around with me so openly if...'

'But we do spend too much time together. That's what Sybil reckons. She reckons I should grow up and stop having boys over to play, as she puts it.'

'Do I?' George paused, suddenly afraid. He looked up at his mate, his eyes begging for reassurance.

'Do you what?'

'Look queer?'

'You're very handsome. Your eyes look like a queer's. How do I know? Do I look queer?'

'No!' George exclaimed. 'You don't.'

'Sybil says...'

'Just shut up. I don't want to know what Sybil thinks. I'm not allowed to cry when you go, and I've buggered you more times than...'

'Enough, George mate, please, enough now. Just drink and enjoy yourself. I'm leaving in five days.'

Their commander had told them to be happy, to make the most of the days before they sailed off to fight the Japs, that this was a time to stand tall, to be proud of the fact that they were going off to defend their country. Des stared at the man sitting below him: George Crossett, handsome, intelligent, a queer. He wanted Sybil to be George, or George to be Sybil; anything but this dilemma. A tempting thought struck Des; it would be better to die in action under the cover of bravery than to carry on like this in New Plymouth. A wife, a boyfriend, a town that was ready to pull his eyes out. Suicide was an answer, like that farmer in Okato, or the chemist he'd had sex with on several occasions and who had overdosed on one of his own concoctions. 'If I come back alive, I'll get help, I'll only be with Sybil,' he thought.

'The booze,' George said. 'Give me another swig, and a cigarette.'

'Pose for me.' Des said. 'Yeah, just like that with your legs crossed, so I can remember what a poofter you are.'

He uttered a drunken, ambiguous laugh, half scorn, half happiness, and pulled a camera from his knapsack.

'You can pin it up above your bunk and say my name is Sybil.' George cocked his head. 'No, wait,' he said. 'I'll take my shirt off so you can have me in the flesh.' He crossed his legs and smirked, simulating the look of a society woman.

'Sybil's tits aren't as big as yours,' Des said. 'Not so muscly.'

'Is that what you'll miss the most?' George said. 'My breasts?' hissing it.

'I would say so. And your...' He remembered to be strong again, to act like a man, and he clicked the shutter. 'Another one,' he insisted. 'Poke out your tongue so I can remember your sarcasm.' George puckered his lips instead and grabbed Des's cap, pretending to kiss it.

'Jesus, mate, and you ask me if people think you're queer!' Des bent down to kiss his boyfriend but then drew back, aware of the proximity of the approaching dinghy. George's eyes swept from Mount Egmont, down to the city straddling the shoreline, along the shimmering beach and the teal sea; and then he realised who was in the dinghy.

He felt a confused flurry of excitement and panic and couldn't decide whether to rush Des off to their own dinghy or go to the other side of the island. Just then the seagulls returned, as if renewed for a fresh attack. Again they swooped, lower this time, and there was something increasingly manic about their caw-cawing.

The American serviceman from the bunker was pulling on the oars, his back to the island.

'Bloody Yanks,' Des said. 'The girls are mad on them. Must have big cocks or lots of money.'

A slight twinge of guilt flashed through George, but he dismissed it and was immediately conscious of a more sinister feeling: Why had Captain Smart still not reported him and the American?

'That one's got a Maori,' Des said. 'And it's not a woman. Interesting.'

The dinghy was passing close to the rocks and the man in the stern lifted his cap and waved at them.

'Good-looking one, too,' George said. 'Know him?'

'The Maori?' Des said. 'Couldn't tell you. Give me the whisky before you get completely legless.' He spat into the sea. 'You do look like a bloody queer sitting there like that with your legs like a bloody woman's. For God's sake, sit like a man!'

George struggled to his feet and looked at the face of the man who had been his boyfriend on and off for the last six years. 'You bloody bastard,' he said. 'You can't take the heat, can you?'

'Heat? Being kicked out of the navy if they... You gotta be ready for the tumble when it happens, mate. You...'

'I what?' George snapped. He'd had enough. He wanted to push Des into the sea and let him flounder there drunk and gagging on the salt water and slimy weeds. The bastard. Everyone was a bastard. For a moment he saw Captain Smart's eyes and heard the curse: 'You'll pay for this.' He stumbled off, his legs unsteady as if they'd been used to nothing more than a boat for several weeks. He turned to look at Des standing with the sun behind him. 'You bastard,' he thought. 'Go and get killed in the bloody Solomon Islands then.'

The American and the Maori were hauling their dinghy up the beach as George staggered towards them across the pebbles.

'We saw you,' he said. 'From that point.'

'Yeah, well, that wouldn't be hard if you've got two eyes in your head,' the Maori said. 'And you've got big ones, I notice.' He gave a long, languid laugh, rolling his head back, and then apologised. 'Sorry, mate, but I like taking the mickey out of drunks.'

'George,' Des yelled from the rocks above. The gulls dived again, and George waved at them with his cap.

'Your mate wants you,' the Maori smirked.

'Yes, we were just sitting there...' he said, looking at the American, who seemed too occupied stowing the oars to take notice. The Maori looked from one to the other. 'I think your mate really does want you,' he said. 'Must be you got the booze...'

'You're with the Marines, aren't you?' George asked the American.

There was a crunching sound behind him as Des approached.

'You got the whisky, you bastard,' he shouted. 'My mate knows how to walk away with the goods,' he added grinning foolishly at the others. 'Okay, come on.' He pulled George by the sleeve. 'It's time we went.'

'How are you guys gonna row back?' the American asked. 'You can't do it drunk. The swell's up high.'

'Mind your...' Des began.

'Des, old mate,' the Maori interrupted. 'You do like the drink, don't you?' He had a winning smile. His big teeth and his big face; a handsome man with thick curly hair. 'Still with Sybil?' he asked. 'Eh, mate?'

George gazed from one to the other, then gave a low knowing laugh.

'We're old mates from camp, eh, Des?' the Maori said. We're both going to the Solomons on Saturday.'

George turned to the American. 'I'm George Crossett. Stores Accountant. Royal New Zealand Navy.'

'So,' the Marine said. 'This some sort of little playground?' He pulled a packet of American cigarettes from his pocket and handed them around. 'Are you off to the Solomons too?' he asked George.

'No,' George muttered, unable to look the man in the face. His eyes sparkled with a hint of wickedness, the way his upper lip curled when he spoke. George was drunk enough to think he could lure the American away from Des and the Maori on some pretext, that they wouldn't be noticed slinking off to a cave on the island.

'The lottery game!' The Marine laughed. 'I'm Frank La Verde, North Dakota.' He extended his hand and the sourness of the meeting lifted. 'You got a drink for Wiri and me?'

'Yeah, well, we're all in this together.' Des grinned. 'Bugger me.'

'Is that an option?' Frank asked mischievously. 'We should be happy to be together, the four of us.' He looked slowly at Des, sizing him up, then at George, without betraying their having met in such circumstances.

George went to the dinghy to get more whisky. It was a strange world. This Wiri character and Des. Himself and the American. His and Des's years together as friends and lovers. The American stood waiting for him, his hands in his pockets, that big grin, much like the man on the Players cigarette packet. They looked at each other; two or three seconds. That was all the time it took George to understand that he had never really loved Desmond Potter.

*

Des's farewell party was taking place on the verandah of the Potters' home overlooking New Plymouth. The same sickly song was playing on the wireless that seemed to be crooning everywhere. Then it suddenly changed, halfway through, as if the announcer too were tired of it. A boisterous male voice then boomed out lyrics of love and war and loss, and the people assembled on the verandah sang along. They even held hands in the throes of patriotism and shared good humour.

'I do hope you don't get sent away,' Miriam Pyke said. She and George Crosset were alone in the garden among the smell of roses and the vibrant blue of cornflowers and forget-me-nots.

'I want to fight,' he said. 'Of course, since the Japs took Singapore, it's only a matter of time before they stick a gun in my hand.' He watched. Des leaning on the verandah above them, standing next to Albert and Sybil, and a familiar sense of bitterness flushed through him. All those years longing for Desmond Potter. Strong or stupid? He shrugged and pulled the top off a flower; Des's games, the fact that he could just pop down to be buggered in the middle of the night, the way he arranged a rendezvous, always at his convenience, for a day at the races or a tramp through the bush. And there was that silly Sybil with her mountain of money and her bobbed blonde hair thinking she'd scored the perfect husband. George felt a delicious temptation to call out to the guests on the verandah.

Sybil, your husband sticks his penis in my bum at least once a week.

His mind raced at the idea of causing a disturbance, embarrassing that cosy group above him, with their lies and deceptions.

He likes to French kiss me. We even did it the night you two got married.

Miriam's mouth was moving, her red lipstick shining in the afternoon sun. Another rich woman in the same category as Sybil.

He'll do it with black men in the Solomons. He'll suck their cocks.

George wanted to charge through the garden, smashing the dahlias and forget-me-nots, uprooting the perfect roses, and go running off to find Frank La Verde. Here everything was suffocating: hypocrisy and denial.

Des darling! Do you love me more than you love Sybil?

Singing up to his boyfriend with his silly wife.

The American. I love him.

'We should bring our troops back from the Middle East,' Miriam was saying. She bent to smell a rose and then invited him to join her, long fingers cupping the petals, fingernails blazing red.

Captain Smart caught us having sex.

'Blue Dolphin, it's called,' she said. 'Ridiculous name for a yellow bloom.'

'It's all ridiculous,' he said, bending to sniff at the rose, which he felt a compulsion to pull out by its roots and present to Sybil.

Here, my dear, a token of hatred from the man your husband has buggered regularly over the years.

The intensity of the rose's scent sickened him.

'The Aussies did the right thing by bringing their men back to fight in the Pacific,' George said to Miriam. 'So why we keep ours in the Middle East...'

'It is ludicrous,' she agreed. 'But the Yanks'll fix the problem.'

'The new gun emplacements down at Seaview are pretty impressive.' George pointed vaguely in that direction. 'Can you imagine the Japs storming our beaches?'

'That's why I wish our boys were here, at home, and not defending Arabs against the Germans in Palestine. Do you get the point about the silliness of things?'

George was reassured again that there were not enough men to defend New Zealand from a Japanese invasion. Smart wouldn't have him and the American decommissioned.

Miriam sighed and for a few seconds she wasn't the woman who could stride down the street with her head back and with her purse tucked confidently under her arm. She leaned forward, close enough for him to smell her perfume, which George noticed was similar to that of the yellow Blue Dolphin. He was compelled to look at her, the proximity forced and unrelenting; those hazel eyes and the red hair swept back, very mannish and very feminine at the same time. He had read a story in the newspaper about an Australian spider that lured male moths in with the simulated aroma exuded by the female moth of the species.

'Tea, you two,' Sybil Potter called shrilly from the verandah.

Miriam reached for his hand and he let it lie limply in hers, too exhausted to pull away. 'George,' she said, 'this is quite uncharacteristic.'

'What is?' he asked.

'That we should hold hands.'

'Is it?' He turned to see if Sybil and the others were watching, but his attention was caught by a cobweb in the hibiscus.

'I know you're a confirmed bachelor,' she said, half laughing, half in earnest.

'At my age?'

She withdrew her hand and placed it above the rose, lightly, so that her red nails contrasted perfectly with the brilliance of the fresh yellow bloom.

'I thought nail polish and uniforms didn't go together,' George said. 'Don't your commanders bark at you?'

'They frown at all sorts of behaviour,' Miriam replied. Again she placed her hand on his and an unfamiliar thrill went through him. He snatched a quick look and saw that the others were watching.

'Uncharacteristic?' he said. 'I've known you a long time, but perhaps my shyness...'

'Shyness, rubbish,' Miriam said, laughing.

George had seen a film the previous week in which Rita Hayworth, full of confidence, hair swept back, mannish in that wartime way, had seduced a soldier. For the first time he realised the full implications of Des's entanglement with women.

'I remember my mother telling me,' Miriam said, her hand still holding his, 'that in the Great War a lot of odd things happened.'

'My father told me the same thing,' he said, recalling the story he would like to tell her now, of Albert's affair with a man from Auckland. The silliness of things. He saw clearly under what subterfuge and with what lies people had to live, in order to conform to what everyone apparently wanted. 'War certainly does very strange things,' he continued, 'but I find that peace doesn't release us from them.'

Processions of army men marching down the main streets of New Plymouth with the crowds cheering, Japanese periscopes out in the Tasman; suddenly George wanted nothing to do with this, because he knew it was them from whom he was constantly hiding and yet for whom he had to fight to protect their freedom.

'This weather's perfect for a garden party,' he ventured limply.

Miriam took no heed of his banter. 'I've noticed that strange liaisons happen,' she said, squeezing his hand.

As she did, that familiar feeling of defeat surged within George; he saw that this was going to be another of those awkward situations with a woman from which he would have to disentangle himself because she, the perpetrator, saw him as eligible even when he had given no signal.

Miriam dropped his hand, took a cigarette from her silver case and offered him one. 'We should go dancing at the Casablanca.'

'I've been a few times,' George offered, 'but I'm not much for that sort of thing.'

'What do you like, George?' she asked. There was something urgent in her voice, and her eyes suggested something mysterious.

'What do I like?' he repeated. Just then Des laughed loudly above them, and Miriam smiled as if she had received the answer she was eliciting.

'I like...' he tried, but the sun was suddenly too hot, appearing from beyond cloud cover as if full summer had timed its arrival for that exact moment.

'Yes,' Miriam said, looking intently at him. 'I'm very much the same way, in fact.'

'Come up, you two,' Sybil shouted down.

'The same way?' George was fascinated.

'Come up and talk to us...'

'People know more than they let on, that's all I can say, George.'

*

A heightened sense of anxiety prevailed as the afternoon progressed towards the inevitable goodbyes to Des. Despite the fact that the guests were all now well practised at such partings, there was the inevitable sadness, mixed with what Miriam had called the silliness, of having to go through this charade of farewelling someone being sent off to kill or be killed for a cause none of them had invented. The talk, as ever, concentrated on various aspects of the war effort. What was unusual, was that the men and women had not separated but stood together in a tight group, as if such intimacy was their defence against what lay hidden over the horizon.

'They say that white women and children were treated quite kindly when the Japs took Singapore,' Sybil remarked, almost jauntily. She had inherited an accent that indicated she had strong links with the Old Country and that she had money.

'But the Americans are here,' Albert Crossett said in a voice that lacked conviction. 'I wouldn't alarm myself about being invaded. The Japs haven't got air cover.'

'Sixty thousand Yanks,' Sybil's mother said. 'We must be worth saving.'

'Too busy spending money on the girls,' Sybil's father added. 'Apparently, Auckland and Wellington are awash with Yank money.'

'Watch out for the Americans, Miriam,' Des said.

'Or find something more suitable sooner,' Sybil snapped, her voice betraying so much.

'I think that women have a role to play in the fight. Marriage would be an irresponsibility,' Miriam said.

Three fighter planes roared low overhead, and everyone strained to look up from the verandah. The noise unsettled the myna birds in the shed and they came clattering and squawking out into the garden.

'To Desmond,' Mr Potter announced, raising a glass of lemonade. 'May he do his patriotic duty and come back to us safely.'

George looked across at the port where four merchant ships were being loaded at that moment with supplies he had ordered. He wanted to be on a ship and away from this humbug, having to pretend like this endlessly, with women asking him to dances and social occasions; having to listen to Sybil, who wanted him married off so that she could reclaim her husband.

'You'll miss Des,' Miriam whispered.

'Will I?' he asked. He glanced up and saw Sybil beaming in what must surely have been the first genuine smile she had ever given him. Miriam took him by the arm and moved him along the verandah.

'We could be seen together about New Plymouth,' she insisted softly.

'Who? What do you know that I don't?' he whispered. Miriam's perfume smelled sickly, but the breeze lifted and the fresh smell of sea wafted in.

'Well, I'm stuck here, and it appears that because of your job, you are too.' She looked behind her as if afraid their conversation might reach unsympathetic ears. 'I've heard certain things...'

'To Desmond!' the others all shouted. 'To victory over the Japs and may he return a hero!'

'What things?' George asked.

'You'll miss him,' Miriam repeated, nodding in Des's direction.

He couldn't answer and felt it would have been useless to try; that look she gave, it sent shivers down his spine, and the image of the Australian spider returned.

'Put your hand on my shoulder,' she said. 'As if you mean it, and then smile.'

'But…'

'Please,' she said. 'There are certain things that are expedient right now.' She put her head back and laughed as if George had said something amusing.

He blushed at the very thought of her having glimpsed the mixed and furious emotions that were running about in his mind. The mynas set up another screech as the returning aircraft roared across the harbour.

'An arrangement,' Miriam said. 'For these troubled times. Dancing, outings, to silence the whispers.'

'What whispers?'

'Oh, George,' she whispered, 'you're so I. This is New Plymouth and rumour is rife. Look at me. Do I look like the kind of woman who wants to marry a man like you? I know what you are.' She pointed her chin towards Des. Suddenly George understood. Her eyes were not those of Miriam Pyke the woman he had known for years, who worked for Military Intelligence. Strange things did happen in wartime.

He took her hand and squeezed it. 'Is there someone?' he asked.

'Yes, there is,' she whispered. 'Anne. You remember her from high school. It's a situation not unlike yours and Desmond's.'

*

It had been two months since Des had sailed from Auckland to the Solomons with the combined New Zealand and American forces. George was at the beach with Frank La Verde lying next to him, basking in the heat from the last of the summer sun. It was one of those days of utter happiness. He stubbed his cigarette into the sand, waved at Miriam and Anne, who were sitting further down the beach, and put his hand on Frank's leg. 'Tell me about San Francisco again,' be said. 'Go on,' he insisted. 'About the bars for men like us.'

'They get closed down,' Frank said, 'and then open up somewhere else. Like mushrooms, coming up in different places.' He scanned the sea before resting his eyes again on his lover. 'I wouldn't want to take you there,' he said. 'You'd get snatched away from me by one of those handsome men.'

'Never!' George laughed at the absurdity of the suggestion. He had a quick, guiltless thought of Des, and then his mind played on the oddity of the way things had turned out. Frank La Verde, ten years older than himself, a senior officer in the Marines.

'I'll come to America,' George said, 'as soon as this stupid war finishes.'

'North Dakota?'

'No, San Francisco. I already live in a North Dakota here.'

'An apartment for the two of us. There's a place called Russian Hill, we'll live there and no one will notice. Lots of men lived like that in Frisco before the war, and in New York too.'

'Frank and George.'

'George and Frank.'

The day shimmered with all the finery of a late summer afternoon as George lay back and dug his toes in the hot sand, luxuriating in the unfamiliar feeling of freedom. This part of the war was wonderful. The Americans had come to New Plymouth, swaggering down Devon Street, with even the old ladies ogling at them. They were different, exciting. The way they smoked their cigarettes and wore their caps and put their arms around their buddies' shoulders. They weren't dry and fastidious like the British servicemen, with hardly a decent word to say about the Kiwis fighting to save Britain from the Germans. The Poms were smug.

'We didn't realise you had electricity.'

'A small minded race...'

Their brittle comments ran through George's mind. Pale, gaunt men; he wanted nothing to do with them after mixing with the Americans.

'Do you suppose Wiri and Des are a couple over there?' George turned to Frank.

'What does it matter? We found each other.'

'I hate to say it, but this war was worth it.'

'It's sure changed a lot of lives. Some in good ways, I guess.'

'Fighting for freedom!' George pointed to a bird swooping above the waves. 'Is that seagull free?'

'Screw the seagull, George. I just want to be in San Francisco with you.'

'Me too! It's really free there, huh?' George said in a pseudo-American accent, excited at the thought of a life away from New Plymouth. He imagined skyscrapers, big cars cruising down broad avenues, and Frank La Verde there, far from this mediocrity.

'Free, yeah, I guess. You don't have to go to toilets to find what you want. But the police do try to close the bars down. Not like in France, where there wasn't any law against it until the Nazis.' Frank flicked his cigarette on the sand, where a gull rushed up to inspect it. 'I'm too old,' he said. 'Seen too much. This goddam war is getting me down, but you've perked up.'

Anne and Miriam approached across the sand. They were the sort of young and attractive women usually seen associating with GIs, smooching on a park bench, doing their best to get silk stockings or a ticket to America for a life of luxury.

'It's hard to believe there's a war out there,' Anne said. 'We were saying how lucky we are, the four of us. Anne and Frank; Miriam and George. The happy couples, always together. New Plymouth must be humming with our romances.'

They arrived back in New Plymouth late in the afternoon. A dense bank of cloud had moved in from the west, darkening the sky and bringing a chilly breeze. George watched Frank's car retreat down

Balmoral Street. A discomforting feeling of heaviness flowed through his body; in his mind an oppressive sensation swirled. On and off; happiness and sadness with no way of controlling events. Death would surely be better than this. Just to drown; to be released. He went inside, where Albert was standing by the window. George greeted his father, who turned to him with something terrible burning in his eyes. For a second or two George couldn't imagine what that look meant, but then he realised. It was hatred, mixed with contempt.

'Did you have a nice afternoon with Frank?' Albert said archly. 'Swimming? I hope so. Entertaining yourselves while others are out there fighting.' He slumped into a chair with an exhausted sigh. 'Get yourself a whisky, George,' he said. 'And one for me.'

'What's wrong?' George asked. He scanned the room for a telegram, trying to guess at the sort of bad news that might explain the need for a shot of whisky.

'Desmond,' Albert Crossett said. 'Blown up in the Solomons while defending our country.'

*

Not even to get his body back. Rotting in some tropical jungle... Sybil Potter sat in front of Desmond's desk, not knowing whether to leave the pile of papers and accumulated bits and pieces or to clear the mess out, as she had his clothes in a fit of despondency a month after he'd been killed. The news had just finished on the wireless. She had barely absorbed the euphoric announcement that the Japanese threat to New Zealand had been avoided thanks to the heroics of the Americans in the decisive battles of the Coral Sea and Guadalcanal. The names barely registered as she sat there looking at the desk; the bank statements, the scraps of paper with his handwriting on them, the invoices. She shook her head to clear the thought of her husband denied the dignity of a headstone in the New Plymouth cemetery. Anonymous despite the congratulations she'd received on his behalf for his valour and bravery, the kind words and condolences from the navy, the piles of telegrams from friends and relatives in New Zealand and England.

'I have to take care of the business,' she told herself. It had been strength of character that had made her get up at three o'clock one morning and empty his clothes cupboard; the shorts folded on the shelves, the socks and shoes. Everything into a huge pile on the floor for the Alleviation of Hardship to come and collect.

Sybil sat bravely at the desk, looking at the papers piled in front of her as if, by clearing those, she would be able to tackle the anguish of being a widow, of imagining Desmond's remains being devoured by tropical insects.

'You bastards,' she said. 'You bloody Japs.' The rain fell outside, dribbling down the living-room windows as the last of the summer faded unhappily into autumn.

'Take the bull by the horns,' her father had told her. 'Everyone around the world is suffering, not just you.' A truism, but he had fought in the First World War and knew how to tackle the terrible things that life threw up. 'Face facts. War is terrible, but Desmond died a hero to save us.'

Sybil sniffed, wiped away her tears and decided that her afternoon would be wasted weeping. Bull by the horns. She began by stacking the bank papers on the table, and then tackled the business correspondence piled in the top drawer of Desmond's desk. By three o'clock she could smile with the satisfaction of having dealt with the worst of the mess. A cup of tea by her side, the cat warming itself at her feet. The rain was steadier now. Relentlessly drumming on the roof, its effect was melancholic but soothing. Sybil tried the third drawer down in the desk. It was locked and there was no sign of a key. She went into the kitchen to get a knife so she could force the drawer open.

2 The metamorphosis of Betty and Neddy Bouzikis

It was early Monday morning, and the wind and salt spray came sweeping in off the Tasman Sea, slapping fish-and-chip wrappings along the gutters. Fareda Bouzikis stood at the window of the ZYX Fruit Shop looking out at Devon Street. A bright Cortina came zooming down and nearly knocked over Mrs Kispest, the poor woman who had lost her husband. Old Mrs Bouzikis shook her head in disbelief at the miseries of life. One minute your husband was alive and the next minute he was dead and buried in soil that had nothing to do with all the scents and memories of home.

'Ye,' she sighed softly. 'Ye.'

'What?' Betty Bouzikis said in Arabic. She was polishing the Granny Smiths to give them that glossy green that her mother-in-law demanded for all her apples.

'Poor old lady from Czechoslovakia. Ye, what a pity. Ye, what a shame,' Fareda Bouzikis sighed.

Mrs Kispest leaned against the lamppost on the other side of the street and, with her hand to her heart, gasped in several deep breaths to recover from her fright. Over her left arm her handbag and in her right hand her woolly gloves.

'What?' Betty asked again, this time in English. She was aware of a sudden whiff of feijoa, more like a perfume than the smell of a fruit.

'Feigowa,' she said. 'Feji...' Some English was really difficult to master. She didn't understand that it was a Portuguese word for an Amazonian fruit. She looked at her mother-in-law, who was rambling on about something, children and husbands no doubt, and then she picked up the feijoa and bit off the end. A cream-coloured pulp oozed out and dribbled down the smooth green skin. She shivered; the fruit's skin made her tongue tingle as if she'd just bitten into soft metal.

'Not even one child she got to give her the comfort now her husband he dead,' Fareda said.

Mrs Kispest opened her handbag and took a handkerchief out. It was as if she didn't know what to do with it now that she had it in her hand: to blow her nose or wipe her eyes? She stood there bundled up in her winter coat with its fur collar like a cat draped around her neck.

'The same year me and Jo we come to New Zealand she come too from that Czechoslovakia with her husband and no kids at all and still now no kids and no grandkids and still she here and he dead and now it 1963 and she all alone and he dead and buried recently.'

Mrs Bouzikis exhausted her remonstrance against the injustices of the world. In fact, she regarded it a sin not to have progeny. It was the worst possible curse not to have children and grandchildren to look after you when you were old and sick. Fareda had the sort of eyes that motherhood had trained to send messages. She focused them on a spot just below her new daughter-in-law's breasts. 'Breed, breed,' her eyes pleaded.

It was six months since Betty had arrived from Lebanon as Neddy Bouzikis's bride. Six months married and still no good news about a baby swelling out that tummy. Fareda wanted to be able to rush off and tell all her old Lebanese friends. She cherished the anticipation of that moment: a plate of honey cakes, some hommos; Silvie Zerihen and Zahia Karameni; Fareda shouting the wonderful news of a grandchild.

'Without kids what it be like in the old age when no one there to look after you like this poor old Mrs Kispest.' Despite the cold, Fareda was in short sleeves. Her arms were thin from the wrists to the elbows, but from there up to her shoulders their main characteristic was flab. She raised her hands and waved her arms as her own mother would have done at such a moment. Her own mother back in the old county half a century before, signalling that all should be done according to the lore of good Maronites.

'Good Lebanese blood Neddy he got. Good for babies. Best family in all of Bechare. Best blood in all Lebanon.' It was an incantation. Again she waved her arms and in Arabic repeated what she had just said, as if English were a language that could not adequately express the seriousness of Betty being six months married and still not pregnant.

'Neddy he the best son in the whole world. When my husband his father he died Neddy he care for me and care for me over and over. Neddy will never leave me.'

Neddy might have been there in the shop with them surrounded by produce. His mother raised her right arm in benediction as she pictured her adored son rearranging the gooseberries and dusting the Fijian coconuts.

The same bright Cortina that had almost knocked over Mrs Kispest two minute before came tearing down Devon Street again. The woman behind the wheel had a beehive hair-do stacked up with a mauve chiffon scarf tied over it. Just then the post office clock chimed eight times and, like clockwork herself, Fareda Bouzikis went to the front door of the fruit shop and opened it to start the new week.

*

Elvira Eliveras went quickly down the path leading out of the apricot orchard. For a moment she stopped and held her hand to her chest in an effort to ease that bump, bump feeling. She took in several deep breaths and then bent down to pick an anemone to put behind her ear, where some hair had managed to stray from under her scarf. She couldn't see the house from where she was at the bottom of the orchard. From what sounded like half-way up the mountain, she heard her brother's mule honking. The pounding in her chest eased a little once she had ascertained how far her brother was away, up there in the fields ploughing. She stopped against an olive tree that she knew the Crusaders had planted. She couldn't think of the word Crusaders without seeing silver helmets, even on a day like this, when she should have been up there in the house, making hommos and tabouleh for the visitors who were coming from New Zealand. Silver helmets like those in the books the nuns had taught her with in the convent. All of those olive and apricot trees down there in the valley below her planted by the Crusaders. All things Christian and worthy that the Maronites believed made up their inheritance.

The Crusaders, the Maronites, the Druse, the Muslims, the Turks and the French; galloping up and down the valley before her, pursuing their destinies. This one a decade's worth. That one five hundred years. She picked another anemone, crushed it gently in her palm and rubbed the blue dye into her fingertips. Only then did she take the letter out of her apron pocket and put it to her lips.

Elvira had received only one other letter from Antoni Hasroun since he had left. This one had the same stamp and the same postmark: BUENOS AIRES 1962. She put the letter down and picked another anemone, just as he would have done for her in that exact spot when they met secretly. Her brother up in the fields and her parents down in Bechares selling their apricots and olives. That was the time of their love. She pressed against her lips the envelope with its smell of anemone and Antoni Hasroun, and what she thought was the aroma of Buenos Aires.

Elvira knew she would say yes even before she opened the envelope. She knew she could even bear her parents' screams about running off to Argentina to marry that Hasroun boy, that treacherous Druse. She held the thin blue envelope up to the sun. No more than a page, she guessed. No more space than it took to ask the question and ask for an immediate reply with the name of the ship on which she would arrive. With her eyes closed she enjoyed the sweet, guilty feeling that Antoni was with her. Antoni kissing her, brushing his hand against her thigh.

✳

'Betty,' Neddy Bouzikis said. He was standing next to his wife in the back of the fruit shop, where the only light came in from a small window near the ceiling. 'Betty.'

She didn't know what to do with this name. It was the sort that office girls had: Betty, Cheryl, Colleen, Elspeth; girls with blonde hair lacquered into sticky nests. Not a name a Lebanese girl felt safe with.

'I'll put the peas away,' she said in Arabic.

'Look, we've got apricots. The first of the season.' Neddy lifted up the wooden crate without taking his eyes from her face. The ochre fruit from the South Island were wrapped in tissue paper as if they were precious objects.

'Betty, for you,' he said. Neddy looked tenderly at his young wife. She had a silk scarf tied over her dark hair so that only a few curls fell onto her forehead. She wasn't like the girls in New Plymouth who wore bikinis to the beach and tent frocks in town, and had sharp little breasts poking from under tight twin sets.

'Just like in Lebanon. At home,' he said.

Lebanon wasn't his homeland any more than it was now his wife's. He saw that in her face as she chose an apricot with a look of painful sorrow.

'From Lebanon,' he said. This time he expressed the same sadness that she had on her face. From Lebanon: he'd always said that in the way a refugee might. Every time a letter arrived from Bechare or Beirut, his mother would wave her arms and ululate. 'From Lebanon! From Lebanon! Ye! From the beautiful place.' Neddy had capitulated to this sentimentality as if he too were an inseparable part of Lebanese rocks and terraces and cedars. But he was a Kiwi, born and bred in

New Plymouth. Looking at Betty holding the apricot, he knew it had been a pretence to think of himself as a Lebanese.

Betty turned the fruit over and over in the palm of her hand and studied it as if it were not a real apricot but something ersatz made in an alien place called Otago. Fake because it hadn't matured in her parents' orchard in the foothills of Bechare under the gaze of Mount Lebanon.

Neddy felt an urge to touch her hand, to put it up to his lips and kiss it because her sadness needed something like that. He wanted to tell her everything was alright. To make love to her like a normal man would have to a gorgeous woman with the creamy white skin of an Arabic princess.

✳

Elvira Eliveras held the letter from Argentina to her chest. It was a sin against God and against her family to allow feelings like these to come into her mind. Feelings that crawled through her breasts and down her thighs and made her think in a mixed-up confusion of love and lust, of things the nuns had warned led to disease and death and an eternity in flames with the Druse and other infidels.

'The best thing to do would be to get out of these mountains and go somewhere else where there are no Druse and Maronites and Muslims,' Antoni had said. He hated that valley with its legacy of Phoenicians, Crusaders, Arabs and Turks. He'd waved his hand at it in dismissal and said that the first country that would take him would be his next home. He was sick of a country that wouldn't let two people marry because one was a Druse and the other a Maronite.

'Argentina,' Elvira murmured to herself. It was a good-sounding name. The butcher from Bechare had emigrated there ten years before with his wife and six kids, and they'd done all right. She had dreamt of a life without her mother and father and brother and those orchards and longed to escape that valley she thought she'd loved before Antoni had taught her otherwise.

The sound of an engine interrupted her reverie, then she glimpsed a car snaking up the road and playing hide and seek between the rocks and olive trees. She realised that she should have been at the house preparing lunch for a guest, a man from New Zealand but with a Lebanese name, who was coming to see them because of some old connections. She stood up hurriedly and the anemone fell from behind her ear, but she didn't pick it up because she was ripping open the letter from her lover in Buenos Aires.

✳

Fareda Bouzikis was in the kitchen preparing dinner for her son and daughter-in-law, who were still down at the fruit shop. Above the kitchen sink, a little window looked out into the back yard with its prolific vegetable garden and the lemon and fig trees.

Betty was a beautiful and good girl, and she soon would get over her sadness. It was the same for all the Lebanese who came out to New Zealand, especially those who came from just a little town and not from Beirut.

Fareda put the potato peelings in the scrap bucket and then went outside to empty it in the compost. She wouldn't let anyone else do this. Not after Jo had performed this ritual for forty years. He'd made this patch the best vegetable garden in all of New Plymouth. It was a bitter night, like those when the wind blew from Mount Lebanon. Fareda didn't like to let herself think of those nights back home in the country she hadn't seen since the day she left on the ship with Jo all those decades ago. It wasn't safe to let the mind wander. That was the cause of Betty's unhappiness. You had to push away memories of siblings and orchards. You couldn't go thinking about what was past.

Fareda paused on the garden path. She could feel the presence of her husband. Jo in his pyjamas. Jo Bouzikis who'd worked hard for forty years to establish the fruit shop and who'd taken the blows to provide for the next generation. It was Jo wanting to put out the compost. Some dried lemon leaves scurried about her feet as she went up the back steps and into the kitchen. A little whiff of grape vines and coriander and donkeys, and for a moment she allowed herself a glimpse of that valley and mountain.

'Ye,' she said. 'Ye, Jo where are you now?' It was a cruel thing to be left without a husband. Marriage was a gift from God but rent asunder by the devil. God wouldn't do that sort of thing. Death was too cruel a punishment to interrupt the sanctity of marriage.

She went back to the sink and looked at herself in the windowpane. Age didn't matter. Looks didn't mean a thing. Fareda Bousikis didn't think like New Zealanders. She knew that. Other old women in New Plymouth were always complaining about hair falling out and the ugliness of arthritic hands and wrinkled lips. What mattered was kids and family, so that when you were old you didn't end life in a rest home, shoved into a lonely room with just your knitting for company, or squeezed into a smelly dormitory like poor old Mrs Kispest. A shiver of disgust and fear ran down Fareda's spine at the thought of such callousness. God had provided her with only one son, but few were as good and caring as her Neddy.

Her heart warmed with the thought of Neddy married to this fine Lebanese girl, who had her hair wrapped up in a scarf even after six months in New Zealand. Betty's humility and shyness. It was good training. Good blood. Not like these Inglesi girls who were nothing but sluts living in sin and who strutted about in beehive hair-dos and pushed their illegitimate babies around in prams as if they had something to show off for their evil.

*

Elvira Eliveras wouldn't come out of the kitchen to meet the guest. She wouldn't even come out to greet Uncle Bishara from Beirut, who'd driven the man up especially to meet the family. She mixed yoghurt and cucumber in a bowl and sprinkled paprika on top, then squeezed lemon for the tabouleh and added olive oil. She didn't need to taste it to know it would be delicious.

'No,' she had said to her mother. 'What have I got to do with a fool from the other end of the earth who doesn't speak proper Arabic but calls himself a Lebanese?'

'You are wilful,' her mother had said, flashing her deep-set black eyes. She put her hands on her stomach and simulated the look of terrible pain that afflicted her when she needed respect.

Elvira knew the hommos needed more pepper and salt, but she delberately left them out. 'Here,' she said, thrusting the plates towards her mother. 'Take these and leave me here. I will not come out like some servant girl for this man to stare at.'

'You're just the same as your Aunty Zita. Bad blood. Bitter like lemon.' Her mother picked up the food and went. From the kitchen the daughter could hear the conversation. Back and forth the polite questions; back and forth that banter about Lebanon and family and this place New Zealand.

Elvira looked at the sharp knife in her hands. It would be as easy as cutting a lemon in half. It would be like slicing a pomegranate and seeing the juice run out over the wooden chopping board. Her heart told her to do it with the same conviction as did her head. End it. End it. She stood there with the voices in the other room rising and falling in her ears, which already pulsated with a feeling of blood oozing through them. They should have been voices happily celebrating that she had been asked to marry Antoni Hasroun, voices of a family rejoicing in the presence of love.

She held the knife above her white skin. It was too much to live knowing that someone else was sleeping with Antoni. It was too humiliating knowing that she had been touched on the thighs with those same hands that would be feeling the intimate places of the woman he said in the letter was now his wife. Rosita. An Argentinian. Sorry. Impossible to marry a Maronite. Your parents. Druse. Cannot.

His words jumbled in her mind as she stood there with the knife poised above her wrist. The hate fuming in her head. Antoni Hasroun with his dark lips and black moustache. A lump of bile rose in her throat and threatened to come spilling out of her mouth, but she swallowed it. Antoni Hasroun. His mouth small, that purple-brown colouring of his thin lips, and in her nose his smell of sweat and pomegranates and crushed olives.

Just there at the kitchen sink with the water hot enough to draw out the blood, as she had read in French novels at the convent. You kill yourself when scorned by love. You cut your wrists and put them in hot water, and your family come out and blame themselves. They wail and lament; and when they find the letter and realise that it was because of that Druse, they rush off to the mountains and start yet another absurd vendetta.

The knife slipped from her hand and, as it fell, cut her foot, but she didn't care. The pain was a respite from the hideous thought that he had not asked her to marry him. Antoni Hasroun, who she had already vowed in her mind would be hers. He was a Druse. He had abandoned her. Never trust a Druse. It was a Maronite saying as old as the cedars.

Elvira had been trapped by sweet lips and sweet talk. And now some wild creature called Rosita was in the arms of the man who had promised to take her away from this religious bigotry.

She had been forbidden to see Antoni, to even mention his name. The black pools of her mother's eyes, and the shadows underneath them like soot, had suggested all the things she'd heard in all of her years in Bechare about Muslims, about Turks, about Druse. That irreversible code of ethics which moulds you, places you irrevocably into that segment in which you were born. 'Never trust a Druse.' The warning pounded in her head as she realised that her parents had been talking the truth.

*

Neddy Bouzikis put on his pyjamas and climbed into bed next to his wife. For a few moments he lay there saying to himself over and over again that he would go to the priest and tell him everything. But that repetition turned into a Hail Mary and he turned his mind off the terrible thought with the opium of prayer. 'Hail, Mary, full of grace. Hail, Mary, full of grace.' Over and over until the pain began to dissipate under the persuasion that good would come from Jesus and Mary and the saints.

In the next room he heard his mother cough. The prayer slipped away and he had a sudden urge to shout abuse at her and her fruit shop and everything that had trapped him here in New Plymouth.

A man forty-three years old with a twenty-two-year-old wife. He was aware of the mocking looks from those he met in the street. Neddy Bouzikis who went to Lebanon and got himself a young wife. Neddy Bouzikis who had bought an innocent girl half his age.

'Arab! Lebo!' The curses rang in his head. All the dark doubts over the years spent in this bed wondering if he were normal, when other men had wives and kids and English surnames. Even earlier, at primary school, the shame of being the only boy in the class with pubic hair. 'Bloody Arab! Hairy Lebo!' In the school grounds. In the swimming pool changing sheds.

Now he had a woman in his bed, a wife, but he was still regarded as a joke. Good old Neddy Bouzikis, whom everyone pitied and gossiped about. He could hear them chatting about him over pints in the pub or in the private bar at the New Plymouth Commercial Club. All those men with their ruddy faces, their blond hair and beer guts. Sitting in their leather chairs with the round of whiskies he'd bought them in his pitiful attempt to make mates.

He knew Betty was awake even though she was breathing as if asleep. Six months of that pretence hadn't gone unnoticed. He returned to the comfort of prayer. 'Hail, Mary, full of grace. Hail, Mary, full of grace.' Suddenly Neddy realised the irony of his praying to the Virgin. He didn't believe in her anyway. The real virgin was his wife, even after six months of marriage.

*

Elvira Eliveras had the inner strength that her people knew came from centuries of domination. As she bent to pick up the knife from the kitchen floor, she put her bitterness back in the safety of her heart, where she had learned that all grief should remain.

'Elvira,' her father called. He was a short man whose face was brown from a life spent out in the orchard. 'Elvira, habibti, lesh?' He came to her by the kitchen sink and put his hand on her shoulder. 'For me, darling, please show our guest hospitality.' She wouldn't let her mother kiss her cheek, but her father was allowed that privilege. He pecked her three times as if she were still his little girl. 'Come into the reception room and meet the man from New Zealand.'

Neddy Bouzikis had a handsome face, and when he smiled it was with all the warmth of someone who had enough money to come to Lebanon for a wife, as all the wealthy émigrés did. Betty bowed a little but didn't take his hand, and Uncle Bishara winked as if his complicity had already reached success with the mere appearance of the girl in the living room.

'She is a fine cook,' Bishara said, looking around for confirmation. He had large yellowish jowls that shook when he got excited. 'Everybody, even in Beirut, knows what a cook she is.' He dipped a piece of bread into the hommos and put it in his mouth, but he was too preoccupied with his mission to realise it lacked the necessary condiments. 'In Zahle they know what a cook she is. In Tyre. In Sidon you will hear about Elvira Eliveras. And the nuns they taught her how to cook the French food, and in... in...' He wanted to eulogise her beauty too, but couldn't mention that in front of the girl herself. Besides, he had been over that point with his guest a dozen times during the drive up from Beirut.

Elvira had nursed her old Aunty Margot through a long illness that the Bechare doctor had said was caused by a lack of blood. The blood just ebbing away somehow, so that there was no hope. Aunty Margot on her deathbed unable to think of the inevitable with any sort of equanimity, even after her eighty years of preparing for the event.

'Save me, Elvira, save me!' she had wailed. Aunty Margot should never have had hope. Fate must be accepted. The Crusaders came. The Crusaders went. The Ottoman Empire rose and then dissipated. Aunty Margot's sin was that she had never accepted that her blood was disappearing. Even on that night when her blood had disappeared completely, she was still whimpering, 'Save me!'

Elvira saw her fate clearly as she sat on the edge of the sofa in her parents' reception room listening to tales of New Plymouth and Fareda Bouzikis and a fruit shop. It was all inevitable. How useless to have believed that she could be different, could have married a Druse. It was like trying to say that history had not occurred.

'Well?' her mother asked. The dim light from the weak bulb accentuated the blackness under her eyes. Everyone else was upstairs asleep, but Elvira and her mother were in the kitchen. 'He is rich, but we don't want our only daughter to go all the way to New Zealand,' she said insincerely. 'What a curse to have an only daughter.' She put her hands to her stomach in that pretence of pain, but she didn't realise that this pitiful ploy had not worked for years. All she got was the grudging acknowledgment that she needed something that couldn't be framed with an honest question.

Elvira still had the letter from Buenos Aires tucked in her dress near her breasts. 'The guest said it's not the same time in New Zealand as it is here in the mountains,' she said.

'No. No. Different.' Her mother took this strange comment as a positive sign. Their daughter was difficult. She was very hard to understand, the direct result of having been educated by French nuns. It wasn't good for a girl to have an education that went past the normal boundaries of reading and writing and rudimentary arithmetic. Education made girls wilful. There was suspicion in the mother's face as she surveyed that of her daughter for signs of acceptance.

'The bottom of the world,' the mother said. 'It'll be day. No, it'll be night.' She couldn't understand the complexities of time zones. But the foreign Lebanese had said the place was very near the bottom of the world and that meant being completely upside down in all respects.

'It's day there, the sun will be up,' Elvira said. It was comforting to think Argentina would also be in daylight at the same time as it was in New Zealand. She couldn't think of herself as being in another bed at the same time as that Hasroun was with his Argentinian bitch. Separated by oceans but not by darkness. Had it been night in Argentina at the same time as Lebanon, she knew she would have dwelt on him in bed with his slut. Elvira could even see that Rosita, a clear picture of the woman with a sneer on her Argentinian countenance, big lips and orange hair. Antoni Hasroun rubbing her thighs and putting his face between her breasts.

'Don't be angry. Don't be upset.' Those words in his letter scrawled in his peasant's script. An uneducated Druse. The words had the effect of those daggers pictured in the nuns' history books. The weapons used by Turks in medieval times to butcher Christians. The nuns' texts: history as hate and revenge. Elvira could see a dagger poised above a heart. Waiting to be plunged in. She was holding it. Antoni's whole village would suffer the same fate. They had all been thrown on the rubbish heap by a lying little Druse. Elvira might have forgiven him if religion had really been the excuse. But the Argentinian wouldn't have been a Druse. Not with a name like Rosita. All he wanted was flesh. Anyone would do if he could get his peasant's hands up a dress. His hands had black hair to the knuckles, and the fingertips were rough from working the soil. Those disgusting hands had touched her thighs. What a sham. What a vile thing to happen to a woman who had allowed herself to be impure on the pretext of love and now to be in a state of disgrace because of Antoni Hasroun the Druse.

'New... New... That place,' her mother said. She was still holding her stomach as if the pain were eating away inside, but she didn't recognise real suffering. She didn't see the anguish in her daughter's mouth and eyes. She was about to say, 'Wilful, wilful. Just like Zita.' But suddenly even she realised that that refrain had been abused.

The Druse had smoked cigarillos and yellowy tar coated his fingers. On the afternoon he'd promised her his love she'd kissed them. She recalled the acrid taste. Antoni Hasroun lying back in the grass with anemones framing his dark hair and stubbled cheeks; the most handsome man from all of the Druse villages. The sort of looks for which you risked a stoning in order to procure. She would have been prepared to be locked up in the house for a year doing penance just for the chance to lie on the grass with a man as beautiful as the Druse. She had even felt the sea salt and the wind of freedom on her face as she stood on the ship sailing towards the mysterious Argentina.

'When we get to Argentina, we'll...' The smell on his fingers. Tar and anemones.

'Mine, habibti, mine, habibti...' His fingers on her lips. Pushing them in and out of her mouth. His hands on her thighs, pushing at her skirt. Then it had been an act of love, but now it had become filth.

'All right,' Elvira said to her mother, whose eyes lit up. The taste of tar was suddenly cancerous on the deceived woman's tongue. 'Do we get married here or do we do it in that place?'

*

A tall woman in a psychedelic tent frock was inspecting a feijoa in the ZYX Fruit Shop. Her index finger was elongated by a false nail. Painted a brilliant scarlet, it shone and arched out hook-like, the sort of thing that actresses in Hollywood wore on gala nights. Betty Bouzikis had seen nails like that in magazines. The woman picked up the feijoa and smelled it. This was something customers wouldn't normally do.

Not New Zealanders. They knew the smell of pears and apples and oranges, and weren't experimental with new fruit. New Zealanders didn't come into the shop to sniff and fondle fruit, and then haggle over the price. 'I'll take two pounds please. Nice weather. Good morning.' That was it. There were no figs, no pomegranates, no aubergines, no bundles of coriander. You could tell this wasn't Lebanon just from a glimpse at a fruit shop.

It was as if the tall woman were fascinated by the fruit's amazing green, which resembled one of her frock's many extraordinary colours. She must have been from Auckland or Wellington to look like that; New Plymouth girls didn't have that same veneer of fabulousness.

Betty should have approached her and asked if she could be of any help, but she stood transfixed. It was the immigrant's syndrome: one day, even months after arriving, you suddenly realised that you were not dressed in the right clothes and didn't speak the right language.

She looked at the woman's bright vinyl high heels and fashionable frock. The immigrant finally waking to the fact that she was different and seeing herself for what she was in the New Zealander's mirror. A reflection of foreignness. Betty put her hand to her scarf, the same one she'd worn on the day Antoni's letter had arrived from Buenos Aires. It had been her favourite piece of clothing because it was bright red muslin, very avant garde for rural Lebanon. But now it seemed like a loud signal of her difference. The post office clock struck ten and a car backfired outside the shop.

'Betty, Betty. The lady waiting,' old Mrs Bouzikis said, waving her arm at the woman by the feijoas. 'She come to attend you now,' she said loudly. 'Sorry. Ye! Betty darling, please attend the lady with the feijoa.'

'If you'd be so kind as to...' the woman said. 'Just fabulous these fruits, aren't they? Just so... so... perfumed and exotic.' Her frock was very mini, which gave her long skinny legs the appearance of a stork's. In one hand she clutched a red vinyl handbag and in the other she displayed the feijoa like an offering of oval green-stone.

'I'm so sorry...' she said as if it were her fault that the fat old woman was being rude. 'But just a pound of feijoas if you wouldn't mind, please.' Even her stockings were fashionable. They looked like the black mesh material that richer peasants draped over their fig trees before harvest. Betty had never before seen anything like those stockings or the woman, not in real life, only in the magazines she'd read since she'd arrived in New Zealand.

Amazing. The woman would have been stoned to death in a Muslim village. In a Christian one, she would have been locked up in her father's house and made to do penance. In West Beirut she would have been jeered at and spat upon, and in East Beirut they would have thought she was a French prostitute.

For six months Betty had managed on the reserve of strength that she believed was the core inside all Maronites. It was what the nuns had always said; the mountain Lebanese have survived against all odds as Christians for two thousand years. It was folk wisdom. It was fact. Not even the Ottomans had managed to drive them out. Not even the Muslims had squashed them, as they had been wanting to do since the time of Mohammed. You endured at the top of a mountain range where no one could reach you. Aunty Margot had had to spend three months under the trees and in caves in 1914 when the Turks had come through to kill all the Christians. Endurance, fortitude and wisdom. Right was on the side of the Maronites.

Realisation strikes at the most incongruous moment. Betty had realised just as the clock struck and the car backfired that she had no more strength in reserve. She didn't want to endure. Saving up just to become bankrupt. Saving just to endure and end up bitter like the rest of them: her mother, Aunty Zita, Uncle Bishara, her brother, Aunty Margot.

Stoning a woman for wearing a short dress. Being imprisoned in your own home for meeting a Druse in the orchard. You ended up holding your stomach in supplication, in a long black dress in a dingy kitchen selling your daughter off to a rich Christian.

'Je suis de... madam. Je suis à vous servir...' Betty said. She felt her whole body fall limp.

'Pardon. Oh, I beg your pardon but I don't speak French. As much as I'd like to. I always wanted... but... *Je suis...* ummm.'

Betty felt the same despair as she had about her clothes. The immigrant's brain in complete confusion; the brain scrambling to form comprehensible language. She spoke very good English, but had suddenly lapsed into French, despite its being entirely inappropriate there in the ZYX Fruit Shop in New Plymouth.

'Well, a little French, I suppose,' the woman said. 'When I was in the sixth form, I... *Quand... lycée'* she said. *'Un petit...* Oh no,' she said. 'I absolutely can't find another word, but...' She had bright eyes like those models who advertised false nails or menthol cigarettes. 'French,' she said. 'The language of a real civilisation.'

Betty could see herself in the woman's eyes: a poor peasant working in a fruit shop with a fat old mother-in-law barking at her. Wearing a red scarf like an Arab, a drab old dress that she'd made in Bechare while waiting for Aunty Margot's blood to completely drain out. Some women weren't from a mountain village in Lebanon, some were educated in the ways of the world. Like Aunty Zita, who was from Beirut, and of course Beirut ladies were different. You couldn't possibly expect to be like a Beiruti if you were from Bechare. Drab and provincial and ugly. Betty felt the prick of tears just beneath her eyelids.

Aunty Zita had told her she was provincial, and Betty knew that this woman was now saying the same thing with her eyes.

'You do speak English, don't you?' the woman asked.

Betty looked to see if her mother-in-law was spying. It was a surprise not to see her there with her arms folded across her large bosom, or casually sorting onions, close enough to hear what was being said. The old woman was outside cooing at a baby in a pram. Just the fact that Betty had to look to see if her mother-in-law was watching sparked another realisation. She'd taken the marriage vows to escape from spies and suspicion in Lebanon, only to be confronted by the same thing in a country that was supposed to be free and modern.

'In school I had French nuns,' Betty said. 'So my French is...'

'But you speak English beautifully, dear. How fabulous. And you speak French. And what else?'

'Arabic,' she said softly, as if not sure of the result. There was a hierarchy of languages in her own country, with French at the top. And in this Inglesi place, Arabic was associated with long noses and filth and deceit.

'Oh,' the woman said. 'How theatrical. I'm from the New Plymouth Repertory Theatre and we need someone like you to take the part of Hermione. Do audition for us. Please. Oh, how I can see you as Hermione.'

Two men walked past the fruit shop and stopped to talk to the woman whose baby Fareda Bouzikis was kissing. One was dressed in a white shirt and tie with short pants and long socks. The other had on exactly the same uniform, with the only difference being a smart blue blazer like those worn by schoolboys. Betty saw suddenly this was all a world in which she had been playing no part. Neddy didn't wear New Zealand clothes. He went in for outfits that Betty knew other people sneered at. A shirt with the buttons undone so that his hairy chest was exposed. In Beirut he had bought all sorts of fashionable garments that men in New Plymouth wouldn't have dreamed of being seen in. Betty wanted to be out there on the street with a man in long socks. She wanted to be like her beautiful customer, wearing something modern, something Kiwi, something that belonged to the 1960s and not something from the Lebanese mountains.

'How exotic,' the woman eulogised. 'Imagine being Lebanese. They say Beirut is the Paris of the Middle East. It must be absolutely fabulous to live in a place like that. New Zealand is absolutely boring.' She seemed so excited, as if all of a sudden her world had opened up. 'French lessons!' she said.

A place like that. The only time Betty had spent any time in Beirut was the week of their absurd honeymoon. And most of that was spent at Aunty Zita's apartment, with her aunt pretending to be all sorts of things she wasn't just for the sake of impressing Neddy. Aunty Zita with her Beirut curls and her Beirut talk.

'Elvira. But that is not an English name. Everyone in New Zealand will laugh. Not an English name at all; Aunty Zita said in her broken French, thinking she was so marvellous, trying to attract Neddy's attention to her sophistication and elegance. *'Non! Non! Elvira, non! Betty. Betty. Betty. Oui. Quel nom!* Betty Bouzikis.' The name had stuck ever since that afternoon because Aunty Zita had the sort of power that made anyone who wasn't from Beirut sure that truth had just been blurted from her painted mouth ringed with its irregular teeth. 'Oh, no. Not Elvira. What a peasant name for someone going to New Zealand,' Aunty Zita had insisted.

'So you really would, would you?' the woman in the tent frock asked, not realising that her grammar was too complex for Betty's limited grasp of English.

'Would would?' the girl asked. She was only just returning from Aunty Zita's as Betty Bouzikis, with Elvira tossed on the rubbish heap as cheap and worthy only of a peasant. The cruel aspect of the name change hadn't struck her before this. At first it had been novelty and gratitude at having avoided the shame of being known as Elvira to English-speakers, but now she descended from gratitude to resentment.

'I mean about giving me French lessons. We are quite bereft of French-speakers in New Plymouth, and I must say my few theatrical lines with the right accent. Oh, do,' she insisted. 'And you must audition.'

*

It was supposed to be one of those delicious moments for which you wait years and then savour for the rest of your life. Neddy and Betty Bouzikis on the first night of their honeymoon in their suite at the Cedars of Lebanon Hotel on the Corniche in East Beirut. He was wearing a white suit he'd bought in the souk, the sort that would have brought jeers at the New Plymouth Commercial Club.

'What are ya?' Dick Banks would sneer.

'Jeez, you look flash,' Jim Birtwhistle would snigger.

These men who had never emerged from the fourth form. Mocking a man who had plump tits or wasn't dressed in long socks and shorts. They were thousands of miles away from the Cedars of Lebanon Hotel, but they were so close after sharing forty-odd years with Neddy.

He went to the window and looked at the Corniche and the apartment blocks. Beirut was the most beautiful city he'd seen in his life, a place where no one knew him for what he really was or wasn't, or what he wanted to be. His sickness was as anonymous here as he was. He felt happy. The air blew in sweetly, a mixture of sea and cooking and diesel.

What he wasn't. That was a thing of the past. Now he was normal. Jim Birtwhistle and Dick Banks would come to accept him. A wife. Children. A marriage certificate to prove everything was all right. He could go into the Commercial Club, order a round of whiskies and say, 'My wife...'

Neddy mouthed the words as he stood looking at East Beirut. 'My wife, my children...' Words that couldn't go wrong, the language of confidence. 'My wife. My kids. Our house. My wife and I. We...'

It was so beautiful standing there savouring the Mediterranean and the lights and the moment at hand that had brought him at last to the end of his sickness.

'Are you happy?' he asked his wife. Betty felt only excitement and confusion. Aunty Zita had crowned her only hours before with her new name of Betty Bouzikis. Betty staying in the flashest hotel in Beirut and wearing a new dress and married to a man twice her age. A travel ticket that read London, New York, Los Angeles, Honolulu, Auckland, New Plymouth. She compared this with Antoni's offer of a steering-class ticket to a boarding house in a place that Radio Beirut a day ago had announced was convulsed in revolution.

'Yes,' she said. 'I like Beirut.' She managed to smile. Happiness almost overtook excitement. She was doing what her mother had ordered by marrying a rich émigré Lebanese, and there was even the possibility for a happy future. But then the truth came back. She was again aware of deceit.

Betty looked at her husband. He should have been half his age. He should have been shorter and darker, with rough hands from soil and pruning. He should have smelled of cigarillos. He should have been called Antoni Hasroun. Money wasn't anything. That's all her mother thought of. She crossed her legs in her new dress in an attempt to look like Aunty Zita on her satin sofa in her apartment. Why had this New Zealand man wanted her so much? Why had he consented to a peasant and not to a Beiruti? She didn't understand. Antoni would never have had the money for a white suit, let alone have ever worn one. The man at the window. The other man she loved in Buenos Aires. She didn't know what to think as the time for bed crept closer. She counted to ten in Arabic, then did the same in French. Then she counted to sixty in English. But that reprieved nothing. She felt sick. She felt evil. She had actually let a man who wasn't her husband touch her thighs and her breasts.

'God's goodness is grace, and grace is a woman's purity,' Sister Veronique had insisted. That was lore, as Arab as it was French. A man would hold up the sheet on the balcony the morning after the wedding in order to show the village that his wife had been a virgin. She tried to imagine her husband on the hotel balcony waving the sheet at Beirut the next morning, the splotches of blood to prove she was pure. Cheers and cat calls and whistles from the multitudes.

For Neddy, marriage promised an end to his disease. He should have done it years before when he was still a young man, and so avoided the toilets and the disgrace and the sin. Avoided that feeling of failure because of his arrested adolescence, that stigma his mother had given him: childless and without even the consideration of providing her with grandchildren.

His mother might have been waiting there in the honeymoon suite, disbelieving until the marriage was consummated. There with Jim Birtwhistle and Dick Banks. She was certainly there in his mind. Wedged between his ears was the irritating echo: 'Ye! Ye! Marry! Get a wife!'

All those old Lebanese women who'd come out on boats as young brides before the Depression. Trotting down the church aisle in New Plymouth, dressed in grim black dresses and pearls, to take Communion. They, too, paraded in his mind on his wedding night. Mrs Karemeni saying he couldn't do it. Mrs Zerihen with that knowing look in her eyes.

'Just because…' he said.

'What did you say?' Betty asked in Arabic.

Just because Silvie Zerihen had found out what her own son was. Just because Alex Zerihen had been caught and Neddy hadn't. That look of remorse and reproach because her son was in Wellington Prison. What a well-kept secret. Silvie who had turned white overnight on account of her Alex's activities with teenage boys.

Lies to the priest. Lies to her friends. Lies to herself. Grey one day and white the next. Standing outside the church after Mass surrounded by her friends. 'The dreams. My husband he come to me in the dream last night and I think I go mad and when I waked up and look in the mirror there I am all white like the ghost.'

Dreams about her dead husband crying to her because he would be trapped in Limbo for ten million years. White hair because of that and not because the police had told her her son was a homosexual who'd been caught being sodomised by a schoolboy in a Wellington toilet.

'Alex,' Neddy said in a remote part of his mind. A hotel door slammed. It might have been in a prison. Slam. Slam. Slam. An entire corridor of prison cells shutting out light and freedom. The moon shone over the Mediterranean. 'Alex, Alex, Alex,' Neddy said.

The muezzin called from a nearby minaret, and the soft breeze from the Mediterranean floated in without the smell of diesel. It should have been so romantic. It should have been effortless to go to his wife, take off her blouse and fondle her young breasts. To kiss her and put her on the bed and make a child as he had been ordered. He turned and looked at Betty. She was beautiful. Jim Birtwhistle would have had her three or four times by now and be down in the bar bragging about it.

Surely it was easy. He took off his jacket and threw it on the sofa and smiled at her. 'Sleepy?' he asked. This was how it should be. The cure was effective; marriage would produce lust and desire, and the reality of being a real man who had overcome his arrested development. He hadn't suffered so much just to fail at this crucial time. Automatic, easy, simple. It was natural to have sex with your wife. It was normal to have sex with a female.

Neddy Bouzikis was married, and would produce a baby. He went to the bathroom and looked at himself; a handsome man who found himself in Beirut ready to have sex with a woman. Easy. He had not committed a terrible mistake. His old mother was right. It was just as Dr Proctor in New Plymouth had said.

'Your people... well, historically speaking... I mean... like the Greeks. They have an acceptance of this thing that our society calls abnormal. Arab culture, if you know what I mean. They are prepared to accept this... decadence. This disease... nothing that can't be fixed up with a nice wife. Someone young, innocent.'

He should have done it when he was twenty-one; found a beautiful girl, married her and had children, instead of succumbing to this disease. He had been weak, allowed himself to indulge his illness by committing sodomy in public toilets, in hotel rooms in Wellington. He was from a culture decadent enough to allow male homosexuality. It was horrible, one of the reasons why New Zealanders showed no respect for Arabs. They all knew in New Plymouth; if Dr Proctor did, then everyone would. All staring at him in Devon Street; a queer, a poofter, an Arab.

In the bathroom Neddy took off his clothes and stood in front of the mirror. Betty coughed softly from the bedroom. She must have been telling him that she was ready. In the mirror he wished himself good luck. One man staring at another. There were two people. He knew that.

One wanted to be in the hotel room in Wellington where there was no worry about achieving an erection. The other was the handsome man in the mirror who looked as if he could seduce a peasant woman without any worry. Doctor's orders. Take the cure.

The moment Neddy had postponed since puberty had come, and it didn't feel so difficult. Change would come from sticking his penis into his wife. Dr Proctor had promised him. It was what his mother must have been trying to tell him during four decades of that ugly ululation. One man walked out of the bathroom. The muezzin called and it was like an alarm clock going off in the middle of a bad dream. Fully awake, but the residual nightmare grasping for more attention. Neddy suddenly realised he knew nothing about Islam. He found himself wondering how many times a day a muezzin called Muslims to pray. Could a muezzin get married? Did he live in the mosque? Neddy wanted answers. There were so many questions about Muslims flooding his mind as he approached his marriage bed.

Betty was in bed with the lights off. Did a muezzin have a script he read from? Was he actually at the top of the minaret, or was it a loudspeaker system that blasted out his message? Neddy climbed into bed and pulled the sheet up to his chin, then stretched out his hand to touch his new wife. It was all right. He could do it because she was his innocent village wife. Another muezzin wailed from another mosque. They were like birds in trees, calling to each other at dusk.

His hand rested on her thigh.

'Yes, Neddy, take my advice and marry someone pretty and young and innocent who won't understand and with whom you can experiment.'

Dr Proctor's words echoed in Neddy's head. For several seconds his hand lay on the warm flesh of his wife and his cock stiffened with desire. It was just as Dr Proctor had prophesied.

∗

Neddy Bouzikis was very generous with his wife. He'd given her her own chequebook despite his mother's protestations.

'She's young yet and only from Bechare,' Fareda Bouzikis was saying. 'Your father didn't have any money when we came here and then the Depression and...' She poured some olive oil over her toast and popped it in her mouth. 'A chequebook of her own?'

Old Mrs Bouzikis had worked every day of her life, and money was something that was put into the bank because of the insecurity of existence. The Turks could come at any moment and destroy your village and burn your crops. In 1918 she'd gone for a week without so much as a lentil in her mouth.

She took another piece of toast and smeared sesame paste over it. 'Ye, you spoil the girl too much,' she said. 'She very good wife but you spoil her and she come out same as the Kiwi wife and no respect the man and turn into the spoiled bitch and want the divorce, one, two, three, like that.'

On the wall above the coffee grinder hung a calendar from Uncle Bishara's business in Beirut. A bright picture of the city under the full Mediterranean sun with the Corniche a strip of happiness lined with apartment blocks.

'Doesn't she work as hard as anyone else?' Neddy asked as he admired the picture.

'Yes, she's a very good worker. What more could I ask for?'

Neddy looked at his mother. What more could she ask for? Her bovine eyes answered her own question. She had bought booties and baby singlets... blue ones because that was propitious.

'Money not important,' she continued. 'What important the baby and now nine month since you have the wedding and still not a baby in sight for me and very old I'm getting. Nine month you been married and where the baby?'

A shiver of disgust went down Neddy's spine at the thought of that wedding night in Beirut.

'Never mind, Mum,' he said. 'It's early yet and I suppose with all the difference in water and food and everything she's...'

'Water? Food? Ye! Babies are sacred for the old age. Ye! Water no excuse, Neddy.' A look of betrayal swept across her face as she put the last of the toast into her mouth.

'Darling,' she said. 'Betty very intelligent and very proud I am in front of Mrs Zerihen and Mrs Karemeni because their daughters-in-law no good. Up to no good business all of them, but our Betty she very good...' Fareda did believe that. So many times she'd stopped in the passageway and thanked God behind his silver frame that at last her big son had done what he should have done twenty years previously. And God had told her to go out and buy blue clothes. God knew what was right and what was wrong, and what would happen, and it was blue baby clothes he had ordered.

Old Mrs Bouzikis was just about to get up to heat the coffee when Betty came back from shopping with Jillian Shingles, her new friend from the Repertory Theatre. The tall Inglesi woman extended her hand and began saying nice things in her posh voice. Neddy's face was at once surprised and pleased. But Betty! Her face was made up with lipstick and powder, and her hair, for the first time in public, was not tied in a scarf but had been pushed off her face and lacquered into a stiff curl at the nape of her neck.

'I'm going to be Hermione,' Betty said. 'In a play.'

*

Fareda Bouzikis and her two friends were seated around the card table at Zahia Karemeni's playing euchre.

'Ye, it's hot!' Fareda said. She took off her cardigan and with her deft hands dealt cards to her friends. The three of them at the table as they were every Saturday afternoon sharing their widowhood. Silvie Zerihen was in black. She'd never come out of it after her husband's death. Just when she'd relented enough to wear grey, she'd realised that her sins had not yet been purged: her son had been turned into a homosexual and locked up in prison for interfering with teenage boys. She sighed the sigh of all Maronite mothers and threw an ace on to the pile in a hope that Alex would be forgotten.

The ritual of Saturday afternoons concentrated upon talk of children and grandchildren, and the prospect of great-grandchildren. Dead husbands were second on the list, followed by in-laws.

'Ye,' Fareda said, 'you'll never guess what the daughter-in-law is up to.' You came to the cards afternoon to crow about your children's successes, but it was also possible to divulge complaints if they weren't of the magnitude of divorce or perverted sex.

'Elvira. She's calling herself Elvira, and not Betty any longer. And more than that...' Fareda collected the kitty from the middle of the table and added it to the winnings already stashed under her handkerchief.

'But Elvira is a beautiful name. She's a very beautiful girl and you should... What do you mean more than that?' Silvie asked. She wanted someone's child to commit a sin greater than her Alex's. Five years locked up for something that in Lebanon was commonplace if done with boys from the souk. The injustice smacked her. Those boys in Wellington were fourteen and fifteen. That wasn't a boy at all. That was a grown man, and if they'd been in the old country, they'd be out working in their fields or the souk or a shop. Lebanese men weren't put into prison for that. Men did it with boys because they had to do it with someone, and you couldn't take a girl before marriage. It was natural, but these Inglesi didn't even... Such injustice! She threw down a card and placed a higher stake. Men having sex with other men. Back home it happened in the orchards. All the women knew that. You only dragged out that information when you wanted revenge against someone. Here it happened in public toilets, as the police had announced. 'Your son has been arrested for perversion.'

Perversion. She'd thought that was something to do with politics. She hadn't understood. There at her front door at seven o'clock in the morning in her nightdress and curlers. Perversion. Sedition. Treason. She'd got them all mixed up. In Lebanon a word like that meant the death penalty.

'What did Betty do?' she insisted.

'Ye! An actress,' Fareda said with trepidation. She looked hurriedly at her two friends. Her opinion of Elvira was in the balance: perhaps it was something to be proud of; perhaps it was something only a slut would do.

'Just like a Kiwi woman and she's only been here nine months,' Zahia said.

'But in New Zealand it's very popular, this acting,' Silvie said. 'Let her be a Kiwi. Let her live. What does Neddy think?'

Neddy was the problem. He had encouraged the young monkey to go out and spend money. This dress and that pair of shoes and that make-up and this ribbon, and now it was even records she wanted. The Beatles on the record machine. Blah. Blah. Blah. Yeah. Yeah. Yeah. Up too loud. Jiggling about in the lounge by herself in a tent frock.

'Music. Ye! In my day...' Fareda shook her head as if she could dispel problems by tossing her old grey hair. Elvira was a girl still, not a married woman or a mother. She'd come from Bechare a peasant, and all this money all of a sudden and dressed up like a tart. A mistake. Neddy should have married a girl from Beirut after all. She shouldn't have insisted on country stock. Fareda looked at her two best friends for the support she sought. Daughters-in-law were the worst sort of relation, especially if they were Inglesi. This one was a Lebanese, but here she was suddenly turning herself into one of these New Plymouth Inglesi and not even in the place twelve months. Her bovine eyes blinked back tears. Neddy her darling. Neddy who deserved the best wife in the whole world.

✳

'Actually,' Elvira Bouzikis said, 'I'm from Beirut.' She was standing next to the ticket box, close to a man. It was the first time she'd ever been entirely alone with a male Kiwi. The sort who strutted down Devon Street past the fruit shop at lunch time or leaned against a lamppost, smoking and laughing with his office mates. He wasn't old. He wasn't dark and hairy. He wasn't Lebanese. He was Inglesi and exotic. The sort of man who would invite you to a barbecue; one of those men Elvira had seen at the beach running down to the waves and throwing themselves into the surf.

'I'm an accountant with Stanley and Stanley,' the man said. He was wearing long pants on purpose. He'd thought he wouldn't have been able to impress her in his shorts and long socks, because he knew that foreigners didn't go in for that sort of thing. He hadn't realised the look she'd allowed him the previous week was because of his big legs and his blond hair and his New Zealand adult uniform of walk shorts and knee-length socks.

'Do all the girls in Beirut wear mini-skirts like yours?' He lit a cigarette, drew in deeply and exhaled a plume of blue smoke.

'It's very modern there. Everyone think we are just peasants. I been here nearly twelve month.' Elvira lilted her accent so that it sounded French. 'They say Beirut it the Paris of the Middle East. We're not peasant.'

'I've known your husband for years,' the man said. 'He's quite well known around New Plymouth, eh.' He fixed his blue eyes on her breasts and sucked on the cigarette. 'He's been around for years, him and his family. Quite a little business they've got. That and their flats on Kowhai Street.'

Elvira experienced a strange and disturbing feeling but didn't want to acknowledge where it came from. She moved away to the window to see if Neddy had arrived to pick her up.

'1 didn't think Arab girls dressed like you did,' he said. He took a few steps towards her. 'I mean, that's a pretty short dress you've got on.' He ran his hand through his cropped hair. He was a strange mixture of beach boy and accountant.

'I'm not a Arab,' Elvira said. 'I'm a Phoenician. Phoenicians aren't Arabs, because Arabs are Muslims and we're Maron... Catholics.' She went to the ticket box and phoned Neddy at the fruit shop. 'So, I get a taxi, then,' she said loudly. 'As soon as rehearsals they finished. We got another couple of hour to go.' She went back and stood next to the blond man. Now that she had surrendered to complicity, she could acknowledge what that feeling was crawling through her veins. It was adoration.

'You ready then?'

'*Oui*,' she said.

There was no need to waste time going elsewhere when there was a back room where the props were kept. There was too much haste to get their clothes off and fall on to the mattress, which smelled of other theatrical liaisons. They disturbed some rats, which began running around and squeaking in the rafters.

The man put his mouth on Elvira's stiff nipple and sucked it. He moved her hand to his crotch. 'Touch it,' he said. 'Like this.'

When she bled, he said, 'Fuck, I didn't think you'd be a virgin.'

At last Elvira was in New Zealand and saw clearly that she no longer wanted to go home to the old country. She had burned a bridge. Just looking at the man's Kiwi face told her that. His bleached moustache and his firm muscles. Even his smell was different, not like lemons and salt. She licked his armpit and tasted disinfectant and sausages.

'Why the hell didn't he fuck you?' the man asked. Elvira didn't know how to answer that question, but she owed Neddy something, especially now that she was involved in marital treason. She wanted to defend her husband, that one aspect of his honour anyway, but she didn't know how to phrase it.

'Why not?' the man insisted. He felt as flushed by the fact that he'd just fucked a virgin as he did by the gossip it would entail.

Sadness crept into Elvira as she realised that this man was just a Kiwi Antoni Hasroun, with a blond moustache instead of a black one. The same disrespect and sleaziness.

'You didn't tell me why he didn't fuck you,' he said. Elvira grasped his wrists and pushed his hands on to her thighs. Up and down and up and down; she dug her nails into his skin as she showed him what she demanded.

'You like that, eh,' he said. 'Thighs.' He managed to be romantic. 'Like cream.'

In the marriage bed in the Cedars of Lebanon Hotel, Elvira had pulled away from her husband. His hands on her thighs. His and not Antoni's. Her husband's stiff penis touching her leg so that she felt like crying. Tears for Antoni. Tears for herself. Her mother there in the bedroom with them waiting for her daughter to lose her virginity and so become the legitimate possession of a rich man, the one she'd forced onto her in the kitchen. Antoni, too, who had renounced his Rosita and come back to claim her. In her marriage bed being watched by her mother and the Druse; the sheet being held up. It was a horrible moment that she'd dreaded her whole life, and she had coiled up like a foetus to avoid it.

'No, all right. That's all right. It'll take time.' Neddy's words in her head as she fucked the blond Kiwi. 'No, all right then, dear.' Even about sex he was understanding. And that had started the trend. From that honeymoon night to this. He was a very good man, her husband. She thought of him in his silk shirt and white jacket. An object of derision. On the next occasion he'd tried to touch her, his hands on her thighs, she'd said, 'Wait yet.' He was too good. She was evil. She squirmed in the blond man's arms as he fucked her. She saw herself coiled up in her husband's bed. She heard herself saying to him in the kitchen, bright and breezy and innocent, 'Can I have some money?' It was a sick idea. She hadn't realised the enormity of the sickness until that very moment; that she had saved herself for the man she loved and had denied her legitimate husband what was his by marriage and kindness.

It was the rats in the rafters that changed her perspective. It was that look at life. Antoni Hasroun with an Argentinian called Rosita. Her mother who knew only about poison. You lived in a Maronite village and learned about the falseness of allegiance and the reality of treason. Druse, Maronite, Muslim. A rat squealed. Neddy was a fool for having brought her to this. For having bought her. For giving her chequebooks and taking nothing in return. She didn't understand it. She'd lain awake in bed on too many nights trying to rekindle his attention with sighs and whispers, and never so much as a touch in return. She didn't know how men thought or acted, because her only reference had been princes in French novels set in the eighteenth century, and that deceitful Druse.

There were rats in life and rats in New Zealand and rats in Lebanon. The one she wanted was Antoni Hasroun, and here he was. She recognised him.

'Well?' he said. 'Why were you still a virgin?' It was a great story for the pub. He wasn't sure if the boys would believe it. But of course the husband was Neddy Bouzikis, and they all knew what a poofter he was. He spurted laughter as he pulled out his penis and shoved it in again.

'Beautiful,' he said. 'Fuck, what a chick.' In and out and in and out. Ten minutes of bliss with an Arab.

Night falling in New Zealand. Elvira assumed that because both countries were in the Southern Hemisphere they would share the same time zone; dusk in Buenos Aires. Black moustache and dark lips. A blond man in swim shorts running into the Pacific Ocean. It was better like this. To have admitted it after twelve months of suffering with Neddy. The cat's eyes of her mother. Marry him. Marry him. Be rich. She wondered why she'd waited a lifetime for this moment. It was only a secret because she hadn't admitted it. There was no one except him.

'*Antoni Hasroun*,' she screamed at the rafters. The same rạt with the long tail was still in the same position.

'What?' the man said. He paused, looked down to where they were joined and then pushed in again. Elvira had to bite her lips. She was being fucked by a Druse, not a Maronite; a Lebanese wasn't inside her, but a Kiwi.

'You like that, don't you?' he said. He was used to having chicks fall for him. This sheila really liked him though, he could tell that. The way she moved her hips. Bit of the tarbrush. He sniggered at the thought of all his liaisons: he was telling his mates at the pub. Each time he pushed in, the image of some sheila in his photo album, his scoreboard. A bit of dark blood. Maori sheilas. They went crazy for this sort of treatment.

'Your old man's got plenty of money,' he said. 'No wonder you stay with him, even if he's a queer.'

She knew what queer meant. Her mother-in-law called half the people who came into the fruit shop queer this and queer that; Miss Jones was queer because she didn't have a husband and lived alone with eleven cats. Mr Simmons above the fruit shop was queer because he collected egg cartons and stayed alone at Christmas.

She felt better after her catharsis about rats. That had answered so many questions. She looked at this man with whom she was having illicit sex. She didn't know his name and didn't want to ask him. Ahmed. Emil. Harry. Max. You could be married to a man for a year and know everything about him; that he waited to fart in the bathroom, that that he liked sugar in tea but not in coffee. But you wouldn't so much as let him put his hand on your thigh, to let him touch you. And here this man was probably giving her a baby. She held on to him and pressed her buttocks up, and he pushed in and out and groaned when she did. When she came for the fourth time it was no longer Antoni Hasroun she loved but his imitation. This man about whom she didn't have a clue except that he was blond and completely Kiwi and had taught her what an orgasm was.

✳

Hermione, the daughter of Menelaus and Helen of Troy, sat on the stage in the New Plymouth Repertory Theatre in a skimpy toga of muslin and every now and then shouted, 'Trojans unite! Trojans to the defence!' Even her few lines in French had been dispensed with because the Repertory committee realised they should have pity on a New Plymouth audience. The play had been made 1960s. The committee was very concerned about the promotion of good theatre. You couldn't just perform Shakespeare, for example, with all that old language and expect a local audience to bother with it. Not with the recent influx of television sets.

Fareda Bouzikis had been quite happy to come along for the first night despite her protests. She was sitting in the third row from the front with her son and Zahia Karemeni and Silvie Zerihen.

'Sssssh!' Neddy warned the old women, who were whispering away. Menelaus was delivering his speech, but his English was so swift that they couldn't understand what was being said.

For Neddy, it was a moment of pride mixed with happiness at the sight of his wife up there in front of the most respectable people in the city. As Jillian Shingles the director had said, 'She's a star. A "born actress."' Neddy felt pleased. He had a hankering for the arts but had never known how to release it. It had always been the fruit shop this and the fruit shop that. And a real man didn't have the time or the inclination to get mixed up with things like theatre and ballet. Not in New Plymouth. In New Plymouth you had to hide your proclivities. The Repertory Theatre was synonymous with people who learned Esperanto and drank wine and ate cheese and biscuits at soirees for arty people. You weren't deemed a normal male if you got dressed up and went on stage. You had to be careful if you were in business. You never knew what normal people might say. The bank manager, the accountant, the people in the tax department. They might take exception to anything that wasn't sanitary and matey. There were prisons full of poofters. The prison where poofters were incarcerated was actually up there on the hill overlooking New Plymouth.

Neddy sat watching this woman to whom he was married. She had certainly been useful. He no longer felt afraid that men thought he was a homosexual; that women thought he was that way inclined. He had a wife. He could actually walk down the street now and not wonder if people were wondering about him. It didn't matter. She didn't even want to have sex. In London, on the way back from Beirut, he'd taken his new wife to see Hamlet, but the whole time he'd been too preoccupied about his sexual dilemma to enjoy the play.

It had been an evening of examining excuses; hers and his. The dangerous thoughts that Dr Proctor's prognosis had been wrong had again flooded in and overwhelmed him. Marriage was not the panacea that it ought to have been. There was no way out. He didn't seem to be able to get an erection. As he sat in that London theatre, there seemed no way to escape the dilemma except through suicide. Even if Betty had allowed his initial advances, he knew he wouldn't have been able to go through with it. A mixture of fear and failure and a complete lack of desire; his disease was incurable. Dr Proctor had given him false promises. Hamlet had been dramatising some minuscule aspect of the human dilemma there in front of him while he, Neddy Bouzikis, sat there with the whole drama of his own life being acted out in his tormented mind. 'What will I do in bed tonight? What will she think?'

Attrition had solved the dilemma. He was married to a woman with whom he didn't have sex. It had taken him six months to understand that it was Betty who was frigid. There were blessings. He wanted to thank the god he didn't believe in for the luck of having a woman with no desire. She was beautiful up there on stage. Her little breasts beautifully formed behind the thin toga. Exotic. Lebanese. He felt proud, of her. She was sweet. She was more like a sister whom he didn't understand and for whom he had no deeper appreciation.

✳

It was 17 April 1935, Neddy Bouzikis's fourteenth birthday. Only he and Alex Zerihen, his second cousin, were at home. They were sitting in the front living room, which had an overstuffed sofa and a view of Mount Egmont. Several uncles, dead and buried in Lebanon, hung on walls behind dreary frames. On top of the wireless the Virgin Mary held out her hands with alabaster rays emanating from each immaculate palm.

'I hate school,' Alex said. 'I'm going to run away to somewhere where…' He closed his eyes in the expectation that a big city like Wellington would suddenly open up before him and sweep him away from Aunty Fareda and Uncle Jo's house in New Plymouth.

'Where?' Neddy said.

'Wellington, because it's big and when we went there for a holiday we stayed in a hotel and ate in the restaurant.' Alex was the sort of boy who knew exactly what he wanted. His teacher had written 'Precociousness leading to arrogance' on his report card. In his mind a thousand cars, and narrow city streets; he leaned back in the sofa and thought about the tall buildings and the handsome, well-dressed men he'd seen.

'Why should I go and work in their bloody shop?' He got up and switched on the wireless and raucous music bounced into the grey room. Neddy watched Alex pirouetting around the room. Alex was different from his other cousins, which was why Neddy liked him. He was accused of being scatty, so unlike a Lebanese boy because he resented working in his parents' haberdashery.

'It's a bloody half-lit dump run by foreigners who speak with Middle Eastern accents,' he had confided to Neddy.

Alex grabbed his Aunty Fareda's patterned scarf. 'They reek of garlic. Why do they allow so many in?'

The sentences picked up from the streets. Alex saw himself in Wellington, where there were more Lebanese and Italians and Greeks.

He placed the scarf over his head so that he saw nothing but the red and white and yellow pattern.

'Dance with me, you queer,' he said to his cousin. They went arm in arm around the room as they'd seen Ginger Rogers and Fred Astaire do in the pictures.

'Ginger,' Alex said.

'Yes, my darling?'

'Will you come to Wellington with me? Run away and go and live down there where there aren't any relatives?'

'But Aunty Basma and Uncle Rouky...' Neddy couldn't think like Alex, for whom there weren't any obstacles like reality.

'Let's go into Ahmed's hut,' Alex said. 'He's at work.' He led Neddy by the hand through the house and into the garden, where Ahmed lived in a converted shed.

'Let's put on these,' Alex said. Ahmed was twenty-two and had all the clothes that a young man should wear. A tweed suit and a racy red tie and a striped shirt. On the hook behind the door was a smart fedora.

'Go on,' Alex said. 'Get dressed up like a man and show me.'

'Show you what?' Neddy asked.

It was a game they'd played often, but each time it had to be just like the first. Dressing up in innocence. Going through the motions of a procedure that would inevitably lead to seduction.

'Get dressed like Ahmed,' Alex said.

'Only if you do too.'

Alex was an excellent actor in this game of seduction. So much innocence. He took off his clothes and moved about the small room pretending to search for the underwear. Stretching up slowly to the top of the cupboard. Bending over to search under the bed.

'I can't find it,' he said. He stood there with his penis stiff and the look on his face that said the game had reached the part where Neddy had to kneel and say, 'Ahmed, will you be my boyfriend?'

✳

Elvira Bouzikis had a couple of hours before she was expected home. She looked at her watch and ran the excuses for her absence through her mind. But excuses didn't matter anyway. Her husband didn't care what she did. Excuses were just something residual from the days in the orchard when there was a huge penalty for the impurity of being touched on the thigh by a Maronite, let alone by a man from another religion. These days, after thirteen months of marriage, she could come home at ten o'clock at night, make a mug of warm milk and flop into her new twin bed without having to say anything to Neddy. It was just the old bitch she had to worry about. The taxi stopped, outside Gary Shingles' house on Pleasant Drive.

'There's no use pretending, is there, Elvira?' That's all her husband had said on the afternoon she'd come home to find the double bed gone and two singles in the bedroom.

'No, no sense in pretending,' she'd answered. And that was it. No sense in pretending except in front of his mother: single beds because of his snoring. He should have taken her in his arms. He should have treated her as her father had his wife. Belted her. Sworn at her. A man wasn't supposed to be weak like Neddy was. It was too confusing. He was nice and here she was being horrible about him and thinking that she should be beaten into respect just to end up like her mother. She had as much money as she wanted. She rarely went to the shop to work. He was a good man; he respected her wishes to be left alone and now she was making excuses to hate him because of her own sense of guilt for being in love with this Kiwi.

Elvira left the taxi driver the four shillings change. It was a lot but she didn't give a damn. It was only her husband's cash. She was being paid to act like a princess, so why not flaunt it? Neddy wasn't even a real man. Not like Gary. Again she looked at her watch. This time she dismissed any excuses with the same bitter casualness as she had just abandoned the change.

Gary Shingles' house wasn't dark and old and full of history like the place she lived in with her husband and Fareda. She walked up the scoria path with its immaculate border of marigolds and petunias. In the lawn three trimmed shrubs. There wasn't a compost heap, reviving the memory of Jo dropping dead. There was no shed at the bottom of the vegetable garden still referred to reverentially as Ahmed's. Elvira took a deep breath of air. Even the mountain looked different from Gary's place. The suburb was new and brick, and lay stretched out on a hill with the volcano behind it. A picture postcard with no history. No valley that had been crossed by Crusaders and Muslims and Maronites.

This was New Zealand, where you could be an actress and the only one who called you a whore was your Lebanese mother-in-law. Everyone else called it art and the mayoress gave you a bunch of flowers and asked you to cocktail parties.

It was the first time she'd been to Gary's house, and the first time since she'd arrived in New Zealand that she felt she really understood what she wanted from this country. New, fresh, bright: a house and real love from a real Kiwi. She saw it all as freedom. Light and breezy. There was a bright wooden butterfly on the side of the house, and a trellis with sweet peas. A woman came out of the house next door and waved cheerily before wheeling a pram down the footpath. It was a thousand miles from her house in the middle of New Plymouth, and another planet from that ancient thick-walled house in Bechare.

Freedom smacked her; right there, on the concrete path to the left of the butterfly, an indescribable feeling of love and newness and acceptance all meshed to give her the clearest insight into her existence that she had ever experienced. New Zealand. New Zealand. It was a sound to her as sweet as the smell of apricots had once been. Just the fact that there was a manicured garden and an expensive fence without a grape vine spilling over it. No fruit trees. No vegetables. No dark shadows that still told those in Bechare the secrets of where Yusuf Adani had been chopped up by the Turks, or where Aunty had been laid out by a heart attack, or where so and so had proposed to so and so and been refused and then thrown himself in the well. No thick honking from donkeys. Here it was clean, and if you got sick you went to a free and efficient hospital, and you had a pension when you got old, and...

Elvira was wearing a tent frock that floated about her if she turned quickly or wanted to appear theatrical. She twirled on the path to demonstrate her happiness at being surrounded by so much that was so beautiful. Gary had dressed for the occasion in fashionable clothes, which didn't suit his thick body and football aura. He didn't look the sort who would appreciate listening to folk songs or smoking pot, but his new clothes suggested that he wasn't really an accountant with a brick house in a provincial suburb who liked to listen to Oswald Cheeseman and his Orchestra. He knew he had to get married one day, and this sheila was a good bet because she had something he lacked. As his sister Jillian had said, 'Elvira has class, and you need it.'

'Want a beer?' he said.

'I'd like wine, please.'

'I haven't got any,' he said. His theory of class had few practical applications. 'What about a shandy?' He wasn't used to sophisticated sorts. His girls were more than happy with a pint of lager and a packet of potato chips.

'Shandy?' she asked.

'Yeah, it's what New Zealand girls like – beer mixed with lemonade.'

'In Beirut we drink arak. We sit in cafés like the French.'

'Well, we're not in Beirut now, are we?'

Gary's long collar didn't match his haircut; he should have had sideburns down to his jawbone instead of the deadly effect of a short back and sides. He looked trapped between what he wanted to be and what he was.

He fingered his tight collar and wished he hadn't spent six quid on a shirt that was fit only for poofters or beatniks. Class. That was the sort of thing that Jillian had gotten messed up in; hoity-toity voice and looking down her nose at football and a man who made good money managing rural accounts.

'But I like New Zealand,' she said. 'Shandy? Okay, good, beauty.'

She was very beautiful. She had the sort of eyes that tart who'd played Cleopatra had, long and Mediterranean-looking. Gary stood there for a moment transfixed by an unusual moment of introspection: this woman was presenting herself to him like Cleopatra had to Mark Antony in the film he'd just seen. He looked down at his new pointed shoes, which were highlighted by the width of his flared maroon trousers. This for her, his foreign mistress, his Cleopatra.

'Everybody in Beirut like the wine and the arak and they all dressing very fashionable and we are not Arab but Phoenician like the white people.' Aunty Zita was speaking through Elvira's mouth. It was as if one's class and culture could be grafted on like a branch to an old tree; new fruit on old stock. 'Everybody in Beirut they know me. They know Elvira.' She put her hand to her heart just as Zita did when she sat on her satin sofa in her Beirut apartment and pontificated in broken French: Phoenician, white skin, dirty Arabs.

'What are you going to do about him?' Gary said. His heart was beating and his gums salivated. It was a physical sensation he hadn't experienced since he'd lost his virginity in the fourth form.

'Him?' she said. 'But he's my husband.' Instead of Aunty Zita it was her mother who now spoke. Even her hand had moved from her heart to her stomach, and she remembered with total clarity the first time she'd associated the cat's eyes in the ruins of Baalbek with those of her mother.

'Ye,' she said. 'My God, I need the drink. Not the shandy. Get me some wine please.' Her mother and Aunty Zita. Her mother-in-law and Neddy Bouzikis. All the old Lebanese ladies in New Plymouth. Her hand was still on her stomach; she thought she felt the thing move inside of her and she panicked.

'All right, then,' he said. 'I'll pop down to the pub and get you some wine. Wait here a minute.'

She was a good-looking bitch. She had class, she spoke French and her family was rich. He could see the future coming together; her on his arm in some place other than New Plymouth, perhaps even Auckland. The thought of divorce was reason for an erection.

He kissed her, put his tongue in her mouth. It was a taste of his honeymoon; he pushed into her. What a gorgeous chick... not like those sluts he picked up at the pub.

She wanted more kissing. She put his hand on her breast and thought about marriage to this man who was so handsome and so blond and so New Zealand, and then she saw her mother and all the old Lebanese ladies who would skin her, kill her, lament and wail and flagellate themselves for eternity.

'Get the wine,' she said pushing him away. 'Darling.'

While Gary was away, Elvira did a quick tour of the house. Three bedrooms, all with new carpet and each bed with a candlewick spread. Everything shone. It was as if nobody lived in this house. She stood in front of the mirror in his bedroom.

'Kiwi girl like the divorce too much. Just like the American.' Her mother-in-law's voice, thick, from the back of her throat. 'The divorce evil. Sin. The Pope and God they no like it.' But divorce was legitimate. Jillian Shingles had had a husband, but he'd gone off to Auckland with another woman. A number of the Repertory women had got rid of their husbands. There was so much freedom here Elvira didn't know what to do with it. This beautiful bedroom. The candlewick spreads. She could see herself in here with Gary and happy to be married to someone who knew she was a woman and would love her for everything she was. You could do anything in life if you didn't live in a Lebanese village. Why live with a Lebanese at all? Injustice went rushing through her like a virus; she almost understood her husband's reasons for not indulging his rights as a male, but instead she had another visitation from the Lebanese. Uncle Bishara shouting at her. He even raised his hand to strike her face. Neddy Bouzikis was the best man in the whole world. Look what he had given her... a new country, money, freedom... and look what she intended to give him in return... divorce, shame, unhappiness.

'Forget it, Bishara,' she said. She'd bought freedom that night in her parents' kitchen when she'd decided to come to this place at the bottom of the world. You didn't come this far just to relive that same old stuff of thick walls and repression. She wanted Gary Shingles; she wanted the candlewick bedspreads and new carpets and the brick house with its butterfly, and a baby with blue eyes who would be a real New Zealander. She twirled in her tent frock just as she had done in the garden; around and around thinking of Gary Shingles.

It was all clear now. A grand plan had been put into motion on the day Antoni Hasroun's letter had arrived from Buenos Aires. Elvira had been meant to come to New Zealand and not end up in poverty with a Druse in South America. Neddy had merely been the vehicle to this moment. She didn't even feel sorry for her husband. Nice but useless.

There was a photo album on the bureau in front of the mirror, and Elvira flipped open the plastic cover. She gagged as she turned from one page to the next, revealing photo after photo of nude girls lying in all sorts of poses. In one picture there were two girls with Gary lying between them, holding his penis for them to worship. In another, the girl couldn't have been older than fourteen.

This was the man she'd fallen in love with and whose baby she was carrying. The man she wanted to marry was a sex maniac who did it with... with... In the next photo a girl who... who... Elvira sank to her knees and vomited on the carpet she had so recently coveted.

This Kiwi belonged to the same class of animals as that Druse Hasroun. Men were vile. Men were animals. Again she vomited, a mixture of her mother-in-law's hommos and tabouleh.

She heard his car in the driveway. The rats in the rafters; she heard them squeaking, laughing at her, their beady eyes yellow with derision. Getting pregnant by a sex maniac when she had ignored her wonderful husband because he didn't fit the image of what she wanted. The lesson learned from rats; she was the chief among them.

'You had to have a look, did you? You fucking fancy bitch,' Gary snarled.

Elvira had heard that just before you die your life flashes before you. She saw herself; peasant, wife, actress, adulteress and whore, mother and fool. People were murdered in gutters or chopped up by enemies wielding swords. But you were never able to envisage what terror those final moments had held. She saw the familiar victims falling and felt their agonies; the adulterer shot in the orchard, the Syrian thief hanging, Uncle Yusuf knifed by Turkish soldiers.

Gary stood above her with a lamp base in his hand.

'No,' she said. 'I'm pregnant.'

'Fucking wog,' he shouted. His arm was raised, but it was entirely symbolic. There was his career to think of. He was too rational for physical violence.

'I'll tell everybody,' he said. 'You wogs are finished in New Plymouth. Fucking poofter of a husband. I know who he's been buggering. He's a queer, didn't you know that?' He backed away and looked at her with such contempt that for a few seconds he couldn't speak.

'Fucking go back to your own country,' Gary finally spluttered. 'Jillian says you don't even know that your husband fucks boys.' He could think of no invectives about her personally. The only ones that were vile enough for the punishment she deserved for witnessing his photo album were about her husband.

Elvira pushed herself up and backed away from him even though she knew she had been reprieved from a bashing. In Lebanon she wouldn't have been so lucky. Her brother, her father, her husband, any male would have been able to kill her for what she had done, and there was no such crime as murder for dispensing that kind of justice. In the mirror her reflection: Elvira Bouzikis from Bechare in a tent frock soiling with colours and stained by vomit. Her hair stacked up in a beehive and lacquered. The nuns would have smacked her across the face and had her wash off the make-up with carbolic acid.

'But,' she said. 'I'm pregnant. I didn't...'

'Don't fucking tell me stories about babies.'

'I'm going to have your baby,' she cried.

'Well, I hope it's got fucking blue eyes,' he snarled sarcastically. 'Just like your husband's.' He put down the lamp. 'Clean up that sick,' he said, 'and piss off.'

*

Neddy Bouzikis had requested that room for the perverse pleasure it gave him. Love. What a thing! He had finally managed it. He lay back in bed and thought about all that had happened in the last six weeks. You could be static for forty years, then suddenly events swept you far from the detritus of everyday existence. He licked his lips at the memories of this wonderful day: the cool white wine they'd been drinking all evening, the delicious food and the scenery. Even the sunset was ideal for the perfect honeymoon: orange, pink and indigo. Love on your honeymoon. Good food and wine and beauty, and the company of one who could sit opposite you at the table and understand and appreciate and love you. From close by the muezzin called, that high shrill incantation to the faithful that had so alarmed him on that first time in the Cedars of Lebanon Hotel.

Neddy was sitting naked on the bed. Freedom was fabulous. He had the idea that it would never end, that it would go on and on now that his life in New Plymouth was over. His body ached for it. He moved his legs apart and rubbed his thigh and laughed. Up and down, his hand touching his own hairy thigh. Just like she'd told him about in her torrent of tears on that afternoon she'd screamed she was pregnant.

'It was my thighs,' Elvira had sobbed.

Touching her thigh on the first night of their honeymoon. On this very bed, the terror of abnormality and sickness. They were still laughing at him in New Plymouth. The whole story had come out and vicious notes had been shoved under the door of the fruit shop. The muezzin called again, and Neddy laughed because on that first night when he'd asked so many questions about Islam, it had been terror that had blocked the answers. There was no fear now, no regrets and no sham attempts at normality. Freedom! What a sublime feeling, and all the more because he had suffered to achieve it.

'Do I forgive her?' he wondered. 'Now that she's dead and buried? An old Lebanese mother who really loved me and never understood what it is to be a man with no feeling for the opposite sex?' All the household stuff had been packed up in boxes, sent to the auction rooms and sold for next to nothing. The picture of Jesus, the one above the telephone, had gone to a Brethren who'd bargained for ten minutes to get the price down to sixpence.

'I'm going to enjoy my life of sin,' Neddy decided. 'I deserve it.'

That bloody fruit shop. He smiled at the intrusion of those haunting smells; the dry, hairy smell of Fijian coconuts and the sweet sickliness of over-ripe apricots. His mother waving her duster at the bins of pungent feijoas and acidic gooseberries. And Elvira and her fate? He wondered for a moment if he'd been too generous with his cheque for three thousand pounds and a house.

Alex Zerihen emerged from the bathroom. Six weeks of attention, good food and freedom had returned his shape and Levantine colouring. He stood at the end of the bed grinning that naughty-boy look through the slackness of his ageing countenance.

'Feijoas,' Neddy said. 'What is it about them that makes me think of semen?'

'Their odour,' Alex replied, holding his purply-brown specimen. 'Spunk mixed with perfume. Delicious. Do you like sucking them?'

3 My Kiwi Prince

On the day of the coronation of Queen Elizabeth II, George Crossett sighed with a mixture of tedium and apprehension in the darkening carriage of a train travelling from Wellington to New Plymouth. It was the last carriage on the train, and empty now that the family of six had got off at Wanganui. George stretched out in his seat, happy in the knowledge that he was alone.

'How magnificent to be in San Francisco or London,' he thought, putting down his newspaper with its multitude of photos of the royal family. Outside, the paddocks rushed by in cruel contrast to his impossible passion for really big cities. A farmer silhouetted on a tractor, and a house lit up behind the ghostliness of macrocarpa trees. The lights there and then gone. Cows dumbly plodding in file through the eerie depths of the last light, another house, then more dark bush and hills, menacing in their remoteness.

George turned his head from the desultory Taranaki landscape and stared at the new monarch on the seat beside him, his depression physical almost, smothering him like a damp blanket. There he was, thirty-three years old and, after years of living in Wellington, returning to New Plymouth to look after his ailing father. He felt a combination of blankness and confusion because today was yet another anniversary of his dishonourable discharge from the Royal New Zealand Navy for licentious behaviour and perversion.

He grimaced at the prospect of having to face the trial of living in New Plymouth again, a hideous circumstance for which there was no alternative. His father wouldn't leave his home and his magnificent memorial garden. Licentious behaviour; it was a nightmarish refrain, constantly repeated in his mind.

'George Crossett, you are hereby dismissed from any duties in the Royal New Zealand Navy.' Captain Smart sitting next to the admiral, and King George VI in a photo behind them. 'From these letters and these photos, it is obvious that you have been involved in sustained activities that are contradictory to the status of the Royal New Zealand Navy. You have heard the evidence.'

George wondered where that photo was now, the one Smart had held aloft during the proceedings. In which file? In which office? In the dock in the military courtroom in Auckland they had made him hold that photo and describe the licentious behaviour that had occurred, extracting it from him, leading him into the ugly confessions of his affair with Desmond. That bloody photo of himself with his legs crossed, posing for Des's camera, with his arm stretched out and his index finger pointing, effeminately puckering a kiss at his boyfriend's naval cap.

'You know, don't you, Crossett,' Captain Smart had told him in the few moments they had met together before the trial, 'that we needed every man, so called in your case, until the threat of a Japanese invasion was over. I didn't want to upset the Americans by telling them about you and that La Verde character. But this business with Sybil's husband. A wonderful woman like that to find such photos and letters in her deceased husband's desk. That was the final straw that brought me to lay charges.'

George picked up the photo of the new Queen; so serene, so beautiful, so manicured for the occasion that he wanted to rip the paper up and throw it out into the passing paddocks, where it would get stuck in cow shit. Wellington had been teeming with well-wishers dressed in their finery; the streets alive with provincials swarming to the steps of Parliament to gather under a giant replica of St Edward's Crown. He'd heard them cheering and singing as he'd waited for the train at Wellington station. Celebrating the coronation of their new Queen, while he, another sort of queen, was obsessed with having to return to the origin of his humiliation.

'One queen comes in and another goes out,' he told himself laconically. He crossed his legs and wondered what it would be like to be an attendant at Buckingham Palace, one of those handsome guards with access to the aristocracy, who were, of course, all queers and eccentrics.

He watched the few lights of a small town that the train rushed by without even a whistle. The countryside was bleak, green and damp, and filled with farmers and bureaucrats who administered the place between them and left no room for anyone who didn't fit within their idealised image. George closed his eyes and listened to the clickety-clack of the train. He felt as though he was going nowhere. Going to purgatory. Going to look after his father. Surely he deserved much better. To have been born as an English aristocrat and have access to those guards. Lord So-and-so with a page-boy with long gold hair to accompany him to operas and concerts. To live in a nation that worshipped freedom and eccentrics.

There was a rush of noise, that swish swish sound when a carriage door opens.

'All alone, then?' the guard enquired, entering the carriage and looking around as if suspicious that someone was crouching behind a seat without a ticket. 'Got off in Wanganui, did they?' He might have been on the line to Brighton so pale was he, so Cockney his accent.

'Thank God,' George said, smiling despite his depression. 'Kids,' he added, emphasising his exasperation.

'She'll make a fine one, won't she?' the guard said archly, nodding at the newspaper. It was only then, because of the exaggerated head movement that accompanied the voice, that George realised he was speaking to a nelly.

'Bit young,' George said. 'How can she grasp the running of an empire?'

'Bad enough trying to get everything done on this bleedin' choo-choo,' the guard said. He looked at George, his thin lips slightly pursed; his eyes, his lips, one raised eyebrow, they told George that there was no room for innuendo or secrets. They were two nellies and this was an empty carriage.

'I'll come back later, shall I?' the guard said. He looked around him. 'The light's very dim in here, isn't it?' He allowed a little knowing chuckle and the tip of his tongue darted lizard-like from between his lips. 'Bye, bye for now,' he said, as he left the carriage.

The train shuddered to a halt at the station of a middling town: Patea, Hawera, Stratford. It didn't matter which because they were all the same. Each with a war memorial for the soldiers who had died defending freedom. Each with little houses, with mothers and fathers and children who had spent the day rejoicing for their new monarch in her pearls and satin. Freedom, hypocrisy, smugness; George saw it all in the houses opposite the railway station. He shifted his gaze from the ill-lit street and attempted to arouse the comforting thoughts of mingling with the aristocracy, of having gentlemen companions in England. But these images were useless in the face of the idea that he should be lying on the train tracks rather than rattling over them towards New Plymouth.

The night had settled in and George lay back on the leather seat and waited for the guard to return. He'd loosened his trousers and draped his overcoat over his lap so that he would appear ripe for the plucking. He soon drifted into a confusing dream involving wintry streets, the stench of ammonia, and crowds cheering as he stood before them with Captain Smart wearing bird of paradise feathers in his uniform. He woke with a start as the guard poked him on the shoulder and said in his crude Cockney accent, 'All right if I sit in 'ere for a while, mate?' He winked conspiratorially. 'No one'll come in 'ere,' he said. I've taken precautions.' Then he expertly pulled out his thin white English cock and wobbled it between his index finger and thumb.

'Do this often, do you?' George asked.

'It's a great job, never know what you might encounter.'

'Servicemen?'

'The best sort. You army then?'

'On leave from the navy.'

'I thought as much. I like navy men, army types.' He wobbled his penis from side to side as it quickly made a metamorphosis from being limp to tumescent. 'In the bunkhouses were you? What's your name, then?'

'Frank,' George replied. 'What's yours?'

'I shouldn't give away secrets,' the man said, 'should I? You never know what sort of trouble… What do I look like? Kevin? Harry?'

'George,' George said. 'George and Frank.'

The guard grinned in anticipation. He pushed his cap back and stroked his penis.

The last time George had made love with Frank La Verde had been in New Plymouth three days before he had learned that there was to be a court martial. Frank whispering the gorgeous words in George's ear as he lay on top of him, 'My Kiwi prince. My Kiwi prince.' These words often returned to George's mind despite the years and his attempts to eradicate them. Sometimes as a sweet refrain worth humming. Sometimes as the niggly lines from a poem learned as a child. Sometimes as the relentless repetition of a scratched record in another room until they became a torture: 'My Kiwi prince. My Kiwi prince. My Kiwi prince.'

The guard lit a cigarette, which remained propped in the side of his mouth while he stroked his now engorged penis. Something initially so insubstantial, within thirty seconds so swollen; it was a fact of physiognomy that suddenly interested George more than the sex itself. Smoke wafted up and irritated the guard's eyes as he bent to take hold of George's stiffening member.

'Like it, don'cha, Frankie?' the false George said.

'I do, George, very much.'

'Come on then, my naval officer, give it to me.'

George again heard Frank La Verde whispering in his ear as he pushed into his lover. So strong, so handsome, the American serviceman who wanted to take him to live in San Francisco.

'Frankie Wankie,' the guard mocked in his wheezy accent. 'Oh, Frankie Wankie, that's it.'

'What?' George asked, suddenly disgusted by this silly nonsense, which was disturbing his dream of Frank La Verde.

George had been sitting in his office in the Queen Mary Buildings in New Plymouth when the telegram, marked CONFIDENTIAL, arrived with the details of his impending court martial. He remembered that moment because, just as he picked up the telegram, he heard the last refrain from a song that was on the wireless in the next room: 'I've always loved you and I always will.'

'What's wrong, Frankie?' the guard asked, turning to look at the face of the man who was buggering him. 'Want me to bum you now?'

'Go on then,' George said. 'Damn it.'

Just three days before that fateful telegram, Frank had presented George with a tiny package.

'I love you, George. This is with all my love. A ring for you to wear always.'

'Oh, Frank. You really mean it.' Two men in the 1940s: one going to war, one staying at home without his lover.

The guard pulled out as the train rushed from a tunnel. 'Oh, matey,' he exclaimed, 'that was a tight one!'

George felt utterly exhausted, and a sourness reared up like vomit. He had been denied the right to live with someone he had worshipped and was now reduced to this momentary amusement with a sleazy Cockney in a dangerous situation.

'Well, bugger me!' the train guard said, astonished. 'You're married, aren'cha?' He looked from the wedding ring to George's face, a sardonic smile spreading with the knowledge that he'd just rooted a normal.

'Married?' George said. 'Widowed, actually.'

＊

Midwinter in New Plymouth. From his office window at McPhail and Sons, George caught a glimpse of Mount Egmont, white-coated, huge, extraordinarily beautiful, before it was again shrouded by an onslaught of clouds. Unable to concentrate on the debits and credits of the Taranaki Farmers' Society, he found himself wishing that he had never left Wellington.

'Tea, Mr Crossett?' Mrs Mutch asked, poking her head into his little office.

George wondered if it were possible to see the mountain without the connotations of what this province had done to him. To be a tourist and see the beauty and think, I'd love to live in Taranaki.'

'Here you go,' Mrs Mutch said. One month employed at McPhails and she still looked at him with her little eyes peering out from behind her little glasses, trying so hard to accept him for what he was: an odd man, rather handsome, still unmarried in his mid-thirties.

'Father well today?' she enquired.

'If the wind didn't bruise his roses, he'd be right as rain.' He knew there was as much truth in that statement as there was humour. Albert Crossett, who'd suffered a score of complaints over the last decade, would still be out in his garden on a day like today, obsessed with his tubers and cuttings.

'A marvellous garden,' Mrs Mutch said. 'The best in Balmoral Street, if not New Plymouth.' She was very modish in her dress: tweed skirts with perfect pleats, all very British and in keeping with the fashions that had come with the ascendancy of the new Queen.

George thanked her for the tea and she left knowing she had been dismissed. 'A marvellous garden.' He had the impulse to go out to the land agent, put the place on the market and drag his father down to Wellington to live in an old folks' home, to be visited once a week. Every spare moment weeding, pruning, sheltering plants from a climate for which nature had not intended them.

Petunias, lacanalias, robustas; his father conversed as if the vernacular of New Zealand were Latin.

'For what?' George asked himself. 'Mother alone?' The Galipoli poppies made him suspect that there was more in the memorial garden than just her memory. You didn't build a glasshouse just to encourage flowers that would never survive the cruel Taranaki climate.

'Good morning, George,' Mr McPhail said, popping into the office. 'Nice weather for ducks.' He produced a big-man laugh, like one of the lawyers or doctors who frequented the Commercial Club, which George had been invited to in his first week at the firm by the senior McPhail himself.

'You did a splendid job with the Gunn account. Saved them hundreds of pounds by my reckoning. Excellent.'

At the club, wary eyes looking at the new man in town. George had sat there uneasily, drinking whisky with the likes of Mr McPhail: affable, hearty, humorous. Those unspoken questions that surfaced every few minutes. Men at the bar drinking, half of whom George recognised as returned servicemen.

'The Gunns themselves asked me to convey to you their gratitude. Great work, George,' Mr McPhail said. 'Well, won't keep you from your work.'

It was George's lunch hour. He went quickly up Devon Street and turned left down Qhakatane Lane. It was ridiculous to have come back to New Plymouth and try to be someone he wasn't. In Wellington he could almost hide. He'd read in the newspaper that Auckland's population now exceeded three hundred thousand and the city was spreading like wildfire. Enough people to hide among, instead of this place, which could barely call itself a city. He passed the Devonport Flats, which had always impressed him as decadently English. A ship was leaving the port: the *Birmingham Queen* going back to England with a cargo of butter and mutton. To go to London, San Francisco. He would do it, George decided. As soon as his father died, he'd sell the house and travel.

Before George had time to cross the road to avoid them, he became aware of a group of soldiers lounging on a street corner. Men in uniforms were unpredictable, demanding a kiss or threatening a kick. He steadied his walk and squared his shoulders in an effort to act like a man.

'Korea,' one of the soldiers was saying.

'Bloody hell,' another said. They took no notice of George, and as he passed, so did his nervousness that they would say something derogatory like 'Queer' or 'Nancy boy'. He didn't care about the Korean war. He'd suffered enough in the last one not to give a damn about this conflagration. The relentless headlines in the papers. Communism, Red Chinese hordes. Korea was nothing to George. He dismissed it as he crossed the road and hurried into Kaweroa Park to look for that foreign boy he'd seen in the fruit van parked outside the toilets on the day before at this hour.

An old, ill-kept park, gloomy with too many unpruned pohutukawa trees. His heart sank when he failed to find the van near the toilets.

The *Birmingham Queen* had turned in the harbour. She looked magnificent as she struggled against the wind, braving her way into the Tasman. There were ships constantly coming in and out of Fort Taranaki; vessels going places. Men inside them. It was a terrible thing to be reminded each day that there was an outside world to which people could escape. Being on a ship for weeks and weeks. Taking a trip to London and deciding never to return. George wanted to curse out loud that he'd been trapped in this provincial town by an ailing father who had enveloped him with the morbidity of a memorial garden.

George had a fantasy of a steward servicing him in a private cabin. The man taking off his uniform, taking a long time removing his underpants. Standing there in the tiny stuffy cabin in his black socks. He should have joined the merchant navy and abandoned this life of servitude to accountancy and caring for an ailing father. The steward's big penis poking out from his shirt front. The wonderful man, tall, dark and handsome, saying, 'Suck it.'

The wind had come up and rain swept in. George felt furious. No friends, no place to hide, nowhere to be but this stupid place that struggled to call itself a city. He pulled a meat pie from his overcoat pocket and thought about where he could eat it. The band rotunda was too exposed to the elements. He wanted to be surrounded by men, to be on a boat, somewhere smelling of diesel and ammonia, where only men like him went.

He turned and went back to the toilets, the place where men with his problem could meet. He sensed the usual mixture of palpable danger and security as he went inside and the reassuring smell greeted him. Entering a cubicle, he locked the door on the world and ate his pie, half fearful yet half excited, as he sat on the toilet reading the rude words inscribed about cocks and cunts and times and places. He had just finished eating when the door in the cubicle next to him banged shut. Someone had made a hole in the wall just above the toilet-paper holder. He was about to peer through it, but the possibility of the newcomer being a policeman deterred him. Then the old thought, tired but nevertheless brutal, flittered there: this was disgusting. What if it were someone young or a man not interested? The ugliness of his preoccupation flooded him and he was about to leave when the person next door coughed that universal signal. George was seized by a mixture of fear, excitement and self-loathing.

Several seconds passed before he heard the cough repeated and a deliberate scrape of a foot. The signals of someone who was interested. A policeman wouldn't do that. He coughed in reply and moved his foot to just beneath the partition. A shoe moved from next door and stopped next to his. George looked at his watch. He had fifteen minutes before he had to be back at work. Quickly he undid his belt and pulled down his trousers. In the other stall Neddy Bouzikis bent and peered through the hole at a big penis, stiff, held upright by a hand, the dark hairs on the wrist, the suit sleeve of good tweed and the shirt cuff of quality cotton. The hand moving up and down the penis, a person standing up and turning to the hole, bending slightly to allow the voyeur a better look. Neddy got down on his knees and saw a good-looking man beckoning him.

George smiled when the swarthy youth entered the cubicle. It was him all right, the one who drove the van.

'Where are you from?' Neddy whispered.

They were holding each other as if neither had ever before received love or affection.

'New Plymouth. Are you a Maori?'

'Lebanese.'

They looked at each other, eye to eye, and again held each other tightly. For some reason George thought of Wiri Thompson, the Maori who'd gone off to the Solomon Islands with Des. His foreign boy's face. Something about him.

✳

It was three days after George had had sex with the youth who looked like a Maori. He had visited the toilets at the same time for the previous two days, but the youth hadn't returned, despite promising he would do so. He was sitting in his office struggling with the tediousness of the Farmers' Society accounts, but his mind was on the nameless youth.

Mrs Mutch poked her head around his door. 'Mr McPhail would like to see you in his office as soon as you can.'

George entered the manager's office and was invited to sit. It was a large room designed with the hard lines and heavy plaster mouldings associated with continuity and permanence. Nothing in it had been charged in the twenty or so years since it had been constructed, so George had the feeling he had retreated to the early 1930s. Only the portrait of the new Queen suggested anything contemporary.

'I admire your work, Crossett,' Mr McPhail said. 'You've been with us a month now...' He paused and his awkward-looking eyes betrayed everything.

'Have you found a discrepancy in my figures?' George asked. A few minutes previously, he had gazed out the window and noted only a few grey clouds, but now the weak sunlight had been eclipsed and rain was pouring down.

'No, no, nothing of the sort,' Mr McPhail shouted above the torrential drumming. 'Well, I should come to the point. You see, we don't have the business to keep you on our payroll so I'll have to ask you to finish this week, tomorrow. Union benefits and such, of course. I'm terribly...'

'But you yourself said I have more work than I can cope with.'

'Actually, what I meant to say is that work is spasmodic, George. Spasmodic.' McPhail felt he had found the right word and repeated it several times, like a toy on which you pull a chord so that it repeats 'Dolly, dolly, dolly'.

'Last week you gave me the accounts of the National Picture House. That's three weeks' work. I've already been to see them about it.'

'Well... work fluctuates; it's spasmodic. You must understand. I'm terribly apologetic, Crossett, but...' McPhail had smoked for forty years and now grappled with one of the disadvantages of having quit: what to do with his hands when he would once have had the intricacies of smoking to occupy his embarrassment.

'You're not telling me the truth, are you?' George said.

'I beg your pardon, George,' McPhail answered angrily. The rain had eased but his voice was still raised.

'Your pay packet and sundries will be ready for you tomorrow at five o'clock. Thank you.'

George felt his saliva run dry as he searched for the reason for his dismissal.

'Thank you, George.' McPhail dismissed him again.

'I won't leave here until you tell me what it is.'

'I'm trying to be above board, Crossett...'

'It's me, isn't it? That...'

'A certain problem has arisen. I can't help it,' McPhail swivelled in his chair and stared at a pigeon sitting on the window ledge. 'I like to be square with a man, I have to dismiss you because you're not good for my business.'

'What's the problem?' George asked. A number of images came to his mind: his mother telling a neighbour to get out of the house, his father saying he had had an affair with a man from Auckland, Captain Smart accusing him of sodomy with Frank La Verde. They flashed like slides on a screen, each a disturbing memory.

'I think I've said all I can, George. It's a personal matter.'

'But I'm the one who is losing his job. You must tell me.' George knew what it was, of course.

Gassing yourself was one way out, like Morris Mills in Wellington six months ago when he'd been dismissed from a government department for acting effeminately. George's fury mingled with panic; he recognised the whole scenario so clearly that he wanted to vomit with rage and inadequacy. A filthy homosexual who had sex in toilets with young men and with anonymous men in trains, boarding houses, parks and empty houses. He'd been discharged dishonourably from the navy. That was it. It was here to haunt him. It was New Plymouth and, like the room he was sitting in, nothing could change.

'I can't be any clearer than that,' McPhail said. 'As a businessman you'll appreciate that.'

'Whose business have I infringed upon?'

'The National. They've cancelled our accounts as long as you are here. And the Potter account, one of the biggest in New Plymouth. Their lawyer contacted me yesterday.'

*

George strode quickly up the steps of the New Plymouth Public Library and went immediately to the section on Earth Sciences, where he had hidden *Homosexuality and the Abnormal Mind* behind books on volcanoes and earthquakes. To have taken the book downstairs and asked for it to be issued would have been tantamount to telling the world that he was that way inclined. Mrs Templeton the librarian peering at the title, then at him. She was also president of the New Plymouth Ladies Bridge Club; George could imagine the gossip over tea and pikelets. Everybody already knew or guessed. Losing his job at McPhails had proved his suspicions. The repercussions of that picture of himself on the rocks kissing Des's cap. Des should never have left those letters in his desk.

George turned to where he had left off in Dr Julius Blumstein's book: 'The homosexual is a neurotic, the product of an insatiable urge to have sex with men in order to overcome the absence of a deep relationship with his father. Overwhelming evidence from the studies on American homosexuals points conclusively to the fact that a dominating mother encourages the abnormality to take effect at any point in a man's life, whether at infancy or maturity.'

George put his hands to his face as if that gesture might release the horror he felt for his misfortune. But his hands smelt of the blood and bone he had been mixing to put around the roses in his father's garden that morning.

He looked about the library; an old woman in 1920s clothing was leading what was probably her grandson by the hand down the aisle. It was all their fault. Women did this to men: a mother to her son, a grandmother to her grandson. The memorial garden was evidence of his own mother's continuing power to demand devotion, and her dying, taking two years to do it with her husband and son in constant attendance. George recalled his life in the house in Balmoral Street with his mother, who had organised all the family finances and bought clothes for her menfolk until she was too sick to do so. Every detail, every decision hers. Obviously, she had made his father and himself into homosexuals. By the time his father had gone off to fight in the Great War, he had been changed by her dominance.

George shook his head, which felt feverish from the thoughts that pounded within. It couldn't be right. It couldn't be true. He turned to the back of the book where the author's credentials were listed: a professor at Yale University who had worked with Freud and studied the lives of two hundred inverts from all over the United States. 'This abnormal behavioural fixation.' The words there on the page and in the look on McPhail's face as he had dismissed George because of this disease. He was sick. It was perversion. The man in the train who had solicited him. The fixation was so strong that these perverts sought each other out in toilets, had anal intercourse and sucked penises. They waited around dark corners at night when other men were at home with their wives...

George saw himself for what he was: a pervert who had been created by an abnormal family. This professor must be right; two hundred case studies to prove it.

'Oh my God,' he realised. 'I can't carry on with this.' McPhail, Captain Smart, Sybil Potter, his father. A week ago he had tried to bring up the subject with Albert Crossett, after dinner when they were drinking tea and eating madeira cake.

'My dishonourable discharge,' he said. 'I've never got over that.'

'Well, surely you should have by now. It's been over a decade.'

'But that's why I lost my job. I can't stay here in New Plymouth.'

'I need help, George. We agreed. The garden... Dr Proctor said that I need care.'

There was a silence in which George waited for his father to continue, but Albert reached out and turned on the wireless. A programme about the new Queen, her history, her pedigree, her favourite foods.

'I'm going to bed,' George sighed. 'Is there anything you need?'

'George,' Albert said, 'there is one thing I must say to you, and I regret it very much.'

'What?' George asked. 'Go on.'

'I made a mistake when your mother died and I allowed you to live like this. I should have stopped it. It was my fault. I should never have allowed you this freedom to become what you have become. My one time, in France, that was wrong and I made amends. I came home to your mother. It was an aberration now that I look back on it. I should never...'

The Queen's favourite dish was roast quail. She adored it, and every week birds were collected from her estates in Scotland no matter whether the royal family was in Britain or not.

'You see...' Albert tried to continue. He was toying with his madeira cake.

'What should I see?'

'You flaunted it, even when I told you not to that afternoon of your mother's funeral. Certainly I had thoughts about it, about my own... but I never acted upon them. I was proper, but you flaunted it. Des and you and Frank. In this house. I should have put my foot down, called in a doctor. It was my fault.'

Apparently Prince Philip had a predilection for black olives and other Greek delicacies. There was some consternation at Buckingham Palace that the royal diet would change. The Christmas stuffing had included chopped olives, and Queen Mary had declined to eat it.

George woke from his reverie in the library and quickly flipped open *Homosexuality and the Abnormal Mind* so that the title would not denounce him. But he must have been too late because the old lady with the grandson looked from the book to the reader and gave a wan smile that said everything.

It was cowardly and George knew it, but he didn't want to go out into the street and walk home. People would see him. Sybil Potter might be about. The McPhail people. Everybody knew he was neurotic, sick, someone who had been dishonourably discharged from the navy for having had sex with other men.

＊

It was one of those gorgeous spring days when the sun actually did heat the air and summer was more than just a dim memory. The few vehicles in the funeral cortege moved slowly down the road and turned into the church grounds, the drive lined with magnificent red, purple and yellow rhododendrons, for which New Plymouth had become famous.

'I suppose I'd better plant some in his bloody memorial garden,' George thought, looking from the car window. His father had dropped dead of a stroke as he was weeding the cinerarias. Sprawled face down, arms outstretched as if he'd been ordered into that position by a gunman. George had been forking the dahlia plot and was unaware of his father's fate.

He had wept when he found the body, already cold, behind the camellias. A quiet life and death. George found that enviable. His father had suffered but three major upsets: when the man from Auckland had been drowned at Brighton, his wife's death, and George's dismissal from the navy. Albert had hidden from danger and never courted trouble. He had occupied an almost friendless world, in which the wireless and newspaper had been his only close companions.

George got out of his car and followed the coffin into the church, with its smell of decrepitude and mourning. The few people present turned to watch the coffin being brought down the aisle as lugubrious music was pumped from an organ. But George didn't see faces. Tears were welling up in his eyes as the funeral director guided him by the arm to the front seat, where he slumped down, exhausted.

'Albert William Crossett was a quiet man, an exemplary citizen,'

the minister intoned. George didn't want to listen. He had little faith
in the opinion of others, because, eventually, these became weapons
used against him. What he wanted was to be on a ship sailing for San
Francisco. On the *Birmingham Queen* sailing out of Port Taranaki. The
smell of salt, that brilliant and liberating essence of freedom: the sea,
the big ships that sailed on it, everything that meant escape. For the
first time since he'd found his father sprawled out in the garden, he
saw himself as freed from the responsibility of staying in New Zealand.

'Bugger it all,' he thought. 'I can get out of this bloody country.'

'...a devoted family man who worked tirelessly in his garden created as a memorial for his late wife...'

George found himself slipping into the fantasy of San Francisco
that he resurrected from time to time, like pulling out a photo album
for a few sentimental minutes. To walk around those romantic streets
he'd seen on calendars and in movies, and a reunion with Frank on
the now mythological Russian Hill. He had no idea what Russian Hill
actually looked like; in his imagination it was unpopulated and resembled one of those extinct volcanoes in Auckland. He was on top of the
hill, looking out at the fabulous view of higgledy-piggledy houses and
streets, a larger version of Wellington but without the connotations
that city infected him with, when suddenly from behind him, a familiar voice and, on turning, the familiar smile of his handsome
American.

'George!'

'Frank!'

'... his efforts to defend Britain in the First World War demonstrat-
ed his patriotism... the free world is grateful to such a good and decent
man...'

The Russian Hill fantasy fled as did the smile and voice of Frank La
Verde. He thought of his father, a good decent man who had fallen in
love with a mate from Auckland, the result of which was a life spent
lingering in New Zealand with barely a word about the episode for the
next thirty-five years. The words 'good' and 'decent' caught like fish-

hooks in George's brain, and he started weeping as a confused medley of love and respect and loss and anger merged with the vision of Russian Hill and his own lost expectations.

'You know you flaunted it, George. You brought it upon yourself. You can't blame them, really.' Another dishonourable discharge over a cup of tea and some madeira cake. Albert Crossett had been in love with a man himself, and yet that was his verdict about George and Frank. George's heart felt like a lump of lead in his chest and his mind ran along the pitted path of his terrible existence. Snatches at happiness: the time spent with Des, a few months with Frank, one or two sympathetic friends in Wellington.

'…and so we put this weary soul to rest…'

George felt as if the minister was consigning him, rather than his father, to eternity. 'The weary soul in need of rest.' The barbarities of his existence. It wasn't fair. It wasn't right. George realised that he had to get out of New Zealand; the price of staying was suicide. Those tall cliffs that had brought a sense of freedom… refreshing sea breezes and beneath him the crashing swells… could launch him into the engulfing sea, where there would never again be a McPhail or a Potter or a policeman.

He shook hands with those who hovered at the church door: the neighbours, the grocer, the man with whom Albert had worked for twenty years as a clerk, Mr Steff the accountant. A little cluster of peripheral people in dark suits. Mr Steff with a black armband. Mrs Waugh in an inappropriate floral hat. The coffin was now in the hearse; George had requested that he did not help carry the coffin, and there were no relations to perform the task. The funeral parlour attendants had borne the old man in and out.

'George,' a voice said. 'It's been years!'

For a moment he couldn't think. The face, its lips and eyes and the pointed chin, dimly recognised.

'Miriam Pyke,' the woman announced helpfully. 'My God, George, you do look ragged.'

As she took hold of his hand, a crack appeared in the armour surrounding his memory. The sinister image of the Australian spider that devoured the male of its own species seeped out. Even the recollection of the red of her fingernails against the yellow rose from that day so long ago in the Potters' garden returned. There was delight in his voice as he said, 'Miriam! Of course I remember!'

'It's like that time in the garden. I had confidences for you then and...' She looked behind her as if she still worked in Military Intelligence and expected a lurking spy, but no one was interested in her intimacies. The funeral director was bustling around his hearse as the other mourners wandered in a desultory line in the other direction.

'George,' she said briskly, 'you look as if you need some sun. Come and visit Anne and me in Auckland.'

'What confidences?' he asked guardedly.

'Oh,' Miriam laughed. 'You haven't changed. Still timid. For God's sake, come and see me tomorrow at my mother's. I'm down for a few days and saw the death notice. You poor old thing. Wiri Thompson confessed something to us about a year ago...'

'Wiri?'

'I didn't know where to contact you. Well I did, but I didn't know if I should because it's, well...'

'The Maori chap who went to the Solomons with Des?' George urged.

'Precisely. But Wiri returned.' She meant to peck George's cheek but instead slobbered on him. 'And,' she said as she retrieved a handkerchief and wiped lipstick off his cheek, 'he has news about Desmond that will astound you.'

*

Wiri was in his garden when George arrived at the farm in his little grey Austin. It had been over a decade since the two men had seen each other, and George felt the burden of those years as if they'd been dropped on him, each filled with its hardships and false expectations. They should have embraced, each wanting to, but the second in which they might have done so fluttered and died.

Instead, they shook hands and scrutinised each other to ascertain the changes in the lost years of a decade.

'I've got some beer in the fridge,' Wiri said. 'Let's have a drink.' He was nervous, the sweat had beaded over his face as soon as he'd seen the car coming up the drive.

'How do I begin?' he had asked Miriam.

'Tell him it all, give it to him,' she had replied. 'It's time George knew what happened.'

'Well,' George said, 'there's plenty of peace and quiet out here. I wish I had somewhere like this to hide away in.' He'd decided not to leave New Plymouth once he'd returned from his holiday with Anne and Miriam in Auckland.

'Miriam said you gonna stay in New Plymouth even though your old man kicked the bucket,' Wiri said. 'Though you probably want to go, eh. But I've got the same problem here because this old place belonged to my old people and I can't march off.'

'And your nephews? Do they understand about…'

'They don't really know. They're bloody Mormons, but even if they did, I don't think they'd say much. I don't let them into my secrets.'

It was the same with George. Flaunting it had led to the disasters he now wanted to avoid. His father had been right; if you flaunted your perversion, you were bound to get into trouble. It was an equation as easy as one and one makes two.

'There's this Pakeha bloke, a farmer in Stratford, who lives with his mad mother. I go over there once or twice a month. He doesn't like Maoris much, but he's happy enough as long as I keep my legs open.'

'I think being quiet's the best way,' George said. 'I'll make enough money from doing a few private accounts. Anything for the quiet life. I enjoy digging in the garden. It kept Dad content and out of trouble, so it's good enough for me, I suppose.'

Wiri examined George and compared him with his memory of ten years ago. He was still a good-looking man; a bit frayed around the edges maybe, a bit fatter around the stomach, but still that knowing smile, that secretive look in his eyes and the slightly queer way of sitting and moving his hands. A few tell-tale signs that he'd always displayed, even in the navy.

'My nephew knows about me,' Wiri said. 'But he won't say anything because we look after each other.'

'As long as we shut up and act normal,' George said. 'Sometimes I even think I should get married just to stop feeling odd when I walk down the street as a thirty-something bachelor.'

'I tried living in Auckland,' Wiri said. 'But bugger me, it's the same up there. I got beaten up by some navy types when I was drunk and made a remark to some Maori bloke. He told the others and the bastards beat the hell out of me. It's better here. Nice and quiet.'

They were sitting under the trees, the dank, dark bush quiet except for bees and tuis.

'Penny for your thoughts, mate,' Wiri said.

'No, I'm all right thanks.'

'Yeah, I haven't got much to say either.' How do you tell the truth? Wiri wanted to be able to look George in the eyes and tell him what had happened, but honesty wouldn't emerge and the pretence... a false camaraderie that nothing was untoward... had trapped both men.

Wiri searched for the right words to say. 'Bloody hell,' he began. 'Memories don't go away, do they? It was tough in the Solomons. Bloody hot eh, and we were about to land. I mean, on this beach and the mines were going off and...'

'You were with Des?' George asked.

'Yeah, well, we were in the same company, same place. Just friends...'

'No, not that. I don't care. I mean when the...'

'The Japs blew him up?'

'I don't want to know the details. I don't want to know anything about the war, but Miriam said...'

'The navy treated you badly, that discharge nonsense. Lots of the boys got the same bloody treatment. Simmons blew his brains out in Christchurch when they told him they were on to him.' Wiri paused and took a swig from his bottle of beer. 'Frank?'

'I tried to contact him, but his...'

George couldn't finish because there was nothing to say on the subject of Frank La Verde. Memories of passion had to be terminated before they terminated you. It was like his new promise to live quietly in New Plymouth and abandon the old dirty and dangerous habits of sex with men in toilets. Don't flaunt it. It was George's new way of life. The life he had taken over from his father, a life of dignity in a garden.

'I've got something for you, George,' Wiri said. 'A letter. I meant to give it to you, but then I lost contact and one thing and another...'

'A letter?' George's blood felt as if it had been replaced by the cold beer he was holding. A freezing sensation went rushing through his arteries.

'From Des, to you. The night before he was killed he gave it to me.'

*

At first glance, Sybil Potter appeared not to have aged. That same smug face, a look of deep concentration, as if she were still dispensing lemonade into a row of glasses on the day of Des's farewell party. That was how George had imagined her during his years in

Wellington. When Sybil came to mind, there she was with a glass pitcher in her hand, in her too-blue party dress, and on her pursed red lips that look of money and hypocrisy.

'I really don't think we have anything to discuss.' She sat on the edge of her desk, then thought better of it and stood up.

On close examination, George saw that she had aged. Tinted hair, hard lines around the eyes, the provincial attempt to keep up with the times. She looked like one of those women in the advertisements who sported pointy bras, hair pulled back and curled, cheeks highlighted with rouge and a waist cinched with a tight belt.

'It's been a long time, Mrs Potter,' he said.

She laughed at the bitterness in his voice and the reference to her as Mrs. 'Indeed, George,' she said. 'What can I do for you?'

He laughed in return. They were like actors rehearsing lines for a play in which there was too much emotion; the words false and gooey. 'You can do nothing. You've already done what you wanted to – made me lose my job.'

His gaze couldn't leave her face. Those eyes and those lips. It was horrible to think that he had shared them through Des. 'Nothing,' he reiterated, still playing the bad actor. 'As I was told by the Discharge Committee, I have no rights.'

'No rights?' she snapped. 'I don't see why you're here telling me this.' A flicker of something went across her lips; for a moment she wasn't the capable person who prided herself on being one of the few independent businesswomen in New Plymouth: Sybil Potter who had inherited. Sybil Potter who was the first woman elected to the New Plymouth City Council.

'You remember the letters that you gave to Captain Smart? The photos that belonged to me and Des?'

'Desmond died a hero. He laughed at you, George Crossett.' She looked at her watch. Fury had made her cheeks redder than any rouge she could have applied.

'They were *my* letters,' George said. And photographs.'

'I inherited his estate. He was my husband. What do you want?' She immediately suspected that he wanted to blackmail her, but she couldn't think for what. But then she saw that money wasn't his object; she knew enough about greed to see that that wasn't the source of his anger.

'What do I want? No. It's what I can give you, Sybil.'

He felt a rare moment of true happiness go flushing through him, as if ten years of suffering were worth this moment when everything the past had dealt him was suddenly illuminated for what it was; the priceless knowledge that life was ghastly but worth the effort for the few retorts he could manage against those who made it so ugly, so unbearable an effort.

'Why are you here?' she asked, a note of desperation creeping into her usually measured voice.

'I lost my job, my dignity, because of you,' he said. The decision to live in New Plymouth had been the right one. To vindicate himself, to put this upstart hussy in her place, to tell her in no uncertain terms how he felt. The happiness hadn't abated in the least, and he saw how easy it was to murder. You got in the mood for it, it became inevitable, hate turned to happiness, killing for the pleasure of ridding your life of something so evil. He wanted to see her slashed, dead on the carpet of her smart office.

'You're quite insane,' she said. 'It's true what everyone says about you. Mad as a hatter. Queer. I can't have you working on my accounts. You'll sabotage them.'

'Oh, sabotage? Do I have a good reason for revenge?'

'Get out,' she shouted. 'Go back to Wellington. I loathe seeing you around New Plymouth, fiddling about in that monstrous memorial garden when I go past.' She made a nasty noise, quite unintentional, but the sort a mouse might make being squashed underfoot. Then she flicked her tongue as if the repugnant action had just been performed in front of her and the mouse lay on the floor.

'You're vile. You corrupted my husband, and yet he died a hero.'

'Hero?' George said. 'One who wrote such letters?'

'They've been destroyed. It was you behind that vileness.'

'You wouldn't destroy such useful information, Sybil.'

He pulled a dirty, yellowed envelope from his pocket and held it out, as if presenting a trophy.

'Here,' he said. 'This'll amuse you. See what Smart and the rest of them will say about it.'

'Get out,' she repeated. 'Your whole family was vile. You'll die of cancer like your mother.' She was wilting under that veneer of impregnability. The handwriting on the envelope, she saw, belonged to that of her late hero.

'Let me,' George said. He realised that this was not a poor play at all, but, rather, a brilliant performance that had been in rehearsal for a decade. He pulled the letter from the envelope and she took it, too greedy for its contents to kick him out now that the act was unfolding so quickly. She was a businesswoman, she could flick her eyes down a docket or a letter in a moment and get the gist of it.

I came to really loathe Sybil. She took away my freedom to be myself.

She looked up and then down as if the world were spinning in a direction she could not fathom.

You were always right, and it was your intelligence I respected above all else. George the brainy one. George the one who wouldn't stoop to other scruples like I did. Yes, I feared being called names. But that's all old hat now, I married the cow for her money as much as I did to avoid the stigma I couldn't live with. Which is why I'm not returning to New Zealand. I knew I wouldn't the day I saw you and Miriam pretending you were normal. I decided then that life is not worth the trial that I've made of it. To return to Sybil? To have to lead that double life and...

Sybil stared at George.

'This isn't Desmond's handwriting,' she said.

...a bullet in the head... dead in the jungle. It'll be easy to set up. I'll do my bit against the Japs. I owe that at least to New Zealand, but I don't owe it my return, because it's more difficult being a hero in New

Plymouth than it is in this dump.

Forgive me, you made me happy but I'm not brave enough... Your mate Des.

'l'll call the police,' she said. She took the piece of paper and ripped it in two and then again. Her lips puckered and her eyes began to twitch. It was one of the happiest moments in George's existence, and he laughed maniacally.

'It's a fabrication!'

'No, of course it isn't. It's a copy. Here's the original,' George's laughter had eased to a smirk. 'I learned too much about your tactics when I was your husband's lover.'

4 Raskolnikov and the teddy boy

Garth Griffin put the book to his lips and kissed it in appreciation. Just looking at the cover gave him a feeling of superiority. The stark picture of two faces, one an old Jewess and the other a man with a face that betrayed suffering. It wasn't the sort of book that other kids would have taken out of the library. Not Russian literature. Not something you could cuddle up in bed with to transport you far from this life of idiocy.

He reread the passage where Raskolnikov was standing at the money-lender's door, the hatchet hidden under his thin coat and his breathing heavy with the fear that she knew he was there for the kill. The cover had a splash of Cyrillic script in black and dark blue: *Crime and Punishment.* A sixteen-year-old in New Plymouth didn't read books like that. He looked longingly at the author's exotic name: Fyodor Dostoyevsky. He wanted to be like Raskolnikov, the tormented student living in a garret at the top of a decrepit rooming house in the mad city of St Petersburg.

'Revolutionary, Imperial, Tsarist, tragic, *fin de siècle,'* Garth tried out the words that measured the fabulousness of St Petersburg instead of the dreariness of New Plymouth in the 1960s. To be handsome like Raskolnikov and dressed in the ragged outfit of a Russian student who was free to wander through crowded streets. To be Raskolnikov in Imperial Russia, and not to have to drag himself through this pallid life in this New Plymouth suburb in this boring house with these tedious parents. Not to have to endure that television in that lounge room blaring out inanities about the benefits of stupid things like breakfast cereals and soap products.

Garth had his bedroom door locked. It was beautiful to be alone, to read the tiny print in the well-worn book with its cover of intellectualism and suffering. A print by Hieronymous Bosch, full of devils, monsters and damned nuns, was pinned on the wall above him.

'Garth! Phone for you!' his sister yelled.

Garth wanted to blot out his present life and seek another. A quiet flat in Wellington where the Bosch could go above a carved mantelpiece, where his windows wouldn't look out on a pale green state house with a car wreck on its unkempt lawn. And he wouldn't have frock-material curtains like the ones Mum had made. Cheap, bright, floral things, listlessly framing the house next door.

'Are you awake or what?' Cynthia screamed. She knew she was supposed to knock at Garth's door, but of course she didn't, to obey that order was to agree he had the right to keep his door locked.

Privacy was one of those venial sins that the nuns declared to be evil: farting, spitting, saying 'bum' and 'titties'. It was akin to pride. You shut yourself away from family to indulge in the devil's sinister preoccupations. A locked door in a bathroom meant you were playing with your genitals; a locked door in a bedroom suggested bad thoughts and evil intentions.

Handsome, tormented, intelligent; Garth again read the description of Raskolnikov's countenance. It was the face the Smith boy next door should have had. The face of the man who would one day knock on the door of Garth's Wellington flat and ask to come in. A handsome, angular face, white from suffering. The face of someone you could talk to, who would understand what it was like to be different. Someone who could lead you down dark paths to other things that not even the nuns dared mention. For a beautiful moment Garth had Raskolnikov there in his bedroom, the idea of friendship as tangible as it was fleeting.

'You in there, Garth? Mum! He's locked himself in and it's a girl on the phone!'

Garth had met her on the Seaview Road bus. In the stark sunlight glinting off the sea, her freckles were more obvious than her chin's cluster of pimples. He had to sit next to her. It was either her or the old man with the blubbery blue mouth like a sea lion's. Old Sea Lion was Lucille Adams' granddad, and it was Lucille Adams who stood at the end of the school corridor with Cynthia, sniggering and saying venomous things. The horrible Adams who smelled of Nugget because they owned the shoe repair shop on Blagdon Road. She had dry blonde hair and a boyfriend who could cycle up hills balancing on just the back wheel.

The bus was haunted by that yellowish light that the sea cast, along with its seaweed smell. At the bus stop Garth had just read that Raskolnikov had old yellow wallpaper in his tiny garret. The handsome student had traced the flowers in the pattern with his fingers until the paper had worn thin. For hours and hours, around and around, he had traced the yellow petals until he had entered a state of madness. Then the evening would arrive and the crepuscular cover of northern summer nights would allow a man to go out into those boulevards teeming with millions of mad Russians that Dostoyevsky described so well in *Crime and Punishment*. The crowds and that wonderful feeling of being among them; it was Garth's dream to be there, to be transported to some place with some culture other than this one where people stared at you and whispered.

The bus was filled with women returning from town with their shopping. It seemed as if the whole world were populated with women in stiff chiffon hats or garish nylon scarves tied over grey hair lacquered into stiff curls. Some wore winter coats or woolly cardigans despite the day's heat. One woman wearing gloves gripped the metal hand rail as if there were no other support left for her in this world dominated by buses and shopping trips to town.

Garth felt eyes following him, suffocating and oppressive as he moved down the aisle. He could have been Raskolnikov dressed in wretched clothes, such were the stares he felt eating him. Eyes from behind glinting spectacles framed with dull diamantes or the dead backs of turtles. Things hinted at just like Lucille Adams and his sister did at school. To Garth, the bus reverberated with suppressed innuendo.

Raskolnikov with his hatchet raised, about to smash the old hag's face. Garth turned his head away from the aisle, from the passengers, from the words he knew were being spoken. A whole bus talking about him. He wanted to get off and go running down to the beach and walk on the sand. For a moment he thought he might, but the bus lurched and he continued down the aisle. A horse-drawn tram in St Petersburg, the smells and noise and excitement. A Russian tram, and not this Seaview Road bus filled with people who he felt hated him. In a filthy ninetenth-century frock-coat and a battered top hat. Raskolnikov suddenly transported from this simpering provincial town to a tram as night fell. Fresh with his madness of tracing yellow petals and wandering crowded streets in the Russian capital.

Garth slumped down in a seat next to the girl. She stared at his book and said, 'I've read *Crime and Punishment*.' The comfort to be gained from someone with pimples was that they wouldn't talk. Lepers will acknowledge each other by not recognising the sores and thus live for a few moments in peace. But this girl had broken that pact. It would have been safer after all to have sat next to the man with the sea lion's lips.

'It's from the library,' he muttered.

'It's a good library, isn't it?' she said eagerly. She had a pretty smile, which didn't pretend to hide her ugly teeth. Lucille Adams had perfect teeth, which made her smile as potent a weapon as her boyfriend's cycling ability.

'We're from Scotland, and my father says it's better than any provincial library there,' she continued. She wasn't even worried about the gloaming whiteheads on her chin. That they were inflamed didn't appear to bother her any more than her uneven teeth. 'I like

Mrs Marmeladov the best. Fancy having a name like marmalade!'

'I like her too,' Garth agreed.

'Oh, yes,' the girl said, 'Mrs Marmeladov tried to save poor Sonia from becoming a prostitute.' She said the word matter of factly. Lucille Adams and Cynthia would have giggled after saying it, as if the word were filthy or contagious. Spat out like 'pimple' or 'queer' to an enemy in the school corridor.

The bus climbed to the top of Seaview Road, grinding at the corner where the road turned at an eroded cliff. For a few moments there was the remarkable view of the Tasman Sea, the Sugar Loaves and a succession of black-sand beaches. The brakes hissed as the bus began descending the hill.

'My word, Mavis,' a woman said, 'a lot of red about this summer.'

'I like New Plymouth,' the girl said. 'My mother likes it much more than Edinburgh. If my father's company finds oil here, it will quite spoil the place. But that's life.'

She had the air of one who had been in big cities. Garth was focusing his gaze on his knees, but the thought of cities made him look at her eyes, which had the greenish tinge of a cat's. Behind her, New Plymouth stretched its limited streets into a haze of red corrugated-iron roofs and tangles of washing lines. The sun suddenly disappeared behind a cloud, and the Norfolk pines and bamboo and pohutukawa trees slithered in the wind so that everything was an unsure mixture of shade and red and green, and white horses were whipped up on the sea.

The girl looked at Garth's knees and he looked away, then opened his book because there was nothing more to be said.

'We came out on the *Birmingham Queen*,' she said. 'Another girl on the ship gave me *Crime and Punishment* to read.'

The bus pulled up near the Seaview Road toilet block.

Decades ago, when they had been constructed, the word GENTLEMEN had been erected in lead above the dark doorway. Rain and sea spray had made each letter ooze like black blood into the concrete.

Why did the girl's family come here? Garth wondered. Why not stay in a big city where there are lots of things to do?

He liked books about big cities. The one he'd just finished had been set in Peking during the Boxer Rebellion, and before that he'd chosen another book because the cover blurb had promised a detailed look at life in London during the Blitz. Everyone meeting in cafés at night despite the bombs. Riotous parties on every page. It was very easy to imagine being a gentleman with rooms and having a footman called Parsons and a private secretary named Rupert. Garth dreamt of being in one of the bedrooms illustrated in that book, lying in luxury under a canopy of black satin.

'The engines were noisy,' the girl prattled on. 'Absolutely shuddered. Mostly in the Suez for some reason.'

A man in his mid-twenties came out of the toilet block and stood beneath the streaks of black blood. He was the antithesis of what the sign implied, because he was wearing a leather jacket with the collar up in the style of Wellington bodgies. His greasy hair was slicked back, with one lock flopping forward at the middle of his forehead.

The girl seemed to guess at Garth's silent question. 'As my mother says, the schools are better here in New Zealand and there's lots of fresh air. If we have to live somewhere else, then this is safe and clean. Edinburgh, well...' Her comparison petered out. It could have been that she couldn't remember what her mother or father had said, that without their ideas she couldn't articulate exactly how she herself felt.

An unlit cigarette drooped from the man's mouth. He was the sort the newspapers were ranting about: teddy boys, bodgies, uncouth louts who danced all night with slutty girls called widgies. Garth desperately wanted the man to signal to him. It was like being in his bedroom with the door locked, waiting for the time when he could pack up his prints and books and leave for a flat in Wellington, where a man might knock on his door.

'You're blushing,' the girl said, and Garth was forced back into the hot and smelly world of the bus.

'Have you been to London?' he asked. From all of the pictures of

London he'd seen in magazines he knew that the bodgie would have fitted into that city. There was a place in life for everyone. The girl wanted New Plymouth with its provincial library and fresh air. Garth began thinking of the ship she had arrived on: the *Birmingham Queen*, which docked in New Plymouth every three months with another batch of immigrants from England. Its moaning foghorn echoed around the town when it sailed away with a hull full of dairy products.

'New Plymouth is the largest butter- and cheese-exporting port in the world,' Garth announced out of the blue.

'Of course I've been to London,' the girl said. 'It's ever so busy and dirty, but there are lots of picture shows.'

'Did you ever go to the Victoria and Albert Museum?'

Garth could see the grey edifice clearly in his mind. At the pictures one Friday night he'd seen a newsreel of London, with red double-decker buses and streets lined with blocks of flats. People in long coats and fashionable hats. He had envied their having been lucky enough to have been born in a place where there was real life, a place that had the best museums and clubs in the world, instead of the distinction of massive loads of frozen meat and cheese. In the film, a man like the one in the grotto door of the Seaview Road toilets had turned to face the camera. For a second he seemed to stare straight at Garth. He, too, wore a leather jacket and his hair was greased back. He had winked at the camera, then turned and took quick, confident steps up the stairs and disappeared into the Victoria and Albert.

'It seems just like yesterday since we left all that behind. How time flies, doesn't it?' The girl patted her tussled hair. Cynthia would have sneered because it wasn't lacquered. 'We're not the usual sort of British immigrants,' she said. 'No assisted passage or anything like that. First-class cabins actually.' Her accent, everything about her, was different. Garth had read a novel about British people in India, and he now realised what that author had meant about 'tea-party nonsense'.

'Could I just flick through your book?' the girl asked. Garth found himself admiring her smooth, unblemished hands. Raskolnikov's sister had hands described as lily like. Not like Cynthia's and Lucille's, which were like bits of Egyptian parchment. Hours spent in the back yard in the sun getting brown so that they would be perfect on Saturdays for the boys at Ngamutu Beach.

'Isn't it ghastly,' the girl said in her prim voice, 'the way people don't appreciate good books.'

Garth glanced at the toilets again and saw that the bodgie had disappeared. He sensed a thick surge of loss. If only the man had winked at him, indicated with a jut of the head that Garth should get off the bus and join him in the toilets. He felt nervous and depressed, the same sort of feeling that accompanied those times when he imagined all eyes staring at him, all mouths ready for attack.

'I don't know where I'd be without books,' the girl said. 'Quite lost, I imagine.' She held *Crime and Punishment* in her lily hands with the same devotion as Sister Chrysoganus caressing the Bible. The book Garth adored held as if this girl, too, had discovered its significance.

'Boys and girls, here is truth,' Sister Chrysoganus had told them all in standard four. The Bible held aloft in Sister's bleached hands, and the children's believing faces staring at her.

✳

'Hullo?' Garth said suspiciously. It was unusual that someone should telephone him. None of the boys at school did, except for the occasional request for help with homework.

'It's me,' the girl from the bus said. He recognised her voice immediately because of the accent. 'You remember asking me to call?' The same television programme was on in her house. The same voices made the same laughs down the telephone line.

'Are you there?' she asked. 'You're so shy, which is why I like you. You're just like Raskolnikov.'

'I...' he tried to reply.

'You reminded me of a boy on the *Birmingham Queen* who took a picture of me but never sent it like he said he would.' She sighed, as if all males were unreliable.

Cynthia sniggered at the door. She puckered her lips to simulate a kiss, and attempted a look that might have been pride, but it could have been one of relief because her poofy brother was smiling and talking to a girl. This was the gossip she had been waiting for. In the corridor at school she could let the word out and denounce anyone who insinuated that her brother was a queer. Garth puckered his lips back. It was a rare moment of complicity between a brother and a sister whose only strong sibling pact was based on hate.

'Yes, thank you,' he said to the girl. 'I'd love to go to a fancy-dress.'

∗

'It's a jolly good thing,' Mrs Griffin said. She felt quite elated. 'It'll get you out of the house, a boy your age.' She was pounding away at a garment on the ironing board. 'It's not normal at your age to mope about with no friend to speak of.' She was adamant about that. The Smith boy next door had a constant string of mates coming and going. She never minded that Bruce Smith played his music very loud when his mates came around. Not even when the windows rattled and the boys threw beer bottles against the back fence. That was normal. A boy needed mates to go to the football matches with. It was good for boys to go out together and have a few beers and sing dirty songs. It let steam off.

Mrs Griffin looked up from her pleats. She was wearing the garish lipstick that Cynthia had nicked from Woolworths for her birthday present. 'When I was a teenager,' she said, 'I wanted to go out all the time with my friends. There was so much to do in those days what with the war on.' She returned her attention to the ironing. It could have been that she didn't want Dad to notice the sudden smirk that creased her orange mouth. Mum sitting on top of an American tank, riding around the race course with the GIs. Phil and Bud with their presents of bubble gum and silk stockings, and their exciting accents.

'It was all above board,' she said as she hung a skirt on the hanger and picked up a blouse with a crinoline collar. 'Those Yanks were as polite as could be, and a good job too. What with so many being stationed in New Plymouth, word would soon have got out if they'd misbehaved. Isn't that right, Dad? They were very decent, those GIs.'

'What are you going to the fancy-dress as, eh boy?' Dad said, looking up from the racing page. He was so relieved that Garth was going out with a girl that he didn't mind being distracted from the problem of choosing between Big Chief and Florence Nightingale in the third race at Wanganui.

'Eh?' he said. 'Speak up so your mother can hear what you're mumbling about.'

Garth knew they wouldn't have a clue what he was talking about. Just to mention Dostoyevsky would have made Cynthia say something disgusting like 'What are ya?'

It was embarrassing to parade his love of reading in front of them, and he hesitated. They had been proud of him when he'd gone up on stage to receive the English prize, but if he said anything at home about books, he was considered a show-off. It was impossible for them to understand that a man in a book could be your best friend.

'Garth's a great reader, but he won't get out and about like he should,' was the sort of thing his mother said. Being a great reader meant you were weird, that you weren't the same as Bruce Smith, who could talk to Dad over the fence about fixing cars. Mum did try to find some consolation: 'Garth'll be a journalist.' But it wasn't normal to read so much. Not highbrow books at the age of sixteen when you should be going out instead of moping under that ghastly picture Garth had on his wall.

'Well, son,' Dad said. 'Cat got your tongue? What're you going as? A pirate?' He was still undecided about Big Chief. Garth's silence was ominous. It meant he might come out with one of his strange questions like 'Why does the Prime Minister think that the Red Chinese are so bad when all they are doing is making everyone in China equal?' 'Why doesn't New Zealand choose philosophers for their leaders like the French do?'

'Raskolnikov,' Garth said quietly.

'Sounds like a bloody communist,' Dad said.

Mr Griffin collected bottles from around the world, and there was a row of them right around the lounge wall. He'd obtained many from the *Birmingham Queen* sailors he'd met while working on the wharf. All sorts of bottles with labels in languages he didn't know, and he looked at them now with pleasure. His favourite bottle was labelled 'Tequila' in red and green and had a man with a poncho over his shoulder, a foreigner's thick moustache.

'What the hell's this Ras... Ras...?' he demanded. You had to stand up to a kid like Garth. You couldn't just let things get out of hand with a smart aleck trying to pull the wool over your eyes with a big word.

'Let him explain,' Mrs Griffin said. It was Mrs Smith's advice to Mum that Garth was too clever for his own good, but that psychologists said that brainy kids had to be given a chance to express themselves. 'Or else they'll get all strange and never say a word to anyone and end up in the nut house.' Mrs Smith had heard that on *Plain Truth* on the radio and had thought of Garth immediately. 'There's a lot of truth to what those Americans have to say about these things.'

'Who is this bloke Raskolnikov, dear?' Mum asked.

She shot Dad a look to indicate that he wasn't to interfere. 'Is he like that painter... Bosch?' She learned the name because she was really trying to understand her boy. He was the sweet one, always had been. The other mothers had always remarked what a lovely little boy he was in his pram. Different from the rest, never a snotty kid, never the sort to demand or scream. As she finished ironing Cynthia's blouse she recalled Mrs Armstrong's words about Garth: 'Those eyes'd make your heart melt. He'll have trouble when he grows up with eyes like that.'

Mrs Armstrong was an odd fish and she could say strange things.

She was still the same all these years later, living in her flat on Whakatane Street all by herself. A bit of an old witch with her prophesies and forked tongue. She hadn't left it at that. 'Just the sort of big brown eyes that nancy boys have.'

'I like Bosch even though he's a bit spooky,' Mrs Griffin said, then yelled to Cynthia for some hangers. 'Some of those pictures are all right, though,' she said. 'I mean, it's all life.'

On the wall above the television set was a painting of a Dutch windmill, like a giant's skeletal arms with the hands cut off. Around and around, the fleshless arms; after all these years Garth had the ability to see them treading the wind.

'Elspeth said she sent a postcard of the *Mona Lisa*, but it never arrived. That'd be the French post, not ours.'

The flat, soggy fields and a mist that was meant to be romantic but was just ugly. Garth remembered the day that Dad had hung it up, stood back and said, 'Now that's what I call art.' To look anywhere in the lounge room was an affront to the eye: Dad's bottles, Cynthia's pink cats on the mantelpiece, and the green carpet that clashed so violently with the red fireplace.

Garth understood what Mrs Ramprasad, who owned the corner shop, had meant when she replied to his question of whether she liked New Zealand or India the best. 'Sometimes you are standing on one side of the cliff and you are looking out and you are knowing you will never be getting to that other side,' she'd said. That look in her eyes. It was one of those pivotal lessons when he had recognised for the first time what it was to be alone in a world in which you had no place. It was a struggle to remain sane in a society that didn't want you. It was as Dad always said: 'Immigrants shouldn't be allowed into this country unless they pass a test. People have to fit in.' The social studies teacher called it assimilation, belonging to the group, being part of it, absorbed in the mainstream. Garth had learned the words for the exams, and he understood them now for what they really meant, because they applied to him. He was the same as the Indian shopkeeper, with her sense of loss and bewilderment.

'Mind you, Elspeth did bring me that linen tea towel with the Mona Lisa's face on it. She bought it in a French museum,' Mrs Griffin said.

Garth wanted to fit in, to appreciate the tea towel hanging above the fridge and his mother's efforts to talk to him about art.

'That was nice of her,' he said. 'That's how the teacher taught us the meaning of "enigmatic". She said you can't tell what the Mona Lisa's thinking.'

'These bloody horses are enigmatic,' Dad said. 'I think I'll take Big Chief.'

'Elspeth said they queued for an hour just to see the *Mona Lisa*, and then it wasn't even as big as the tea towel, so it was hardly worth going all the way to Paris, was it?' Mum continued.

'She did say that France is really beautiful,' Garth remarked.

'It might be beautiful,' Dad said, looking up from the racing page, 'but those miserable Frogs don't appreciate that our boys died defending them.'

'You can't trust the French,' Mrs Griffin added. 'I wouldn't trust them as far as I could kick them. They might have all the museums in the world, but what Elspeth said is right, no personal hygiene.'

How Garth longed to see those museums and to have a friend to talk to about all the paintings. Hieronymous Bosch and Dali and da Vinci. The names ringing beautifully, strung together like the words of the language he invented for himself when he pretended to be a European in his bedroom.

He wanted to say to his parents, 'I'm going to London. I'm leaving for Paris or New York.' That would be easier than trying to fit into a place in which he knew he couldn't live any longer. It was too much of a battle; Mrs Ramprasad's cliff was as high as a mountain and the gulf was broadening. The arguments about not playing football, the constant battle about locking his bedroom, and the sneers about wearing pimple cream, which Dad said was nothing more than girls' make-up.

Garth wanted to please his parents, to announce that he was going to the party as a pirate or an Arab or a lumberjack. Or talk cars with Dad. To be normal like Bruce next door. He turned in the direction of the Smiths' house as if they could help him to accept and not to taunt his parents by mentioning a character from a Russian novel. But Mum was pulling the curtains so that the carpet wouldn't fade and the moment was passing too swiftly. He felt something metallic swilling through his body like some illness.

'Anyway, that girl you're going with,' Cynthia said. 'She seems posh.' His sister had an irritating way of chewing gum, making it smack in her mouth. She'd been experimenting with her mother's lipsticks so that her mouth had a mixture of unnatural sheens. 'Lucille says she's a snob like you are.'

There wasn't much you could do in a world like this except run away. His eyes told Cynthia how much he hated her, and his mind boiled with the injustice of having to put up with this sort of existence.

He wanted to scream at his family, to cry and throw Cynthia's pink cats against the brick fireplace.

Mrs Griffin put down her iron and looked at her two children. It could have been a photo album she was looking at. Flicking through the pages and seeing the years pass by. Cynthia at five with all that confidence. At age ten holding her brother's truck above her head, and Garth at her feet surrounded by her dolls. Now Cynthia was standing in the lounge with that repugnant mixture of lipstick on her mouth, and the two of them were acting as they always had. Nothing had ever been any different, and Mrs Griffin wanted to know which side of the family had produced this terrible mixture of hatred and silliness. It was Cynthia who was always in the wrong with her vicious mouth and her willingness to be cruel. She had come to no good; it was there for all the world to see.

As much as Cynthia talked Garth down, he was clever and a nice boy, despite Mrs Armstrong's predictions. Mum looked at his big brown eyes; no, he wasn't like that. Mrs Armstrong had been a bitch because she didn't have children. Garth was sensitive and intelligent, and had an eye for nice things. Now he had a date with a girl, the sissy stage might now be passing.

Cynthia was grimacing at her brother. She was a slut. It was hard for Mum. She had resisted those GIs at the race course during the war. She'd tried all her life to be a good Catholic and to bring her kids up the same way. She couldn't figure out where she'd gone wrong.

'Bloody families,' she said. They could all go to hell. She thrust an armful of ironed clothes at Cynthia. 'Put this bloody stuff away,' she said.

Garth knew there was no way out for him. He had his mind made up for him with his mother's own summation of the truth: bloody families. It was there in the bad taste and the waste of life in the lounge room. His hero was Raskolnikov, a beautiful man who wanted nothing but the privilege of being left alone in a garret, without a family to rebuke him for being different. Garth's father let him have the Humber to go to the fancy dress party. At the girl's house he parked and rang the bell. On his head a battered top hat like Raskolnikov's. Dirty, unkempt, as close a replica as he could manage. Raskolnikov wandering furtively through the night alleys of St Petersburg in his crumpled overcoat and wearing those sinister gloves with the fingers cut out.

'She's going as an angel. She looks awfully sweet,' Mrs MacDougal said. She was a big woman and wore the sort of clothes that would have frightened Garth's mother. The brogues and tweeds and silk scarf proclaimed immediately what she was. Mum wouldn't have known what to do when confronted by a woman in clothes like that. Garth had an awful image of his mother arriving at the MacDougals' for tea, wearing her special outfit, the one she'd worn to Elspeth's wedding reception at the Livinia Lounge. The flowing mauve dress trimmed in feathers with the bust gathered in elastic. Garth could tell the MacDougals were rich just from the sort of clothes they wore around the house. Mr MacDougal had on a jacket and tie, even though he was at home in front of the fire with a book in his lap. Lamps glowed on small polished tables, softly illuminating the room. They didn't have light bulbs hanging on long wires from the ceiling as other New Zealand houses did. Garth summed it all up while politely sipping lemonade, his Raskolnikov hat on the satin seat next to him. These lucky people had lived in Britain; they were from the upper class.

'I shouldn't have said how she's going, should I, dear? You wait until she comes down,' Mrs MacDougal said. 'We had such a problem making her wings.' She indicated to the stairs as if announcing the appearance of a señorita who would slowly descend with a rose between her teeth.

'What sort of work does your father do?' she asked. When Garth replied, 'He's a wharfie,' she shifted slightly in her chair and smoothed her tweed skirt.

'Our daughter informed us that New Plymouth is the largest butter- and cheese-exporting port in the world,' Mr MacDougal said. 'That must keep your father very busy indeed.'

Garth wished that he'd taken his mother's suggestion and come dressed in something that would have made him carry his head high. As Cary Grant, perhaps, sophisticated in the tuxedo Cynthia said she'd seen in the second-hand shop. He shouldn't have let himself down like this,with dirt deliberately smeared on his coat to simulate the filthy, desperate Raskolnikov.

'It's very encouraging to see how New Zealanders read,' Mrs MacDougal said. 'Fancy a boy of your age loving *Crime and Punishment* so much. We thought it was just our daughter who was so obsessed by books.' She got up and offered him peanuts in a pewter dish.

'Russian literature was born and bred from Slavic suffering,' Mr MacDougal said.

'Dostoyevsky said that strength came only through struggle,' Garth offered.

'I'm sure he did, because he suffered enormously for being an intellectual,' Mr MacDougal replied. He tapped his pipe on the ashtray and stuffed in tobacco. When he lit it, blue smoke wafted through the room. Garth knew the smell was the same as in the filthy cellar bar where Raskolnikov had bought with his last kopecks the concoction that had led him to decide that murder is acceptable if perpetrated for a just cause.

'My teacher told me that New Zealand could never produce a writer like Dostoyevsky,' he said. 'I mean, just the part in the smoke-filled bar where he decides to help poor people by murdering...'

'Fortunately for us, there aren't the social conditions in New Zealand to produce that sort of torment,' Mrs MacDougal said. 'Which is why we like this place, it's so much more wholesome than Europe.'

'Yes,' Garth said excitedly. 'Yes, I know, but if I were a Russian I would have become a communist too.'

'Perhaps communism is another Russian extreme. We're socialists, the middle path,' Mrs MacDougal said.

Garth looked from one to the other; they were the people he should have had as parents. He wanted to blurt out all his secrets to them, tell them that he'd always wanted to live in London, that he loved Hieronymous Bosch and Raskolnikov, and that he didn't understand how he had been produced by the likes of Mum and Dad, who thought all communists should be shot.

'The Scottish are great socialists,' Mr MacDougal said.

'More lemonade, Garth?' Mrs MacDougal asked. 'Of course suffering is the main theme of this favourite book of yours, where crime is committed against the haves to benefit the have-nots. Didn't Raskolnikov have some of the socialist in him just as the Scots and the New Zealanders have now?'

She had poured the lemonade in the kitchen and brought the glass back on a pewter tray. Mum would have had the bottle sitting on the table. The MacDougals and the Griffins, they were as different as the extremes Mrs MacDougal was talking about between Russia and New Zealand. This was the nicest house Garth had ever been in; there were candles on the mahogany dining table and real paintings behind beautiful frames. He realised he had never before felt that he belonged somewhere so much. If the MacDougals had been invited to his house, Cynthia would have sat there smirking and ruined it all by playing her records too loudly. Or the television set would have been blaring. In the Griffins' house there had to be constant noise to cover the embarrassing lack of social intercourse. Mum would have sat there trying to sound posh while she rabbited on about keeping Dad's bottles dusted. Garth could now see that people lived other lives, there were other ways to say things and drink lemonade and to talk to teenagers.

*

'I'm the Good Angel,' the girl said. 'You must call me that all evening, and I will call you Raskolnikov.' They were driving in the Humber down by Ngamutu Beach. At the port the bright lights of the Birmingham Queen flicked through the wind and splattered in the choppy sea.

The Good Angel was forced to sit forward to avoid crushing her wings. Her chiffon and lace smelled of washing powder and scent. She snuggled up to Garth as best she could in the confines of her abundant dress and touched his neck with her fingertips. 'We could park down there at the beach for a little while,' she said. 'Under those trees, the ones with that unpronounceable Maori name.'

'Pohutukawas.'

'If you insist. I shall never be able to remember that as long as I live. One has to be born into a culture in order to understand perfectly what…' She stopped in mid-sentence as if she had recalled someone saying she had an annoying ability to sound like a know-all.

'I'm afraid of Maoris,' she said. 'They appear so… so… different from the rest of us. But there's always someone unusual in a crowd I suppose.'

Garth knew what she meant, but he was applying that to himself.

He saw how Maoris must feel every time someone pointed them out: huhu-bug eater, Maori runt. It was the vocabulary of people who hated anything different from themselves: Maoris, queers, poofters. The Good Angel's fingers had moved more longingly over his neck. As they travelled up Seaview Road, she said, 'This is where we travelled on that bus. You're different from other boys. I noticed that immediately. Park here, Raskolnikov, so we can re-live where we first met.'

Garth noticed the toilet block with the dripping GENTLEMEN sign lit by a weak light. As soon as he'd parked she leaned over and licked his cheek and then buried her nose in his ear. Peter was betraying Christ in Garth's mind: 'And then for the third time the cock crowed...' It was a message from the Bible he had listened to with only half an ear, but the meaning had remained implicit; it wallowed in his mind as she rubbed the back of his neck. Sister Chrysoganus with her tattered Bible in her bleached hands. Sister Chrysoganus standing in front of her desk in her black habit, saying 'Virgin' and stepping back theatrically so the statue of the Virgin Mary on her desk was revealed to the class.

The Good Angel giggled in a way that Mrs MacDougal wouldn't have. Her metamorphosis was at the transitional phase; giggles interspersed with grown-up talk. 'I'm awfully fond... awfully...' she said. Again she giggled. In and out of her dual roles of mother and daughter. 'Go on, let's do something.'

It was Raskolnikov who had been thinking of Peter's betrayal as he had hit the old money-lender on the head with an axe. The act of righteousness a just reward for Peter, who had betrayed Christ. The blood staining the old hag's carpet was the symbol of purification for her having taken advantage of Raskolnikov.

'Go on, I'll let you,' the Good Angel urged. Her face was ghostly white in the unflattering street light. She looked as if she had died and come back to life in her desired caricature of an angel, but one that had never known blood in its veins, a dead creature that needed lipstick and rouge to simulate the presence of life. The powder on her face was the same sort that Mum patted on before going to Mass.

'I liked you the very first moment you chose to sit next to me on the bus,' the Good Angel said. She was trying to move closer to him, but the handbrake lever jabbed at her buttocks. 'It was something about your knees, the way your knees looked. You do like me, don't you?'

Garth wondered in what order the betrayals had come; it was such an important part of the novel that he would have to memorise it. Peter falling asleep during the most crucial moment of Christ's life. The scenario came back. It was interesting how the mind worked. The novel playing on the reality of life. The novel was the highest form of being alive because you lived according to the plan it laid out for you to follow. The woman murdered. The release from constraints.

The Good Angel must have driven in Humbers before because she knew exactly where the seat-release lever was. The back sank lower and lower; she giggled each time it did.

'One should never wear wings in a small car,' she said in that voice he found increasingly irritating. It could have been Mrs MacDougal advising on the best way to decant sherry or prune roses; the voice just a little too shrill, just a little too grown up, even for an adult.

'You're nervous, aren't you?' the Good Angel said. She was lying back in the Humber's seat. 'Take off your hat, Raskolnikov,' she said. 'Go on. You can.' She sat forward a bit because her wings were jabbing her in the back. Garth needed reassurance, she could see that. He was different from other boys; that was obvious in his reticence and the way his hands shook. Men were not as confident as women. It had been Mummy who had to put the pressure on Daddy to leave Scotland, who had forced him up the managerial ladder.

'Closer,' the Good Angel said. 'You mustn't be afraid.' She had been on ships and lived in London and attended the best school for girls in Scotland. Fear didn't affect her. Not in the front seat of a car with someone from the working class.

Garth hadn't thought it would be like this. He knew he was different; that was a daily fact of life, and it hurt to be reminded of it by someone who was supposed to have gleaned sensitivity from books and whom he'd met through Raskolnikov. But it had been the same for Raskolnikov with the old Jewess who hadn't let him in the door. Life didn't go according to plan. Dostoyevsky had proved that with Raskolnikov. He was such a good writer you could almost see the page stained with the old woman's blood.

'You needn't worry about pregnancy,' the Good Angel said. 'I've taken precautions.' Her wings wouldn't allow her the luxury of reclining, so she had to stay propped on her elbows surrounded by her heavenly swathe of white chiffon and lace. She gazed at Garth with understanding and forgiveness as he pouted at the dark Tasman. This was the same sort of problem she'd encountered with working-class boys in Scotland. She was the one who had to do the seducing. The sailor on the *Birmingham Queen* had acted in the same reluctant way.

'What are you thinking?' she asked. She was trying to be nice, but to Garth she might have been Lucille or Cynthia in the corridor at school with their taunts about sissies. He looked at her propped there in the seat with the powder covering the colour but not the contours of her acne. A car drove by slowly and stopped just down the street.

'Who's that?' she asked.

'Stay down,' he replied. 'It's just a car. It's gone now.'

She took his hand in hers and she moved it to her right breast, encouraging him to rub and squeeze it. Just then a flurry of rain splattered against the car and the squall obscured the city lights.

The Good Angel's hand pulled Garth's head towards her. He felt helpless to resist. His mouth was forced against hers and she pushed her tongue between his dry lips. The smell of her powder reminded him so painfully of his mother at Mass that he wanted to scream. When he broke away from this long and awkward kiss, he turned to the window to gasp in some fresh air. He noticed that the rain had stopped and the driver of the car along the road had climbed out and was standing on the footpath lighting a cigarette.

The Good Angel pulled at his neck again. The wet hole of her mouth was the black door of the old money-lender's flat in St Petersburg. To enter it was to be trapped. To be trapped was to suffer and to suffer was to have to repent. The novel's enormous equations went zing, zing through his head.

'Kiss me again,' the Good Angel begged. Her wings were flattened now, their complicated wires poking into her back as she tried to drag Garth on top of her. She slipped her hand into his fly, and began fondling his flaccid penis. 'What's wrong?' she said. 'Tell me.'

She didn't smirk or twitter as other girls might; you didn't do that sort of thing when you were being cheated. She had learned her lessons. Her mother loudly complaining about being fobbed off by cheap sherry, snorting with derision at her husband's suggestion that they should stay in Scotland rather than risk emigrating halfway round the world.

'It's this angel's outfit, isn't it?' the Good Angel said. 'You're a Catholic. That's why you can't get a stiffy.'

'No,' Garth muttered. He knew that he had only a few seconds in which to effect change or else accept that he would be lost for the rest of his life. He reached out and put his hand on her breast without being helped. Beneath her singlet, he toyed with a girl's nipple for the very first time. Sinking back on her flattened wings like a debilitated insect, she sighed with pleasure: this was what happened when you wouldn't take no for an answer.

Garth understood why his father had winked when he'd offered the use of the Humber. There was a time in every man's life when this had to happen, and this was his encounter with reality.

'Come on,' the Good Angel whispered. 'Quick.' She opened her legs and guided his hand under her dress. The sailor had stuck his fingers into her. It was obviously what men wanted. She giggled with anticipation.

Garth found himself erect and manoeuvring on top of the Good Angel. Suddenly he pictured Raskolnikov in his wretched garret, nude, with his penis sticking out, thrusting into Garth's arsehole at the same second Garth slipped his penis into the Good Angel's cunt. He pushed in and out, amazed that it was possible for him to do this against all the odds. He glimpsed his mother at the ironing board, but quickly brought Raskolnikov back into focus. The man he adored, with his hairy legs and superb white arse. Garth opened his eyes and Raskolnikov fled. He felt himself go limp.

It was raining, again. The man from the car was lighting another cigarette as he stood in the shelter of the toilet block entrance. It was the same man, the bodgie with the leather jacket, he had seen from the bus.

Garth turned to look at the Good Angel. 'I'm sorry,' he said. He was sorry for the whole world. Raskolnikov had committed murder in the name of social justice. Evil had become joy, but for Garth the opposite had happened. Confusion and contempt battled in his mind.

'Go,' he said. 'Get out.'

'But it's not a sin. You Catholics...'

'Catholics?' he spat. As if it were as simple as that. As if it had anything to do with the silly notions of virgins who could bear sons, of turning wine into blood.

'It's your religion. It's not a rational kind... it's... Please, can I help you? I know you can do it.'

She didn't have an inkling. The very word 'help' made his skin crawl.

'You're ashamed,' the Good Angel said. 'That's why you can't do it.'

Garth saw everything with the same clarity as he saw the man smoking in the toilet door; the grease on his fallen lock shone in the light reflecting from the puddles. At the convent there was a statue of the Virgin Mary standing in a grotto, looming like the bodgie in the arched door of the toilet block.

'Of course I can do it,' he said bitterly.

'Let's try again,' she said, sinking back and reaching out for him.

He looked at the Good Angel. This must have been how his hero felt at the moment of hitting the old hag on the head and seeing the blood gush out.

'Get out,' he yelled again, pushing her out the door.

She was weeping when she poked her head in the window. Her tears had streaked the powder on her face and her wings were soggy. She begged desperately in her attempt to comprehend.

'It's raining,' she sobbed.

Garth turned away and she trudged off into the dripping darkness.

It was the first time in his life that Garth had felt an urge to smoke. He understood the urgency of an addict craving that fix of nicotine and the smooth flow of smoke in his throat. He crossed to the toilet block and asked for a cigarette.

5 Judas Iscariot was a blatant homosexual

George Crossett walked quickly and slightly self-consciously down Devon Street as if it were still the days of six o'clock pub closing. He had not come to terms with the fact that it was 1967 and that pubs remained open until ten. Groups of men no longer spilled out into the street all tanked up and ready to accost any man they regarded as abnormal. It was part of George's character to walk purposefully and to avoid eye contact. To saunter was to look unoccupied, which might mean you were on the lookout for little boys to molest. That was the sort of thing he knew mothers and fathers thought unmarried men over the age of forty were all about. Loitering with intent. Soliciting. George knew the terminology of his oppression. It was regularly in the newspapers. Loitering with intent at seven thirty on the fifteenth of July in Whangaroa Street: So-and-so of Such-and-such; six months' imprisonment. He'd never been bashed up in his life, and attributed that to the fact that he had always been careful to disguise the fact that he was a queer. He'd perfected his walk. He no longer cared about that tell tale aspect of a homosexual's identity because he knew he walked like a man.

It was a chilly late May evening, with the wind rushing off Mount Egmont and slapping the frigid streets with icy particles. George was wrapped up in his smart new overcoat, signalling his professional status. He continued down Devon Street, alert as usual. He had changed in some respects during the last thirteen years, but there were some things that were habitual, innate almost, like the fear of being anywhere near teenage boys in case he was accused of soliciting. Despite the cold, the gathering darkness offered a modicum of comfort. Outside the National Insurance Office, where the old ZYX Fruit Shop had once stood, he paused for a little remembrance. It was the one part of Devon Street where memories didn't make him feel melancholy. If the whole of New Plymouth felt like that corner did, he wouldn't have had to spend half of his life entertaining ideas about running off to Wellington or London.

Neddy Bouzikis had run away, and George admired him enormously for having done so. The New Plymouth grapevine had buzzed with the detritus of gossip.

'Neddy Bouzilds has run off to Beirut, and he didn't go with his wife.'

'Well, she's better off without him.'

'That's what killed the old lady. Apparently she just dropped dead from the grief of it.'

'Jillian Shingles told me that Bouzikis took off with some man, another Lebanese.'

'Yes, a homo Lebo. They must all be like that.'

George had been having tea in the staff room at the Farmers' Equity Group, where he had been employed as an accountant for several years, as he listened to the gossip. He knew all about it himself, everything that Neddy had told him about whom he was taking to Beirut. The very thought of it there outside the fruit shop on that freezing evening, hearing the staff ramble on about what they knew nothing of; never dreaming that the silent Mr Crossett drinking his coffee next to them had been penetrated by that man on so many occasions.

But what a shame Neddy had gone. Those delicious liaisons in the fruit van, with him always as willing to ball as he was to bend. It was exciting just thinking about that hairy man performing the things you might expect from an Arab. George shivered at the thought of Neddy's luscious penis. Neddy had been his most regular sex partner until he had quit New Plymouth a few years ago. And not a word since then. Never a letter with a big bright stamp marked LEBANON.

Life was peculiar in so many respects; you could suck and fuck, but share so few other intimacies as normal people did.

Intimacies all right, despite George's promise to himself years before to be celibate like his father. He'd had intimacies with strangers in strange places: Fifteen minutes of passion with a sailor. Three or four times with a policeman from Wanganui who liked to be masturbated while he stroked his own uniform. Yes, intimate to the point of deep, dark secrets that lived and grew, like the memories of Frank La Verde. Passions grabbed for the moment and sucked dry because they couldn't be continued like those enjoyed by normal people.

George lingered by the smart new swing doors where the old wooden entrance of the ZYX Fruit Shop had been, with its piles of boxes outside. There was nobody else in the street on this cold night. They were all in the pubs or at home in front of the television with a cup of tea and their feet up. Neddy had got out alive, had dumped his wife and gone somewhere exciting. An apartment in Beirut. Hot days and fresh oranges and beautiful boys. Where there was the freedom to be a homosexual because, as everyone knew, the Arabs didn't mind it before marriage. That was the life. Anything was better than Devon Street on a cold May evening, all alone and wrapped up in a gaberdine coat, thinking about freedom outside the memory of the ZYX Fruit Shop.

'Imagine Beirut,' George said to himself. 'Imagine life in the Middle East.'

He sighed in the dark air and felt angry at himself for not having run off like Neddy. History happened, it had to occur. It was all there with the smart doors of the insurance office instead of the old fruit shop. Things moved on. Nothing was static. George regretted having done so little with his life. He hadn't gone to Beirut with a man.

History hadn't affected him in the least, except to bypass him. The panic that arose when he allowed himself to remember that he was still doing accounts after all these years now attacked him. It was the thought of Neddy taking off his underpants and standing there with his huge penis sticking out and that happy-go-lucky smile working his lips, making its way to his dark eyes. Beirut and the image of belly dancers and curved streets and minarets.

So much had been lost in George's life. Neddy could have been his if only he had been a bit more alive and not stultified by fears and accountancy. It was an enormous loss. A whole lifetime stranded in New Plymouth when he could have been in Neddy's arms in Beirut. But he'd thrown all that away by being so pompous with Neddy. In bed and out. A curt little nod as he went by the fruit shop, as if the two had never performed mutual fellatio in the back of Neddy's fruit van. Never wanting to be too chummy in case he was caught and punished.

A man came out of the insurance office, and George guessed that he was an accountant: the drab attire, the lost-looking eyes, all that ugliness that possesses a man trapped in a boring life. George himself wore the same clothes. Two tedious twins in the main street of New Plymouth. He wanted so much to live, to reverse the mistake of loneliness and tedium: Beirut, Neddy, boats, even England.

'London,' he thought. 'At least that.'

The man was fumbling in his briefcase. 'I'll do it,' George said aloud. 'Once and for all.'

'Eh?' the man said. 'Do what?'

George sweated despite the chill wind. He was so unaccustomed to enthusiasm that his excitement had a physical quality.

This was to be the last run for the *Birmingham Queen*. The *Taranaki Herald* had suggested that the familiar ship might be scrapped or sold off to act as a coastal vessel in Africa. George changed his plans about going straight home, even though he had steak-and-kidney and dumplings waiting. In his new mood he decided to farewell the

Birmingham Queen. His only regret was that he would not be able to pack a bag and get on the ship before it left on its last voyage from New Plymouth the following morning.

From the corner of Brighton Street and Hinemoa Lane he could see her at the wharf. The ship didn't seem old to him, not something one should scrap or sell off to some African country. It had so many lights; it breathed excitement and secrets and history.

The Seaview Road toilet block was one of the few things that hadn't changed over the years. Not even the old sign in lead letters above the door. It had always appeared as if something nasty were oozing from each letter. George's heart beat with fear and expectation as he walked through the arched entrance.

A couple of weak lights cast a pallid glow in the cavernous building, where water dripped from ill-fitting fixtures. There were some twenty stalls. It was a remarkably large facility considering its isolation up there on the hill overlooking the port. One might have wondered why the architect had had the idea that twenty men would have needed to defecate at the same moment at such an isolated location.

George was no longer a smoker, but he always carried matches and cigarettes for such occasions as this. The decision to leave New Plymouth had emboldened him. Usually he would have gone into one of the stalls, locked the door and sat there for a very long time because he was too afraid to solicit in the open. But there was already somebody standing at the urinal. Despite the dim light, George could see that the man was wearing a denim jacket. He went up and stood next to him.

'You again, eh?' the man said. His voice was heavily accented. He was the sailor from Liverpool with whom George had had relations on three or four occasions over the past few years. His voice seemed full of disappointment. 'You again.' George understood: you couldn't expect someone so young and slim to want a man as prematurely aged as himself.

'Unlucky, aren't you?' he said. 'Who were you expecting? Prince Charles?'

'A hole's a hole, I suppose, matey. Come on then,' the sailor said, grinning despite his disappointment. 'In the stall. I ain't waiting for no prince.'

'This is your last trip. You should count yourself lucky to have me again,' George said. 'After all, if my hole was good enough last...'

'Shut up, you old tart,' the sailor snapped, and pushed George into a cubicle. 'At least I know you're clean and ain't police.'

He was wearing an intricate belt that took some time to get undone. George had already positioned himself with his hands against the cistern. It didn't occur to him to indulge in foreplay or hope to take an active part. He knew this sailor wouldn't want to muck around.

'Wait. Listen,' the sailor said as a car pulled up on the gravel outside. Men didn't usually arrive at the toilets so noisily; there was always something secretive, slinky almost, about an entry, as if each approach had to be made fearfully. Noise meant police, who didn't understand that raids wouldn't work like that.

For a second George felt fear, then a burst of excitement, but the situation was so expected that the fear and excitement turned momentarily to tedium. 'Piss off,' he said in his mind. 'Leave us alone.' There was just enough time for the sailor to slip into the next stall before George heard the door on the other side of the sailor being bolted.

'Three men in a boat,' he thought. He knew he should have his excuses at the ready; prostate cancer makes me want to piss all the time... an attack of diarrhoea...

'Why should I feel like this?' George wondered. In London there were pubs that homosexuals could frequent. No need to go to toilets. He'd heard there were clubs where men danced with each other, not a heterosexual in sight. He lit a cigarette and smoked, sitting on the toilet thinking that he should have decided twenty years ago to get out. In the past, depression would have entered his mind like concrete pouring and setting; that old refrain and the failure to act on it:

London, London. He had not so much as taken a trip to Wellington for the past six or seven years. Stuck. Glue. Inertia. Whenever George thought about why he hadn't gone away, he felt panic. He had a sudden impulse to pull up his pants, extinguish the cigarette and go back to that bloody house with its bloody memorial garden. He would throw things into a suitcase, close the door and walk out. 'Bugger the roses,' he said. 'Let the whole bloody garden go to pot.'

'Yeah,' he heard the sailor saying. 'Wow!'

George put his eye to a peephole above the toilet-paper dispenser. A very large penis was poking through a hole from the stall that had just been entered, and the sailor was admiring it.

'That's it, matey,' the sailor said. It might have been his mother plonking down a plate of bangers and chips and saying, 'Eat up, sonny'.

George winced at the lost opportunity. Why hadn't he, rather than the sailor, gone into that stall? He peered again, but now all he could see was the back of the sailor's head bobbing up and down.

'Jesus, matey, that was a mouthful,' the sailor said after a few minutes.

George left his cubicle as the sailor did. 'I'm coming to England soon,' George said as they reached the door. He put his hand on the sailor's shoulder. 'I'll buy you a drink if you can show me around.'

'What the bloody hell are you doing?' the sailor said, brushing the unwanted intimacy of George's hand off his shoulder. 'You fucking poofter!'

George was left standing there as the man disappeared into the cruel blackness of the night.

'Excuse me,' a voice behind him said.

George turned to face a tall blond man with a thick ginger moustache stepping out of the third stall. George could tell a mile off he was a policeman.

'You're under arrest for soliciting that man.'

'But... but... but...' George stuttered. He felt as though he had just been injected with a lethal substance and had only seconds to live.

'That's right, soliciting leading to sodomy. I was in that stall watching the whole time. We'll get you on buggery. Nice one. Accomplice fled. Unidentified. We've been after you for a long time, Mr Crossett. Buggery *in flagrante delicto*. Hasn't that got a nice ring to it?'

*

George had been in Her Majesty's Prison on the top of a hill overlooking New Plymouth for a week. Not that he actually got to overlook anything at all; there was nothing to see from the window in his cell except wire and dirty glass. Mount Egmont could have been in Gisborne or Timbuktu for all the prisoners saw of it. The Tasman Sea, which had always given George such solace, might have been crashing on some shore a million miles away and not just down the bottom of Dawson Street. He was facing five years shut up in this dump with the smell of sour cabbage and greasy sausages to affront him. 'At least I don't have to deal with farmers' accounts,' he thought wearily.

He was sitting in the counsellor's office between two other prisoners, Jock Howley and Benny Puhoi. Three homosexuals about to be locked up for years because they'd been involved in sex with males.

'Doesn't matter if this counsellor joker Palmer keeps us waiting. Nothing else to do here, I suppose,' Benny said. He had the cheerful grin associated with people who didn't go around being morbid about their situation.

'When did you get here?' George asked.

'Yesterday. Two cops brought me down in a van from Auckland. Nice Pakeha bloke, but the Maori was up himself.'

'And you?' Jock asked.

'A week, and it feels like a lifetime,' George replied. 'Yourself?'

'Yesterday too. Flown up from Dunedin.'

Each of them politely sitting there as if the headmaster were about to enter or they were waiting to be interviewed for a job. Identically dressed in grey outfits, like big schoolboys: shirts, trousers, socks and black shoes.

'This is like my first day at boarding school,' Jock said. It would have been forty years since his school days.

'What'd you do to get in here?' Benny asked.

'Long story involving a tribe in Papua New Guinea. Let's just say I got caught.' An intelligent-looking man, he had the long, gaunt face found in one of those Spanish masters' paintings full of dark greens and blacks, in which a ray of light illuminated a face of suffering.

'A whole tribe?' Benny grinned again. 'That's a story to string out for us over the years.'

George studied the eyes of his companions. After a lifetime of interpreting signals, he'd learned that eyes were much more revealing than speech. They didn't lie. His father saying, 'I understand,' when his eyes proclaimed that he didn't. Eyes and lies. He could just see the eyes of Mrs Lynch, his secretary, indicating to her friends that she knew what he was.

He contemplated the swiftness of punishment. There had been no chance to return to his house to get anything he might need for the next five years. Nothing as sweet as a goodbye to his cat. Then that bastard, the agent provocateur, sitting up there in the dock and giving evidence with his big blond eyebrows frowning with innocence. For hours in that courtroom listening to the accusations and knowing that the police, the judge, the newspepper people, the voyeuristic public, were all enjoying the titillation.

'Soliciting in public toilets. Is that what the public must put up with, George Crossett?'

The arrival of the prison counsellor interrupted George's sad recollections. Palmer couldn't have been more than thirty, the sort of hearty man who went bush-walking at weekends and mountain climbing at Christmas. George's heart sank. Another blond man. Another virile type. Another heterosexual who was going to reprimand him, remind him that he wasn't normal, wasn't allowed to go back to the sanctuary of his home for five whole years. George had to push himself into the reality of the counsellor's room in order to avoid the despair of madness. He stared at the Queen, smiling benignly in her frame behind Palmer, hating her serenity and her agents of punishment.

'I'm Jonathan Palmer,' the counsellor announced. 'You've been asked to come to meet me today, gentlemen, because you're going to share the same cell and you need to get to know each other. You're mostly homosexuals in this prison. I guess you know this is what's known as the "homosexual's prison". You've been brought here from various parts of New Zealand.'

Unaccountably, George found himself thinking about seagulls. He imagined one flying over the Tasman, elegant, free and happy. He recalled them taking off from the cliffs above beaches around New Plymouth. A draught of air and up and away. They had sometimes rested on the rail of his verandah at home, gorgeous white and black creatures with bright red beaks and legs. He wondered how long they lived. Two years? Three? One had returned regularly. Brown feathers in its wings had set it apart from the others. It had turned up once or twice a week for the bread he provided. Or was it for more than crumbs? What made that bird come back to try to gain his attention? He should have taken more notice and read the signs it was giving him. That bird was different, the way it ran up and down in a tormented fashion.

'Well?' Palmer was saying. 'George?'

'What was that?'

'I was just asking you to give us a little run-down on your life, so you...'

'A run-down? I'm run down all right.'

A gull lived for maybe five years; surely not much longer than that. George didn't know much about the working details of nature, but birds, surely, had no longer than five years. Cats got seven or twelve, and dogs at least a decade.

'Seriously, George. Benny and Jock have both provided a few details about themselves,' Palmer said.

'Well, all I want to say is that I'd rather be a seagull for five years than me for fifty,' George offered.

'And why would that be?' Palmer didn't give a wink or a nod to the other two to indicate that he agreed that the man was mad.

'That's clear enough,' Benny said. He looked at George with relief in his smile. This stiff-looking lawyer type with the hoity airs answering like that. 'Anyone'd rather be a bloody seagull than stare this place in the face for five years. Right, George?' Benny asked.

The three prisoners laughed, but coyly, like a group of children allowed into some adult secret they understand entirely but are ashamed of admitting to grown-ups.

'It's ludicrous. We're three men incarcerated for doing nothing wrong,' Jock said.

'Nothing wrong?' Palmer said. 'That's a bit subjective.'

'No big words, please,' Benny replied. 'If we have to live together, remember that.' He had the huge hands of a wrestler, and thick glasses that were tinted slightly green, like those worn by Russian scientists in comics.

'You must have used a few big words in your time, Benny, as a science teacher,' Palmer said. He was doing his best to use the skills he'd learned at university to help patients recover from psychological impairment. He pushed back his long hair and looked from one face to the other.

Palmer had recently read a research paper published in New York stating that fifteen per cent of gay... He balked at the new word the research document had used. 'Gay' was offensive somehow, old language used flippantly for something criminalised. The report stated that fifteen per cent of gay men had more than ten partners in a single week. Crossett, Howley, Puhoi; these three prisoners would have had thirty men among them in just seven days, when he himself held had intercourse with only three women in three decades.

'Well, George,' he said. 'We'll get your story at another time. I just want you men to know that I'm here whenever you need me. Life in prison for educated men isn't so easy.'

He was like the rest of them, the nice smile and the slightly hippy touch were just pretences. George recognised more lies and deceits and half-truths. He looked at Jock, who winked back. There was no use having a discussion with this counsellor man who had been born to fuck women and have kids, a life so utterly different from the three other men in the room. He was trying to be nice, but you could see in his eyes that he didn't understand.

George saw himself in the Seaview Road toilets bending down to get a good view of a penis. Terrible? Hideous? Criminal? Worthy of years in prison? The agent provocateur free and wandering around toilets looking for more victims; the injustice of that policeman getting sucked off before making his arrest went reeling through George's mind. He had a quick vision of Palmer rooting his wife; a nice, easy time of it with no fear of being compromised by police. Doing it legitimately. The world was filled with homosexuals, but they were still... The image of the heterosexual with his woman fluttered and extinguished itself. Wet wood in the fire. Heterosexuals were so different and they held the power. Maybe Palmer was right. Men seeking each other in toilets was disgraceful. George felt sick at the thought of his perversity, his vileness. He laughed bitterly at himself and the two queers with him and the innocent blond man behind the desk.

'I understand that you've been through a lot in the past few days,' Palmer said. He looked at his watch. In another hour he'd be putting on his shorts to go surfing.

'A religious group called Exodus will visit one of these days. They've had a lot of success with changing homosexuals to...' He stood up. George saw him as the judge, the agent provocateur, merely another bastard he'd had to listen to for decades while pretending he was a real man. 'I merely wanted you to get acquainted before you're locked up tonight in the same room,' Palmer added, smiling.

'Cell,' George said. 'It's not a room. And it has a stinking toilet.'

They looked at each other: Jock, Benny, George. Then they looked at Palmer, who was smiling that same smile, like a barometer forever stuck on WARM.

✳

George was angry that he had to attend the Exodus meeting with some of the other prisoners. He would miss the second round of beginners' table tennis, in the first round of which he had been runner-up.

At five o'clock he finished his accounts in the tuck shop and locked the cash in the safe. He handled all the financial details in commercial ventures to do with the prisoners. George lingered in the shop, waiting for Billy Hewitt to arrive with his broom and mop. Of the sixty or so inmates, Billy was the one who, as he had told Benny and Jock, 'stirred' him the most.

'He was a truck driver in the King Country,' George had told them, as if defending Billy against gross allegations. You could see toughness and hard work in his face, the way he wore his uniform and the way he completely shaved his head every couple of days in order to avoid the regularity of short back and sides and the conformity of prison mediocrity.

'A real man. I mean, if I like men, then why not choose a real one?' George had explained the previous night while sitting on his bunk talking to Jock and Benny.

'He's not your sort,' Benny had scoffed. 'He's a wanker. Tough men aren't tough at all.'

George tidied the bags of sweets and the packets of cigarettes, then turned off the lights in the tuck shop. He felt nervous but giggly, like a young boy doing something naughty. Billy Hewitt always came by at about five to collect the rubbish, and the guards were all out of the way down at the workshop.

'My mother always told me to marry someone like me,' Benny had said. 'She said that like-minded people should stick to each other.'

Benny's mother's words surfaced in George's head as he waited for Billy. George believed himself to be a man, just like Billy was, not the sort who threw sheep onto a truck, for sure, but he had managed to perfect a real-man style of walking and talking. He knew he played table tennis without the effeminate affectations of some of the others. He didn't affect a slight tendency to lisp, and nor did he turn his head to the side when he wanted to say something sarcastic. George was an expert in picking queers. He'd been doing it all his life: 'I wonder if he is?' was a phrase as much used in the corridors of his mind as 'I wonder if they think I am?'

Billy entered the small room looking around as if wondering why the place was so dim.

'Gidday,' he said. 'Much rubbish?'

'I've put it in a pile for you, Billy,' George said. He pointed, as if the cleaner might be unable to identify it as rubbish. The beauty of seduction. Those tender moments of fearful pleasure with a man next to you, poised, the muscles in your jaw twitching as you decide whether to say something to aid the process or to make an irresistible movement.

'I find you very attractive, Billy,' he said. 'I like men like you.'

There was a pause punctuated by a bell in a distant room.

'You do, do you?' Billy said. He put down his buckets and moved towards his fellow prisoner. George heard another bell ringing in another part of the prison. So many distant bells, hollow, sweet, clanging, delicious, Billy coming closer to him, rubbing his hands on his shirt front. Billy with his big man's face, his three-day beard and rough-shaven pate.

George felt a flush go through him. The bells ringing in his mind as Billy, his nostrils going in-out-in-out, neared him, breathed on him. But instead of a kiss or a rough hand grabbing George's balls and a tongue being forced with pleasure between his lips, Billy poked his

Sucking Feijoas

index finger in the older man's abdomen and, screwing up his eyes in derision, turned and spat on the wall near George's face.

'You stare at me every fuckin' time I come near you and I'm fuckin' sick of it, mate.'

'You seem to have...' George's anticipation of lust instantly became panic.

'You seem to have... You seem to have... Isn't that just what I mean. Posh and stupid. You want to fool around in my pants? Fuckin' sissy. All the winks and nods you give me every few minutes, I'm sick of it. You're as queeny as a dairy cow.'

'But I just wanted to be friends,' George lied. He was suddenly fearful that he would be beaten up – a fate he had so far escaped, although it was part and parcel of being a homosexual.

'Friends?' Billy looked amazed that such a girl, such a fairy queen as Crossett could ever have imagined that. 'With a queen like you? A fucking dairy cow?'

Billy turned and gathered the rubbish together, then paused and looked back at the wounded man. 'Look,' he said, feeling a moment of remorse for having inflicted so much pain. 'I... You're not my type. You gotta be strong in prison. Tough. Be a man and not so bloody camp. It's for your own good. Don't mince. Don't sit like a queen.' He picked up his buckets and left, farting as he went out the door.

Walking down Devon Street wearing a fedora and a long gaberdine coat. Strolling in Pukekura Park by himself in a tweed jacket. At Ngamutu Beach or Kaweroa for the afternoon, enjoying the waves and trees and the mountain. Those walks came rushing back to George. Those afternoons, people in cars passing him. Women in shops and men in offices. Mrs Mutch, Mr Faithful. Miss Jenkins, everyone who had ever met him, filing past in his mind as he went wild with grief. They had all known he was a queen. Every one of them. Mincing down Devon Street. Touching his hand to his fedora at Miss Jenkins as she passed him. They'd all known, when he thought he'd been covering up so splendidly. He hadn't wanted to believe it. But he was a queen. He did walk like a girl. He'd deceived himself over the years. He conjured up his image reflected from a mirror or a shop window and knew that he had always been recognised not only as a homosexual but as a queen. It had taken another homosexual to tell him.

George saw all the things that a queen did. She flapped her wrists and sat cross-legged and spoke with a lisp. She was the most hated sort of homosexual, the one who is camp. The word seemed to dribble down his face, infecting his lips as he said it.

'Billy lied,' he said to himself. 'He's just a rubbish man.' He tried to retrieve his dignity. The sort of life that he had led had given him the ability to turn his cheek, to bear the slap. But now he saw what he had never wanted to visualise. It was true. He could see it in his eyes, the way he held his face; he was a queen, he was camp. His whole life pointed to that. The photo they had used to kick him out of the navy. Always a queer, always a poofter, no matter how hard he tried to talk and walk like a man.

George clenched the tuck-shop key in his hand. Prison hadn't been so bad until this moment, in fact he'd been enjoying the respite from the tortured world of New Plymouth. He had made new friends and shared secrets about love and sex, things he had never had the opportunity to talk about with men in the outside world.

'Billy's just a bitch,' he consoled himself. 'A bully bitch.'

Billy had worked in the bush, shorn sheep and driven trucks, and now he was marching around the prison with as much authority as one of the guards, calling him a dairy cow, a poofter, a mincing queen.

Tears smarted in George's eyes. 'I'll show you who's camp, Billy Hewitt. You wait.'

'We're looking for you, Crossett,' a guard said, his head suddenly popping around the door like a jack-in-the-box. 'You're wanted in Palmer's office for the Exodus meeting, so stop bawling like a fuckin' sheila and get down there.'

*

Dorothy Lewis was a small, pretty woman with a soft voice that mesmerised with its mellifluousness.

'You see,' she was saying, 'our group has had much success in changing homosexual men into heterosexuals.' The Queen of England and of all the Dominions was above her. The Queen. Billy Hewitt. Prison. Being camp. George was so filled with anger that he could not bear to listen to this woman, who was sitting there toying with a pencil and talking the sort of nonsense that he knew was just another way of making him feel inferior.

'Everything is behavioural,' she continued. 'Mr Palmer tells me that you're all educated men.' She produced the sweet smile a wife gives her husband when he returns from the office in one of those American movies. 'So you'll understand what I mean by that. We're taught things, and we can change our behaviour.'

Inside his mind, George laughed derisively. Change our behaviour! He'd been trying to walk and talk like a man for forty-odd years, and not ten minutes ago a so-called he-man had told him that he was a poofter, a queen, a dairy cow. He couldn't even manage to correct his deportment after such laborious practice over four decades.

'I'm a Mormon,' Benny said. 'Can I join Exodus and still be changed to the sort who can get healed?'

'Of course,' she replied. 'And so can Catholics. It's a disease with a cure.'

For a few seconds George thought he would explode from the indignity of the thwarted love tryst with Billy Hewitt. Being rejected. Being told he was camp, a dairy cow. He wasn't sure what a dairy cow really was – not in homosexual lingo. It was camp in itself to even use that sort of language.

'Camp. Camp. Camp.' George thought. 'I'm a naughty little Noddy and I don't like anybody and I'm camp.' The thoughts as daggers in his head. Staccato bits and pieces searching for a whole, and each one accompanied by an image, so that his mind sped from the portrait of the Queen to a cow in a paddock blinking with big girlie eyes, a bovine beauty with enormous lashes. Noddy kicking his little car, smashing it to pieces.

'Well, I was married and I erred,' Jock offered, 'It's all fated. I was fated to marry and I was fated to be a homosexual. Confusing, isn't it?' He moved his hands and looked at them as if he were delivering a sermon, a calm rational man with a look of suffering. 'As a Catholic I've lapsed and it's because…' He seemed exhausted by this declaration. A lifetime of struggle to produce those few faltering words. 'Because…' he tried again.

'Because you've allowed in the devil, lost your fear of God,' Dorothy said. 'I'm offering you a normal life.' She held her hands out oddly, as if trying to show them the particular choice she'd made in nail polish, then she splayed her fingers and joined them to form an archway. 'You see,' she went on. 'Life is like God's temple. There are ten doors. Nine lead out and one leads in, and I will guide you with His help to that small entry.'

The three men glanced at each and tried to suppress a snigger.

'Jock,' Dorothy inquired, 'you look puzzled. Is there anything you'd like to share with us?'

'God help me,' he said, 'if I did.'

'Precisely,' she said, pleased that he was asking for the help he needed. 'All behaviour is learned,' she continued, 'so you must follow my instructions. Homosexuality is an evil so pernicious that the devil is laughing at his invention. It's like a weed, one that grows and grows.I don't know about you, but I have oxalis in my garden, and oxalis is a bit like homosexuality. You need constant weeding to get rid of it.'

George looked at his two friends; one wringing his hands, the other talking as if he were applying for sainthood. It was nonsense. This business of God and Jesus and having to listen to trivia about being like oxalis.

'You can lead normal lives. A wife and children.' That smile again, fixed for a moment on each pervert.

George had read that Florence Nightingale had been a real bitch, a tyrant according to the biography he had perused while passing his lunch time in the library. Miss Magnanimous who had represented kindness and civilisation for a century before being exposed for what she was. Like this Lewis woman spitting poison on men who were fucked up by others' derision, and hatred.

'Look,' Dorothy said, eying George because he was the one, she could tell, who was the most undecided about joining her crusade to righteousness. 'I had a vision not long ago in which I saw the Last Supper. Jesus was with the twelve apostles, but in that gathering there was one bad man.' She might have been preaching to children. Jock Howley had been an instructor in teacher education for catechists in Papua New Guinea and he recognised her condescending technique. He looked at George, who was being singled out.

'Judas Iscariot was…' she paused. 'I could see it quite plainly, I've had a lot of experience dealing with homosexual men. The way Judas appeared…' It was obviously a vision she had related to many groups in her time with Exodus, and she held her sweet voice for effect. Again she gazed at George, with her eyes set as if receiving a celestial vision, and announced: 'Judas Iscariot was a blatant homosexual! Blatant!'

George had never been a religious man. Prayers at school had bored him. To him, it was very simple and straightforward: there was no God. He had been given no encouragement to believe as a child, so he hadn't. He realised at that moment that he owed a great deal to his father that in fact things at home hadn't been so bad. It was certainly bizarre, this belief system that encouraged Dorothy Lewis's vision that a two-thousand-year-old Middle Eastern man had been a poofter.

'What does that mean?' Jock asked in a voice that suggested both sincerity and scepticism.

Jock was an educated man, a former preacher. He saw another

truth about poor old Judas, that he had probably loved Jesus. He'd probably fallen head over heels and been rebuffed, and so he'd hung himself. Poor Judas vilified just as he himself had been by the bishop, who had discovered that more than just Holy Communion had been administered to the male parishioners. Jock saw the picture of the Last Supper in his mind; Judas slinking off in the corner of the painting because he was a queer. He was probably a very nice man and hadn't sold Jesus for silver at all. Judas who'd been forced to commit suicide because he was queer, and then all the stories about him in the Bible about his being a betrayer for silver. Lies and betrayals; not even allowed to exist as a queer in history, but turned into a sleazy traitor. Homosexuals were everywhere: in the Bible, in the Holy Land, in Papua New Guinea, in New Plymouth. 'She's right,' Jock thought, 'Judas was one of us, a brother, a homosexual.'

'You're very quiet, George,' Dorothy said.

'What made Judas such a blatant homosexual?' he asked. 'Was it the way he lisped and crossed his legs?' He wanted to be sarcastic, but his remark came out as being merely half-hearted, like a polite question being asked at a cocktail party.

'My vision merely shows that homosexuality is not condoned by Christianity.'

'I see,' George said. 'So we should all commit suicide like Judas.'

Dorothy Lewis had dealt with such bitterness on many occasions. She knew George from having lived all of her life in New Plymouth. She had seen him on the streets and, on one occasion, had come into his office and had had her suspicions aroused by the way he turned his head slightly to the right when he talked.

'Society has a duty,' she said, looking directly at Benny. 'To protect our young from perversion. And I play my part by training perverted minds to think normally.'

Religion hadn't worked with George, she could tell that. One thing that always amazed her in these meetings was that there were actually men who had no belief in God. That there were atheists in this world, those who actually rejected His truth and compassion, was extraordinary to her. But George's question had struck a chord and her vision returned; she saw from her vision that Judas had minced, that he was the only one to wear robes in effeminate colours while all of the other apostles wore dark brown and green.

'But I cannot help you, George, until you come to Jesus,' Dorothy insisted. That was supposed to work. He was supposed to feel vile and weak, and then stand up and say, 'I do! I do!' in an act of spontaneous and ecstatic contrition.

'Judas Iscariot,' George thought, 'a blatant homosexual!' It was amazing. You could rewrite biblical history because of a vision experienced in New Plymouth. George realised that he had been through a conversion in the last few weeks in prison. He sighed with anger and passion. A conversion. The word sounded both hollow and magnificent as he repeated it in his mind. A conversion from caring about being spat on and vilified, and it had taken another homosexual to bring him to it. He suddenly recalled a moment from a movie seen forty or so years ago. Cowboys were riding down a hill when the Indians had opened fire and killed all of them. Then the white women and children were butchered; not a pale-face left alive on the screen and the Indians jubilant. The audience had hooted in disbelief that the goodies had been butchered by the head-scalping savages.

'Billy and Judas,' he said. He slapped Benny on the back. 'Don't listen to this religious hype,' he said. 'It's time you grew up and stopped believing in fairies.' He got to his feet and, deliberately and delicately, he brushed his collars with his fingertips. 'Excuthe me pleathe, mith,' he said, lisping over a deliberately thick tongue. 'Pleathe, mith. I mutht pith urgently.'

6 The secret diary of Ho Chi Minh's daughter

Garth Griffin stood on Ngamutu Beach. Three days earlier he'd been pushing his way on to the metro in order to get to work in the world's most congested city. A whiff of Mexico City came back as he stood absorbed by the teal and white and grey of the Tasman Sea. That smell of dirt and smog and cooking wafted in his mind. Mexico City in all of its glory. A five hundred year old cathedral with towers which he now knew were as much of him as this sea was. His apartment built before the Revolution. Sitting on his balcony drinking coffee he had imagined Emiliano Zapata and Pancho Villa clip clopping triumphantly down the Avenida beneath him. Armies, carriages, pedestrians; year upon year blending into new movements and fashions. That was the Mexico he had come to adore and cherish. Colour and revolution. Immensity in everything. That was where his teenage imagination had become reality; the teenager in his New Plymouth bedroom dreaming of big cities and Raskolnikov and freedom.

'At least I escaped,' Garth thought. He turned to look at the volcano. Objects and emotions; they crowded in and merged and formed a composite labelled 'My Life' and he saw clearly how he was a part of them as they grew and grew in both complexity and number. This sea and that mountain joined those big city smells and the ancient cathedrals and the thought of his avenida being the one which Zapata rode down in revolutionary glory. Funny how life worked. A kid in New

Plymouth yearning for other things. Then came that magic day and under the pretence of seeking higher education the escape; a train to Wellington and then on to the rest of the planet.

He wanted to be able to get into his car and drive back to his apartment through the crowded streets of Mexico City and cook dinner for Alfonso instead of going back to his mother for a meal of boiled potatoes and chops and sauce. Two worlds; fabulous nature and fabulous culture. Mexico versus New Zealand, the dilemma of a true exile.

'God, it's beautiful here, so why the introspection?' He shook his head. Even nature couldn't make you forget and not search out the poignant and ironic. His friend Sylvester Martinez had an answer for that. Sylvester had the same problem, not being able to live in his native Mexico City because of the connotations. 'Like a dog. You can only train it when it's a puppy and my childhood in Mexico was like that. I was trained to hate myself in that city for being a queer in a macho family.' Sylvester, exiled in Paris. Jorge from Buenos Aires now exiled in New York. Jack in San Francisco. All those gay boys running from what they wanted to love to somewhere they could love within the passion of dislocation. Place and dislocation: they were the Palestinians, the gypsies; homosexuals forced into exile and subterfuge and deception by their history. A wave sluiced across the pebbles. When it retreated it left a slight scum. Being a queer was like that. He wasn't quite sure how but the image suited his emerging depression.

＊

Time was up. He had to get back to the house because Mum had shouted at him as he'd left: 'Tea's at six o'clock, dear.' He took another deep breath of sea air to trap the memory. Store it up for those days when the putrid air in Mexico City really did insult his senses. He walked up the black sand to the street lined by a row of cottages each tightly fenced with their tiny tidy gardens. In there behind the windows lurked...? A surfer came out of one of the cottages and looked across at

Garth before picking up his board and disappearing behind a house. From somewhere came that hideous sound of canned laughter. The late afternoon sun glinted off a window. Someone was there, peering through a half inch of space between the curtains, their fingers gripping one edge. Garth couldn't tell if it were a man or a woman but he felt like a queer being stared at. He was Garth Griffin in New Plymouth and suddenly it was 1965 and not 1980. The feeling that he had never left this provincial city pounded him. He was again a pimply teenager who hated himself for being alive and for being different. The surfer came from behind the house and walked across the road and smiled like a man should to a stranger: 'Gid'day mate,' he said. 'How ya' goin'?' The masculinity and the bare chest and the long golden hair. The curtain opened wider and now two people peered from between the faded curtain. The surfer looked at him from behind his grimy car window in a way that mates didn't look at each other. Then he lurched the vehicle into the road and sped off. Garth Griffin standing there on the footpath feeling like Sylvester did in Mexico City.

'I'm paranoid. It's in my blood,' he thought. 'Nothing but a paranoid queen in her home town on holiday. They think I'm stealing the car, not that I'm a poofter. Be rational.' New Zealanders were tough and unsentimental and didn't gush smiles at strangers. A surfer was a surfer. A man who went into the sea for hours and took solitary pleasure in fighting waves wasn't expected to cross the road and grab your hand and say: 'Gid'day, be my mate, don't be afraid of the past.' That was how the rational mind thought. He tried to tell himself that. In the garden opposite a gnome wearing a little red hat stared at him and a mermaid with her scales painted individual colours posed on a plaster rock by a rose trellis. In the next garden several plaster swans froze on alighting. An immortalised fantasy world. There were more such creatures in this street than there were living humans. Just people peering from behind windows. He felt isolated and exposed. In an avenida with a million people you felt safe. Surrounded by skyscrapers and cathedrals and the hustle of twenty million people you were hidden.

'Oh, God,' he said. 'So much drama for one simple queen to cope with.' He got into his car and started the engine. He could now see an old man staring from behind the curtain. The other figure had moved away. Then the curtain closed completely. A blackbird landed on the surfer's fence and skipped about ceremonially. Peace and tranquillity at a New Plymouth beach. This was the essence of New Zealand. The quintessential everything which was why he thought he loved it and knew he hated it. A very sweet street with charming cottages and ancient pohutukawa trees lining it. Nothing pretentious or commercial. The only things sinister were in his mind. Garth wiped the sweat from his upper lip and saw it all as it was; a reflection of the damage from the past. He'd been gone since 1967 with only one trip back and that had been seven years ago. 'Things aren't like then and even if they are, fuck them.' Again the curtains parted and the elderly couple stared out at him. It was as if people weren't allowed to visit a public beach or as if the couple behind the curtains felt guilty about shutting out the sun. What was their motive? It was funny; they stood there like the old couple in one of those Swiss clocks; a couple marinated in their own paired obscurity, unaccustomed to the sight of people on their own. He laughed sardonically, in relief almost, because they were as tragic in their own insecurity. There was no telling what their fascination was about. They might have been thinking he was a thief, a homosexual, or a tourist, or maybe their long lost son who'd disappeared in 1957. Just vanished and since then they'd kept a vigil, every afternoon waiting to see their Harry return as Jesus had promised them and now here he was sitting in his car thinking how silly he'd been to give them so much agony for so many years. Harry home at last. The misery of all these years of waiting ended.

'That's how life is,' Garth said. 'I only think in terms of my own problems. They think I'm Harry.' He wished he had a magic wand to zap the people behind the flowery curtains to the main avenida in Mexico City at rush hour; small minded, claustrophobic, content to peer through chinks in curtains, silly enough to waste their lives waiting for Harry when he'd left them.

'Agoraphobia more like it,' he said. He drove off but he couldn't bear the thought of the tea and Mum so took the turn for Moturoa Beach where there weren't any houses with windows.

'The year of my deliverance,' he said. 1967 when he'd been pulling at the bit to get to Wellington and go to university.

'I want to go to Uni, Dad. I want to study literature and languages.'

'I don't know why you just don't get a job and save up. You'll lose three or four years of earnings by going to university. Your cousin's got a job at the bank.' Dad's advice and Dad now dead and buried. Wellington, Sydney, San Francisco, New York, Mexico City; the great cities behind him and a job teaching literature in the Universidad Nacional de Mexico his prize for having escaped from mediocrity. A doctorate in Latin American literature and already a senior lecturer with the promise of a professorship before he turned forty. He walked down the steep bank to the beach with such thoughts preening themselves in his mind. High above him the cliffs covered in flax and the sky pink, blue, white. A grey cloud hovered alone above the horizon, incongruous amongst the hues of sunset.

'Alfonso. Alfonso. Alfonso,' he said. 'This is the part of me you don't know about, even after five years.' Alfonso de Reyes. Garth looked at his watch and calculated the time in Mexico City. Alfonso would be in bed with some man he'd picked up or in the steam baths, cramming in as much sex as was possible in the few weeks they were apart. Gorgeous Alfonso. Alfonso de Reyes with eyes inherited from the Spanish and the Aztecs. A breeze arrived; a lover blowing sweet nothings in his ear. It smelled of kelp and ice and palms as pungent as the thought and smell of the sex and excitement of the bath houses in the Avenida Obregon in Mexico City. The working class boys' rough sex and the fabulous Egyptian who met him at the baths every Thursday afternoon.

'Alfonso, Alfonso, I miss you,' Garth said.

There was no one on the beach despite the enormous beauty of the setting sun. They were all at home watching television and eating chops and boiled vegetables. It was as predictable as the Mexican middle classes eating grilled beef and a salad and a flan at seven thirty.

*

He lay in the dunes and rested his head on a piece of driftwood. That urgent smell of sea-salt and islands. The breeze from the South Island and the Antarctic. All that moss and ice and the sub-tropical forests. This was why he had come back to New Zealand. His eyes were closed and the tears struggled out and ran down his cheeks. You got kicked out of home and went to another country and thought you'd adopted it, but the smell of an island made you yearn for the normality and inevitability of your birthplace. That feeling was as unavoidable as the knowledge you could never return; the currents going in different directions. The blue line of one current pulling north and the grey line of the other pulling southwards and the choppy surface where the two met was the ugly scar of childhood which was much more powerful than the appreciation of nature.

*

Day six of his trip back home. He'd been lying on his bed all afternoon reading a literary biography and dreaming of Alfonso.

'Just about, dear,' Mum sang out from the kitchen where she was mashing the potatoes. It must have been five to six because she added: 'Tea'll be ready in five minutes.' He wandered into the kitchen and watched her.

'I suppose it's not fancy like you like nowadays, dear,' Mrs Griffin said setting the table with her nice things in order to impress her big son from Mexico City.

'When's Cynthia coming to stay?' he asked, to avoid a hurtful answer.

'She's got fat,' Mrs Griffin said. 'On Wednesday.'

Garth hadn't put on weight, she thought, and he was as good look-ing as ever. Now he looked rich and successful. His mother studied him as he chewed his chop. Garth with his neat hair and his neat clothes and his ability to speak foreign languages. She wanted to pat him on the hand and tell him how proud she felt and that if Dad were still alive he'd be proud too, no matter what, and that the best thing he'd ever done was to get out of New Plymouth and see a bit of life and get a job in a University. Only...

'Mint sauce?' she said in a voice which only just covered her anxiety.

'No thanks. The chutney's good.'

'Mrs Armstrong's tamarillo and feijoa. She's been very good to me since Dad passed away, Garth. She'd love to see you. She's always got heaps of feijoas.'

Mrs Armstrong. He imagined her in the same old coat in the same old house in the same old everything. He'd always thought of her as a witch and fifteen years away had only cemented that idea of her as someone beyond changing.

'She wouldn't mind at all if you went and picked some,' Mum said as she chewed her chop and chutney.

Mrs Armstrong. In Mexico she'd be in a long black dress in the village church putting candles in front of the Virgin. She'd be the one on the front doorstep pretending to sweep her stoop but look-ing at the villagers going up and down the cobblestones; a few words here and there with the same tired innuendo and then masticating the gossip with sugar cakes and coffee later that afternoon with her cronies. There were types like Mrs Armstrong in every country. Types as much a part of existence as the predictable conversations that people had with one another instead of telling each other the real things from their emptiness. The conversations with his mother over the past few days attested to that and he braced himself for another evening of dialogue in which the same old clichés emerged before they'd take themselves off to bed for another... He stopped himself in mid thought from the depressing cynicism he knew had found him wishing for escape and excitement.

'She helped me wash Dad's clothes after he...' Mum said. 'You weren't here but then of course... And it's old friends and Mrs Armstrong was...'

Mrs Griffin had bought red paper napkins for Garth's visit. She didn't bother with them usually, just on special occasions, and she wiped her lips on one and looked at him above her glasses. 'And Cynthia had another bun in the oven when he died and I tried to tell you all that in the letters but what with one thing and another it's just not easy to put things into words and the telephone is all static so...'

Alfonso had a blue suit he'd bought in Rome when they were there on holiday. A fabulous suit in a mix of silk and linen. Alfonso in his blue suit, white shirt and red tie. The English shoes. Spiffy, sexy, Alfonso. The way he held his knife and fork and the way he could use his hands to converse, moving them up and down. Those long, elegant fingers, the sort that belonged to the class of man who'd never been inside a house like this. That blue suit and those conversations seemed like they were from another era, another world, another galaxy. Garth applied a little more chutney to his chop and saw Alfonso raising his eyebrows and putting back his head in an attempt to make conversation with this woman who was chewing her chop and talking at the same time. Dear Alfonso who didn't feel guilty about anything. Darling Alfonso who didn't care about being a snob. Sweet, handsome Alfonso who really only cared about architecture and sex and Garth.

'Penny for your thoughts,' Mrs Griffin said. She had thoughts of her own. She felt quite sick about bringing up the subject but she knew she had to even though she'd been dreading it. She looked at his soft hands and coughed politely.

'Garth,' she said.

'What?'

'I bet you don't say what to your friends in Mexico.' Her heart was beating. She didn't know how to approach big subjects without that anginal feeling. She fiddled with the little diamond on her left hand.

'Well…' she said.

'What?' he said. He could feel it coming. The topic had had to come up, it was as inevitable as the day's habitual acts but he felt himself pale nevertheless. All Alfonso's mother had said was that it was the disease of the aristocracy so now she was pleased their family had finally joined that elevated class. Mum twisting her engagement ring, the dull diamond a tiny star from a very distant galaxy. He watched her movements knowing they signalled something she found difficult to express. She'd always pushed her diamond to and fro when she was on the verge of a serious subject. Señora de Reyes didn't wear diamonds because she thought they were boring. She preferred the very red subtlety of rubies and the ruthlessness of turquoise and clumps of silver. Again Mrs Griffin opened her mouth in an attempt to divulge her secret and a stray thought emerged from the fright of the expected question. She's never had the money to repair the chip in her dentures and the sudden thought that he could pay for her to do so jumped in for a second. He counted his heartbeats. Mrs Griffin twisting her lips and looking at her diamond ring as if for the very first time in all those decades since her engagement.

'It's about Barry,' she said. 'I have to have it out.'

'Barry?' He couldn't think of any Barrys. For a horrible moment he thought she was referring to the boy down the road with whom he'd had sex in the bamboos all through form six and seven. That by some chance he'd spilled the beans to her when drunk or that Mrs Armstrong had found out and…

'Barry,' she said. 'You know, my man friend. It's not easy to tell you this. You've got your own life overseas and I can't run away and do things in secret like you kids can because I'm stuck in New Plymouth.' She looked at him like a little animal might from a trap with its little paws stuck under the steel snap: whimper, whimper, help me. Mrs Griffin looked suddenly old. That sort of old, that decrepitude when your dentures don't fit and you chomp chomp on your meat but it won't masticate properly. She was only sixty but she was working class. It was as plain to see as the living room decor. He didn't know how he'd escaped, why he wasn't a wharfie drinking himself to death to cover his reality. He should have put his hand out and touched hers and asked her not to weep but the strangeness of the familiar surroundings was suddenly surrealistic.

'Barry's been very good to me, Garth. I can't rely on my family for comfort. That's what I wanted to tell you.' She pushed her plate away as if both food and intimacy had been dispensed with. But her eyelids flickered. She'd always had the propensity for tears. At the clothes line if a thrush had shit on her sheets. Tears if the rubbish man came before she'd put her bin out. She was waiting for an answer. She looked at him, a little girl disappointed by not receiving a dolly for Christmas. But he couldn't respond, not knowing what it was she wanted from him. He couldn't relate to her any more than she could understand her own child. Now she required something that she hadn't given him, he couldn't find succour in return.

'Off my chest,' she said. 'I feel better for that.' She got up to get the pudding while he gathered his thoughts. He lectured on Latin American literature in Spanish at the most prestigious university in the Republic, but he couldn't think of what to say about Barry. He knew how to discuss tragic irony in the works of Mario Vargas Llosa and he gave lectures on the emotive content of Chilean poetry. But responding about Barry was too difficult. He could only guess that she was hinting at some intimacy he didn't want to contemplate, and wanted his blessing. He wasn't sure whether it was relief he felt for having not being asked if he were a homosexual or disappointment at the lost opportunity. He fiddled with his fork dejectedly and then went into the kitchen.

'A watched pot never boils,' Mum said.

'I love you, Mum,' he said. 'You and Barry should get married and come to Mexico for your honeymoon.'

'Oh, Garth,' she said. 'I knew you'd understand.' She wiped her hands on her apron even though they weren't wet but the drying motion was the habit of a lifetime.

'God,' he thought. 'Tell her you're queer and that you've been with Alfonso for five years.' The price was enormous. His lips actually quivered as he stood on the verge of his statement. It was so stupid; he'd fucked men in freighters and had gained a doctorate. For years he'd lived a life of adventure and excitement in the world's most populous city. He knew his way around Europe and Latin America and could name arias in operas and who could best sing them. But he couldn't tell his own mother in the family kitchen what even his cleaning woman knew and accepted. This kitchen was a more formidable environment than the world's largest city: that yellow Formica table and the spotted vinyl chairs. The empty vinegar bottle and the jar of Mrs Armstrong's tamarillo and feijoa chutney. Everything was ugly and changeless. It could have been 1966 with Cynthia shouting. He heard his father say: 'Make me a cuppa, Mum.' The past closed around him. There was not a hint of distance. He shivered at the thought of the Tasman Sea and Mount Egmont, all that vastness and wonder polluted by this human idiocy. He saw himself, a silly human in a silly house filled with the need to tell his mother he was a homosexual, for her to accept him as he accepted her trivial news. He was a wimp and he knew it. But he realised as he stood there tongue-tied as the thirteen year old boy he felt like, that he finally just couldn't be bothered with the nonsense. There was no other reason to be in New Zealand than to tell the truth and he couldn't. Seven years of thinking about coming back and telling Mum: coward, silly, wimp. He looked out at the living room in order to avoid her seeing his eyes blinking back the tears of need and frustration. The picture of the windmill above the sofa. The pink china cats and the indentation in the sofa where Dad had always sat. He couldn't stand it. He was trapped in a time warp in this house aged thirteen. It was suffocation. He wanted to be at the steam baths hiding with a hundred homosexuals in darkness and hot showers. Lying next to the Egyptian on his Thursday afternoon of illicit sex. So anonymous. You could share more intimacy and love with a stranger than with your mother. He looked at her; he felt repulsed that he'd once sucked her nipples and yet rejoiced in those of the hairy Egyptian.

'You're not upset about Barry, are you dear?' She was stirring the custard and didn't look at him.

'No,' he said. 'Of course not. I'm very happy you have company. I hope I get to meet him. It's good that you told me.'

The moment forever passed, lost forever. He couldn't get out the words he wanted but at least he now knew why.

I love Alfonso.

She removed her glasses and wiped off the steam.

I'm a homosexual and you've always known it.

'These damn glasses,' she said. 'I must get them repaired.'

I've been happy for five years with Alfonso. And I think I love the Egyptian. We always have mutual anilingus.

'This custard's lumpy. Bother it,' she said.

I'm gay, Mum.

'You've got to stir in warm milk but I was too lazy to heat it.'

I've watched men fuck each other in New York, San Francisco, Mexico City, San Salvador and my abiding fantasy is to get fucked senseless in Damascus by a platoon of Arab infantry men.

'You're very quiet,' she said.

It wasn't worth it. Not even the most simple formula of: I'm homosexual. The words would make her cry her ready tears, scream and gnash her teeth and ring up Mrs Armstrong for counselling. '*I have sex with an Egyptian in a Mexican bath house.*' He wanted to yell it. He wanted to grab her by the shoulders and tell her he loved her and needed her to understand that he was different and the same and was as entitled to be a homosexual as she was to have a man to whom she wasn't married. But he knew that acknowledging the truth would destroy her.

'Barry said we could go to Rotorua. He'll drive us,' she said. 'I'd like to see the geysers.'

'Mother...' he said. 'I...'

'Oh, no,' she said. 'The screw's fallen out of my glasses. Help me find it.'

On their hands and knees together looking for a screw the size of a pin head. He wanted to weep as he had done at the Tasman. The medieval argument about the number of angels that could fit on a pin head; the thought was as funny as it was sad and he suddenly understood the full enormity of it's religious implications as they searched on the spotless linoleum. The trivia in avoidance of the profundity. Gone forever in the kitchen, that moment to grasp reality and understand her son. She would take her suspicions to the grave because she had decided that was safer; he knew she didn't want to hear them verified by anything as dangerous as facts or logical argument.

*

'You're looking good,' Cynthia said. She pecked him on the cheek and stood back and admired the glamour and finery that Garth represented. Then she soured. A hard life did that. He read hardness and insincerity in that false self-confidence of too much make up. She resembled one of those Mexican women after midnight in the Plaza Garibaldi. A sweet smile for a man she wouldn't recognise in twenty-four hours. He couldn't believe he'd come back to encounter this. It was the same seven years previously when he'd come home for two weeks. Seven years of postponement until he believed he wanted to visit these people again who were called his family.

Nostalgia was the problem. That desperate need for sentimentality and the inability of the human mind to ever escape from its upbringing. He knew all that intellectually. He could dismiss or eulogise sentimentality in his lectures. Those Chilean poems he had his students analyse to increase their critical awareness of the insubstantiality of the present. The themes of sentimentality and loss and the illusion of what was reality. He could quote lines and lines of it. He saw his prissiness and intellectualism as he stood there at the door of his mother's house welcoming his sister. Chilean poetry and the influence of nostalgia. Here it was incarnate in a sibling pact; the responsibility of hypocrisy and its connection to false nostalgia. It was better to cut ties, to forget, give up. A sister who despised her brother for being successful and a sissy and a brother who despised his sister for being lower class and a slut. Lower class? No, he corrected himself. It was not to do with class it was to do with being awful: these people were merely ghastly. But they had to stand there and believe that all this piety was necessary.

'You haven't seen Darrell,' she said. Darrell was in a push chair. He must have been eating chocolate biscuits all the way down on the bus from Hamilton. 'And Shane's eleven now. Shake hands with your uncle, Shane. Make a cuppa, Mum,' she yelled. 'Shane, your Uncle Garth lives in Mexico. You ask him all about it. They haven't got Maoris there, just cowboys and Indians.'

Grin and bear it. He'd learned to do that when the subject of blacks or the poor or Zapata arose with middle class Mexicans. He shook Shane's hand and picked up Darrell.

'Oh, Garth,' she said. 'I've been talking all about you to my friends. What a professor you are and Lynette reckons you'd be eligible only I told her you're not a Hamilton type and that you wouldn't really want someone with dyed blonde hair.' She laughed at her own joke and again he saw the problem of type casting. It was a theme in literary analysis; that people should not be types in fiction but that defied the facts of observation in real existence.

He sat there laughing at her jokes and asking questions. Her humour and the way she seemed to be accepting him for what he was. Her gabbling allowed him to think she liked him after all. In this very room where they had fought out their childhood and youth together. Talk talk talk non-stop about herself. This supermarket had opened down the street from where she lived; the government was giving her a bigger benefit than she was entitled to but she hadn't told them.

Gary had a new diesel engine and had promised her he would keep himself out of prison.

'Janine telephoned you, Son, from Wellington,' Mrs Griffin shouted from the kitchen. 'When you were at the shops. She'll be up here tomorrow just in time for Christmas with her parents.'

'I suppose you came back to get a Kiwi wife, then,' Cynthia said. She turned away as she asked him. She pretended Darrell had a dirty nappy. 'Isn't Janine your old girlfriend from university? I remember her. She was very pretty and brainy. Just the sort for you.'

Christ had been crucified at thirty-three. Garth saw himself on a cross on the top of a hill overlooking New Plymouth. It was a glimpse of himself funny enough to laugh at. Cynthia below with a sponge dipped in urine for him to suck on. This thirty five year old invert nailed up there with his view of the Tasman and Mount Egmont and the knowledge that he was being castigated for the sins of others, such was Cynthia's ignorance, his mother's prejudices and his Dad's belligerence. And suffering equally for his own sins, for not having the balls to stand up and say: 'Mum, before you make the cuppa, I want to tell you I'm a homosexual and proud of it.' Christ up there on the cross above New Plymouth. Garth saw Him, like one of those hideous, tortured renditions in a Mexican church, all bones and blood and sweetness through suffering. Poor old Jesus, spat upon and vilified for trouping about with a bunch of riff-raff who showed no inclination to get married. Jesus crucified for his ideas and for not being normal and settling down with a wife and kids and a nice house in Jerusalem. You could just hear his mother shouting: 'I've tried to talk him into carpentry but he will knock around with the likes of Judas.' He laughed at his own joke and rubbed his hand in his nephew's hair.

'Oh, Garth,' Cynthia said. 'I hope my Darrell grows up to be like you so that he can...' The room was too hot. The curtains had been drawn against the sun fading the carpet.

'So he can what?' Garth asked. He'd been wrong, he felt it. Cynthia was nice, it was just that she didn't know how to relate to his foreignness any more than he knew how to relate to her attitude about Maoris and supermarkets.

'Well, I never had the opportunity to study hard at school because I was a girl but I want Darrell to be like you and swot and get a good job.' Darrell had shit his nappy and the stench was of old baby food, a yucky mixture of pumpkin and spinach.

'You'll have to encourage him to study,' he said. 'I'll pay any expenses. Extra classes, whatever. Maybe he could take music lessons, the violin.' He was thinking about Alfonso's nephews: violin, piano, painting. The de Reyes had their children in training to be great Mexicans. Nationalism at the forefront; a Rivera or Kahlo or Fuentes, somebody great for Mexico and their family. But he saw the look in Cynthia's eyes: piano and violin. The question right there in her pupils. It was one of those looks Dad had given him when he wore pimple cream; a homosexual in this living room. Violin and piano; it was almost pederasty, an open suggestion that he would fund her son to become a homosexual.

'I was thinking more about something like a pilot because he's sort of practical.' The child wasn't a year old; it couldn't hold a knife or fork. It didn't even have the ability to control its bodily functions. Garth saw the poverty-struck peasants in Mexico bending beneath their statues of a Christ bedecked in gilt and jewels. Absurdity and nonsense; the bowing to the greater ideal no matter how unrealistic and fictional. Such delusions were being enacted here on his mother's sofa.

'He's a bit young to decide his fate,' Garth said. 'But I'm willing to help in whatever way you think will be good for his education. Maybe you should be thinking of Shane because he's eleven and I can help him, send him to a better school or something.'

'Shane's as thick as pig shit, can't get anything right at school no matter how much I shout at him. Eh, Shane? He's like his father and he's inside for eight years. He had a tattoo of a headless policeman on his arm so I reckon they gave him a few more years just for that.'

How did one escape from class restrictions? Garth raised his hands involuntarily and looked at them; the lily-white fingers and the soft palms. They'd never been near an engine or oil but that had been their thwarted destiny. It was no different here than in a rigid caste system; Darrell was trapped unless there was some major stroke of luck or a perversion like his uncle's to motivate him to rise above this silliness.

'I bought a sponge,' Mrs Griffin said coming in from the kitchen. 'It's not mock cream.' Mrs Griffin was in her element. She'd chosen the best tea pot and for a few seconds she stood in front of the china cabinet wondering if she should get out the nice tea cups as well.

'Fuckin' hell, now he's wet the sofa,' Cynthia said. 'Little bastard.' She smacked Darrell on the bottom as if he should have known that penises weren't for pissing or that practical babies should wait until they had a clean nappy to pee in. Garth looked at his hands again for verification that he had had the strength and the wherewithal to get out and leave this particular class system for one he could manoeuvre in more effectively.

'I wasn't encouraged to study, either,' he said, taking up her offer to discuss iniquitous education. 'Mum and Dad didn't want me to. You know that.'

'But you were brainy. You passed your exams.'

'But I studied. Dad used to make me go out and mow the lawns and find all sorts of things for me to do to but I still... In the sixth form when I was studying for University Entrance he insisted that I paint the roof.'

'Oh, I know,' Cynthia said. 'But I was a girl and then in those days...'

He stared at her hard face. It was true. Girls weren't encouraged to study but boys weren't either. Not in this sort of house with the races blaring all day and the idea that education wasn't for the likes of them. Was it only because he was queer that he'd escaped this life of detention? Somehow he'd grabbed education as his escape from a bad situation; Doctor Griffin, formerly of New Plymouth. But then not all working class homosexuals were university lecturers or even

well educated. It was confusing and he wanted a neat academic reason for his being where he was in Mexico City while she'd ended up
in a welfare house in Hamilton with a series of boyfriends who all
eventually went to prison.

He shook his head and laughed and made a joke of it and tried to
think of something neutral to say to her. Something about Hamilton.
Something about what music she liked or what Shane would like for
Christmas. But his mind was ravenous; it needed the sort of food he
didn't get in New Plymouth. By itself, on remote control, seeking
explanation for all of this inanity it went racing along looking for the
usual sustenance it got from conversations with his friends and
Alfonso. He was watching Cynthia wipe her child's bottom. Caste and
fatality. Had Cynthia really been a product of her environment any
more than he had been? Couldn't she have escaped this?

'Turn it off,' he thought. 'Stop thinking.' But rational requests
didn't work. He stuck a finger with cream on it for Darrell to suck on.
Caste and class consciousness and snobbery. He was the snob. That
was what these people thought about him without ever realising that
they were as snobby and protective about their tattoos and anti-intel-
lectualism and heterosexuality as he was about his proclivities. It was
the ultimate snobbery of the working class to not know that they were
as exclusive as the ones they despised for being hoity-toity.

'Well in Hamilton there's a lot of single mums and we get about
together. There's a club sort of and we help each other,' she said in
that way that everything came out nasally.

He wasn't sure if it were ennui or snobbery or both but he felt sick
at the thought of two weeks of this carry on. She hadn't asked him a
question about himself in an hour of conversation. The only thing
Mum had asked was if the weather in Mexico was nice or if he'd ever
thought about coming back to settle in Auckland. It was nothingness.
He hated Gary's diesel engine and Hamilton and babies' nappies. He
sat in his chair thinking, pursued, burrowed into the synthetic, a little baby himself looking at the world as if for the first time but with

an innate filter from Latin American literature. Terrified by it. A baby knowing it will never escape from nappies and breast feeding. The magic realism of fate and eternity on a crucifix above New Plymouth. Trapped in the Taranaki proletariat. A snob. He saw himself in his poncy clothes. Ever so understated, no bright colours. Garth Griffin dressed with all the subtlety of the Mexican intelligentsia. It was awful. It was horrible. It was vile. He felt his anus contract. Traitor. Mum was whistling in the kitchen, so full of happiness that her kids were getting on while she put real cream in her sponge and not the mock sort. And here he was undergoing existential miasmas because of who he was and the fact that he'd never be able to bring Alfonso into this house and say: 'This is my boyfriend.'

The sudden, familiar smells of sex and chlorine revived him. Entering those doors after a hard day's work: sex and forgetfulness in Mexico City with men. The adorable smells and the comfort of males seeking the same refuge from being different.

'Snob?' he thought. He looked at his sister and glanced around the room. 'I'm no fucking snob just because I don't like this room.' He sat up. An El Salvadoran peasant had once told him he was the kindest man she'd ever met. The woman's lined face and her hand squeezing his. Garth's mind was rebelling, it was almost a physical sensation. He wanted to be with that peasant in her hut and not in this suburban house filled with his dead father's bottle collection. He pushed back his shoulders and straightened up. He had the impulse to get his bags and walk out and go to where he was appreciated. Cynthia's baby looked at him. It had all the wisdom and ignorance of a creature still largely untouched by conditioning. Garth got up and then sat down again because there was nowhere else in the little room to be that wasn't a memory or untidy or confronted by bottles. If this were all snobbery, then so be it. That was the prize for having been a baby on that sofa thirty-five years ago and for having crawled out of this existence.

'There must be nice cake shops in Hamilton, Cyn,' Mrs Griffin said as she put the sponge on the table.

There. That was it exactly. Mum asking about the cake shops in Hamilton but never about those in Mexico City. They could call him a snob but he'd asked Cynthia forty questions about her life and she hadn't asked him one. They negated him; not a mention, not a murmur of anything. Fear? Distrust? Ignorance? He closed his eyes against his women folk. That delicious combination of hot water and soap and sweat where men went to hide from this sort of thing. An hour of solitude amongst men who lived with the same need to avoid oppression. To not be confronted with the eye which sized them up; out there in the street or in the office or in their family's living room so pungent with subterfuge and discontentment.

Mum quickly drank her cup of tea and then jumped up to put her coat on. 'What's wrong, Mum?' Garth said.

'I'm just going to pop down to the shops to get some things for tea.'

'I thought you went shopping this afternoon,' he said. Coat and hat and handbag. 'I'm off,' she said. She stood at the front door looking apprehensive in her old coat, like Queen Elizabeth would in cast offs after a republican revolution.

'Go and play with your cars, Shane, ' Cynthia said. 'And shut the door behind you.' She was burping the baby. He must have been full of wind because he brought up air and sick.

It was just like in the old days; Cynthia getting at something. Her lips waiting to pounce. Garth swilled the tea in his mouth and smelled instead the chlorine and sweat and bodies.

'I have to know, Garth,' Cynthia said as soon as Mrs. Griffin and Shane had departed.

'Know what?' He was suddenly bored and sick and dissipated. Alfonso fucking in the bath house. He imagined him with the Egyptian. The only jealously he felt was that Alfonso was enjoying himself and he wasn't. He wanted warmth and steam and companionship.

'Are you a gay or not?'

He stood up and went to the window and pulled back the curtains.

There was the Smith's state house which had always represented depression and ugliness. Nothing had changed it, not even the futile attempt to eradicate its uniformity with new metal window frames and chateau-like shutters. In essence, nothing could ever be different. That state house was as marked by the presence of class and the 1950s as he was himself by his sexual proclivity. The moment of truth had arrived and he wanted to feel nothing. A thrush landed on the fence, fluttered and flew off into a struggling pohutukawa.

'Are you a gay?' she said.

He felt like correcting her semantic error. 'Are you a straight?' he asked.

'Don't be sarcastic,' she said. 'We've got a right to know.'

'What right do you possess?'

'Mary Toogood said it could run in the family, and I've got two boys.'

'From two different fathers.'

'This is not about me,' she insisted. 'It's about you.'

A woman he'd never seen came out of the state house. She was in bright pink slippers, the fluffy sort, and an equally pink dressing gown. This inevitable moment. The moment he'd paid two thousand dollars in airline tickets to enjoy. It felt as if his whole life had ticked on just to confront this moment. Cynthia on the sofa under the windmill. Cynthia burping her baby. There was no Mexico. There was no education or scholarships or best friends or travel or restaurants or nature or books or Alfonso or accolades or El Salvadoran peasants. No life. It was just family. This house and them and this question. It was so stupid. Why did he persist in coming back to a stupid family when he had wonderful and accepting friends? Those weekends endured back here when at university? He saw his reflection in the window; the good boy stuffed with an absurd filial piety.

'One of your breeding stock might have had queer genes,' he said. 'Who got them, you reckon, Darrell or Shane?'

'Don't be sarcastic,' she said. 'This is hard, but...'

'But what?'

'I'm not the one who...' she said.

'Who what?'

She still wore the same fuchsia lipstick she had worn as a teenager. Sticky stuff, something cheap from Woolworths. He watched her lick her lips as if the gloss were delicious.

'Who? Who? You who's shaming Mum. And me. You being a gay. You've broken her heart. Dad died of a broken heart when he found out you were a gay.'

'Don't use *a* with gay or even gay,' he said.

'Why not?'

'You wouldn't understand.' Everything outside seemed pink suddenly: The curtains next door and the rhododendron and Mum's daisies. Even the cap on the stupid plaster elf standing on a toadstool.

'Are you?' she asked.

'You've already determined that. There's nothing ambiguous about...'

'Don't use big words,' she said. 'I've got a perfect right. If my boys are...' She looked down at her baby. She might have been looking for signs of tuberculosis or nits instead of homosexuality.

'You want to know who I sleep with?'

'Mum... I mean I just wanted...'

'But you already know that I'm queer. So? Okay, make it official. Feel better?'

'I need a fag,' she said.

He was furious but he sniggered all the same. She needed a fag: his friends would adore it. Sitting around the table in his apartment trying to make the pathos funny in Spanish.

'I am homosexual,' he said in a voice so tired it alarmed him. 'Anything else? For your information, homosexuality is not a disease and nor is it hereditary.'

'Don't you tell your mother this,' Cynthia said. 'Promise me. It'll kill her. You killed your father, when he found out.'

'You fucking bitch,' he said. 'Why? What right have you got? Has Mum got?' He stared about him. His mother running out like that... 'I... I...' he uttered. 'This is a set up... you... Mum...' He wanted to punch her. It had always been the same. There she was, some cheap bitch in lipstick with two bastards and he was being accused of matricide and patricide and giving her sons homosexual genes.

'I'm a Catholic,' she said. 'And Mum, and it's difficult for us to understand.'

'Yeah, really difficult,' he said. 'Which is why I'm not one.'

'Eh?' she said. 'I thought...'

'How did I kill Dad?' he asked. It was so preposterous that anger turned to interest.

'Broken heart. Look, it's your life but I just wanted to know if you were a gay or what because of the kids.'

'I am, so what do you do about them? They'll be infected.'

But she stared at him smugly, like a punk after he's beaten someone senseless.

'It's what you hear,' Cynthia said. 'Dad heard it from Mrs Armstrong. He never told Mum but he told me and it'd kill Mum 'cause Dad was absolutely devastated.'

Again, the predictability of the whole situation sucked him down. It was exactly why he had never taken them into his confidence. Of course they would say things like this: disease, killed your father, sick, contagious. He'd heard this conversation from gay friends a hundred times on a hundred occasions. He'd waited decades for it to be his turn but absolutely nothing different was being said from the dialogues he'd had recounted from friends in Idaho and London and Mexico. The predictability was what most offended him. He wanted some new twist, some new plot, something which hadn't been spewed by millions of straight people against their victims. If it weren't for the hurt it would have been genuinely boring. No wonder men went to bath houses to escape. No wonder they had to hold each other anonymously in dark corners in affirmation that they'd survive. Jews and

retards and homosexuals. All the ones the Nazis had tried to elimi-
nate. And here was one of the persecutors patting her blond son on
the sofa. This was one of their propagandists. He stared out the window in a mix of ennui and anger. The pink woman was going up the
path with her milk bottles but when she saw him she hunched her
shoulders.

'I'm so sick of you, Cynthia,' he said. But what he was saying was
just as predictable and he caught himself saying it like an actor in a
feeble movie mouthing the words the audience needed to confirm
their own desperation.

'I...' he said struggling for new lines along a different story. But
there was none, it had all been set in stone forty years previously. Had
he expected them to say they believed in gay liberation like some of
his friends' families had? Not for Garth, so he realised. There was no
use. She had him. She was legal. The way she twisted her mouth told
him she'd achieved her victory. Patting the new nappy into place,
looking disgusted.

It was amazing. Nations could change overnight. Revolutions happened. Whole continents metamorphosed. His academic interest was
the effect of violent upheaval on the Latin American novel. Change.
Flux. Only Cynthia couldn't. She was static. She was as fixed as one of
those 1960s pop singers forever in a bee-hive hairdo and a tent frock
on the front of a record album.

'I've said my bit. Dad's gone. But for Christ's sake don't let Mum
know. There's no need to get her all upset 'cause she'll never accept it.'

'But why did she go running off now? Isn't this a set up? he said.
'You both...' He fought back the tears but they wouldn't stop flowing.
One after the other, drip drip off his cheeks on to the floral carpet.
Shane came back into the room and stood there watching. Even the
baby stared from its push chair.

*

'God, it's fabulous here,' Garth said. 'Maybe it is only nature that saves us.'

'Tongaporutu is my favourite place in the whole world,' Janine said. 'Sometimes I think I'm missing out on things by not living in New York or somewhere exotic, but a beach house in Tongaporutu, a huge old flat in Wellington. I'm lucky.'

'It'd be great to have an address like this, Tongaporutu, Taranaki, Aotearoa, the beach house by the dunes.'

'Maybe I would have found a man if I'd gone to Mexico instead of staying in Wellington,' she said.

'Don't be wistful,' Garth said. 'When you lived in London you mourned for pohutukawa trees. Besides, you didn't have to run away from New Zealand.'

'No wonder you fled. You were lucky with everything else, looks and brains and Alfonso. But not family. I don't understand why you come home.'

'Home? Well, I won't anymore unless it's a pilgrimage to see pohutukawa trees, I guess. Nature. And I'm a New Zealander.' He didn't feel like one standing there at the window, but then he didn't know what one was. New Zealanders had an image of a Mexican as wearing a sombrero, a big moustache and lying in a hammock. There were stereotypes of New Zealanders which were just as stupid. 'I am, aren't I?' he said. 'Even if it means identifying myself only by trees and black sand beaches and fabulous volcanoes.'

'No,' Janine said. 'You're not. Don't envy this windswept place when you've got so much going for you.'

'Should I go into permanent exile? Deny my upbringing in a working class house in a provincial town in a country which hates queers and intellectuals?'

'Don't be bitter. You have pretty well done that anyway. I think it's just your sister that sent you into exile.'

'Jesus, Janine,' he said. 'You mean a million times more to me than her. I thought women would've been more understanding, but that's the thing I've learned. You can't make generalisations and that's my lesson from this trip back. I tried. Families. Jesus. Why do we bother?' There were no answers, the only solution was personal and one that shouldn't be found in bitterness. He trained his eyes on the sea and studied the motions of the waves as they rose and fell and rose and fell.

*

'What are you preoccupying yourself about now? More mania about being a repressed homo?' Janine asked.

'Yes,' he said. 'That. Quite simply. What it means to be a homosexual.'

'Well look how much better off you are in New Plymouth in 1980, darling,' Janine said. 'It's not that bad.'

'Poor fucking homos generally. It makes me boil to think... When I was in the Soviet Union a couple of years ago and got fucked by the biggest cock under communism at the Dostoyevsky Museum, the guy told me...'

'Enough. Enough. I've heard that story a million times. Fantasy stuff that's all it is...'

'What? About Dostoyevsky... You...?' He shut up. He probably had thrashed that anecdote from Leningrad. For a few seconds he dwelled on Dimitry's giant penis. 'Ooooooohhhhh,' Garth said. 'Couldn't sit down for a week.'

'Garth, spare me. I don't want to know about your sordid lifestyle in all the grim details from every city on the planet. I thought a visit to the Soviet Union might involve culture and not only sexual exploits. Especially at Dostoyevsky's Museum. But look at me, please.' Her thin blond hair was cut boyishly and she wore an Indian dress of white diaphanous muslin. She beckoned to him with her index finger.

'Come,' she said. 'Listen.'

'You're looking at me like my students do when I set an assignment,' he said.

'I'm older than you,' she said.

'You look like Katherine Mansfield sitting there with the kowhai tree framing you.'

'I'm getting old, Garth. Be serious.'

'Age, dear. Look at me.'

'You're still gorgeous. All the boys... But be serious. I've an important request.'

'But I want to have a good time after dealing with Cynthia.'

'Okay, but be a little bit serious because...'

'Only a little bit serious? Then I should be literary rather than facetious. This should be a literary holiday. In conversation at Tongaporutu with Katherine Mansfield, discussing the great New Zealand novel. I should write a novel about this very moment and all the drama which has brought me to this peace and harmony with a friend as opposed to family.' He put his hand over his heart in mock seriousness. 'I want to write a novel about the destruction of the nuclear family so that the world will read it and be liberated.'

'What'll you call it,' she asked. '*Camping It Up? Sex and Danger in the Provinces?*'

He suddenly understood why Katherine Mansfield had exiled herself permanently. 'I wonder why she never wrote bitter things about New Zealand?' he said. 'Just lovely nostalgic things with no anger or twisted venom like I would.'

'She took it all out on others in book reviews,' Janine said. 'Listen darling, this is dramatic and I haven't got the time or inclination for literary theory. I work in a university library so academic theory's been frozen out of me by male academics. I'm thirty-seven.'

'Are you being neurotic about age?'

'I'm old and I want a child.'

'Get a Salvadoran baby. I can arrange it.'

'No, my own hormones need...'

'A bit of pumping?'

'To sound camp, yes.'

'So. There must be some fisherman around here. Cynthia seems to be able to find men to pop her brats.'

'You're so camp sometimes, and it doesn't become you.'

'Fuck you, too,' he said. It was odd. He realised for the first time the different feeling between being put down by a sympathetic friend from that of an enemy and for a second he wondered how really large was the distinction. 'I'm gay, I'm camp, okay?' he said.

'I'm not altogether happy with camp,' she said. 'It's too mock. Just be normal.'

Normal? It was not worth pursuing, but questions lodged foully in his head.

'What I need is a man with your brains and from what you say about Alfonso, I need someone with his looks.'

'It sounds like a recipe but you're the one who's sequestered herself in a university library. Go to Senegal and find a fabulous black man who speaks Patois and French.'

'I have a very important request.'

'I was never a matchmaker,' he said.

'You're so lucky, I mean Alfonso and being a lecturer in Latin American literature in Mexico City.'

'Darling, what are you getting at?' he said in the campest voice he could muster. 'The price I paid was being brought up in a cultural and emotional swamp in the 1950s and my just reward is a perfect expatriate marriage.'

'Which survives multiple sex partners?'

'Is enhanced by it.'

'I don't understand how it survives.'

'Heterosexuals don't. Alfonso and I have a marriage which defies analysis merely because it works perfectly.' Straights couldn't understand the subtleties of homosexuals. Her slight discomfiture with his camping it was merely another manifestation of incomprehension, dislike even. 'So, Katherine,' he said exaggerating further. He realised that homosexuals were like Maoris in that both groups were trying to claim recognition for what they really wanted to be, alive with their own culture, and up from under the oppression of the... He stopped his thought and told himself not to be paranoid or serious, as she had suggested. Fuck the heaviness. There was that in Mexico at the University with his professional duties; a symposium looming when he returned, a lecture on the influences of revolution on indigenous poetry. For a further moment the whimsical and fabulous nature of his existence vanished, and what was there was the reality that life was fucked, that what peasants wrote about in their verse was not whimsy and sweet, but filled with the vileness of oppression and suffering. That his relationship with Alfonso could collapse precisely because there were other men prowling for such a good catch as a handsome and sophisticated Mexican.

'You're so bohemian, especially for someone who doesn't believe in marriage and yet is married,' she said.

'Don't have a little mind, darling, don't be so New Zealand.' He laughed at the recognition of his bitterness, but dismissed it as belonging to reality rather than to cynicism. A country that still imprisoned homosexuals in 1980 didn't deserve to be treated sweetly.

'Don't you have people with little minds in Mexico?'

'There are lots of little minds.' Alfonso's parents didn't care that there son was a homosexual but they treated their three servants like serfs. 'Everything is ironic,' he said. 'Ultimately. But at least Mexico is the broad canvas. History, darling. Invasion, colour.'

'Yes, so romantic. No poverty or hunger or homelessness, just beautiful homes painted indigo and pink and happy natives. All is bliss in Mexico and New Zealand has no colour or cultural diversity, no colonial invasion, no literature, nothing romantic, nothing to speak for it.' She rolled down her muslin sleeve. 'Sometimes your own story overwhelms everyone else's. Sometimes your fabulousness is just arrogance.'

'Oh,' he said. 'Time to take notice.'

'You're a bitch but you know it Doctor Griffin,' she said. She knew he was listening, taking it in. He went to the far wall and straightened a lopsided painting. 'But since you want drama,' she said, 'I'll give you some: Impregnate me.' She was leaning against a fifties cushion with cowboys and Indians embroidered on it and at her right elbow was a red cushion emblazoned in gold lamé with VISIT FIJI THE SUNNY ISLES. The soft light seeping through the kowhai and the faded curtains.

'Moi?' he said. This time he placed both hands over his heart.

'Toi.'

'But darling. I'm a homosexual. The baby might catch my disease.'

'Like Cynthia says?' They both laughed. 'It'd be better if it did so that I'd get a caring, sensitive, artistic...'

'Don't be silly. Aren't there any horrible gay men?'

'I don't want a straight man's baby. They're all so boring and tired and I want a child who can run off to Mexico City and be vital and interesting and teach Latin American literature to the Latin Americans and send for me in my dotage to live in an adobe bungalow. An indigo and pink one.'

'Oh, you want an arrogant baby then, do you?'

That was the sort of vindication, the praise he'd always wanted from his family. A card to congratulate him on getting a doctorate. A pat on the back for not having to get up at five every morning for forty years to go to work on the wharves until he got worn out like Dad had.

'You really do love me, don't you darling?' he said. It was true every time; it was the family you made not the one you were born with. Rosa Luxembourg had tried to have the family banned after the Russian Revolution had succeeded; a brilliant idea lost in the dead weight of a patriarchal and straight reaction to real change. This was the amazing thing about life, the constant thought process: bang, bang, bang in his mind the ever present thinking about how it all fitted together. It was wonderful, delicious. He said a little prayer of thanks to the waves which were approaching the dunes and then he turned to her, half in wonder, half in earnest:

'What are you saying? Me, impregnate...?'

'Oh, go on,' she said. 'You fuck all over the world so you can stick your cock in me for two minutes.'

'One child. It'll look good on application forms. A heterosexual for the job.'

'Will you?' she said.

*

It had gotten dark. He'd spent the afternoon nervously going over in his mind the legalities and ethics of such an occurrence. It was one of those evenings that people on the West coast pray for throughout their tormented winter. The light on the waves and the black sand a ribbon of pink beauty.

'So crepuscular,' Garth said emphasising his favourite word with a deliberate lisp. He couldn't stand the idea of having to fuck a girl, let alone his best girl friend. It was all both odd and fascinating. He could whip down his pants for a quick one with a Mexican barrow boy and thirty minutes later be in front of a hundred students discussing the influence of Pushkin on Uruguayan poetry. But he'd had to get drunk just to initiate these preliminaries with Janine.

'Show me your thing so you can get used to the idea,' Janine had asked him.

'Can't I just stick it in?'

'I'm just interested in seeing the penis that makes my baby.'

'You're not trying to seduce me into marriage or anything deeper than sperm giver, are you? Nothing remotely romantic or clingy?'

'Such an inordinate distrust of women, Garth. Show me your dick, come on.'

'You're making too many demands.'

'Just out of curiosity.'

'Limp or erect?'

'Either way.' She took a long draught of wine and lay back on the cushion.

'You won't seduce me by looking languid on a cushion. I think you'll have to cover your whole body in cheese cloth and cut a hole where I have to put it. Should I take my pants right down or just pop it through the zipper?'

'As long as he doesn't grow up as camp as you're being at this moment.'

'So sexist. What about if it's a female?'

'Shut up and think about something really sexy. Take your clothes off so we can get it over and done with.'

'Oh, God,' he said. 'There's nothing in Latin American literature about this although Carlos Fuentes has a scene where a boy masturbates in front of the statue of Jesus.'

'What a shame it wasn't in front of Jesus himself, then whole course of history might have changed if he'd been caught with a minor.'

'It's all very well for you. You don't need an erection for the sexual act.'

'We have to pretend in other ways, dear, but just do it. I won't look.'

He went into the bathroom and had a hot shower in order to limber up and relax and make himself clean for the encounter. The New York bath houses; wildly, fabulously decadent. The sort of things men had been longing for since the beginning of time. Every fantasy catered for. Garth with his eyes shut and the hot water running over him; imagining New York style sex in preparation to enter his best friend's vagina. The man who insisted on being fucked through a hole in his jockey underpants. The man with the ebony skin and the ebony erection; Garth opened his eyes at the thought of the delicious pain of being pumped like that twice in twenty minutes. That Haitian in San

Francisco idling at the doorway of his bath house cubicle and using his eyes to buy Garth with. Being bought. Up and down, the eyes which said where lips should be placed and what would be slurped up and... and...

'Thank God,' Garth said, still dripping from the shower.

'What?' Janine asked.

'I'm erect.'

'Then hurry,' she said. 'Stick it here, look.'

'Oh, God.'

'What now?'

'I'm going limp.'

'Be serious and think dirty for five minutes and you'll come.' Such an admonition worked. The rational and the emotive: with his eyes closed he thought about the Haitian. What an afternoon. What a week. He and Alfonso together with the man from Port au Prince; a whole week of sex fun in San Francisco. He and Alfonso on holiday in San Miguel Allende in the Pension Cubana with the Señora's parrots squawking in the courtyard and the bedroom so stifling that their sweat washed them. Alfonso licking Garth's mouth and their saliva mixing and sucking on each other's lips. Beautiful and sublime and exotic and Aztec and Anglo-Saxon and Latin. The new race. Men and man and Alfonso and being sucked off by an Egyptian.

'I'm thinking madly,' Garth said. 'Like D H Lawrence. Procreation and loins and all that.'

'Ready? Good. God, it's enormous. Quickly. Shove it in here like this.'

'Call it Alfonso,' he said.

'Shut up and think dirty.'

'The last time was with an angel.'

'Shut up and concentrate.'

An owl hooted as he realised what a bastard he'd been to that poor thing on that wet night but what a fabulous first fuck it had been for himself in the Seaview Road toilets. The Good Angel, his first and last girl fuck until this moment and he laughed with the happiness of knowing that things could and did change for the best. Janine knew he was a homosexual and wanted him to fuck her for a beautiful and intelligent child. Fleeing the tedious and the repressive. Twenty-odd years later having sex under such bizarrely different circumstances so that it was almost all right, kinky even. She loved him. She knew he fucked in New York bath houses. It was Raskolnikov he'd managed to stay erect with last time he'd been inside a vagina. Raskolnikov the fabulous and tormented Russian he'd loved as a tormented teenager and the smell of the Russian's perineum there, wonderful, that magic essence like the Egyptian's, with his face close up, licking. Raskolnikov bending over him, guiding him to the dark corner. Garth opened his eyes and met Janine's rather than the Russian's.

'Close your eyes or you'll get distracted,' she said.

Raskolnikov's gorgeous arse and the freedom to lick it. A whole New York bath house of Raskolnikovs. He laughed at his old fantasy and renewed his strength with the modern one, the one he could indulge in: me in fetish clothing, underpants and leather and cock rings. It was amazing what freedom had done and... Raskolnikov in a New York bath house putting his hairy dick into Garth's arse. All those wonderful men in Mexico City, Veracruz, Acapulco, throughout his adopted country being fucked by men he understood for something as indefinable as sex and lust and loveliness. Freedom. That night in the car outside the Seaview Road toilets with the Good Angel. He'd moved on, fled, escaped the life he thought he'd be trapped in forever and forever as an unhappy, mistreated teenager. Raskolnikov's beautiful torso melting into the memory of the bodgie in the Seaview Road toilets and his first anal experience. Losing his virginity in the toilets because there was nowhere else to go to find the man he craved. Nowhere else to lose his supposed innocence. That fuck which had been so fabulous. Monty from Birmingham. Monty in the urinals every time the *Birmingham Queen* had berthed in New Plymouth.

'Call him Monty,' Garth said.

'Why?'

'Another time.'

'Are you getting closer or are you going to ride me all night?'

He'd always thought of sex as being as profound. The very oddity of putting his lips in a very intimate place on a man's anatomy. The combination of sex and love with Alfonso. He opened his eyes and looked down; pushing it in and out of the sort of hole he'd shunned for twenty years. Sex, the ethos of the twentieth century, like death was in the last. Silly things floating through his mind as he pushed in and out while attempting to make a baby called Monty who wouldn't grow up demented and torn like Cynthia or be put through hell like he himself had.

Oh, God,' he said. 'I think I'm enjoying being a heterosexual.'

'You're actually a very good fuck. It's slightly off-putting knowing its been up so many arseholes.'

'Raskolnikov,' he said.

'I'm not calling it that.'

Raskolnikov and the smell of bath houses and Alfonso's magnificent cock and the Egyptian licking his armpits while making love. Alfonso and Raskolnikov and Monty and the Egyptian: his best friends were his loves and family. They were lined up against the damp plaster in the Mexican bathhouse he frequented. Each one inviting him, each one in lust with the other.

*

Mum was sitting at the kitchen table. A bit of honey dribbled off the crust. The dribble, plop, plop on to the table-cloth.

'A long golden drop of semen,' Garth thought. Two weeks in New Plymouth and the only sex with a woman. He spread peanut butter on his toast and was about to bite it when his mother said: 'You're a homosexual. Cynthia told me over the phone last night.' She might have been saying why she preferred one brand of detergent to another. It was that matter of fact. The peanut butter was suddenly dirt smeared over his toast: lumpy, vile, something indescribably horrible on his fingers like dog shit. Very calmly he replaced the offensive food to his plate. For several moments he closed his eyes and understood the bizarre collusion between his sibling and his mother, this 'don't tell Mum' bullshit of Cynthia's, the ludicrous lies and porous subterfuge. Then he opened his eyes, they felt very tired, very sore suddenly, and he looked at her. Was this perhaps one of those great moments of life? Being born, surviving those first moments of realisation in a world which would erode you into self-preserving cynicism. The great moments. He didn't take his eyes off her and she had to shift her gaze to the curtains while she waited for his meditated reply. Mum calculating. Mum thinking. The thoughts going through her mind: tick, tick, tick; anal intercourse, men kissing, Mrs Armstrong saying that homosexuals had venereal diseases, Cynthia's worry that her two boys might be poofters. Mum shuddered. Her shoulders were shaking. She had a horrible image of Shane and Darrell playing dirty games or being interfered with.

Those great moments. He saw them one after the other, listed by the sequence of their inevitability: realising you were different, realising you wanted to be, the first love affair followed by the first heart break. The first foreign country. Alfonso. This moment of truth with Mum in the kitchen. Death.

'Well?' she insisted. 'I deserve a straight answer.' Only this wasn't one of those great moments after all. Truth; he deleted it from his list. Not for her with honey dribbling down her chin. Not Mum. At his age he had no room for love or compassion. The only great thing about this moment was he knew definitively that he hated her and everything she represented. Hatred; he added that inevitability to his list. Then he added Freedom.

'A straight answer?' he said but she didn't grasp the black humour.

'There's no use denying it,' she said. 'And I was hoping that you and Janine, but...' She actually popped the rest of her of toast into her mouth and began masticating it as if nothing more serious were happening than the planning of a picnic. A lifetime of this. He felt he hated her as much for her habit of talking with her mouth full as he did for her homophobia.

'You better answer me,' she said. 'Cynthia's told me all about it.' The crumbs soggy and mixed with butter and honey and stuck to her tongue and teeth.

'Which detergent do you prefer Mrs Griffin? The blue coloured one or the white?' The Virgin Mary with a sample displayed in each hand. 'Granules or liquid? Which do you find does a better job on your aprons and son's underpants?' The Virgin Mary standing before them with the incontestable evidence of purity. 'White seems nicer. Yes, white definitely.'

The Virgin Mary in Garth's mind as he sat in his mother's kitchen. There she was in plastic and aluminium above the toaster on the second shelf above the ironing board. What a monstrous fabrication she was. The very concept of glorifying virginity and using that mad notion to repress healthy sexual impulses. His mother ruined by mythology and misguided concern for the right hole at the right time. No freedom. No human rights. Nothing but the perceived norm laid out in an old book and sanctified by single men called Popes and Bishops in league with a celestial virgin. He understood how a peasant girl in a Portuguese field could see mirages and have illusions. The mere fact of a brief education by priests and nuns could do that to a susceptible mind. The Virgin Mary in her grotto bending over a pail of water with her box of white soap granules. Mary washing Joseph's undies. Cleaner somehow than putting one's undies into a blue liquid. Yes, definitely, white granules for a good wash, white like my soul. My Son will be so pleased with the white because He constructed sin in order for it to be erased in the same way that it appears; we dirty our clothes, so that we can wash them again. Souls, absolution. All mothers know that. The Virgin Mary. Mrs Griffin. The entire universe.

'Did you conceive immaculately?' he asked his mother bitterly.

The erosion into cynicism had become a landslide. Another word for the list. Cynicism; he wondered where to slot it. Where would it fit neatly or did it act like a liquid, infiltrating all of the other conditions on the list, flooding each of them in its own sticky, intrusive act of osmosis? Another particularly great happening and she had produced it in him. The years of this. Mum and Dad and Cynthia and being alive to understand life's realities through the hideous experience of history; the Germans' extermination of homosexuals in concentration camps. The fact that families had turned their own sons in to the Gestapo.

'It's repugnant and a bitter disappointment and Cynthia told Mrs Armstrong. Cynthia promised she'd never tell anyone. That's what kills me. Fancy telling that bloody old telltale fish wife and now they'll all know right up and down the street and... I... I...' She picked up the tea towel and rubbed the honey off her chin. 'I suppose you let men stick their whatsits up your rear. I didn't sleep a wink and poor Cynthia telling me and up there crying all by herself in Hamilton and upset because you turned out to be a homosexual.' He wondered where she had learned the word 'repugnant' as he watched the expected tears forming. There they came in the corners. The old tear ducts pink and loose from years of peeling onions and weeping over spilt milk. Then one dropped out, a slow dirty droplet off a clothes line. Mum's tears over his being abnormal. Her boy. His chest felt tight. Around his heart anginal feelings. She was folding the tea towel and blubbering.

'Well? Just don't sit there. What've ya' got to say for yourself what with all your university degrees and being high and mighty.'

This was boring. For some reason the eerie music of the hurdy-gurdy man who played on the avenida struck up a symphony; dozens of hurdy-gurdies in his mind. And the hurdy-gurdy man's old wife in rags with her out-stretched hand begging for pesos was his mother. He understood why Carlos Fuentes had pictured a boy masturbating in front of Jesus Christ. The anguish of being alive under the influence of such a narcotic as Catholicism. His mother was as addicted to it as any old peasant in an adobe church who'd been harangued for years by some rural cleric about sin and damnation.

'I demand an answer. It wasn't me. It's not my side of the family and I wasn't dominating like Mrs Armstrong said and now the whole street knows and I'll be the laughing stock because... because...'

'Cynthia said not to tell you because the knowledge had already killed Dad and that it would kill you. Why did you pretend you were not a part of this inquisition? That you knew nothing?' He wished the so-called news would kill her. He visualised her having a heart attack in the kitchen chair. One of those quick clean ones, instantaneous, plop, dead, over so there'd be no need for mouth-to-mouth resuscitation or weeks of hospital visits. Letting her gasp for air on the floor like a fish in its last minutes. Refusing her something life saving like an ambulance or her rosary or mouth-to-mouth resuscitation.

Depressed. Bored. Full of ennui and existential tiredness. The toast with its covering of dog shit. Garth shifted slightly but couldn't find the energy for anything else, an arm movement, a yawn, an explanation. Even the plastic Virgin wouldn't conjure any more images of suburban washing-day tricks to avoid dirt and dullness. The great moments arrived: hatred, tedium, truth. And they were great precisely because of their momentum. The momentum of this one crushing him; he had the feeling that Dad's concrete mixer was pouring out the wet sludge, all over him, burying him under crushed bottles, pained windmills, under wet concrete, under the very foundations of this kitchen where sin had been invented. The whole morass. The Virgin in her grotto saying silly things about detergents. The arguments from decades ago which still clung to these walls like the fly shit.

'Barry'll think it's filthy. He won't trust me. Just when we were getting on,' Mrs Griffin said through her tears.

'Why don't you ask me if I'm happy? Garth, are you happy, son? Go on, ask it.'

'You'll be lonely when you're an old man sitting on a park bench trying to get young boys. I've seen them. Mrs Armstrong said there's one in Pukekura Park and shows young boys his whatsit when they're on the swings.'

'Lonely!' The blood came rushing back into his veins as if activated by an intense, artificial stimulant. His blood boiling in response to the right cue. It was as if she'd had the intelligence to really think about his existence before leaving home and then finding the word to describe it. The most pain. The most anguish. Paging through the thesaurus of her mind and then seeing it there in black and white and waiting to be chosen. Loneliness. Alone. One. Garth with his family.

'Lonely? Jesus Christ! Do you think I wasn't lonely in this house when I was growing up? Lonely!'

Injustice was the most common theme in Latin American literature. He gave entire courses on it. Genocide in El Salvador and Argentina. Peasants and intellectuals having their tongues ripped out by generals professing the preservation of the Christian nation. Lonely when he was an old man and condemned to sit on a park bench. That fate was as fictitious as harmony had been in this household. As unjust as refugees, as the children he'd seen with beri-beri when on aid missions to El Salvador and Honduras.

'Lonely!' He thumped the table three times. 'Fuck you!' he screamed. He threw the peanut butter covered toast at the cupboard behind her but she didn't flinch. She was one of those generals watching her enemy squirm. The toast stuck to the cupboard for one or two seconds. He watched it. Then it began to slip, slowly down, down, down, leaving its filthy trail.

'Lonely when I'm an old man! I've loved more than you have. Lonely? You and Dad and Cynthia made me lonelier than I could ever imagine. I've got a man who loves me and who I love and what's Cynthia got? Has anyone ever loved you or her? Did Dad ever say to you: 'I love you?' And Cynthia just opens her legs when she sees a tatoo. This place is a spies' nest of lying Mrs Armstrongs. You knew all along, you and Cynthia.'

'You've broken my heart, Garth. I tried to shut my eyes last night but all I saw was you as a little boy in your pram and then that repugnant... that repugnant... I can't tell you what I kept seeing. All night. Not a wink of sleep because I kept seeing you with another homo doing it like Mrs Armstrong explained.' The tears started flowing again. This time he realised they were authentic. The way she sobbed. Her shoulders shaking. Up and down her large old shoulders in her faded dressing gown. Her hair had thinned; age had really struck her. She should have been enjoying herself playing the pokies in Surfer's Paradise or taking a bus trip around Wanaka. But she couldn't do things like that. She wanted this sordidness. Mum's thin hair and old body and the tears falling out of her eyes. And then again he relented; always looking for another aspect of the author's intention. It was because she loved him and didn't understand and was afraid and didn't have an inkling. He was at the point of reaching out, of touching her shoulder but the general came back into focus; the general who'd ordered Argentine homosexuals to be rounded up and dropped from an aeroplane above the Mar del Plata. Homosexuals in the Middle Ages having hot pokers shoved up their bums in punishment for buggery. But even more than that. He didn't love her. He didn't want to succumb to the pity and sentimentality of thin grey hair and hunched shoulders and visions of a happier life she'd missed out on because of her own pig-headedness and stupidity.

'I killed Dad, did I?' he asked. The blackness there like sour milk in his stomach. Then she looked at him. There was honesty in her eyes. He could see that. He knew enough about life to tell when people were being deceitful or sad; you could tell true emotions when you had lived the sort of life he had. But it didn't matter. It was too late. He couldn't love her just because she was being honest with him for the first time.

She shook her head and some more tears dropped out. 'Dad,' she said. 'He did tell me he loved me. Many times. He told me the night he slipped away and he would have told you if you'd come home to see him, but you didn't. He loved you, Garth.' She dabbed the tears with her tea towel.

'Did I kill him?' The list was written in concrete, unchangeable. Cynicism and hatred.

'I wouldn't like to say. Not really.' A few more dirty tears slipped out of the ducts. 'Cynthia reckons so. She said your Dad was devastated. It was a secret they kept from me but it finished him off. Cynthia said so.'

'She told me not to tell you I'm gay.'

'I never suspected a thing. Not till last night when Cynthia called me up and right out of the blue and says you're a queer. It was a bloody good thing you were at Janine's 'cause, well, I think I would've frightened you with all my crying I was so upset. A bolt from the blue.'

Never suspected a thing. Not in her life. Bolt from the blue. Garth shook his head in disbelief at the lies and the injustice. They'd known he was queer since he was a kid. They had always tortured him in one way or another because he was different. But this was the culminating torture, the *coup de grace*. The ultimate guilt trip: Mum didn't know her son was a homosexual. The brave and saintly Cynthia had tried to keep the terrible secret from Mum but couldn't due to the deep hurt and disgust that her brother was queer. Garth saw the idiocy and vileness of his family's plot to increase his torture. Patricide had been stirred in. Now matricide was included. Torture him, make him feel really guilty: it was a sport almost. Taunt the homosexual. He sat in the chair in his mother's kitchen as if he had his hands tied behind his back, his mind thick with ennui and hatred. He saw the bodies of live men falling from a cargo plane above Argentina. A henchman with a searing poker.

'Never in a million years,' she said.

Of course not. Mum going down to the shops to get some things for tea when he'd known she hadn't had to. Mum putting on her hat and coat and rushing out not ten minutes after Cynthia had arrived from Hamilton. The winks and nods. The generals in collusion.

'You were such a lovely boy. You didn't do bad things like Cynthia but now she's the one who's a comfort. Giving me Shane and Darrell. Your Dad loved them. He must have known way back then 'cause he absolutely lavished attention on them.' She began buttering another piece of toast. It was incredible. She was accusing him of murder and there she was thinking about her stomach. He watched her as she shifted her eyes from the honey to the peanut butter; the indecision for those few seconds. She chose the peanut butter and smeared it on. His hatred boiled over into searing words.

'I don't believe this,' he said. 'You can stick it. The next thing you're going to say is that I'm responsible for maybe making Shane and Darrell queer. Well, if it's genes to blame, then it can't be me who's passing them on. It's you. It's your fault you've got three queers. Didn't Mrs Armstrong tell you that it's passed on through the mother's genes, not the man's. It's you who did it.'

Enough. He stood up and looked about but he didn't know where to go because his head was spinning. Victim. Always a victim when it came to sexuality. A victim of queer bashers in big cities. Victims though the ages. A victim of this family. No wonder Alfonso could never understand this aspect of his life. *Qué será será*: what an insensitive thing for Alfonso to say. As stupid as the song Alfonso quoted it from. *Qué será será* if you came from a family who accepted your homosexuality. He saw how people could murder. He raised his index finger at her and was about to shout but he saw honesty. It was there, pregnant, in her eyes, shining, beseeching.

'Mum,' he said. 'Mum.'

She'd pushed away her plate with the uneaten toast on it. He'd misread her. His heart went to her. She hadn't wanted that toast at all. It had been merely something to do with her hands in her anguish of confronting this issue which she had postponed as much as he had. He saw himself for what he was. Selfish. Pompous. Arrogant. Her slow dirty tears were genuine. She believed that he, her only son, had been seduced as a youngster, that he had bad hormones, that is was her genes and that she'd mollycoddled him. It was all there in her eyes. She was saying sorry, begging him to reach out his arms and hug her and say it was all silly and not worth this pain.

'Mum,' he said. 'Mum.'

'Hateful!' she screamed. 'Repugnant!' She threw the toast at the linoleum. 'And you want me to say it's okay! But... but...' She didn't know how to articulate her deepest feelings. There was no precedent in their family for evoking emotions with speech sensitive to human needs.

'I got a book out of the library on it,' she said shakily. 'It said they have dozens of partners and group sex and sex in the mouth. Those sorts of things. I'm a Catholic and it's disgusting.'

Go back to Mexico and never again contact them. Take out Mexican citizenship. The beauty of it. Never again see his family. Not even be an exile, but a Mexican.

'Don't go away,' she said.

'But you hate me.'

'Sex in the mouth. Can't you get married? There's a group called Exodus which changes queers into real men.'

'I've been living with a wonderful man named Alfonso for years. He's a Mexican. We love each other, Mum. Can't you understand that?'

'Why couldn't you live in New Zealand? Not good enough for you? You wouldn't have to be a homosexual in this place. It's healthy.'

There was no way around this. It was something from the theatre of the absurd. One of those plays which twisted everything so that it appeared unreal and ridiculous but utterly believable. Here it was being acted out in an untidy kitchen in New Plymouth rather than on a stark stage in Berlin. Art as reality struck him as he stood there. The toast finally plopped onto the linoleum after its slow descent down the cupboard. Alfonso listening to samba. Sitting by himself in their living room under the soft lamp-light reading a book on Barcelonan architecture. Señora de Reyes calling to ask them to dinner. The normality of his life in Mexico.

'Leave now,' Garth thought. 'To not leave now is to stay bound to this bullshit.'

'I'm going out,' Mum said. She blew her nose into the tea towel and dried her tears. 'I need fresh air.'

'And if I'm not here when you get back, you'll know you'll never see me again.'

She looked at him. Her eyes said something but he didn't dare read them after the last misinterpretation. And she didn't have clichés which said the lovey dovey things Americans used in the shows she watched on television. It was just those little animal eyes all puffed up from crying and confusion and a life made sordid by her inherited prejudices. She cast him a glance as she went through the door, the sort of look that had turned Lot's wife into salt. She didn't say good-bye or anything, just that desperate look of disbelief that her boy would go to Mexico forever and leave her.

'*Adios,*' Garth said after she'd shut the door.

He'd killed his father. The injustice of that accusation made the hatred and sadness really sting. His father. His bloody silly, bottle collecting, whinging, never satisfied father. He went into the living room and picked up the tequila bottle with the moustachioed Mexican in a sombrero that adorned the label.

'Dad' he said. The tears came flowing down. He was unnatural and dirty and nothing better than vermin; the bottle was Dad's wholesome interest. The passion of a good family man who loved his son and wanted the very best. Not homosexuality, sterility, this filth where Mum was upset and forced to leave her own home to avoid her dirty minded progeny. Anal sex and anilingus and sucking men's nipples. Dad's thoughts coming through the bottle. Dad's hatred emanating through the glass and into Garth's hands and into the blood vessels and travelling to his brain.

'Repugnant,' Garth shouted, repeating his mother's word. 'I hate you too.' He threw the bottle at the windmill above the sofa on which Dad had sat for so many years looking at the racing pages. But the bottle didn't smash. He wanted to see it break into a thousand pieces, the punishment for its oozing out the cruel thoughts and accusations but the hated receptacle only dented the windmill.

'As it has to be,' Garth said.

He went into his mother's bedroom to get a picture of his father. Again the feeling that there was something wrong with his blood, that a disease was rushing through it, his chest tight, choking him. His mother's room was mauve and purple and the picture of his father wasn't on the duchess where it had sat for years. To stare at that picture of Dad and so verify that he hadn't caused the old bastard's death but that a lifetime of bitterness, lamb, hogget, cigarettes and whisky had.

Mum's top drawer was slightly stuck and he had to pull it firmly. She'd probably hidden Dad from Barry, under her hankies and underpants. There was a bright woollen tea cosy stacked in with her underwear and everything smelled of mothballs because of her horror of insects.

'All this shit comes from a lack of education and too much Catholicism,' he said through his tears. The tea cosy had been made by his long deceased grandmother and he had an impulse to steal it and take it to Mexico as a reminder of the one family member who had loved him.

'I hate you all,' he said. 'Hate you.'

Under the singlets in the second drawer there was a book which Garth fished out and held up to the light. The red cover with an Asian girl sprawled across it enticingly, her lithe legs parted, the satin night gown not even covering her pubic hairs.

THE SECRET DIARY OF HO CHIH MINH'S DAUGHTER

17th April, 1967: Today Cong came in from the Ministry of War. He looked tired and I told him to come into my room so that I could make him happy. But it would be more like Mo making me happy because he has the biggest cock in all of Hanoi. Cong didn't need any coaxing because he is a real man, a man of fire and a man of passion and love and slowly I ran my long red fingernails up and down the shaft of his huge cock so that he was soon writhing in ecstasy. Because I had been entered by seven or eight men that day already, I made him fuck me in my arse on account of having a sore pussy. He did it beautifully. Cong doesn't mind where he puts it and for me, I feel just the same.

*

The seventeenth of April was Garth's birthday. He felt that this was the birthday present he had always wanted. Sitting on his mother's bed hoping she'd gone for a long walk and wouldn't be back any moment.

*

4 August 1968: Today was difficult. The bombing has been going on for many hours. The customers are very troubled by the noise. Or some actually enjoy it and when the bombing gets fiercest, they perform like lions. They think they are going to die so they fuck extra hard. I love it when the bombs are falling. I think that this could be my last hour and I am at one with my customers and encourage them to do the things to me that not even I would do unless death were about to wipe me off this earth. The seventh customer must have been a soldier but he didn't tell me. He was strong and handsome. The only words he said to me were : I have to urinate, lie on the floor.

*

Mum's birthday. The fourth of August 1968. She would have invited Aunty Gladys and Uncle Victor over for a few beers and some peanuts and chips. They'd probably bought her some of those hankies in the top drawer which she'd used to cover this book. Garth was flushed with excitement because this was one of those extraordinary moments in life. He added another word to the list: revenge. It came neatly between hatred and freedom and it was, in essence, not that much different from irony. Ho Chih Minh's daughter was performing fellatio on an American prisoner of war when he heard Mum opening the front gate.

'Well,' she said when she came into the living room, 'I had a little walk.'

'You went to Mrs Armstrong's, didn't you?' he said. 'To gossip about all this, because you enjoy it. It's really good drama.' He'd left the light on in her bedroom. She looked from him to her room and then back at his eyes but she said nothing.

'Go on,' Garth said. 'What have you got in your life except Mrs Armstrong and the gossip you two spin? You couldn't wait to tell her the latest instalment.' She wasn't able to lie. She went white, even under her powder.

'She's been very good since your Dad passed away.'

'Since I killed him.'

'Now, now,' she said. 'He was sixty-six, not a bad innings considering, and he'd worked very hard for you kids. That's how you got your education.'

'I think actually that the government paid for my education and you never gave me a penny in the eight years I spent at university.' She was still in her coat and hat with her handbag hanging over her arm.

'You made your father very proud,' Mum conceded. 'Even if you did go on demonstrations and get yourself arrested. He never forgave you for that time in Wellington.'

'No, never forgiveness. But you mean over the Vietnam War demonstration?'

'We saw you on the telly protesting for all New Zealand to see when the boys were fighting against communism.'

'Did you think I'd be gone by the time you got back?'

'No,' she said. 'Mrs. Armstrong's advice was that...'

'I don't want advice,' he said. 'I want to ask you about...'

'No,' she said. 'Garth, no more. After a cup of tea perhaps because Mrs Armstrong has some suggestions.'

Mrs Armstrong's advice brewing; he could just imagine it. She was probably on the phone at that very moment rejoicing to her other friends about the Griffins' latest titbits.

'She's not dumb, you always underestimated her powers.'

Her powers. He'd always thought of her as being a witch. He could just hear her advice and Mum taking it all in, fortifying herself for this conversation with her estranged son: Mrs Armstrong recommending a psychologist she'd read about who could give shock treatment. There was a ward at Tokanui Hospital which took in deviants. Mrs Armstrong sitting across the table from Mum, the teapot the crystal ball. Mrs Armstrong saying she'd heard the treatment had worked wonders on a lesbian from Auckland.

'I...' he said. But a thought unrelated to Ho Chih Minh's daughter entered his head. You didn't need a doctorate to see that this conflict was no more or no less than any of the conflicts in the history of this household. It was like the war in El Salvador or Lebanon or Palestine, all the current conflicts that came with repetitious sadness on the television. The pattern was there for a blind person to see; you never resolved anything just because of the sheer complexity of the human condition. This was a family which bred on discontent as a form of relating. Mum had just performed a part of the ceremony; off to Mrs Armstrong's for a bit of a gossip about it and now back for the next round, but first a cuppa. Of course she knew he wouldn't have gone off to Mexico just like that. That wasn't scheduled in the family's form of conflict. There'd be another round and she believed she held the trump card because she was the mistress of this game; she'd played it so successfully with Dad's willing participation for so many decades that it would be the loss of the game which would kill her, not his homosexuality. He was staring at her and she at him; she was waiting for the first call, like bingo.

'It's ghastly,' he said.

'I know,' she said. 'That's why I'm so devastated by it.'

Ghastly. He realised he used words like she did: Cynthia thrashed *hideous* just like Mum did *repugnant*. Ghastly, hideous, repugnant, it was family institution to select and abuse the vocabulary of discontentment. He and Cynthia were as much a part of family addictions as they were products of their parents' genes. Around and around viciously, like the cycle of malaria.

'I don't know any more,' she said as if tired. 'I must wet my whistle before...'

The malarial cycle; at some point a prophylactic had to intervene.

'The Vietnam War,' he said. 'We used to run about Wellington yelling long live Ho Chih Minh.'

'I know,' she said. 'And it's a bloody good thing he didn't win because you wouldn't have been free to come and go as you liked everywhere around the world as if there isn't any responsibility. If the communists had've gotten down here it would have been a different story. The Japs nearly got us.'

'Ho Chih Minh,' Garth said. 'I wonder if he had any children?'

'He...' Mum said. 'I...'

'You don't think Ho Chih Minh had a daughter, then?'

'What?'

It was another one of those great moments. He made a mental note to record it for his expanding list. Shock. Mum's face going whiter and whiter. The look of terror and anguish and betrayal. She looked at her bedroom where the light indicated everything.

'You bloody little bastard,' she shouted. 'That's my book... I mean... That's Barry's. He... I mean... It's private...' The more she blubbered the more he enjoyed it.

Mum didn't know what to do when she'd finished trying to say who actually owned the book. But the truth was all over her face. He could tell. She and Barry had been reading it. It must have been their bed time reading at night; just a few pages of filth before lights off. First she lurched forward as if to snatch the book when he brought it out from behind his back and then she pushed an empty cup off the table and it smashed on the floor. Another round in the long history of the Griffin feud. He laughed just thinking about it: ghastly, repugnant, hideous. He wanted to add *predictable*. How clear it was; learned behaviour, as if in a play in which he had been unwillingly conscripted. The only sad part was he hadn't understood its nature until this minute.

She looked around her living room. It was then that she noticed that the windmill had been punctured, but she didn't stay to comment.

'A play,' he said, 'called *The Secret Diary of Ho Chih Minh's Daughter* in which the main theme is comic tragic irony.'

7 La Virgen de Guadelupe

A freezing shiver slid down Janine's spine and she coughed as the metro car surfaced from beneath the city and went rushing noiselessly through rain and grey suburbs towards the Basilica de la Virgen de Guadelupe. It should have been fine for this pilgrimage. A Sunday afternoon in Mexico City with Garth, her son Monty, Alfonso, and his mother Hortensia de Reyes. She wanted blue skies and sunshine and the warmth that would make her feel well and rested instead of this low lugubrious depression amidst twenty million people trying to enjoy a Sunday afternoon in dampness. Her hair was wet and dribbles slipped down her neck but she didn't have room to stretch back her arm to wipe them. Everyone squeezed together in the metro car in that peculiar amalgam of anonymity and intimacy. The thin mestizo faces of young men in tight jeans and loose sweat-shirts and the chubby mestiza countenances of their girlfriends in identical outfits; Sunday pilgrims from the downtown slums and inner suburbs dressed like Gringos for their peregrination to their most holy of virgins. She wanted them to be laughing, breezy, languid people in loose calico shirts and trousers and sombreros who conformed to her stereotype of what Mexicans should be, a scene of people who weren't trying to emulate Los Angeles teenagers, something much more romantic than this obeisance to all things Californian. Those baseball caps and the denim jackets. Everyone should have been enjoying their families in parks and plazas instead of this cramped technocratic nightmare which didn't fit her tourist's expectations. A sneeze worked through her nostrils, begging to come out. She could feel it marching across her forehead, her whole head infected with that thick feeling; her eyes tingling from influenza and pollution. She could barely see Monty whom Garth was holding, the two of them barely distinguishable through her misty vision.

'Get me out of this bloody death trap,' she thought. She stifled the impulse to elbow her way out, to push past the señora with the face of an old baby and the businessman with a briefcase clutched to his chest. 'Quiet,' she told herself.

A man, perhaps twenty years of age, was squeezed next to her, his elbow digging into her side. He had the face of an angel about to visit its Holy Mother Guadelupe, the virginal Queen of Mexicans. Janine concentrated on his profile in an act of meditation. An angel who smelled of camomile and hot-dogs. She sketched his profile with her eyes; nose, lips, forehead, the profile of one of the Aztec statues she'd worshipped in the Museo de Antropologia the day before. It was extraordinary. In this polluted megalopolis someone of such pure beauty. Someone so angelic. His eyebrows tantalising her as she stood there trying not to sneeze or sniffle or cough. This was the magic Garth went on about. The skies heavy and sooty with industrial pollution but beauty in corners. Beauty because of the pollution. Those yellowish grey sulphuric clouds hovering above the cathedrals and contamination-stained buildings. The surrealist imagery of it, so many millions of lives over so many hundreds of years in this very spot. Just there at that intersection through the window; a huddle of people in the rain and the four-storied buildings all grey, all bleak, all beautiful. Life and death in the latter part of the twentieth century. Another shiver slid down her spine, a cold pin prick on each of the vertebrae. The angel moved slightly so that she could see the length of his eyelashes. The next shiver, even colder than the previous one, went scuttling down her spine and rattled her bones, then running up the way it had come. She had an image of those famous Mexican skeletons. All of the skeletons of all of those millions of souls who had inhabited the area they had just rushed through. Centuries of souls in the Valley of Mexico. In her mind the men and women being held down on the sacrificial altars. She shook her head but the obsidian knives in the museum, the ones tucked neatly, clinically, behind glass, emerged there in the metro car and lunged into the hearts of their victims. The angel would have been one of them; this beauty taken in battle or on his own volition laid out on the stone altar to appease the sun.

This was the whole existential nightmare of history. Reading behind the racks in the university library when she should have been shelving. Any bit of knowledge in the pages for her to pluck at random. History on pages. A degree in the stuff. All of those scenes coming back to haunt her there in the metro, but larger, more vivid; the obsidian knives and the willingness to be victims. The substantiated and the abstract; the enormous reality of the present fused with the past in the faces of these inhabitants of the megalopolis. The shiver went running up and down her spine like a rat in a pantry. This was the exhaustion of knowledge. To have read so much. Sociological treatises. Anthropological studies. Historical analyses. The dozen books about Mexico she'd read before this trip. She saw everything piling up; books on shelves, a hundred million of them. Books and journals and print, but the events actualised. Yet all she wanted at that moment was to run her finger down the perfect line of the angel's left eyebrow. He was supposed to turn and look at her. An Alfonso for Janine after all this time and loneliness; this heat, this claustrophobia, this illness. She felt fraught with the disease of knowledge and the burdens of history.

'Why did I come here when I should have stayed at home to get better?' she thought. 'I'm so ill.' She could see the top of Garth's head above the damp blue suit of the businessman; Garth who had managed a successful migration. Garth who had done it all: the academic career, the spectacular boyfriend. Even a gorgeous son he didn't have to tend.

'Stop being so fucking morbid,' she told herself. 'You're acting like a depressed librarian, not a tourist.' It was difficult to defy her intellectual preoccupation under the influence of influenza; she tried the meditation again and it worked for a few seconds but the faces drew her back. Each person getting off at his or her station and disappearing from her forever to continue life for its allotted span. Other people's lives. It seemed an absurdity not to know about each one, not to have the ability to see everything. Not to be able to look out that window and see Mexico as it was when the Aztecs ruled it. The señora with the baby face: what sort of house did she live in and what were her secrets? A baby-faced señora worthy of a novel who merely got off the train and disappeared forever. The passive faces of the businessman and the angel. All of them mestizo with that look that said things are modern but things haven't changed at all over millennia. The heat in the metro car, the electronic tunnel lit by fluorescence and speeding, hurtling through existence. She was sweating, all over her body the cold chills, now hot ones, and yet the fabulousness: the angel's beautiful lips, the centuries' deaths and her own eclipse. Standing in a train in Mexico City for twenty minutes with a headache and the feeling of pins digging into her. In the great span of things it was her whole experience of life encapsulated and it weighed on her as if she were seeing it all as one is supposed to as one leaves this life, the soul ascending. The soul going around and around and the mortal mind looking back; seeing itself, seeing everything melted together.

'Oh, God,' she thought. 'I feel so sick.' She had a quick glimpse of herself looking down at her own person from above or as if through one of those image distorting cameras used for security purposes in banks and apartment buildings. In a crowded bus in her own small, windy, coastal city on the edge of an isolated island. Crushed up next to old ladies with blue rinsed hair, elderly Wellington ladies who bundled themselves in frumpy coats in any season. Above her own body and looking down and seeing everything so clearly, everything fitting together as if it were not the mystery that religion and myth and reality begged humans to wallow in.

'I came here to relax and get well,' she thought. 'Not to be haunted.' She wriggled her arm free and wiped her forehead with her sleeve and begged God not to let her sneeze until she got outside. The heat and claustrophobia: the angel's face not six inches from her own and that attempt to be human enough, to be the trained and social animal and so avoid the impulse to pull the emergency chord and push the angel and the businessman and scream and scream.

*

'Devils,' Alfonso said looking around him at the street scene. 'It's a city of devils.'

'What a perfect family outing and I'm the grandmother of my son's boyfriend's son. Is that the modern Mexican family?' Hortensia said. She looked at the wet sky and then at her cigarette as if it too symbolised the catastrophe of pollution they were so proud of for having to survive and battle within. 'Our city...' She might have been at her dinner table involved in another conversation with the right people about the right topics and not on a street corner in the drizzle. 'Our city is filled with devils. This city's literature and art I mean, how could it not be alive and passionate with death and black flowers?'

Death and black flowers; the way Hortensia's red lips moved over the words and then pursed themselves together like something slightly obscene and blood clotted. Everything in Janine's mind drifting in the unreal; washing in and out of what seemed to be and what wasn't and then very clearly what it was all about. It was the stabs of clarity, those shots of truth which hurt the most. Those questions which had always been asked but which by their very nature could not be so clearly answered until now. The very shape of Hortensia's head and the severity of her beauty and her blood clotted lips and the words which spilled from between them: class, haute couture, hypocrisy. It was a stereotype as grand as the one she knew she desired as a tourist, to see all Mexicans in traditional Mexican outfits. The Spanish woman descending an elegant staircase with a rose clasped in her teeth. Hortensia was that señorita from the Mexican cinema of the 1930s, in black and white, the image slightly shaky, only now she appeared as a middle aged señora in 1982, as archetypal as any peasant in a sombrero and leather sandals leading a burro through the cactus fields.

'It's hard to tell whether this is rain or dripping pollution,' Hortensia said. 'I remember when it was all clear skies and...' It seemed too long ago or the memory too cloying to continue. Hortensia in her beautiful outfit. The whole group beautifully presented and not at all ashamed, as Janine was, of being a cluster of wealth amongst the pilgrims flocking to the Cathedral. Janine's eyes sore and misting and her mind hurting from the thought that her friends were hypocrites; so much talk over the last few days about the nature of the Mexican Revolution and about the need for equality. All those demonstrations she'd been on in Wellington in the seventies which demanded social justice: Ho Chih Minh, Mao, South Africa; a long list of political affiliations she'd devoted her time to and here she was a middle class woman with upper class friends who spouted hypocrisy about justice. Just then Señora de Reyes said something stupid, something inane about poor people migrating to the city. The Señora in her flouncing skirt, her red lips and her perfect everything. The pretension oozing from her and Janine hating her for it. Pretension in Mexico City; those women who marched about with stiff blonde hairdos and manicured lips with an Indian servant trotting behind them. It might well be a culture based on passion and extremes and the fabulousness of an enormous history, but it didn't sit well with a girl who still believed in socialism. She laughed bitterly at her own image of herself on that street corner in her raincoat within the ridiculous situation: Mao, Ho Chih Minh, South Africa. All that time and wasted energy leading to nothing but her own inexorable inclusion into the ranks of the privileged. Janine stared at her companions with momentary hatred. The thoughts sharp, staccato through her feverish mind. She sneezed onto her sleeve and saw the image of someone somewhere screaming, but it was only the vision that had been recurring since this depression had hit her in the last couple of months: the Edvard Munch painting of the screaming woman. That face at the end of the pier and the tortured expression. The scream. She saw it as she fished for a clean tissue in her bag; she heard it in Spanish on the radio in the disjointed half-understood message on that morning's news: Israel invading Lebanon and Beirut being bombed. You couldn't excuse that outrage. Thousands dead. Even in the quick fire Spanish from the local radio station that morning she'd perceived the gist of the horror. She had an image of that city; the outrage of the 1970s bloodying the new decade. Each night the two minute clips on the television news and now more desperation. The concrete apartment blocks the symbol of everything. Bombs. Bombs. From Beirut to Mexico City, the huge populations dying from being smashed and bashed by explosions. In her nightmare there was no colour, just the black and white finality of news documentaries of the Blitz in London, Coventry, Berlin, Rotterdam, the hideous sensation that life was being exterminated by...

'God in heaven. Why do I think like this?' she thought. The documentary playing out, fizzing into grey with the Spanish language edition of the day's outrages in Lebanon.

She put the sodden tissue into her pocket and hated her friends because they didn't recognise her ill health and the fact that they were enjoying their privileges so much in a city as divided like this class ridden atrocity of Mexico City.

'Loosen up,' she told herself. 'Relax.'

The mundane things as acts of history: washing hanging on a balcony and a child's bicycle leaning against the railing. Television clips of the whole thing going up in flames. The heat of the cold and the coldness running up and down her arms; each hair on her body pin pricking like each of the thoughts invading her mind on that street corner in Mexico City at that particular moment in history. Her friends were talking as they waited for the traffic; something – she couldn't grasp the Spanish – but it must have been something so... so worldly because they were laughing and using their arms and hands to explain like puppets in the drizzle. Alfonso in his perfect attire and his mother gesticulating. In the gutter some unrecognisable rotting remnants, the water dribbling over it oily and brown like the seepage from decomposing bodies. This was a sea of hypocrisy and she felt she was bathing in it, her body shaking from fever, and her mind tormented. How could one be freed, released from this? She stared at Hortensia and couldn't understand. She wiped the perspiration from her forehead and sneezed. Hortensia had three large rings on her middle finger and her hand had the appearance of one of those severed, alabaster hands displaying rings in jeweller's windows.

'*No hay contestas ni hay razones, al contrario,*' Hortensia said. She used her Spanish as if it were something delicious, luxuriating over it, licking the consonants and syllables in an effort to delight her foreign guest and indicate the beauty of her cultural privilege. Then she changed into English with its hint of a US accent. 'Look at all these pilgrims trying to make sense out of things by worshipping some pure mother saint who never existed,' she said.

'We never brought an umbrella,' Alfonso replied.

'We can buy one here with an image of the Virgin of Guadelupe on it,' Garth said. 'Faith on everything.'

'What's wrong with faith?' Janine said. They were like characters in a play, *Pygmalion* or *The Cherry Orchard*. Effete and privileged and late nineteenth century.

'Our pilgrimage,' Garth said. 'Let's advance on the Virgin.'

*

Standing on the street corner in a lower middle class suburb of Mexico City waiting for the cars to pass so that they could cross a street and walk to the Basilica. Alfonso, Garth, Hortensia, wealthy by definition of their having pale skin. Wealthy in every respect. She would rather have been with the mestizo family behind them. Mama with the child in a rebozo on her back. The three girls holding hands and dressed in tulle and black patent leather shoes and the boy holding his father's hand, his huge eyes wide and staring. Janine didn't even like her own child at that moment. Monty who was so gorgeous and so spoiled and so much like Garth.

'EM Forster is Garth,' she thought. 'That pompous arsehole.' *A Passage To India* and those British Raj elitists with their inherited pomposity. Decked out in their impeccable outfits, looking down while astride elephants. She was Miss Quested seeing herself all these years later in a situation in Mexico City not unlike that which had happened to that insignificant heroine in India in the 1920s. It was clear, Garth was Forster. He said the sorts of things that Forster did: 'What is life but the pursuit of beauty and adventure?' Stupid things which were meant to be graceful but placed you firmly on the elephant. Pompous, elitist. And Hortensia some British official's wife in a white pith helmet and they were all going off to some place of pilgrimage, some caves to view the extraordinary. That odd angled camera, the vision through it. Miss Quested knowing she would be the victim.

'I've got the flu. I might…' she said.

'Quickly,' Alfonso demanded. 'Get Janine out of this drizzle.'

On their left was a pastry shop with its window filled with skulls and skeletons dusted with different coloured sugar powders; theory and no action. You could dust a skeleton with sugar but it made death no sweeter. Janine looked at her reflection against the skulls looking out. She couldn't even find herself a real man to give her a child. She'd had to beg a homosexual to impregnate her. Not even love was legitimate and that was the main thing she wanted. Miss Quested in the caves seeking passion. It was no different from having asked Garth to fuck her at Tongaporutu. The next shop contained virgins; rows and rows of Guadelupes standing on a rose or in a grotto or under a lampshade.

'I hate coming to the Basilica,' Hortensia said. 'It depresses me. Look, we should buy you an amulet to get you well quickly.'

'Shall I buy you some Guadelupe key rings?' Garth said, pointing to the trays of junk tourist merchandise outside a small shop. He laughed mockingly, holding the key ring aloft as if he'd just discovered the concept of kitsch. He was wearing a long black coat, one he'd bought in New York on his last vacation. She suddenly loathed him for it. The coat and his voice and his insincerity, the way he mocked at everything for its aesthetic as if everything had to be seen through high culture, through some gauze called gayness.

'I...' She sneezed into her sodden handkerchief. As she did, she saw Miss Quested going into the caves where the disaster happened.

'A Virgin magnet for the refrigerator?' Alfonso said. The family with the three girls in tulle were selecting pencils with the Virgin's image on them.

'Or wall hangings?' Garth asked. 'Is this hideous enough?' He held up a mauve velvet square with the Virgin's image disfigured by bad painting.

'I'll wait to buy some peasant handicrafts,' Janine said.

'And not these ones?' Alfonso asked. 'Made by Taiwanese peasants in factories.'

'The Mexican peasants prefer plastic to adobe handicrafts,' Hortensia said. She lit another cigarette from the ember of her previous one. 'It's the intelligentsia who want peasant purity.'

'The peasants don't stand about discussing what's philistine,' Garth said. 'We're the intelligentsia. That sounds uppity to a New Zealander, eh Janine? Here it's a proud term because the intelligentsia helped fight the revolution.'

As if on cue, a peasant woman with a striped rebozo tied around her leaned in front of Hortensia and grabbed a handful of pencil sharpeners. She counted out six sharpeners with the intense deliberation of the semi-numerate. She could have been the Virgin of Guadelupe incarnated as a peasant woman in a cheap shop, sent to perform a miracle with pencil sharpeners to provide evidence of the peoples' faith for these educated sceptics watching her. Janine wanted her to raise her arms in some kind of benediction or manumission. Even Monty stared at her. She picked out the green pencil sharpener and put it back in the bucket and as she did she smiled up at them, the Señora, the handsome gentlemen, the blond child and the tired looking gringa.

'Buenos tardes, señores,' she said. She had bright white teeth that were too small for her large brown gums. The Virgin of Guadelupe. She was there in the form of a peasant woman with a face as intelligent and gorgeous as one of the market women in a painting by Diego Rivera.

Janine wanted to attach herself to this woman, to let Monty experience this side of Mexico and not have to listen to this bullshit about the intelligentsia. It was horrible recognising that one's beliefs were arrogant, that one was a member of the intelligentsia; she saw it all through the fog of flu and bitterness. EM Forster and the gang in Mexico City. This peasant woman there as a convenient symbol of something to draw them to the same conclusions of their inescapable destiny. It wouldn't have been astonishing if the woman had manifested a bunch of roses as evidence of her sanctity as the original Guadelupe had done for the peasant Juan Diego in the mid-sixteenth century.

'Go on,' Janine thought. 'Perform a miracle.' To see Hortensia and Garth confronted with that evidence would be beautiful. The Virgin levitating. Roses falling from heaven. To touch the Virgin's hem and recover from this illness.

'Juan Diego saw the Virgin, don't you believe him? He was a peasant and you think the peasants have the real social impetus in this country,' Janine said.

'The Church needed a miracle to prove its colonisation of the Americas was right,' Hortensia said. 'Invent the Virgin, a brown one. Very clever. All the Indians follow.'

'All my children go to school,' the woman said in Spanish with the enormous dignity of one who hasn't herself had that privilege. She was a soul, a spirit. She was the only person Janine had felt love for since she'd arrived in the country.

'I'm not well,' Janine said. 'I want to go back to the apartment.'

'We'll just have a quick look and at the Basilica and then get a taxi,' Garth said.

They reached the vast square and entered through the porticos. Janine shivered at the sight of the Virgin's immense twentieth century edifice, at the power and the glory. She shivered from cold and fever and tiredness and oppression and the hugeness of everything before her; the crowds and the majesty of it all. The wet sky hung down over them and reminded her of dirty laundry.'It's fabulous and hideous at the same time,' she said. 'I thought it was going to be...'

'Colonial? Majestically Hispanic?' Alfonso asked.

'It's so Arizona.' She wanted to offend them. The angry current of discontent was as pervasive as the illness making her feverish. She wanted to see Hortensia try to avoid having to defend Mexico, to see if she were sophisticated enough to accept criticism gracefully. Scratch a Mexican and find the hurt passion of nationalism. The intelligentsia who moaned about their peasantry's Virgin worship were the first to defend that right if a foreigner condemned it.

'Is modernism only the privilege of the first world nations?' Hortensia asked.

'This architecture represents Mexico's coming of age,' Alfonso said. 'The 1960s were its take-off into modernity.'

'Mexico is a stupid country so filled up with problems and contradictions,' Hortensia said. She was too wise to be completely taken in by Janine's encouragement. 'Come, darling. Leave the men and we'll go into the Basilica.'

Several women shuffled on their knees along the aisle. Crawling up towards Jesus hanging above the altar in a 1960s rendition of twisted black steel and wire.

'Guadelupe, from one woman to another, let me get better,' Janine begged. She sneezed violently into her handkerchief. Snot on her fingers and nose, her forehead burning. The illness drawing into her being like water into parched soil. Her body opening up, swaying internally.

'You don't like us today because the poverty has gotten to you. It always happens like this to foreigners,' Hortensia whispered. She had a hand splayed across her flat chest like an old ballerina posing. 'Meet real Mexicans. Those women on their knees and that man in rags,' she insisted.

Meet real Mexicans. She turned away from the veined hand from a shop window, severed and attached to a chest, bleeding, vile; Jesus' hand at the crucifixion. Janine's mind hot with the cold afternoon and the rain pouring down soaking her; rain running into her shoes and through her whole being. Stumbling into a child stuffing a tortilla into its mouth. Meeting real Mexicans. For a moment she looked back, Lot's wife taking her last glimpse at the city of sin; the Basilica streaked with wet, a monstrous edifice as ugly as anything in the history of architecture. For another moment there was complete clarity: the silliness of her escape and the childishness of it. Running away from Mum and Dad and seeing it as if from very far away in time, at the beach house in Tongaporutu. Mum in her 1950s swim suit and Dad holding a beach ball above his head. Six years old? Seven? The camera and the inverted telescope. In her wet swim suit running along the beach and into the flax, hiding because something was wrong. For another flash she saw it all and what it meant and then she turned because again the torment of lucidity was too immense. The flax clapping, making that harmful sound. The waves crashing, swallowing her up and Mum calling from very far away: Janine! Janine! A procession of dancing Indians and rows and rows of masks and feathers and more masks of kings and queens and snakes and the sackcloth rubbing against her legs and body and like the waves and flax the tintinnabulation of drums and the hollowness of old wind instruments and that poignant hysteria of accordions.

'*Señora, un peso.*'

'*Hijo, mio, venga. Juan.*'

'*Somos cristianos, Señora por al amor de dios un peso.*'

'*Responsibilizite, niña. De rodillas para la Virgen.*'

'*Un peso, Señora. Por el amor de la Virgen de Guadelupe. Un peso.*'

The outstretched hand at her hem, tugging at her ankle.

'Never look back, girlie,' her father said. Her father's very strong hands grasping the beach ball. Grasping her. That hand at her ankle and moving into the cave. Miss Quested with the Indian doctor behind her. 'Don't tell your mother anything. You're Daddy's little girl.' His strong arms above his head and throwing the ball at her. Mum's eyes. Mum in her swim suit and looking at them oddly. The hand at her ankle and her dress being lifted. A vision as horrible as the one perceived by the woman who was turned to salt because she looked back.

The image staring back from the glass case in the wax museum just as it had at the pastry shop with the skulls. '*Emiliano Zapata,*' she read. '*Hero de la Revolución Mexicana.*' Her image distorted by his; black mustachios and an enormous sombrero. 'I'm going mad,' she said. 'To be this ill, to be thinking like this. Me. The strong woman.' She breathed in deeply but the air cut her lungs, rasped her, made her faint with pain and the lucidity that comes with drowning. She struggled to get out of the maze but she couldn't. This was the place with the hidden camera. Spying on herself through that inverted camera. Her father saying: 'Tell no one, you are my special little girlie'. It had come to this. Madness in a wax museum in Mexico City. She had glimpsed herself glimpsing her own vision. A group of school children had just piled in. There seemed to be hundreds of them shouting in Spanish. That deep breath had set off a chain reaction of pain and with each breath more pain until it was suffering she encountered.

'Cancer?' The question stunning her as if she were asking it of herself for the first time and not the thousandth over the past weeks of fatigue and illness. The word on her lips in the library as she stacked.

The word in her brain in the bus or in the shops or while playing with Monty.

'Overtired and stressed. You can see that from the state of your gums,' said the doctor in Wellington. The doctor peering at her, looking into her mouth with a torch. You lost weight with cancer. You got sores when you had cancer. You were susceptible to influenza. You got diarrhoea. You ran away seeking sun and Acapulco instead of going back to those bastards who poked you and told you that perhaps it was because you were stressed from being a single mother. You felt ill and angry and had silly thoughts about Miss Quested and you alienated your friends. Emiliano Zapata in the glass case in front of her. He had the waxy skin of someone who'd been dead for centuries and stuffed with some fluid and laid out in a glass case to demonstrate the inevitability of mortality. She was pressed up against him and her reflection by the schoolchildren pushing past. An elderly gentleman said something to her in broken English. His head nodding like one of those toys on a wire; nodding at her, nodding at his wife and then his hand on her shoulder, reaching out as if it were Zapata himself reaching through the glass and trying to grasp her. Her father taking her hand, moving it in his firm grasp to his erect penis and the flax clapping and the waves going swish swish swish and mother shouting from the bottom of the cliff: Janine! Janine!

'*Pancho Villa! Mira!*'

'*Si. Pancho Villa. Qué maravilloso.*'

'*Qué caracatura! Qué caracatura!*'

'*Zapata! Emiliano Zapata!!!*'

The shrieks in her ears and mind and tears streaming down her face and her lungs stabbing her.

'Señora, we help you.'

'Where is the one you coming with to Basilica, Señora?'

The elderly gentleman and his elderly wife. Boys and girls and a policeman, all wax figures in their glass cases looking down from a very far distance. The mother with a handkerchief looming down to mop her forehead. A long time ago. Something. The flax clapping at the beach and Daddy throwing the beach ball and then running very hard and the iron sand too hot on her heels and climbing far up the cliff and looking down at the waves and her father looking up at the cliff: Janine! Janine! Come back! Shivering on the dirty wooden floor of a decrepit wax museum in the suburbs of Mexico City. The images simultaneous: high on the cliff looking down; so clear, so lucid; Emiliano Zapata in his case looking down at her from a place of black flowers and grinning devils.

'*Una gringa.*'

'*Nueva Zealandia, mira, aqui está su pasaporte.*'

'*Necesitamos ambulancia.*'

'*El doctor, inmediatemente.*'

'It couldn't be cancer, darling. None in our family.'

'Señorita, drinking now water.'

'I saw them,' a girl said. 'With her friends, on the metro.'

The angel's eyebrows coming into focus, his face and the profile. The angel wiping her forehead with a tissue.

'I go,' the girl told Janine. The people crowding around where she was laid out on the filthy floor. 'I find your amigos. I know them on the metro.'

'Monty,' weakly. 'Monty.'

'*Pues, tienes hija? Hijo? Señora?*'

'*Ruega al Virgen... la Virgen.*'

'*Señora Virgen de Guadelupe.*'

'*Señora Virgen de Guadelupe.*'

*

'Double pneumonia. Very serious,' the doctor said.

They were all standing at her bedside.

'Pneumonia? Pneumonia?' Garth uttered.

'These red welts on her legs,' the doctor said in Spanish. 'It's a sarcoma. Kaposi's Sarcoma. I saw it recently in New York. It's associated with... I think we need to have a serious talk. Who is her next of kin amongst you?' He looked from one face to the next. He had that soft white skin of someone who appeared never to have surfaced above ground and the fluorescence made him appear even more ghastly.

8 Jesus, I'm a Maori

Neddy Bouzikis was sheltering in the basement of his East Beirut apartment block. 'Ace,' he said, throwing down a card. The man from apartment sixteen sighed heavily and pushed across the winnings. 'Even in war you make money,' he said. 'Even at the point of death.' He grimaced at his unpleasant joke. Neddy Bouzikis the rich man with the famous ZYX Delicatessen. But the smile was as forced as the nerve needed to concentrate on a card game in a basement on the third successive night of bombs blasting Christian East Beirut.

'Deal another round,' Neddy said. 'Hurry up, we could get blown to bits any minute.' He looked around the basement: candles and a single lantern left eerie shadows on the faces of the twenty or so people gathered there in an attempt to thwart death. Odette Raai with her hands to her face and her thick lips moving: 'God in Heaven, God in Heaven, God in Heaven.' Neddy didn't need to be a lip-reader to tell she was miming the language of fear.

'You all right, Odette?' Neddy asked.

'Of course,' she replied. She placed her hands in her lap and pretended not to hear the series of explosions. They were very close, to the west.

'St Pious of the Holy Sepulchre. St Thomas of little animals.' The man from apartment seven had a thin, waxen face and was known as the Morbid One. He knew the names of the saints and their particular sponsorship in the same way that other people had a knowledge of shops and what they specialised in: Moran's for haberdashery, Nadia's for spices, Mansoor's for orthopaedic footwear. 'St Christopher, patron saint of sickly mothers, St Veronique of fruit sellers, St Augustine of the Holy Shroud of Turin. St Francis, patron saint of those travelling on ships.' Over and over he beseeched his mistaken identities for a safe passage from this world to the next, using the same obsequious intonation as he had with the rich during his career as a stockbroker.

'Shut up,' Neddy shouted. 'Enough!' He stared at his neighbour. The shadows on the thin face gave him the appearance of a sinister rug merchant ostracised by the souk.

'Jack of diamonds...'

'He's right,' Odette said. 'You're driving us crazy, pray to yourself.'

A particularly loud explosion burst nearby. 'I can't stand it. I can't stand it,' Alex Zerihen cried. He threw down his ace of hearts by mistake, and when he went to pick it up, the man from apartment sixteen placed his hand on Alex's wrist.

'You played it.'

'I didn't mean to.'

'What card player says that? I win.'

'It's the bombs and that Morbid One moaning. I can't stand this another moment...'

'You played your card and I'm playing mine. Ace of diamonds. I win.' The man from number sixteen scraped his winnings towards him.

For a few moments those in the basement forgot the onslaught of death. You didn't argue with a man who held connections; not someone like Monsieur Pettit from number sixteen.

'You son of a bitch,' Alex said. 'You cheated. I saw you.'

'Gentlemen,' Odette pleaded. 'This is war, not a time for fighting over cards.'

'That's what the Lebanese are doing. Fighting over who wins a game.' It was the student who boarded with Odette. He had the pale face of someone who had known only classrooms and bomb shelters.

'Alex,' Neddy said, 'you played the card, so put up with the consequences.'

'I can't take any more of this shit,' Alex exploded. 'Say what you like about supplying people with their needs and not being rats leaving a sinking ship.' He was shuffling the cards furiously. 'You think we can endure this forever. Here in the middle of a civil war saying it'll be over and…'

'If this is the middle of the war, then we have another twelve years to wait for it to finish,' the Morbid One said.

'Christmas is coming,' Neddy said. 'They promised a truce for the new year.'

'Have you really got fresh quails eggs in at the ZYX?' Odette asked, holding up her head proudly. You didn't give in to fear and morbidity, not after twelve long years of civil war, not even when the bombardments were as severe as tonight's.

'Fresh from Bechare, sixteen dozen…' Alex replied. 'If the refrigeration…'

'Of course. I also want some fresh salami. Do you have any of that in stock?' It was an absurd question; they could hear the rounds of ammunition no more than two blocks from their basement hide-out.

'We have French salami. It lasts better without refrigeration,' Neddy said. His hands weren't steady, but he played his card nevertheless.

'I prefer Belgian,' Odette said. 'It's less salty, and my doctor told me not to eat too much salt on account of my heart.' She paused for a moment and the ludicrousness of it all melted her fear and she laughed. A heart attack. It was like that man who won the national lottery; on the morning he went to collect his prize, he was shot by a sniper and his cheque had to be returned to the bank for reissue to his wife because it was too blood stained to be cashed.

Nothing was normal. Odette looked at Neddy and Alex the two wealthy homosexuals who owned East Beirut's most famous delicatessen. There they were in full health and just like man and wife. Never a thought about God or Christianity, but still alive and still together while here she was a pious widow of forty, her three children and her husband dead in the Israeli attack five years ago.

'They can kill us all,' she sobbed.

'What about your salami and quail eggs, Odette?' Neddy said. 'I'll give you a dozen if...'

'If what?' she snivelled.

There wasn't any answer. The Morbid One was right. This was just the middle of a civil war already twelve years in the making. Another ten, another twenty? Trapped in a basement with a lot of smelly people who knew nothing but suffering.

'I think the bombs have stopped for the night,' Alex said, rubbing his jowls. He looked like a concentration-camp victim with just enough spark left to suggest he was alive. 'I want to go up to the apartment. I'm not staying another night here,' he said. 'Not four in a row, please, Neddy.'

'But, darling,' Odette said, 'the bombs haven't stopped. Stay here, it's too dangerous up there. Keep us company and be...'

'Be what?' Alex snapped. 'Brave? Keep up the good fight till the finish? Through thick and thin?' He laughed bitterly and threw his cards on the floor.

'If you were a true Lebanese...' Odette sobbed. She took a handkerchief from her pocket, blew her nose and again started weeping.

'Now, come on,' the student said. 'Enough.'

'St Abibus...'

'Shut up,' Neddy said. 'No more about your saints.'

'I'm going upstairs to my own bed.'

'Stay, Alex...' Neddy begged.

'Alex what? If I'd had my way we'd have got out of this place and gone with Michael and Anton to Cairo when the going was good, but just because of your Palestinian boys... Is that why you can't leave your precious Beirut? Zita was right. You're a patriot only because you like teenage Palestinians. A few pounds for an afternoon; two at one time. I know you, Neddy Bouikis.'

'All right,' Neddy said, 'you queen, you win.'

Together they crawled up the stairs in the dark. The lights were not working and they couldn't use candles for fear of attracting snipers.

'I feel so old,' Alex said. He took hold of Neddy and they kissed. 'I love you so much, Neddy. All those years in New Plymouth and now this. Whoever would have thought…'

Neddy looked at his lover, who was still beautiful though battered and suffering.

'… that we would end up here in war-torn Beirut still suffering.'

'But we had years of everything we needed and more, and each other. We decided to stay here, remember? It's our city.' Neddy said.

'This is the conversation people have every day, isn't it?'

'Ten times a day, whether rich or poor.'

'I'm too old for this, Neddy,' Alex said. 'Can't we go to Algiers?'

'Or New Zealand?' Neddy said.

'Never! Not after what they did to me.'

'Surely nothing as bad as this? We could have a house in the country and…'

'Two old poofters with silk cravats together in a place that hates queens. I should know, I was the one raped with a broomstick in prison.'

'I'll make some tea,' Neddy said. 'Go and lie on the bed and rest. I'll boil water for you to wash.' He went into the kitchen and fumbled for the matches to light the kerosene stove. Two old queers in Beirut, a city that had loved them and which they had loved in return. A house with a herb garden and roses and a fresh South Seas breeze was just a dream, remote enough to fantasise about during bad bombings. It was crazy, the two of them clinging to a business that sold quail eggs to rich Christians and Phalangist generals to feast on in order that they could forget their sins. Champagne by the crateful for the aristocracy.

Neddy turned to go to the bedroom to tell Alex that he was right, that they should go to Cairo or Tangiers as soon as the airport reopened. 'Alex,' he said. 'Come off the balcony, darling.'

His lover was silhouetted against the orange-red sky. It could have been one of the sunsets Beirut was famous for, the sort that required martinis on the balcony with friends. Alex turned. He might have been sharing the same pleasant memories, because he laughed and seemed about to say something. But he didn't get the chance. A sniper's bullet smashed his head, and by the time Neddy grabbed him he was dead.

*

Two months had passed since Alex had been cremated and his ashes stored in the Egyptian urn they'd bought in a Cairo bazaar while there on holiday.

A truce had been in place for three days, the first real peace for over a year, and people were out in the streets. Neddy took the long way to the Bank du Libnan in order to savour the freedom. At the Corniche it was odd to see that the Mediterranean was the same azure shining with a million sparkles.

'I am a Beiruti,' Neddy said. It was an old refrain that he and Alex had repeated proudly. He turned his back to the Mediterranean and studied his devastated city. The Paris of the Middle East. At the bank, an ornate building left intact by some miracle, he was frisked by a soldier before entering its cavernous realm of gloom and fallen plaster.

Neddy had come to clear out Aunty Zita and Uncle Bishara's deposit box in which they had kept valuables to protect them from the bombing. He picked up Zita's wedding ring, which she said she'd put in there because she didn't want the Palestinians to come in and rip it off her finger. A sheaf of letters, tied with string, caught his eye. On one faded blue envelope he recognised his mother's awkward attempt to write in English. The New Zealand stamp, a triangle with a picture of the young Princess Elizabeth, was postmarked the year of his birth. For a moment the smell of an old house, of a loved garden, even the sour odour of Dad's compost heap, seeped into his memory.

He opened the letter and began reading the squiggly Arabic script.

New Plymouth
Dearest darling Zita,

How happy I was to receive your letter from Bechare when I got to the post box this morning. Happier than happy because I too have happy news and you will know what I mean because you see darling after all that unhappiness about not having a child and what the doctor said and me and Jo never having a baby well listen. You see darling, we were in Whangamomona where we started the little haberdashery business and we were at this farm in the bush and one day, well, very happy to write this good news to you Zita my darling. And there was one house and me and Jo went up to it and knocked to sell the people some ribbons or a shirt or something because we bought a horse and a donkey and we go all over this province selling things because to have a shop is too expensive and with everyone so poor now no one's got the money to buy things in town and at this house there was one Maori girl, young darling, young, she came to the door with a baby, sweet, ye! Darling, sweet baby and the Maori girl was crying and all upset, the girl crying and one thing and another and she told me and Jo: this baby's from a Greek and when I saw you two come to the door I thought you were the grandparents and I see you coming up the driveway and I think you two coming to get the baby because he, the Greek, went back on the ship to Greece and now maybe you the grandparents come to get this baby. And her own parents they don't know anything about the baby because she's not married and it's all a secret. Darling Zita. She gave him to us. She didn't want her own baby and she's happy to give him, skinny and lovely baby just like a Lebanese, true, the Lebanese looking dark and white all the same in one. There and then she gave him to us like from God Blessed Jesus. Half Greek boy half Maori and he looks just like a Lebanese and we call him a New Zealand name Neddy...

✳

Neddy found himself out on the Corniche again, staring at the sea as he grappled with the images from half a century of deception. Beirut. Lebanese. His parents. A Greek sailor and a Maori. All mixed up in a melange. His mind reeled as if from the effects of a hallucinogenic drug.

'Jesus,' he muttered. 'I'm a Maori.'

9 Are you having a nice day?

In the Soviet Union in 1978 Garth Griffin discovered that you can actually fuck your way into a teenage fantasy. He walked down the wet Leningrad street and across the Nevsky Prospect where Raskolnikov had stopped to peer at the freezing waters in *Crime And Punishment*. Just to stand in the imagined footprints of his literary hero was the sort of thing that made Garth Griffin's life worthwhile. Garth had steered Alfonso away from visiting Dostoyevsky's apartment; there were things he didn't want to share. This was a moment for himself, one that didn't belong to the non literary Alfonso. 'I get your drift,' Alfonso had said. 'I'll go to the Soviet Academy of Architecture.' The path to Dostoyevsky's apartment was the path to the fulfillment of a fantasy and the route to the tragedy that he would obsess about many years later. But he knew nothing of that as he walked in the slushy snow to that place for which, as a boy in his bedroom in New Plymouth, he had dreamed so much of in his yearning for brilliance and freedom. Dostoyevsky's apartment building was tall and narrow and discoloured to that dingy yellow that old gilt picture frames turn to. He went up the wooden stairs to Dostoyevsky's abode with the memories of being a youth in New Plymouth. From that to this; that world of pimple creams and repression to this one of freedom and romance. The accomplishment of the mission exciting him as he paused on the landing and imagined Dostoyevsky returning home from a bad night gambling his royalties. On this landing three floors up the inventor of Raskolnikov would have paused for breath and looked at the door in front of him. Garth was just about to push open the door when three schoolgirls suddenly emerged and shoved him aside as if they were being pursued by the ghost of the old writer.

'You English?' Only the speaker's head appeared around the door; his icy eyes inspected the visitor with a tight precision; a flick-flick of the eyeballs, the movement like those of a lizard.

'Yes,' Garth said.

'Museum closed now,' the man said. 'Schoolgirls last visitors today, noon now you see.' The man was about thirty and had high cheek bones and skin that said he had lived all of his life in a wintry city without the luxury of trips to the Caspian or Black Sea for summers.

'But I'm going tomorrow. I must come in. Please.'

'Museum close at twelve o'clock.'

'Look,' Garth said. 'I'll give you this.' From his overcoat he pulled out his copy of the famous novel which he had brought to read on the trip in preparation for his pilgrimage, a faded copy of the Penguin edition of *Crime and Punishment*. The man came from behind his barricade and into the foyer and looked around him. It was that look in his eyes that Garth had begun to recognise after ten days in the Soviet Union. The eyes narrowed in the expectation that someone might catch you doing something you shouldn't do, like speaking to a foreigner or changing roubles to dollars. In his own culture that was the look people had when they threw rubbish in the street or took a newspaper from an honesty box without paying.

'For me?' the man said. His icy eyes melted and the blue changed to iris. 'Dusty, it looks dusty like a beautiful old edition. Penguin,' he said in appreciation. 'An old Penguin.' There was no one about. Dostoyevsky's apartment was obviously not a scintillating destination for tourists. Just then a door slammed in the foyer. The whole ambience was the perfect accompaniment to the expedition. For a second Garth had a glimpse of the disheveled Raskolnikov at the door of the old pawnbrokers as she attempted to shut the door on him. The hag with her watery, suspicious eyes judging his poverty as she stood half hidden by the door. Her eyes searching him, seeing the shape underneath his rags, feeling in her heart something was there, the axe under his wretched garment.

'I'm not going to murder you like Raskolnikov did the pawnbroker,' Garth said. The man's eyes moved from the proffered novel to the tourist and then he laughed with excitement: 'You know all about Dostoyevsky's characters,' he said.

'Of course I do. Why else would I come all the way out here to his apartment?'

'You're not English,' the man said. 'Your accent is something different.' His own English was near perfect but for a heavy drag in his glottal and a slight hiss in his sibilants.

'I'm from New Zealand.'

'Ah, why did you not state this immediately, then,' he said. 'We can be friends with this information. English bore me. Come in,' he said. 'I lock the door because we don't want the school girls intruding.' The vestibule was something immediately claustrophobic, as if by entering the great man's apartment you accepted the cloak of his novels' form and character.

'New Zealand,' the man said. 'Many beach and plenty of sunshine. You going to take me to it?' His eyes were the bluey purple of an iris and were made more remarkable by the gold eyelashes that flitted about them. His hair was the same gold, the colour of hay in hot weather harvests. The combination was both fabulous and repellent like something that had been assembled to be extraordinarily beautiful but rather straddled the cusp into weirdness. Inside the apartment with the door locked against the public his eyes took on another character.

'My name Dimitri, very common name, your name John or something usual too, my guess.'

'Garth. But sometimes I think I'm Raskolnikov.'

'Sometimes I think me too because of my madness. There's the kitchen. There's the book collection. Enough. We look later. You want to see Fyodor's bedroom? Most glorious room. From sleep come the dreams of writing.' They went through what was the living room, a small space cluttered with spindly chairs and a vile green sofa and vases from some indeterminate period. A spooky chandelier hung down from a cream ceiling; the whole effect was one of a hesitating elegance with whiffs of depression mixed in.

'The wallpaper's yellow,' Garth said. 'That's the colour which symbolises prostitution in Russia.'

'Ah, a scholar. Like red colour in your culture. Red light district, no? Here it is yellow. Look,' he said as they went into the tiny, dark bedroom.

'Dostoyevsky's bed,' Garth said.

'Dostoyevsky's bed. Very beautiful, no?'

From below hurdy-gurdy music started. That thick ancient sound, both melancholic and exciting, the most appropriate theme music. It came heavily up the walls from the outside of the building and seeped in as if was triggered the moment someone entered the author's bedroom.

'There are no spies in this place,' the man said with distinct meaning, its significance tantamount to an understanding of the Soviet Union and its paranoid political culture. 'There is no secret cameras like in the hotel bedrooms. You know we Russians do that?'

'I hope not in the bedrooms,' Garth said. Without intending to, he had said it prissily. Just the way the prissiness had come out so spontaneously made him realise he was in the presence of another homosexual. He would have erected a stronger guard if he had been with someone who wasn't a faggot. That innate knowledge. Giving himself away with a short sentence emphasizing campness. A warm feeling went running through him; in the presence of a homosexual in Dostoyevsky's bedroom. Their eyes met and locked. The Russian was enjoying the seduction; he was at ease, he had the assurance of someone who had had plenty of practice in this very situation.

'Why? You are not with your wife?' He raised his golden eyebrows in mock irony, but there was a certain ambiguity as if, at the very last moment, he were not sure he had made the correct gamble with this stranger. There was a string cordoning off the writer's bed and the Russian moved it so that they could enter the holy arena. He gesticulated that Garth should join him in feeling the mattress with his fingers, to poke it as if the comfort of the mattress were an important aspect of the writer's literature.

'I'm not with my wife,' Garth said. 'Are you married?'

It was a needless question but the game was all the more exciting for it. Seduction by words, like painting by numbers. You filled in the appropriate space with the required hue and bang, you got what you wanted by following the set procedure. The Russian merely scoffed at Garth's question. The colouring exercise was almost completed. The two men looked at each other, one on each side of Dostoyevsky's bed while the hurdy-gurdy music sent its mixed message of sadness and excitement throughout the apartment.

'You want to see Dostoyevsky in the nude?' the man asked.

'He's here, is he?'

'Take off your jacket, shirt, trouser,' the man said. The complete whiteness of his face had been transfused by a flush that rose to a pinky hue and merged in the shadow of the golden fringe which fell low over his forehead. 'This is not Chekov, all crazy words which mean nothing. Real words which mean something bigger, like what Dostoyevsky said.'

Chekov and Dostoyevsky being discussed with a handsome Russian in Dostoyevsky's bedroom; it was a fantasy, a moment so enormous that Garth felt his erection subsiding. It was a situation which had never before occurred in any form as fabulous as this and the fantastic, the amazing nature of it, chilled him. There were few events in life which amounted to the truly amazing, the fabulous, despite the use of those words to describe the mundane events of ordinary living such as a day at the zoo or a fun dinner party.

'You first,' Garth said.

'Precisely.' The Russian undid his trousers and took of his shirt and threw it theatrically over the bedpost. His body was taut, like that of a ballet dancer's; his nipples stood out and through his underpants Garth saw the enormous erection. This was life, this was how it was meant to be daily: adventure, beauty, passion.

'Dostoyevsky was a Christian conservative,' Dimitri said. He slipped off his underpants and stood there holding his giant penis. It didn't seem real, like a commercial dildo manufactured for the sadists' market. Garth decided not to comment; he threw his clothes on the floor and sort of half crouched on his knees on Dostoyevsky's bed in a position which suggested he was about to worship something. 'Which is why we should fuck in his bed,' Garth said.

'For so many reasons we should have sex in his bed, but the number one is you are so exquisiteful,' said the Russian.

'Exquisiteful.'

'Exquisiteful.'

What was real and what wasn't? The moment was one of fantasy and reality all mixed up in one of those brilliant episodes that compensate for all those moments that defeat you. The Russian must have been refused the right of penetration on so many occasions that he pre-empted such a refusal from this sex partner by offering a solution: 'Just the head, see it's not so wide as the how do you say in English? The base, stem… stick of the penis?'

'Shaft,' said Garth as he realised that fluency in a language comes only through multiple experience and practice in appropriate situations. They kissed for a long time: it was the passion of two men enjoying themselves for minutes which were hours; sex when it is seamless. He fucked the Russian from behind, holding the famous writer's bed posts as he did so. Amazing. Fabulous. He wanted to be there forever, to never leave and return to the mundane, the inanity. Until the Russian insisted on fucking Garth; then the pain set in. Squatting over the enormous prick and trying to get it in his arsehole.

The cusp between weirdness and beauty and between fun and seriously stupid: 'Ah, keep it there just the head in…now…now…like you are being fucked by your famous author,' Dimitri said as he ejaculated into Garth Griffin.

'I never would have thought, in a million years,' Garth said, when the fuck was over. He lay back with his head resting on Dimitri's chest. 'In my life there have been a few coincidences, a few things strange and wonderful, but to think that…' He heard himself being gushy and sentimental, but the feeling was one of both disbelieving bliss and a searing pain in his backside.

'Me too,' Dimitri said. 'I fucked with many men here sorry to say you not the first.'

'Just don't tell Dostoyevsky.'

'Americans, too. I like that one because they are the enemy. The capitalist and they really know how to fuck. Like you.'

'It comes from freedom.'

'You don't like Communism, eh?'

'Yeah, before I came to Russia, but this is too creepy. I had enough of repression as a kid being queer. I can't stand all this stuff about spies and cameras.'

'Prison for queers here, too. So we all do things to make us better. I sex with men from all over. One question.'

'What?'

'Why so many queers they love Dostoyevsky?'

'I didn't think they did? What makes you think that?'

'I am loved by so many. Blonde. Blue eyes. Dimitri Dostoyevsky, great, great, great nephew of Fyodor Dostoyevsky at your service.'

*

The lobby in Alfonso and Garth's apartment house had been re-decorated during the Porfirian era of the early twentieth century in that bourgeois Mexican preoccupation with all things French.

Architectural pretentiousness was smeared and dangled throughout the interior to allow middle class people to think that, really, they belonged to the aristocracy; the chandeliers, the ersatz candelabra on the balustraded banisters, and the marble walls and floors were the inhabitants' symbols of place and achievement. What was piss elegant in the 1900s had turned into a decadent, slightly sleazy ambiance by the 1980s, but still with upper class pretensions of grandiosity. Alfonso had bought the apartment with a legacy from his grand parents for precisely that *fin de siècle* aesthetic of decadence and pseudo-elegance just before he'd met Garth. It was in this lobby of such class delusions that several inhabitants of that architecturally notable apartment house had gathered.

'You see,' Señor Beauchamp insisted, 'we have them living here, here, here in our edifice.' He looked at the others, from one face to the next, as if he expected them to flee in horror at the very thought of Aids in their midst. Señor Beauchamp's face was as pretentious as the decorations which surrounded him. He still wore wide silk ties from the 1960s, the era of his hey-day, when he'd amassed his money by selling fake shares for casinos on the French Riviera. His ties, like his mentality, were gaudy and linked to that golden era in which he'd suffered no recriminations for involvement in a scam so preposterous that he'd had to flee France forever. He wore his Frenchness in pseudo-elegance and pomposity and stirred in machismo to produce what he thought was a person of distinction and culture. In his lurid mind the elegance that surrounded them meant continuity and wealth and order, all those superficial attributes of the decadent Porfirian era that the Mexican Revolution had exposed as being indefensible and had attempted to obliterate in a decade of extraordinary violence.

'Well, apparently and astonishingly...' Lucidia Zamora said pausing dramatically with her withered hand over her withered breast. She expected Garth to appear at any minute through the swing doors from the Avenida Gallegos for he often returned from the University about this hour. She seemed to be counting the seconds, one, two, three, four, five in the hope that he would appear before she continued so that he might guess from their looks and innuendo that they were discussing him and his homosexual partner. She wanted him to arrive in his linen suit, his long dark hair swept back off his face, one which she always thought of as looking louche and jaded, so that she could tell him to his face that they didn't need his kind in this respectable building.

'Well,' she continued, referring to Garth. 'Apparently, that one, the foreigner, he was married.' She had always referred to him deferentially as Doctor Griffin. Seven years as Doctor to be now reviled as the foreigner, un-Mexican, a nobody, nothing but a disease carrier. 'Yes,' she exhorted. 'A queer who married.' She turned to the others, from one face to the next, as if that appellation were the moral equivalent to someone who'd spat at the Mexican flag or raped and mutilated her daughter. 'And she... she...' Lucidia Zamora had been married to a famous art critic who had died while performing a solo piece on the stage at the fabulous Casa de Opera. It had been his one and only professional presentation, but it was this artistic legacy to her that she was able bask in; death on the stage, and at a location no less salubrious and fortuitous for his reputation than the Casa de Opera, the most glorious edifice of culture in the Republic. She had aspired to and had attained the theatricality of someone famous, of someone who would live in this sort of apartment house, who would put her hand on her chest when she spoke in confidences to her friends and neighbours. It was what had endeared her to Garth and Alfonso, the campness, the drama, the theatrical demeanor. And it was in such confidence, in a mood of gin-induced hilarity, that one day, years before, over drinks in her apartment, Garth had mentioned that he had been 'sort of married to a New Zealander who had had his child.'

'And then of course he had given her that homosexual disease,' she whispered. As a group they peered up, the collective eyes amongst the marble and ersatz interior, as if they would be able to see inside the homosexuals' apartment, as if the spirit of Janine still hovered there listening to the terrible saga that had overtaken her and her son and now her queer husband. Disease seemed to linger above them, that group of aged pseudo-aristocrats in the dingy interior, disease descending in aerial spores from the homosexuals' apartment.

'It is my contention,' said Señor Beauchamp, 'that we cannot have these... these... things here any longer. Think of the scandal. Think of how they are spreading...' It was a word too vile to be enunciated. The media was full of it; the disease from homosexuals and Haitians. Mexico imperiled, the United States filled with the contagion, and the terrible truth that it was now being spread by mosquitoes. One newspaper report suggested that very morning that within five years, by the end of the eighties, there would be few people in Mexico without this infection. Señor Beauchamp had been in communication with his priest that morning, a telephone conversation as he drank his coffee in number eighty, immediately under *the* apartment. The priest intoning about what was right and wrong; the priest in full agreement at how the dilemma should be handled.

Spreading. Mosquitoes. The group listening to the deliberations about self-preservation and justice. Alberto Santisteban, thin, frail, with that hunched look of an aging academic, but dressed in a suit which signaled his preoccupation to be forever youthful, attempted an objective look at the situation. His mind fluttered over the debits and credits of the situation, a task inspired by an academic training as an art historian. He stuttered as he tried to wring meaning and reality from the situation for his less educated neighbours.

'I think,' he said, 'that we need to remember that the media is not always correct, and that this news about mosquitoes could be sensational.'

'But of course it's sensational,' Lucidia Zamora interrupted. 'Sensational. That's why we're upset. Isn't it sensational when an infected mosquito bites you? Or perhaps you have no blood, no hot Mexican blood to defend yourself with against these homosexuals.' Everyone looked at him. The inference and insinuation from her words and voice had them all straining for what she might next burst forth with: homosexuals, no real Mexican blood, not a real man. Santisteban the bachelor, no woman, alone in his apartment with his collection of marble busts and alabaster males.

'Spreading,' Señor Beauchamp said. 'It's spreading from such deviants, and I for one must sleep with my windows open to get fresh air but they live right above me and so the fear of contagion is... is...' The neighbours' eyes bored into him, fixated by truth and terror. Old Señorita Zfaz shook as she began her slow understanding that that nice man, that handsome foreigner, that doctor was in fact... in fact... she could barely imagine that such preposterous goings on could occur within the world let alone her apartment house. She spluttered and wiped her mascara and spread the awful green down her cheek as she realized what horror was occurring.

'Spreading by mosquitoes, by air, by breathing,' Senor Beauchamp insisted at his audience. They had all taken a step closer together so that their circle was now huddled, intense, as if they had gathered specifically to peer at something on Señor Beauchamp's face, to witness on him the effects of having been bitten by an Aids-spreading insect.

'And furthermore, I mean surely you all know this,' Lucidia Zamora said proudly in the knowledge that they didn't know at all. When she uttered these words they all strained towards her as if it were now her turn to be inspected for insidious effects of airborne insects. She looked at them with a mixture of paternalism and contempt for their ignorance at not knowing what horror she now had the honour of imparting: 'The foreigner's child died from Aids. And yet... But the Mexican one, that Alfonso de Reyes. His mother is a nothing yet she thinks she is from one of the oldest families. She'll tell you she's actually a Gorgonzaza but really, honestly, if the truth be known, she was a nothing until she grabbed that de Reyes for a husband. She was not a Gorgonzaza anymore than I was a baboon or a Rothschild.' She had a trump card and she knew how to play it with her neighbours. She paused with it and searched the faces. From her little purse she took her little handkerchief, licked it, and passed it to

Señorita Zfaz and said: 'Wipe your mascara, darling.' Several sirens screamed in the street outside. 'Well,' Señor Beauchamp said, almost beside himself with the mixture of intrigue and suspense. No one even looked at the direction of the sirens; all danger was firmly lodged within the walls of their apartment house. 'Alfonso,' she said when the screech of the sirens had abated. 'Alfonso. We haven't seen him for weeks, have we? Well, my dears. The lottery woman has seen him. She saw him leaving in a taxi from where she sells her tickets just outside. He's very, very sick, the lottery woman told me. Very, very sick indeed. Weak to the point of having to be supported.'

Alberto Santisteban had always wondered what his reaction would have been had he been alive during the Mexican Revolution. To support the oppressed majority who demanded social and economic liberation from the arch-conservative oligarchy of Porfirianism? Or to side with the reactionary forces and thus preserve intact his own privileged position as a member of the upper middle classes? It was a little game he played with himself in his apartment when surrounded by his books on architecture and Mexican history. This was his chance at last to voice a real life decision and not a fantastical one like those he had toyed with about the Revolution.

'It is their apartment. We can die in the street from a bus or a mugger. We should be neutral,' he said. 'Mosquitoes have been disproved. This mosquitoes link is a fabrication by ill-informed opinion.'

'Oh, my dear,' Lucidia Zamora said. She looked at the others – they had been joined for their informal meeting by the Bravos, that very wealthy El Salvadoran family in number ninety seven. Lucidia Zamora searching from one face to the other with her pencilled left eyebrow raised as if she were acting the lead role in *Norma*, an opera she sang to alone in her apartment with the mimicking of a truly disappointed artist. 'Oh, my dear. As an academic you will think like that, but as humans with our minds very much in the living, we do not feel that we can take such chances. Do you not look to see if the bus is coming, or if you go out at night, do you not take a taxi to avoid the muggers?'

✳

Alberto Santisteban drew in on his cigarette with that intense satisfaction of someone who controls himself to one or two cigarettes a
day. Garth, who never smoked inside because Alfonso hated it, stood
on the balcony where he blew the smoke into the polluted atmosphere of the vast city spread out beyond him. The city was indeed
grey; the buildings were half absent in the mist of industrial grit, the
fumes from three million automobiles and the aerial remains of dried
human and animal effluent.

'So much trouble with smoke, in this city,' Garth said. He still
didn't know why Santisteban had come to their apartment. He had
been in there on only two occasions previously, once to a drinks party
Alfonso had organised, and once to ask Garth to take some lecture
notes to the University when he himself was ill. Santisteban moved
uneasily on the sofa, he was a thin man with an immaculate coiffure,
the sort that looked as if each hair had been individually arranged
with tweezers. From the bedroom he heard the high wheeze of
Alfonso coughing but he didn't look in the direction of what was the
sound of a sick person. He remained uneasily poised, as would have a
wealthy society girl trained in the arts of social deportment.

'Alfonso isn't well I hear,' he said.

'No, he isn't.' Below, there was a sudden lull in the traffic. Garth
wanted to say something sympathetic, or to actually blurt out the truth
of the matter, but he saw in a moment of ironic and bitter clarity that
such a disclosure was like telling people you were gay. The traffic
moved *en masse* from the lights below them and the street was again
filled with noise. It was better sometimes just to shut your mouth and
live with your secrets in silence. It was called expedience, a useful social
device that Garth had learned to apply. Especially to a hypocrite. Garth
looked at the man; hypocrisy was evident in everything: the faggy fea-
tures which tried so hard to pretend they were straight, the prissy smile
of a man who lived the indulgent life of an aesthete.

'Is there anything I can do?' Santisteban said. It was an odd question for one who had always seemed so detached from the social links one might have expected from a fellow homosexual and colleague. Garth looked at his annoying neighbour; the fruit salad plant immediately to the left of the pallid man appeared, from where Garth stood, to be actually a part of Santisteban's adornment, the spindly, pollution spotted leaves, a weird tiara set on, or rather emerging from, his tweezers coiffured hairdo.

'No, there isn't, thank you,' Garth said.

'Illness is a terrible thing. So many people have it.' Santisteban said in a sweet voice infected with an affectation of true sincerity. 'My father was always ill when I was growing up and it marked me indelibly, so that I have a certain understanding for those affected.'

'Alfonso's parents are marvelous.' Garth gesticulated vaguely, his movements uneasy in front of this limp homosexual who had never had the courage to even insinuate he was one, let alone to say it. 'They take turns to help me and of course we have employed someone, Jaime, an El Salvadoran man, a nurse who...'

'The El Salvadorans in the building. Do you know them?'

'The Bravos.'

'Precisely.'

'Why do you ask?' Garth said. A bleat of fear passed through him.

'Well, there are certain things he knows about.'

So this was it. That sinister Emilio Bravos and his equally sinister family. Garth had seen them in the lobby, the four children, the parents, in a file going through the doors into the Avenida like ugly ducklings wobbling after each other. It was amazing to watch rich people, the oligarchy who were responsible for the misery of others. How close you could get to them. You could reach out and touch their clothes, or smile at them as they passed in the lobby. But they were members of another galaxy, an unfathomable horror, Central American caricatures of their own absurd existence. Garth always thought of them as if he were the refugee begging, wanting to touch their hems and, in such a miraculous moment, change them into poor people seeking justice against the very sort of people who they themselves - military, powerful, murderous – represented. Garth shook his head to dispel the ridiculous fantasy. The refugee was not himself but them. He had seen their world, this one of the rich Central Americans, he knew it from repeated visits to El Salvador where he had gone on various assignments for the International Human Rights Commission.

'There are some times I wish I didn't live in this building,' he said. 'With the likes of them. This building is not for people who... who...' Irony again infected his thinking. This smart apartment house, for all he and Alfonso laughed about its *fin de siècle* decadence and piss elegance, still represented the mentality of the Bravos family. Wealth and power. In a bizarre and sadly ironic twist of his own hypocrisy, he saw that he too was powerful, that he too had made it to the top category in Mexico City; an apartment in the bosom of the affluent.

'They are very strong Catholics,' the crouched Santisteban said. 'Didn't you link the name? Archbishop Bravos y Durrera.'

'Of course. Of course. Is that what you've come to tell me?'

'That there is, how do you say it in English, monkey business? Monkey business about politics. You are known for your political work and brave work too, but...' He stubbed out his cigarette. In his nervousness, he reached for the packet again and pulled out another. But something happened. It was as if he had a quick glimpse of an X-ray showing his diseased lungs, or a vision of a cancerous tongue. He replaced the cigarette and shut the packet.

'There are some weird people in this apartment house,' Garth said as his eyes met those of his eccentric neighbour. Again the brittle cough from the bedroom but he didn't take his eyes from Santisteban. His dislike for him increased suddenly, an acceleration and a deepening of that sour feeling he had for any closeted homosexual. There was something cynical, dried up in Santisteban, a soul that had no energy but for the gratification of its own perfidious little expectations. An effete little man from the lower aristocracy who might have been better served in this city in an earlier century. It was just as Garth had that thought that the corollary struck him; everyone in this apartment house appeared to be living in another age and that was both the charm and the danger of it.

'My involvement with El Salvadoran refugees?' Garth said. 'Is that what this is about?'

'No, not exactly.' Again Santisteban reached for his cigarettes but again his fingers played there nervously as if the event of lung disease would be utterly immediate. 'It's lifestyles, as they say in the United States.' He put down the cigarette packet.

'So,' Garth said. 'There is a witch hunt against... um... um... Let me guess... communists?' He wasn't sure if it were irony or anger or ennui that infected him so swiftly but sarcasm was what he emitted. He pulled a cigarette from his own packet, went over to Santisteban and handed it to him. 'Smoke it,' he demanded. 'Set yourself free from frustration.'

'Not a fear of communists. Oh no. Not a fear of communists,' Santisteban insisted. 'Mexico is free of that political preoccupation. Our Revolution enshrined much that is leftist and so...'

'Shut up Alberto, and tell me what you came to discuss,' Garth said. Sarcasm was replaced by bitterness. He stood above the little man then bent and lit his cigarette. As he did he had the idea that this was a play, the dialogue from Chekov, but even more bitter, more stilted and very poorly acted. He had an impulse to squash out his own cigarette on the balding head beneath him.

'Well, I want to warn you. It's...'

'Oh, say the fucking word, you are one yourself.'

'Homosexuals,' Alberto Santisteban said in a voice which could have been emitted from a child's toy, the sort you must stand on end so that the voice mechanism is activated: peep peep, dolly, peep, peep dolly. The silliness of its unreality and uselessness in a plastic gismo with which to fleetingly amuse little children. Garth had wanted to see the man squirm, this effete person who would no sooner be open

and truthful with one of his own kind than he would with the brother of the right wing Archbishop Bravos y Durrera. And now that
Garth got what he had wished for he smiled.

'Queers,' Garth said. 'That's what you've come to warn me about,
isn't it?'

'Well, sort of,' Santisteban confessed. He took his packet of cigarettes in a gesture to hide his nervousness and he waved them as if to
loosen the compacted contents, but instead they fell out all over the
floor in front of him.

'Are you afraid of what people are saying about you?' Garth asked.

'Me? Why me?' he said. To cover his embarrassment he stared at the
ceiling and the thought occurred to him that the ceiling designs were
the exact replicas of those in the Musee de Paris. He was so taken aback
by this fact that he forgot about Bishops and homosexuals. A wave of
jealously went through him, and he looked from the ceiling to Garth
then back to the ceiling with disgust spreading from his eyes to his lips.
The ceilings in his apartment must have been renovated and these fabulous details done away with. It was an architectural nightmare, one he
had never before imagined in all of his years in his habitation. Imagine.
These ceilings so fabulous, so historic and those in his apartment merely ersatz renditions of another style more in touch with the 1950s. It
was preposterous; he sucked his cigarette and studied the details and
only when Garth barked at him did he look back at his neighbour who
again reminded him of the reason for his visit.

'Well,' Santisteban said eventually, 'there are homosexuals in all
societies.' He could see the conspirators at the bottom of the banisters:
Zamora and Zfaz and Beauchamp muttering and sneaking glances
about them. Searching with their eyes for infected mosquitoes. They
did know about him. He could see their claws. He wanted to get up
and go to Garth and say exactly what had happened and what course
of action was possible to avoid it; but from somewhere very distant a
huge shadow floated back to absorb him.

'Homosexuality is legal in Mexico,' Garth said. 'This is not a tin pot village the queer gets hounded out of…' He felt bored and wanted the man to go. Having to explain himself at this stage of his life, having to seek rationalisations for his existence. It was boring. It was again like being in his mother's kitchen. It was like talking to Cynthia.

'I must…' Garth said looking at his watch. Alfonso needed some soup and would be wondering what was happening. He looked nervously at the bedroom door at the end of the passageway. He saw in his mind the emaciated man with the sunken eyes and the skeletal figure, his lover.

'Oh, sexual inclinations may not be the problem… Well, the link is and that seems to be what is upsetting your neighbours. I just wanted to… to warn you.'

'Warn?' What?' Garth went to the window and looked down at the street in order to avoid the grey eyes and the grey demeanor of the seated homosexual. The lottery woman was talking to the water melon vendor and three curs were sniffing each others arses. There were moments that grabbed you and flooded you with what felt like molten toxins. That moment when the penny dropped and you saw everything for what it was, negative or positive. Just as one cur mounted the other and the third in the party sniffed the arse, the dog doing the fucking Garth saw it all for what it was; the world was inhabited by passive and active players but the roles were interchangeable depending on the moment and the way fate decided how the balance of power was to be enacted. There were no set procedures for ensuring safety and happiness anymore than there were for danger and sadness. The clock ticked on and at any moment there was the possibility that you could be tipped from one extreme to the other. His life had been like that: smart, handsome, loved, admired. The metamorphosis into a cosmopolitan man sure of himself in the world's largest city. A man working for both a university and for the International Human Rights Commission. A lover. Health. Everything. And then Aids. Death. The clock ticking him into oblivion and all those he had loved and supported. Negative. Positive. Even the language that bespoke of binary fates was the language that described the medical condition that had fated him and Alfonso, the same conditions that had killed Janine and his child. It would be his turn at any moment.

'Garth Griffin, you're a homosexual. Mrs Armstrong said so.'

'Garth, the doctors say its Aids.'

'Monty's got it. Monty's got the virus.'

'Your mother died and left a letter which says she disowns you.'

'Garth, your results show you are HIV positive.'

'Monty died this morning.'

The lines which pilloried you to a future that the past had never entertained. Santisteban was about to deliver another blow and as he did Garth saw it all, life, for what it was: a silly quivering game involving enormous hurt and enormous consequences.

'Your neighbours want to have you evicted under the Contagious Diseases Act,' Santisteban blurted.

'What?' Garth said. The lugubrious reverie about the fuck up of life dissipated and he turned his eyes from the street to Santisteban who, at that very crucial moment, was picking up his cigarettes which were still tumbled about him.

'My neighbours? The Contagious Diseases Act?' Strength through struggle. That old maxim he had learned way back in New Plymouth whilst reading *Crime And Punishment*. It had struck him then as being the only way to get by, and he had incorporated its tenets into his life ever since. He didn't think of it consciously as he moved from the balcony to the wall immediately behind the effete man now sitting with his legs crossed in the Italian armchair, but it was what underlay his current action. On the wall were rows of masks which Garth and Alfonso had collected over the years in their travels throughout Mexico. Devils, ogres, caricatures of Hispanic lords and nobles, frogs and demons, faces from the opera, faces from the Aztecs. He reached up and took hold of a mask and dislodged it from its nail. Santisteban twisted in his seat and watched. The mask Garth held aloft, as he would have a trophy, was of a woman, or it could have been a man, but whatever its ambiguous sex, it spoke of malice and cowardice and cynicism. Its left eyebrow was raised on its powdered countenance in high camp affectation of drama and ugliness.

'Here,' Garth said handing the mask to Santisteban. 'Wear this when you tell your neighbours that homosexuals are not going to buckle under Nazis.'

*

Three weeks later Garth Griffin stood outside the tenement building where his friends Victor and Margarita Izos lived with their five children. The day was close and the pollution particularly heavy over the city. A shroud so grey and yellow that the thought that a bolt of lightning had actually found its way through and selected Victor Izos from the twenty million other people in this megalopolis added to the madness of what Garth felt inside of him. Crazy. Mad. How did a bolt of lightning come from the sky and zap a man who had been merely collecting bottles in order to feed his family?

A man emerged from the dark entrance of the dirty building, he might have been a priest for he had that look of old fashioned piety that came from being dressed in a clean combination of gabardine and acrylic. For a moment he looked around him as if he were afraid of spies or private detectives, the odd searching movement of a paranoid or an agoraphobic. Garth didn't want to go inside that entrance, a cave to his own insecurities and sadness. A black mouth to be absorbed in; up the stairs and into the hovel that the Izos' called home on account of being destitute El Salvadoran refugees. The man was a priest. Garth could tell. The clothes, the weariness. It was hard to tell in Mexico because priests and nuns were forbidden by law to wear a habit publicly but this man had somehow achieved a secular version.

'Excuse me, have you been to see Margarita Izos?' Garth asked.

'Yes. Are you a friend?' A foreigner and a well dressed one. The priest looked Garth up and down. 'You're from the Association of

Concerned Citizens on El Salvador, aren't you?' the priest said.

'I am. Do you know me?'

'I heard you speak a few weeks ago after you got back from El Salvador.' He had a harsh voice. It could have been from the fact that he was a chainsmoker because he lit another cigarette. 'And now he's been struck by lightning.'

'It's unbelievable. I don't get it. Out of twenty million people it was Victor. I was walking home yesterday, why wasn't it me who got struck?'

'You probably had the money to go into a café until the storm ended. Victor had to hide under a tree.'

'Is that what god would say?' Garth asked. 'That it's economics?'

'There is no god, so he couldn't say anything,' the priest said. 'Marx would say that it's economic. You know that. I must go. I have a whole archdiocese to look after.' He smiled and he meant it and he inclined his head towards the Izos' apartment and grimaced: 'Sad,' he said. 'Tragic. Your speech the other day was excellent. Goodbye.' He went off with quick little steps across the dirty plaza and Garth laughed at the funniness. The priest was like a toy wound up and walking. He imagined him in a confessional dispensing no nonsense penance to old ladies with sins that were no more than little social infractions such as saying they'd liked someone's curtains when in fact they hadn't. Penance. Forgiveness. Absolution. The Catholic in him, those rotted roots deep in his psyche, itched for a moment as he watched the priest disappear into a cantina. The bizarre, the tragic; the hegemony of these infractions against the smooth life of a normal existence: the madness all seemed to have increased with the disease; life had changed so irrevocably since its onslaught that normality had forever changed around him. A godless priest blessing himself; a refugee struck by lightning. A lover with Aids. The disease no doubt bursting in him. Garth was at the point of blessing himself in a god-less benediction, but the old maxim about strength returned; you didn't get strength from the silliness of belief in an abstraction that dumped on homosexuals. He laughed again because just then the priest emerged from the cantina with two peasants on either side of him and together the three of them wandered off across the plaza: the drunks, the priest, absolution and forgiveness. A little infusion of something beautiful ran through him. He saw love and strength and goodness going across the plaza and that was a sufficient satisfaction. 'Alfonso. Darling,' he said. 'You will survive death. You will inherit goodness. Monty, I will always adore you and beg your forgiveness.'

There was very little light in the interior of the building because of the washing strung on lines from balcony to balcony. What had once been an attractive water well, tiled in colonial designs, was now a stump of concrete with weeds growing over it. It was the region of the impoverished lower classes, a crowded dirty hovel of an ancient building, but one with the attraction of being in the city centre and not stuck out in the infinity of the dry, endless, city outskirts. On the landing of the second floor a dog that might have been dying bared its teeth at Garth. When its feeble threat of yellow fangs and arched ears didn't work it retreated for effect to pathos. Garth stopped and stared at the mange and the fleas and the desperation with all the pity of one who understands the mortally ill and the dying.

'I should go home,' he said. 'Alfonso, why are you doing this to us?' The hurt which until recently had gone rushing through him as if from a sudden and violent attack felt merely sluggish this time. Too much had happened. The build up to the loss was too fraught from its expectation. It must have been from tiredness, the brain saying it could no longer exude further excitement or sentimentality because there was just too much effort to produce more of those particular stimuli.

Garth heard the weeping before he got to the open door of the Izos' two roomed flat. It could have been a child or an adult, the noise was so eerie that it defied analysis, but when he looked in he saw it was Margarita Izos. She was leaning over the coffin so that his first thought was that of the painting by Xavier Vargos where the distraught woman in the dark green shawl is herself half in the sarcophagus. The scene had all the poignancy of a medieval painting; the shadows and the poverty and the illness. He felt the tears rise as soon as he entered the dwelling and saw them all, the five Izos children and the mother. It really was the scene from... for a moment he couldn't think, his mind searched for it. He had a quick glimpse of his bedroom as a child in New Plymouth and then of the Dostoyevsky Museum in Leningrad and then the image came to him; it was an exact replica of that brilliant passage in *Crime And Punishment* where the distraught and consumptive Mrs Marmeladov is weeping over her daughter Sonia the prostitute in their impoverished room in imperial St Petersburg.

'They brought the body back an hour ago,' Pedro Izos said. 'From the morgue, but his body is burned.' He had dry eyes. The whole of him seemed dried up from worry and poverty. A youth of fifteen who should have been happy. He should have been kicking a football in a soccer field in his home city of San Salvador. A youth with a happy girlfriend and a happy constitution. Everything should have been pleasant and happy. It shouldn't have been like this.

'Should,' Garth thought. 'What a useless word.' He went to the widow and hugged Margarita but she couldn't speak through her anguish. Some neighbours came into the room, one of them carried six gladioli, their bright orange blossoms a dramatic but incongruous beauty in a room filled with such disbelief, poverty and sorrow.

'But how?' Margarita Izos asked. 'He was just collecting bottles. I've got five children under sixteen.'

It was all a sham, this persistent belief in happiness. It seemed ludicrous as he stood by the window looking down into the dirty narrow street where peasants wheeled barrows of corn husks and bright fruit. The only logical thing was the priest who didn't believe in god. It seemed like the logic of madness had one moral representative to act against it. Madness and ill health; the scene before him straight out of *Crime and Punishment*. Alfonso home in bed dying of Aids and bleeding black blood and shitting water in the ghastly process of leaving. Janine. Monty.

'It was wet yesterday,' Margarita said. 'I told him to take the umbrella but he always hated taking them. He said he looked like a queer, especially with that bright pink and yellow one. And I told him it was better to look like a queer than it was to get wet.' She shrugged with a movement that summed up all the despair of a newly widowed woman with five children. 'But he didn't listen and then he had to hide under a tree and of all the people who were sheltering in this city yesterday from the down pour it was my husband...' She looked at Garth as she might have a priest a few decades earlier when she still believed one was necessary and that such an entity could bring relief.

'A queer,' she said. The tears had come again and she hid her face. 'Because he didn't want to look like a homosexual.'

The street was now empty except for a midget walking along with packets of pink candy floss pinned to the long pole she was carrying. What the godless priest had said about Victor being killed by economic forces had struck a note, but the more plausible reason was that it was a death caused by fear. *I might be taken for a queer if I carry a yellow and pink umbrella.* Perhaps there was a god after all; perhaps god had said *you stupid prick for being such a coward* and the long finger of fate had pointed from the sky and eliminated Victor Izos for being so prejudiced.

'A god for the new age,' Garth thought. 'I certainly need one.'

The extraordinary thing was that nothing changed. You got stuck. The midget must have felt that very keenly when she was three and didn't grow up like the rest of the kids in her tenement. A tall man was fishing in his pocket for money to buy some candy floss and the short girl had to step on her tippy toes to pull off a packet. The themes that surrounded the events of his life, he thought watching her, didn't seem to change that much either. He was friends with this family and they didn't know that he was a homosexual precisely because he had never told them. He'd even insinuated that he had a girlfriend. In the closet after all that work to get out of it with his mother and New Plymouth. The hypocrisy when he chastised other homosexuals for being so hidden. Hiding still from the reality in a macho culture like the one inhabited by these Latins.

'I want you to come to the funeral,' Margarita Izos said. 'You've been so good to us. If it wasn't for you, we wouldn't have been able to come to Mexico.' For a second he thought she meant it spitefully but she didn't. She looked at him and a tiny smile infected by irony appeared through her grief like a peek of blue in the polluted sky above the city. The facts of their lives in El Salvador were such that Victor would have been selected for execution by the death squads long before he was struck by a bolt of lightning in Mexico City.

'It's just that I don't understand the madness of it,' he said. 'Lightning.'

The funeral would cost money and he knew that they had none. What money he had left in the bank was swiftly disappearing now that Alfonso wasn't working. A funeral was always expensive. 'Shit,' he thought. 'I can't be bothered collecting from the Salvadoran community. Not again.'

'I don't know what we'll do,' she said. She was actually wringing her hands. These were all the motions of complete grief, the very sort displayed by Mrs Marmeladov that most fabulous of dramatic characters in *Crime and Punishment*. As Margarita Izos put her hands to her face she looked at her eldest child, Hilda, a girl of sixteen. 'Hilda should be in school,' she said. 'Victor and I were both teachers, bourgeoisie, and now look at us, beggars. And Hilda.' Garth looked at the daughter he'd never known very well. It was like looking at the man at the bottom of the tenement, the one he could tell by instinct was a priest. In the same way, Garth could tell that Hilda had taken to the streets.

Sonia Marmeladov had been a prostitute in St Petersburg in the late nineteenth century, a victim of politics and repression and aristocratic greed. Denied what was hers by a system as foul as the one in operation in Latin America a century later. Garth saw it for what it was, a static world in which greed and irony were the main ingredients. He was about to say: 'I'll pay for the funeral. You can have half of what I've got,' when he thought: 'Fuck it. She doesn't like homosexuals and we could do with that money ourselves.'

Hilda got up, went to the coffin and lifted the lid to peer at her father for a few seconds. She had the same dried up face as her brother, the sort of skin you got when it was no longer well nourished. It was a syndrome of the middle classes who had been affected by poverty. Their skin, their faces seemed to take it worse that those who had always known the affliction of not having enough. From one face to the next, she looked at all of them. Then she picked up her jacket and left the tiny apartment.

'It's all a series of events,' Margarita Izos said. 'It started the day Victor yelled at the headmaster because he would no longer allow the children of subversives into the classrooms. I can see my husband now, arguing for the rights of the children, but look what happened to us. From that to this in Mexico City with my daughter supporting us with prostitution and my husband killed by lightning.'

It was then that he should have told her. He opened his mouth but it struck him just as he was about to insinuate something, that it was not only not the right moment, but that he was trying to pacify her about her daughter's sleazy occupation with reference to his sexuality, as if that were also something sleazy and disgusting.

'Yes,' he said. 'A series of events.' Garth's had started in Leningrad in 1978 in Dostoyevsky's apartment. He felt that, even if he didn't know it was the source of the infection. That great, great, great nephew. It had been a wonderful story at camp dinner parties for a couple of years: giant cock, being fucked on the great man's bed... But the humour had died along with the deaths of his friends and family. From that to this. Garth knew, he felt it instinctively, something deep and emotional and therefore valid, that it was from Dimitri Dostoyevsky that he had been infected and so had passed on the virus to his lover, Janine and Monty.

*

The effects of the visit to the Izos family in their tenement weighed on him as he walked down Avenida Juarez towards the metro station. 'I've known the Izos' for over a year and I've never mentioned Alfonso,' he thought. In the middle of the busy road a yellow taxi swerved to avoid an Indian blowing fire from his mouth and Garth stopped to watch the commonplace scene which to him, because of its brutality, had never become familiar. The man swigged more kerosene and with his cigarette lighter he lit the liquid as he spurt it from his mouth. City of devils. He saw the man as a victim in the same way as the godless priest had seen Victor Izos as a victim of arch capitalism. Devils. Black flowers.

'I should go home,' he thought. The Indian had exhausted himself from the effects of blowing kerosene and he hunched over as if about to collapse but another taxi honked at him and he jumped to avoid being hit. 'I really ought to,' Garth told himself. But sex was forgetfulness and he needed forgetfulness more than anything. The image of the nude Egyptian. Hamid in the bathhouse lying back on the bed in the cubicle with his arms behind his head and his hairy torso and erect nipples. The dilemma started in Garth's mind as he watched the skinny Indian weave his way through the traffic. Alfonso sick in the double bed being attended by his tired mother; the Egyptian smiling at him, his arse, the smell of him, sucking his penis. It was almost two o'clock, the time he always met Hamid on a Thursday at the Torres Bath House in Calle Obregon.

'No,' he said. The image of the ill man coughing and shitting himself and Hortensia reading to him or wiping his forehead with a wet cloth; that image disappeared because he forced it out. Too ugly, too commonplace, too disgusting. He could leave it for a few hours before the next round had to be fought. 'I'm sick of being Florence Nightingale,' he said and a woman standing next to him at the lights looked at him and smiled. The smell of the bath house with its ambiance of forgetfulness and pleasure was the only sweet sensation he could think of. As he got off the metro and entered Calle Obregon that familiar, excited rush assailed him. His step quickened towards the green and red and yellow building with the steam pipes emitting vapors into the tortured atmosphere; in just a minute he'd be inside that purdah where he could forget there was an outside world where he had to hide and be Garth Griffin the professional, the heterosexual in a macho society, the man who was stressed from the effects of the world around him, the nurse, the everything...

'Ah, señor,' the woman at the ticket counter said to him. 'Welcome, it must be Thursday afternoon.' She had said the same thing to him for over six years. Week in and week out the routine, one of delight, in that he could step in off the street and pay twenty pesos and get a fresh towel and go upstairs and get undressed and be surrounded by men just like him. At the telephone booth on the second floor he stopped and called Alfonso.

'I know,' he said. 'Yes, I'll be home in a couple of hours. Tell your mother to wait until I get back. I'm at the bath house for a bit of a relax. I'll bring you some fresh things for a salad.'

In the showers he began to revive. The steam and the heat and the men washing themselves all around him. The man under the shower next to him he knew from having been here almost every Thursday afternoon for six years and they exchanged greetings; a thin dark man with a huge cock which he exhibited as if it were his only point of reference.

'It's not sex I want, dear,' Garth said. 'It's company.'

'I'll give you that,' said the man.

'Well, put a condom on it, Jorge, you've got a wife and kids.'

'Yeah, no worries, I'm healthy, meat on meat's best. You still at the University?'

'I am. My usual Thursday here.'

'With that Turk. You two must be lovers after all this time.'

'Egyptian.' Talking broke the pact between that life out there and

the one you wanted in here which was about anonymity and forgetfulness. He wanted only the hot water to hit his back and neck and
release the tension of this life that had gone sour.

'I bet you fuck like a rattlesnake,' the man said.

'You still with the wife and kids?' he asked merely to be polite to
the man.

'Ah,' he said. 'Why bring that up when I'm here for my recre-
ation?'

'Exactly. But you need to put a condom on it.' It was the same pattern and he recognised it: Garth Griffin as social activist. Put a condom on it. Seek out Salvadoran refugees. Feel bad about the world and
try to better it by a few silly ineffectual actions.

'I can tell if someone's healthy,' the man said. 'Mexican men won't
get this disease because they eat good food and look after themselves.'

There was no answer. He thought *fuck you* to the man and turned
off the shower and went into the steam room and let his muscles rest
in the deep heat, the bliss of the room. Then he went to find Hamid.

'How's my Egyptian?' he said. He closed the cubicle door behind
him and they kissed, two old friends, lovers for years and years. They
had only divulged their names to each other after two years of meeting when they had finally formalised their Thursday assignation. They
had never phoned each other, had never met outside of the bath
house, a perfect arrangement of love and devotion to each other within the secrecy and romanticism of their bath house cubicle. If one of
them did not show on a Thursday, it was taken for granted that something unavoidable had come up to prevent them. It was the sort of
arrangement – passionate, devious, sophisticated – that Garth associated with French men and their mistresses. And above all it was sex,
glorious sex, with a man who never, never became boring or predictable when it came to love making.

'I need you today, Hamid, I really do.'

Hamid spoke perfect Spanish. He was the assistant secretary at the
Egyptian Embassy and was married with a wife and two sons.

'How is Alfonso?' he asked.

'Not well. He keeps vomiting black blood.'

But there was nothing left to tell. It had been said in a few sentences twelve months previously when Hamid had said: 'I had a test and it's positive.'

The cubicle was small, the sort of cubicle that belongs to any bath house in any part of the world. It could have been a sex room in Auckland, Baltimore or Cairo except that the music was definitely Mexican. The high screech of sentimentality that only mariachis could produce with their violas and violins wailed around, the words of love lost and love abandoned in the State of Chihuahua accompanying the two men's love making. They held each other, two friends in a small room with the sounds of other men outside laughing, shouting above the steam and the pipes fizzing. Garth loved Hamid, he told him, the words more beautiful, the meaning more poignant for being uttered in Spanish which was neither man's first language. The hair on Hamid's chest, the dark eyes saddened by the events they shared, the man's beautiful lips the colour of tinned raspberries. Hamid held his lover's head, stroked it, his fingers through the thick hair and rubbing Garth's stiff neck. He kissed Garth again and again and whispered in Arabic what Garth knew were the same words he had just whispered in Spanish.

'What will you do when he dies?' Hamid asked. It was a cold transition from love making to their reality. The sperm on Garth's stomach felt cold and clammy and its deliciousness of a few minutes previously was now poignant with its invisible and fatal qualities.

'Ask you to marry me,' he replied, wiping off the semen.

'Joking aside, my little one.'

'Who knows. Go to New Zealand and grow vegetables in the countryside?'

'I don't know what to do about Fawzia. It goes round and round in my mind but if she's positive... if I've infected her. We no longer have sex so...' He buried his face in Garth's neck and dry sobbed for several seconds. 'Being honest isn't possible. I don't know how to tell her to take a test. It's all wrong,' he said.

'No more right or wrong now than the last time you and I had this conversation.'

'How to be good? How to be responsible?'

'It's like the end of the world, isn't it?' Garth said. 'This disease has ruined our lives. It sounds inane, trite to say such a thing in the face of the enormity of it but everyone seems to be dying.'

'It's only a disease. It could have been typhoid or cancer. The reason why I don't tell her is because it's from being a homosexual, sex… and that's the stigma.'

'Fucking in a bath house with men?'

'Death is a bad moment that passes is what the Palestinians say about dying for the Intifada. Same with us. We all die.'

'Is that Islamic fatalism?'

'Must be.'

'My mother had many clichés to help get through life. She would have been very successful in dealing with Middle Eastern politics.'

'If Fawzia begins to get sick, there are ways out of the dilemma.'

'Like?'

'This is Mexico City. You can hire anyone to do anything and pay some money and, well, you know the situation. Who finds the person who killed her?'

It had come to this, but as nightmarish as it was, it didn't seem out of the ordinary, because what was anymore? A vegetable garden in New Zealand, a place by the beach in Tongaporutu; was that the answer? Garth kissed him on those lips he loved so much; sweet and full, that delicious colour. The stubble of a day's growth on his Arab's chin and cheeks. He got another erection and Hamid's cock got erect next to his. Sex and forgetfulness and love; that delicious, fabulous combination which was always a savior for Garth Griffin.

Garth took a taxi from the bath house. 'Calle Lugones, Colonia Mercado,' he said. The taxi driver looked at him through the rear vision mirror, a wealthy looking tourist going to one of the inner city slums wasn't a usual request. It was now late afternoon, the effects of the day's pollution pretending to be the crepuscular hues of the setting sun. Outside the Izos' tenement building Garth had to push his way through a crowd of Indians who were lined up waiting for something, their restlessness agitating the already overheated late afternoon.

'Margarita,' he said when she opened the door on the dark room. The coffin had been taken away, the room even emptier as if something that had always been there were now missing.

'Garth,' she said. She had no capacity for further speech. He noticed how her tongue stayed at her lips as if too swollen to retract back inside. Hilda sat in the dark corner with the youngest child on her lap. When he addressed her, she turned her face to the wall.

'Firstly,' he said. 'When is the funeral?'

'In three days. The priest has arranged it,' said Margarita.

'I will be having a funeral too sometime soon. We're old friends, Margarita, and I'd like you to come to it.' She put her hands to her face in a confusion of fear and disbelief. She looked about the room and then stuck her tounge in and out as if trying to find some wetness to lubricate it: 'For who?' she said.

'For my lover, Alfonso de Reyes. He has Aids and he's going to die within the next few weeks.'

'But...' she said. She took a step back into her dark room. 'I...' she said. 'You...' She blessed herself. Hilda laughed and said something which he didn't catch but when he looked at her she raised her left thumb in a salute of appreciation.

'I never told you about my being a homosexual, about Alfonso,' Garth said.

'But Victor's brother is a homosexual. The world is full of gays. Do you think we don't know about this thing, about what you are?' said Margarita.

Hilda laughed from her corner. 'Uncle Fernando is one of the biggest gays in San Salvador,' she said. 'He even wears yellow to mass.'

'We said nothing. It was never our business. You said nothing to us Garth... Garth...' Margarita said. 'Victor said many times: that boy is a *maricon* and if *maricones* are all that nice and that good, then we can all hope we have some children who are queers too, like him. Victor loved Fernando, it's just that he didn't want to look like one himself.' She smiled. Then she laughed. For a second the lines went away. She was again a happy woman. She might have been at a party with friends and family and listening to music and having a drink and sharing hilarity. Just for a few seconds. 'But he didn't want to carry a pink umbrella,' she said. She laughed louder; Hilda joined her. The two of them balancing their grief in well-deserved humour 'Ah, Victor... Victor. He would have been laughing his head off too if... pink umbrella... Latin men... Latin men are so ridiculous.'

'The other thing I have to do while I'm here is to give you this,' Garth said. He handed her an envelope. He knew he shouldn't be this generous because his finances were such that they needed to think about money, about the loss and expenses from Alfonso's illness. Margarita's laugh turned to joy. Her eyes showed the relief from poverty, from total destitution. A second of joy followed by several seconds of love as she looked at Garth and then hugged him. 'You will be blessed,' she said. 'You will be spared something ghastly.' For a few moments her eyes were those again those of a middle class woman freed from sheer terror. Then the eyes changing to gratitude. They said: I am from El Salvador; I have been reduced to this, without help, without a husband. Even her hands said it; she gestured with them to her surroundings, to her daughter the prostitute, to where the coffin had been standing. Then she began weeping.

It was a matter of selfish joy and he knew it as he went through the torpid streets of central Mexico City on his way back to his apartment. And the selfish glee of it made him laugh to himself. Happiness came bouncing out of him like a bubble up a bottle of still water; unexpected, alone, but a bubble of happiness nevertheless. Selflessness was the only way to redemption. It was a lesson he had learned as a Catholic and his selfish joy was the corollary of the purity of his action, an inevitable aspect of the human frailty which demanded payment. Give and you shall receive. The payment may be ambiguous. At the corner of Juarez and Isabella another emaciated Indian was performing his horrible show. A life in the middle of the road defying death from insane traffic and toxic tricks with flammable liquids: Garth laughed at the madness. 'Such a planet,' he said fishing in his pocket for a handful of pesos. 'What should I care if we go broke in the face of this fucking bitch arsehole of a pandemic?'

Why was it always on stairways that he had thoughts of who had infected him and to whom he in turn had passed on the virus? It was a useless question he knew, more of a nuisance after all the times it had been asked, like an unwanted refrain from a song which keeps returning, over and over, the annoying words banging their repetition; Dimitri Dostoyevsky infected me with it. Dostoyevsky in some hideous, ironic retribution. At the top of the stairs he had the urge to just turn back, go somewhere. For a few moments he stood with his head against the door thinking of where he could escape to, but there seemed nowhere. The pleasures of the bath house were mere incidentals to the expressions of nothingness and tiredness that had returned by the time he reached the top of the stairs. The images of rural bliss in New Zealand just abstractions infected by memories of rejection, of infection, of the city of the devils. That door had to be opened. He had to go in and tend to Alfonso.

'Mother left half an hour ago,' Alfonso said. 'Are you having a nice day?'

'Fabulous,' Garth said, laughing. 'And you?'

The bedroom looked beautiful. A puff of relief emerged with the recognition of beauty, the sheer joy of beauty from objects: the embroidered Porfirian curtains across the balcony windows and the soft light from an antique lamp bought in Seville. Successful, beautiful, young, attractive, intelligent, professional, affluent, exotic; there were a dozen adjectives he knew had been applied to them, that they had applied to themselves.

'I'm fine,' Alfonso said. 'But such a shame I didn't get struck by lightning.' Successful. Monty and Janine had died of a disease he had infected them with. Attractive. Alfonso's face bloated and shrunken at the same time. Affluent. No income from the architect for eighteen months and so much less since Garth had cut back on work in order to attend to Alfonso. Exotic. The neighbours complaining about having an Aids victim in their building.

'You don't want to think like that my love,' Garth said as he tidied the sheets and plumped the pillows. 'Kiss me,' he said.

'Why not think of it?' Alfonso asked avoiding Garth's lips. 'Because this doesn't end in death after another few months of shitting and vomiting and night sweats? I'm killing Mother, she's got old and unhappy and I can't stand seeing her like that, and you.'

'Old and unhappy? Thanks. I'll get you some soup and salad.'

'Wait, I don't want that.'

'Well, what do you want my lover boy? Anything. You name it.' He was thinking of pizza or cannelloni or tuna salad. Instead, Alfonso made a little noise, the sort a little animal might make when cornered; a whimper, a squeak, not so much from fear but resignation.

'I want you to help me commit suicide,' he said. 'It's that time. We agreed. And now I have decided.'

10 The end is the beginning

George Crossett adored his art deco flat, which he had acquired after quitting his father's old home and that increasingly tedious memorial garden. His abode, high up in the Devonport Flats, made him think of the big cities he'd never visited and the decadent lifestyle he'd never enjoyed. He looked at his watch and went busily down the passageway to the lounge.

'I shouldn't worry about dust,' he said, flicking a lampshade with his feather duster. 'Not an ancient queen like me.' He was very excited as he entered his tiny kitchen to check the refreshments he'd made for the impending occasion.

'So camp,' he said, looking in the hall mirror. He was dressed in bicycle gear: skin-tight black shorts, a black and red T-shirt and the thick white sports socks that jocks wear. He was very 1986 and, at the age of sixty-four, George took pride in being sexily dressed and up to date in both thought and fashion. Again he looked at his watch and then at the front door. Suddenly the doorbell rang and George felt as though it was tingling in his heart. A rush of nervousness at having advertised in the *Taranaki Herald* for all the world to see.

'Oh blast,' he said. He fumbled with the safety pin and card he'd written on but forgotten to pin to his T-shirt: George Crossett, New Plymouth Gay Men's Action Club.

'Stuff it,' he told himself. 'Why be nervous?'

The doorbell rang again, this time with urgency as if the person waiting could wait no longer to join a gay men's club. But George paused: it might be somebody who wanted to bash him up; you never knew these days. In Auckland queers got beaten just because the Homosexual Law Reform Bill was seeking freedom for homosexuals of sixteen. Bashings and a public hullabaloo about pederasty and Aids being spread by queers who wanted liberation to do it more openly.

'Blast them,' he said, opening the door. A good-looking man in his late thirties stood there, dressed in the sort of clothes one might wear in Paris or New York, but definitely not in New Plymouth.

'Good evening,' the man said in a voice etched with education. He had that seedy, naughty-man look of someone dissipated somehow, either by too much alcohol and fast living or... or... George didn't know what. Everything was happening so quickly, it was all so exciting. But the man's eyes; they were beautiful big dark eyes. George looked into them more closely and saw suffering.

'You won't bash me up, will you?' George asked, a big smile on his face. He was still holding his duster, purposefully posing with it as he beckoned in the man with the affected gestures a dowager might display with dinner guests.

'I've made these tags,' he said. 'A bit camp, but it's so we won't forget each other's names because this is the first meeting, and... and...' He stood back with a hand splayed over his heart and studied the visitor. 'I mean all two of us.' Then he stood up very straight and very proudly; George Crossett with his shoulders back and his head held up like a man receiving a medal for a lifetime dedicated to converting heathens. George Crossett being as camp as he wanted to be.

The stranger sat with his long legs crossed and thinking how dried-up and sun-tanned the creature in front of him was, like an elderly raisin or long-time nudist, 'Thank God, for that,' he thought. 'Someone decadent in New Plymouth.' He pulled out his cigarettes. 'Mind if I smoke?' he asked.

'As long as you offer me one. I'm so ancient, some more nicotine won't hurt me,' George said. 'And do we have a name, dear? Just so I can make a little name tag. Can I offer sherry? I'm afraid I haven't got proper glasses, and you look the sort who would notice.'

'Oh, I don't know,' the stranger said. 'I've drunk all sorts of things out of all sorts of vessels, if you know what I mean. Perfect deco apartment you've got.'

It was so nice to have someone so sophisticated and appreciative. George wished he did have crystal sherry glasses.

'Apartment?' he said. 'That does make a flat sound grand. I think you must be from Auckland.'

'Auckland? That big Suva. No, I'm not actually.'

'Or small Sydney. Depends how you look at it. So, no name?' George queried.

'Names are so boring,' the stranger said. 'You're George, and that makes no difference. What if I call you Dotty or Dixie instead of something as ho hum as George?'

'George, and that's it definitely. It's taken me a long life to like myself, and there's no mistaking my self-devotion these days. There's no need to be sarcastic about my... my...' He fumbled for the right word. 'Pedigree?' George felt a combination of disappointment and happiness; the former because he knew he could never become the lover of this handsome young thing, and the latter because he knew they would be friends. 'You're not a local boy, then?' he asked.

'I *am* a local... born and bred under Mount Egmont.'

'Well, you haven't been local for some time, dear. The mountain's now called Mount Taranaki.'

'I'm staying at the Hinemoa Hotel. I've been living in the world's largest city for the last umpteen years. I've been back a week and saw your advert.' He drained his glass and George immediately got up to fill it.

'I'd love to go to Cairo,' George said. 'The army boys reckoned it was the best place to be in the war. All those Arabs. I wish I could have an Arab.'

'Mexico City, actually. But I had an Egyptian lover, the Egyptian Consul's First Secretary. We met once a week in a bath house until...'

'Until?' George asked.

'Until the inevitable for a faggot.'

'Oh,' George sighed. 'That.' He got up and fetched some dainty savouries in an effort to avoid appearing disturbed at the very thought of that gay disease. Then he sat down and, with a turn of his head, decided not to even think about it; not after such a long life. Surely he would be spared this final indignity.

'In a way,' Garth said, 'you must be stronger than those of us who left places like New Plymouth and fled to gay ghettoes and thought we were being so very liberated by holding hands with our boyfriends. You stayed here and fought the battle in the front lines.'

'Bunch of stupid cunts if you ask me,' George said studying a savoury. 'We stayed and put up with a lot of crap. I knew someone who was too weak to defend himself when an agent provocateur caught him in a public toilet. He went to prison, where he had the best time of his life and learned what it was like to stand up for himself.'

'You?' Garth said.

'Might have been, but I want to know more about you. You show me just how provincial I am.'

'We've all been around, some in our minds and some geographically, but it's how you use it. I've met some tedious travellers,' Garth said.

'True,' George said. 'Hasn't everyone been around and done things? Sex, I mean. As if sex were so important, something to legislate against. Sex is so trivial, so natural. Oh, my dear, I've had a very long life indeed, and seen a lot of hypocrisy. But the Egyptian... let me live in a fantasy.'

'An Egyptian lover called Hamid. And a Mexican boyfriend, partner I think you now call them in New Zealand. His name was Alfonso. I...' Garth stopped because he wasn't sure how far he should go in divulging secrets, even to this person with whom he felt a cosy and trusting affinity.

'Now that I come to think of it, I had an Arab. A very, very long time ago. I wonder what happened to him? We used to do it in the back of his fruit van down at Ngamutu Beach.' The smell of oranges and bananas and semen wafted back to George. 'My God, I really am getting ancient. I can't remember the name of the man I taught how to perform fellatio.'

'Was he a New Plymouth man?'

'He became an expert at it, thanks to me.'

'I have a vague recollection of an Arab in New Plymouth. Or was that...?'

'No answer unless you tell me your name. No more secrets between us.'

'Garth Griffin at your orders, señor.'

'Oh, señor, how romantic!' George pulled his elastic bicycle pants at the crotch because they felt uncomfortable. He'd bought the smaller size on purpose, but it meant his balls often divided, one down one side of the elastic, one down the other. 'They owned the ZYX Fruit Shop in Devon Street. Arabs of some sort,' he said.

'I remember them. I used to go in there just because it was different. Even when I was a kid I recognised them as exotic. They used to make me think I was overseas and out of this dump. An old lady with enormous bosoms, and a pretty younger one, and there was a handsome man with really hairy arms and thick black hair. Of course it's been...'

'Donkey's years. You're not as young as you look then, my dear.'

'Fellatio with an Arab in a fruit van. How exciting! I think that's what kept me going back to my Egyptian for so many years. Fellatio's much more exciting than penetration.'

'Exactly,' George said. 'Oh, I wallow in fellatio.'

'Usually Arabs want to just screw you without foreplay, bang, bang, and that's very boring. I got tired of the men in Morocco.'

'It's my one regret that I never got out of this place. I should have gone to the world's largest city and had an Egyptian.'

'It sounds as if you did all right here.'

George could feel love emerging, gliding over him. That delicious sensation spreading from his perineum to his head within seconds. It fluttered around his heart as he downed the rest of his sherry.

'I don't think anyone else will come to my meeting,' he said. 'All the local queens go to Wellington on a long weekend, or else they'll be out cruising. I'm trying to get a club together where things don't have to be sordid, and then there's this whole homosexual law reform thing. Everyone in Auckland and Wellington's doing something against the bigots, but not in dear little New Plymouth, so I called this meeting and...'

'Perhaps you should have advertised it in the toilets. We've never had anywhere else to meet each other, and now its enculturated.'

'Enculturated. You could put it like that. At the Seaview Road toilets. What an excellent suggestion. If anyone ever opens a gay bar here, it'll have to be called the Seaview Road Toilets in honour of our only meeting place.'

'They're still there?' Garth said. 'I remember their particular stink. The same taps leaking, I suspect.'

'Even if the law reform goes through,' George said, 'us old queens... Toilets are like scent and lingerie are for straight men. They get excited when they touch lace and silk, so what's the difference with our desires?'

'You mean chlorine and concrete? Frankly, I think cruising toilets is ridiculous.'

Garth went to the window and parted the curtains. Outside, the half-moon and the yellow street lights cast an eerie combination of the natural and ersatz. Across the street stood a colonial church and the silhouette of a war memorial. Beyond that the Tasman, its great black expanse dotted with moonlit sparkles.

'Monuments for death or bravery?' he thought. His parents were dead. His child and Janine were dead. His lover was dead, and so were half of his friends. He looked at the dried-up man in the armchair enjoying his sherry and then turned back to the sea. The waves were constant; drawing up and drawing back, driven by the moon. You could swim out there and let the sea claim you rather than submitting to the horrors of a protracted death. End it definitively, like the Egyptian had arranged for his wife and himself in a suicide murder because they both had Aids. End it as Alfonso had done with Garth helping him: a syringe, some heroin, Alfonso laughing at a spelling mistake in his own suicide note. Alfonso's eyes as he died looking at the Porfirian ceiling.

'I'm getting morbid,' Garth said, turning to George. 'Tell me something funny. I didn't come here to get depressed.'

'I don't look like a French prostitute, do I?' George asked. 'I just wondered. The way you're looking at me.'

'Perhaps a New Plymouth one. Tell me something fascinating about your life here. What I missed out on by fleeing.'

'As I was saying, I was arrested in the Seaview Road toilets and spent years in prison on trumped-up charges, and as a result had the best years of my life with the most wonderful man in creation.' George went to the bureau drawer and pulled out a framed picture, which he held aloft like a trophy. 'Gorgeous, isn't he? If he hadn't dropped dead of a heart attack, I'd still be rapturously happy. It was a glorious time. He was a real man, my everything, and we had five wonderful years together. He died three weeks before I got out.

'The reason why no one else will come tonight,' he continued with a sudden bitterness, 'is because they saw the address and recognised it as my place.' He reached over and took two cigarettes from his guest's packet. 'Everybody knows me. I'm an institution in this dump. The effete homosexual. And no doubt when you've been here a while longer you'll feel the same about me. Someone to sneer at and avoid. "A tired sunburned queen" one of them called me not long ago, and she was only eighteen and hasn't seen anything. She thinks she can judge me on age and condition, but I could beat her hands down at survival.'

It still hurt, even at his age and with his belief that he was too tough to be touched by such silliness. George stood up and purposefully minced across the room to hand Garth a lit cigarette. He wanted to be camp. There were so many reasons to be. He wanted to know whether this young man could accept a camp and bitter old queer. If he didn't like it, he could piss off before any more time was wasted.

'They've got more freedom. We...'

'We?' George interrupted. 'We? My dear, you weren't even a sperm in the 1940s when I was floating around here trying to make sure I walked like a real man and didn't mince or lisp.'

'What was it like here for a homosexual in those days?' Garth asked.

'Oh, they've always done it here,' George replied. 'Whores, these New Plymouth men, but hypocrites. It was a blessing to meet an American after these New Plymouth drips. I used to do it with him, he was a serviceman from North Dakota, gorgeous, gorgeous. I can still smell and taste him. We did it in his tank at the race course. Can you imagine it? A tank going around and around the New Plymouth race course doing training exercises while there inside two homosexuals were sucking each other off. He had his hands blown off in the Philippines, and when I wrote to him, his mother replied saying I shouldn't write again because he'd married his childhood sweetheart.'

'Didn't she notice it was a man writing a love letter to her soldier son?' Garth asked.

'Of course she didn't. I signed it 'Matilda Crossett'. I think I even asked for silk stockings to make it look authentic. Frank La Verde. A real man. A real American. Absolutely yummy, and he ended up being forced to marry some half-wit because he had no hands.'

'What a tragic but fabulous story. You should write a novel,' Garth said.

'Oh, not with my bitterness. It would be like sucking lemons,' George insisted. 'Bitter. Bitter.' And then he laughed at his own drama and downed the remaining sherry.

'The happy times?' Garth asked, looking at the photo. 'This...'

'Benny. Benny Puhoi. Intelligent, witty, I could eulogise all evening.'

'That must have been...?' Garth said as an image of Monty distracted him from what he was saying.

'Look, darling, I don't know you from a bar of soap and, not wanting to be rude, I don't think being a homosexual is all that much fun especially when you've made yourself stay in this place for six decades because...'

There were a few moments of tense silence, each man in his reverie.

'Why don't *you* write a novel, dear?' George said sweetly, his mood lifting.

'Perhaps I haven't got time.'

'Time, dear! Before I went to prison I had enough time on my hands to write entire encyclopedias. It was prison that taught me how precious time is.'

'What about Frank?'

'A small pocket of happiness destroyed by a dishonourable discharge and that letter from his mother. If I'm bitter, I'm allowed to be. It's what this new generation doesn't understand. An old queen. Yes, true, but an old queen because she's had to fight for every liberty. These ones you see nowadays wearing earrings, well... It was us who suffered, and they don't understand that.'

'Well spoken,' Garth said. 'It was a struggle. I saw Quentin Crisp speak in San Francisco in 1978 and there were only about fifty men in the audience. The rest were all out being liberated. They didn't want to hear Crisp because he was a self-declared effeminate homosexual, and yet he helped liberate them. It's so easy to be liberated in a gay ghetto.'

Neither spoke for several seconds. George stared at the picture of Benny, and Garth watched the Tasman. Its surface looked like an old vinyl record, black and flat and glossy. It would be so easy to disappear into that nothingness. He shivered at the memories, deep, dark, black ones, of those two years nursing his partner through his illness. He saw in a dark recess in his mind Alfonso dead in their bed from the overdose of heroin. He watched himself kiss the dead man's lips then leave the apartment; down the marble staircase, Garth saw every step from that hideous night. He saw himself walking like a somnambulist about the streets of downtown Mexico City, creating an alibi so that the police would believe his story of it being a bonafide suicide.

'But don't you have time?' George asked him.

'Time?' Garth said. 'I have secrets.'

'Secrets are just things you're ashamed of,' George said, 'and you shouldn't be ashamed of anything in front of me.'

Garth looked at him. It was possible, in the profile, to imagine George as a twenty-year-old, his pants down around his knees with a Marine servicing him. He had that aura of someone who had always been sexy. 'Every homosexual has secrets,' Garth said sadly.

'Well, I've known a lot of homosexuals I wouldn't breathe a word to. Vicious queens,' George said. 'Vicious. You would tell them nothing. Nothing.'

'We're friends, aren't we?' Garth asked. 'I...'

'Of course we are, darling. Such an immediate rapport. Two very old friends. I feel it.' George went back to the bureau, poured them both more sherry and put the photo of Benny back in the drawer. This cosiness and friendship was like being back in prison. He looked over his shoulder and their eyes met.

'We're the same,' Garth said. 'The same person almost. What do you suppose all this is about?'

'I'm not sure. Are you?'

'Love of life, I think,' Garth said. 'And the fact of suffering. I can see that you've loved it all and have had a prick of a time too. I can see that in your bravado. But you're an old man in a twenty-year-old's outfit, and your eyes tell me you've suffered. Nothing can hide that.'

'We suffer because we're homosexuals,' George said.

'No,' Garth replied, 'not by exclusion. Everyone in this world suffers. But we have our own line of suffering, which creates our culture. Like Palestinians or American Blacks, each group is shaped by its own form of discontentment.'

'Goodness,' George said, 'I must be inebriated. What sort of music do you like? I haven't got anything too sophisticated. Do you like waltzes?'

'God, I do get more and more morbid,' Garth said. 'I must stop it. I feel as if I'm responsible for the entire twentieth century, or that I'm the only one to have been given an unfair deal of worries and suffering.'

'To suffering and getting through it with a smile on your face,' George said holding up his fifth sherry.

'Could I swim to the horizon?' Garth said, looking out of the window. 'Look at that sea. So enticing. So fabulous.'

'There is no horizon, not till you get to Australia.'

'And I don't want to go there.'

'And would you swim back if there was a horizon to swim to?' George asked, realising as he did that he hadn't had an intimate conversation for years. 'You've got a secret. Please tell me,' he said with tenderness as he looked at the beautiful man in front of him. 'Let us be real, real friends.'

*

Neddy Bouzikis sighed with relief at the realisation that he'd made the right decision after all. The terrible feeling that he'd been wrong to leave Beirut eased away as soon as the Air New Zealand craft left the magnificence of Sydney and flew out over the Tasman. That teal-blue and green colour saturating everything in the aircraft, from the carpet to the seat covers to the stewards' uniforms, the colours of a nation he never thought he'd belonged to suddenly made him sniff with emotion. The woman next to him was reading a New Zealand newspaper with a headline screaming about the nation being sold off to foreigners: forests, fisheries, banks. Neddy had been out of Beirut for forty-eight hours, and the last headlines he'd seen there had announced the deaths of seventeen Lebanese villagers in Southern Lebanon, blown up by the Israelis. A steward minced down the aisle with a bottle of white wine as he repeated: 'Wine service, ladies and gentlemen, wine service.' Neddy opened his eyes and nodded to the steward to pour some more wine. The woman reading the newspaper was a Maori, the first he'd seen for twenty years. He sneaked another look at her. He wished he could say something to her in Maori, ask her what it meant to be a Maori. The Greek part of himself he understood because Greeks were as mad as the Lebanese, but the Maori aspect?

'Jesus,' he thought. 'From Beirut to Whangamomona. I'd better get a Maori dictionary at the airport.'

'Noisy, isn't it?' the woman seated next to him said.

'Are you a Kiwi?' he asked, staring at her closely.

'Yes' the woman replied. She had the big brown eyes of a Lebanese woman, the sort you saw in pictures ululating at heaven after their homes had been devastated.

'What part of New Zealand are you from?' he asked. He realised what a sight he must have presented with the bags under his eyes from the war and twenty four hours of travelling, and then to lurch at her like that. But he was used to strangers starting in immediately without the preliminaries of soft talk: who had died and how. It was the sort of conversation he'd had endlessly with customers in the ZYX Delicatessen.

'I live in London,' she said. 'I'm going home for a tangi.'

'Where are you from?' she said. ' Are you a tourist?'

'Sort of,' he said, smiling.

'I haven't been home for eleven years,' the woman continued. 'My two kids were both born in England, and I'm sure no one will even recognise me, I've got so old and fat. My hubby reckons I speak like a Cockney.'

'What's a tangi?' he asked, with only a vague memory of the word.

'A tangi's a funeral. My granny died and we're all going home to have a good cry and say goodbye to her, together, the Maori way.'

'I don't know anything about Maoris,' Neddy confessed.

'You'll learn,' the woman said, smiling. 'Actually,' she added, 'when I saw you I thought you were one of us. A Maori.'

Full circle. Neddy saw it as he looked at his splayed hands. You come full circle. Fact is stranger than fiction. You never know what's just around the corner. When one door closes... The clichés describing what was happening to him buzzed in his mind. He looked at the ragged green coastline of the country he had run away from because he was a queer Lebanese. Far below him, huge white waves crashed on black sand. His throat contracted and tears began sliding down his cheeks.

✳

It was one of those Taranaki cottages with a verandah and wisteria, settled-looking, but still with a hint of the late-nineteenth-century struggle that had wrenched such civilisation from bush and swamp. A charming, rather run-down house with a rusty iron roof and vast sash windows that looked out over lush paddocks to the black sand and the ever-changing Tasman. The breeze off the sea cooled the hot day with crisp spurts. Idyllic. Sylvan. A prize Garth Griffin fully appreciated as one he deserved for having cared for Alfonso through two years of horrible illness.

'Great,' he said, proudly looking at the pile of uprooted weeds. 'I've done it.'

Two rows of radishes and two of lettuce, the earth's smell thick and pungent. He breathed in like a sick man intent on recovery. The clear day and the hours of gardening had obliterated his worries. For once there weren't those images of Alfonso that often seeped into his mind. He'd just smoked a joint and now he looked up at the sun with a thin, elevated feeling penetrating his head. A plane left its trail of vapour as it soared above Mount Taranaki.

'God,' he thought. 'I don't understand this disease at all, but for this moment, these few weeks or months or maybe even years, I'm really grateful to be here, to be alive.' He didn't hear the car come down the gravel road. He had his eyes closed, the sun coating him as he lay in his old shorts, with pictures floating in and out of his mind.

'Hello, darling,' George Crossett sang as he sauntered into the garden. He skipped lightly over a log, his arms in a welcoming gesture. Despite feeling annoyed by the sudden intrusion, Garth laughed at his friend dressed up in youthful sports attire.

'Rex has ventured with me,' George said, indicating the man who followed him. 'We're probably disturbing this solitude you keep harping on about, but we don't want you to get morbid all alone out here in Okato, do we?'

'Any excuse to come to the country houses of the rich and famous,' Garth said. In the glare, with the sun behind him, the man called Rex looked like a Mexican. For a cruel second he saw Alfonso approaching.

'Gidday,' Rex said, extending a hand. 'George has told me all about you.'

'God,' George said. 'I used to dream about days like this when I was in prison. You've got no idea what it's like to be locked up when you know everyone else is sunbathing.' He ripped off his T-shirt and carefully positioned his body to absorb the sun.

'I know what it's like to be locked up. I spent twelve years in Mexico City.'

'No you don't, darling. You've been very privileged, thank you. Rex, this man was a professor in Mexico City and he puts himself down the whole time, as if he were a peasant.'

'Please,' Garth thought, 'leave me alone.' He wanted to plant the spinach seedlings or walk to the beach and collect driftwood for the winter fires.

'Well,' George said in a more serious tone. 'This is no idle visit. We need you to help because I can't do it all by myself. That bitch

Dorothy Lewis has a petition going in New Plymouth against the Homosexual Law Reform Bill.'

'Go and get some beer out of the fridge, Lady Ottoline,' Garth said. 'Make yourself useful as a domestic instead of all this political hoo-ha. The dope's on the kitchen table.'

'Well, it's a good thing I was trained by harsh prison warders to tend to everyone's wishes.' George smiled, honoured at being attributed with the campness that an association with Lady Ottoline Morrell entailed.

'I thought you were a Mexican,' Garth said to Rex when George had made his exaggerated exit. 'Same colour, same smile.'

'Mostly Maori,' Rex said. He had a half-beard and a naughty grin. He turned, as if too shy to speak, and wandered to the fence where he looked across the fields and bush towards Mount Taranaki.

'He does look like a slightly seedy Alfonso,' Garth thought as a hint of unaccustomed sex adrenalin flickered.

Rex returned, his hands in the pockets of his baggy, paint-splattered shorts, but he kept his silence. An awkward few minutes passed while George was in the house.

'It's probably fuck thinking,' Garth thought. He closed his eyes against his first impulse of using eye contact to cruise the handsome Maori. The thought of having to say, 'Look, there's something I should tell you.' No. Silly. Embarrassing. It was better to remain intact, your own person, to have a wank and forget about handsome brown men with washboard stomachs and gold earrings.

George came back into the garden and continued his story. 'Tomorrow Dorothy's setting up a table outside the library, so my informants tell me, to get signatures against us homosexuals.' He used strong sibilants so he sounded like a snake speaking.

'How ridiculous,' Garth thought, 'how inane, to have one term to describe men who had sex with other men, men who had sex with both men and women, women who loved women…'

'I want to do something about these bigots, and I demand your help.' George poured beer and handed glasses around.

Garth felt his heart sink as a vague fear seeped through what he now appreciated was but a thin veneer of happiness and rural equanimity. This was not his battle. There were a million others qualified to fight this one. He had experienced too much drama and wanted nothing but the peace of a cottage surrounded by sea and paddocks.

'Drink, smoke and be merry,' he said, unable to think of anything else that was witty enough to disguise his mood. 'For we may die tomorrow.'

'Well, maybe not tomorrow,' Rex said, smiling. 'It's a gorgeous fucking day, and the forecast is the same for tomorrow, so wait it out.'

Garth watched Rex, who was sucking on the joint, and a feeling of horror went through him. He was angry at how quickly all that hard-earned peace had vanished. Here was the intrusion of a handsome man and all the insecurities that entailed. He realised that he was putting his head in the sand in a pathetic attempt to live normally. He took the joint offered by Rex, drew in and handed it to George, who sniffed at it in a Lady Ottoline simulation of smelling roses.

'Damn these anti-homosexual people,' George said. 'We've always been persecuted, and don't I know it! And now with Aids they want to put us in concentration camps.'

'Us?' Garth asked.

'Well, those with HIV,' George replied.

'I can't go back to Sydney,' Rex said, as if losing the chain of their conversation and continuing with another in his head. 'I can't bring myself to walk past the hospital where they're all dying of Aids. I get so angry. Who the fuck put the disease in the water supply in a bath house? The CIA? I wanted...'

'To come back to this?' Garth said. He felt just as he had when Alfonso was really ill and there was no escaping the situation.

'What do you mean?' Rex asked.

'Nature.'

'I just had to get out of Sydney.'

'Are you from Taranaki?'

'Wellington, but I've got a sister here.'

'The Jews in Germany didn't believe they'd be incarcerated,' George interrupted. 'This is our chance to get the law changed. If we don't, people will hide their HIV status and spread the disease.'

'They don't want to legalise us because they think homosexuality's a disease. And now we have Aids, they think they have a good reason,' Rex said.

'True,' George replied, turning to Garth. 'We've decided you can't isolate yourself too much, darling. I mean, Okato!'

'Help us, eh,' Rex said. 'You've got the experience for doing things like this.'

'For years I fought for social justice in Mexico, but I don't want to be involved here. I'm telling you straight. I need...' He didn't want to speak. He couldn't. He saw Alfonso well, happy, walking down the Avenida Juarez in his blue Italian suit.

'If Mexico was so wonderful, why did you leave it?' Rex asked.

*

The Salvation Army Citadel squatted in the middle of New Plymouth, one of those stolid buildings that could have been lifted from a provincial British city and plonked down at the other end of the world for the same sort of people to pray in. So dour, so austere; Garth shivered at it now as much as he did at the memory of it as a child. There was no adornment inside either. In one corner stood an ancient organ that looked as though it had droned away at endless services for a century. Gloomy curtains were draped halfway across the platform, where a table bore a vase of lugubrious white lilies, slightly yellowed at the edges. Dozens of dark wooden chairs had been set out in stiff rows, but only about forty people were clustered in seemingly haphazard groupings. A plump, greying, tweedy woman with a worn-out face crossed the stage and leaned into the microphone.

'I'm Dorothy Lewis,' she said. 'Welcome. We meet this evening as citizens concerned for our integral values as much for the safety of our children. Our objective is to get a petition signed by one million New Zealanders, a third of our population, to stop Parliament passing the proposed Homosexual Law Reform Bill, which would legalise sexual acts between homosexuals, homosexuals aged from...' she paused as if the next word were too disgusting to say in such company ...sixteen.' She shuddered, then looked around at her audience, from one group seated on the far left to another, on the right-hand side of the hall. Back and forth her head swung like a sideshow clown's.

Garth watched her, the whole ambience of dourness and hatred, of repression and loathing, seething inside him. He felt as if his life had turned sour and was unavoidably complicated by a fatal disease and its moral ramifications. It couldn't be washed off, forgotten, paid to leave or commanded away. The farmhouse offered him no escape. There was only one solution and it drummed in his brain relentlessly: an invitation to death. He should do it, and quickly, to avoid this idiocy of suffering and aloneness. 'You were right, Alfonso,' he murmured to his dead lover. 'Why suffer? Just do it. Be brave enough to do it.'

Dorothy Lewis raised her arms, like a Southern evangelist. 'This evening we embark on our plan to halt the evil of homosexuality. We want to halt the rot, the decline of moral standards in our country.' She took a gulp of water as if her few sentences had exhausted her. When she had replaced her glass, she turned and called upon an emaciated-looking man in a Salvation Army uniform to speak to the audience.

'The churches of New Zealand,' he droned, 'are against the legalisation of perversion.' Those in the audience, largely elderly, middle class and, except for Rex, exclusively Pakeha, craned their necks to look at the speaker, who seemed to crouch behind the podium. Immorality. God. Aids. Filth. Disease. Pederasty. He went quickly down a list of horrors.

'I will ask you,' he continued, 'to stand and pray for the cause, for our commission from Jesus to stop this heinous presumption by our elected government to legalise the aberration of homosexuality.' Throats were cleared and chairs scraped as people stood, an elderly congregation shuffling and moving to stand and ask the Lord for whatever the Salvation Army man had ordered. The whole hall was standing except for George and his entourage.

'Lord, we ask forgiveness for those who suffer from this disease, which has afflicted so many in our modern society. We pray that these men, who have taken a path contrary to Your wishes and designs, and who have followed the road devised by the Devil, may be saved in Your name and in the name of moral righteousness.'

'What about lesbians! Lesbians don't want to be left out, you sexist!' a woman's voice shouted from the entrance.

The Salvation Army man ignored the interjection and continued in his funereal tone: 'This petition is a signal to those unfortunate men whose perverse practices traverse the moral code established by common sense, social righteousness and the Bible, that they will be saved.'

'Lesbians are perverse too!' the woman at the door yelled.

'Yeah, lesbians!' another voice added. 'Lesbians are criminals! Don't forget us!'

The confused audience didn't know which way to turn. A woman in a pavlova hat sitting directly in front of Garth kept fidgeting with something at the back of her neck, as if the clothing label was irritating her wrinkles. She seemed more preoccupied with her scratching than the spectacle.

'Oh, be quiet!' Dorothy Lewis ordered in her role as headmistress. 'There are those among us here tonight who have personal witness to the tragedy of homosexuality. As many of you know, I have worked with Exodus for over twenty years and, with the help of Jesus Christ, have been able to turn many, many men with this affliction into normal heterosexuals who have taken their place in society. Tonight I call on one of them, Michael Maxwell, to talk to you.' She clapped enthusiastically as if a famous singer were about to cross the stage and start crooning.

A tall, thin man appeared from behind the curtain and stood with his hands clasped in front of him in pious fashion.

'Homosexuality is a psychological condition that can be fixed,' Dorothy said. 'I invite you to listen to the testament of such a man.'

Maxwell was probably about forty, but he had that indeterminate look of a person so unsure of his own mind and body that he could have passed for either thirty or fifty. And no moral miracles could possibly have changed his campy-looking face.

'I'm a teacher,' he said. 'I'm not ashamed to stand in front of you tonight and say that when I was younger I was a homosexual. Dorothy and the people from Exodus helped me find the Lord, and so I was changed into a man who can now hold up his head. I have never married because I felt that that would be to avoid other responsibilities that the Lord has given me. I have dedicated my life to helping in Exodus because it is of the utmost importance that we keep our values as a nation. New Zealand is blessed with everything fine, as we all know. But there are evils, there are temptations.' His voice was relentless, a mixture of ingratiation and whingeing. 'We want to emulate America in so many things. We buy American cars and products, we watch American television and listen to their music. And now we want to have American organisations like Gay Liberation. This rot, this Americanisation of love, has caused Aids...'

'Oh enough!' George shouted. 'We've had enough of this rubbish.' He stood too quickly, with too much anger, so that his chair fell backwards. 'You may have stopped having sex with other men, but that doesn't stop what goes on in your brain. America? America? Damn it, they saved us from the Japs!'

'Now, now!' a man yelled from the front row. 'None of this. We don't want your sort here tonight. This is our meeting.'

'Whose meeting?' George responded. 'It's a public meeting. Get your facts right.'

'You men are impostors!' a woman yelled.

'What about us lesbians? We're impostors too!'

'You ought to be ashamed of yourselves!'

The hall buzzed like a swarm of angry bees. It was as if the audience had been waiting, pent up for decades, to get everything off their chests about what they considered was wrong with their country. This atmosphere of rage in the Salvation Army Citadel allowed them to voice their hatreds.

The woman in a hat that looked like a pavlova stared at George, then she suddenly realised that here was a homosexual, the public enemy she had always hated but had learned only now to recognise. Her gaze swung from George to Garth, and a further horror became apparent: that she was sitting in front of them and might get Aids from the germs they were breathing.

Dorothy Lewis bellowed from the podium: 'We all have our emotions on this issue but I would kindly ask those here tonight who do not support our cause to leave. They were not invited.'

'This is not a trial,' a woman in George's contingent shouted. 'The disease is spread from ignorance. My own son died from Aids, and I know how it's spread. We must begin by understanding.'

'Let's discuss this humanely,' an Anglican vicar said. 'Please, a proper debate with rational questions and answers.'

'This is not an open meeting,' Dorothy said. 'We're not here to listen to advocates for homosexual law reform. There is but one answer. God's answer.'

'I have something to say,' Garth said, slowly getting to his feet.

'Not now...' Dorothy said.

'Let him,' the vicar interjected. 'If he speaks calmly, let him.'

Garth stood with his arms up as if he were speaking from a hill top above a large crowd.

'Enough, please, this is our meeting.' Dorothy spluttered.

An elderly man who looked as if he had served in the British Indian Army stood up and shook his fist at the vicar. He had one of those moustaches one associates with ruddy faced colonels racing around the Punjab in the 1930's in the service of Empire.

'You Anglicans, you've destroyed wholesome religion for us.'

'Disease is disease,' Garth shouted above the hubbub. 'Cancer, TB, heart attacks...' He paused, seeing instantly that rationalism couldn't work in the face of fundamentalism. It wasn't possible to behave like an academic in such a situation, and he tried to inject some passion. 'I want to say publicly that...' But he was given no time to finish because the lesbian at the door put her fingers to her mouth and whistled shrilly.

'Don't bother, Garth,' Rex yelled. 'The girls are coming in.'

A dozen lesbians, shrouded in black robes, marched into the hall, chanting, 'Save us from our sins.' A shocked silence in the audience was soon replaced by a furious buzzing, this time tinged with alarm.

'We are the sinners. We seek forgiveness for being women with black souls and black knowledge.' The troupe of black-clad sisters made their way slowly down the aisle towards the podium, twisting, turning, surrealistic. 'Flog us! We are lesbians! Homosexuals! We are sinners!'

Suddenly they produced small bags from beneath their robes and, with the slow, sweeping movements of a Greek chorus, scattered handfuls of white ashes at the audience and over themselves. 'We are vile sinners, adulteresses and lesbians!'

'No!' Dorothy Lewis shrieked. 'No! This is an abomination!' But there was no conviction in her voice; her mind seemed devoid of its authoritative pragmatism.

Garth stood with his hands still raised, his mind a spinning mixture of excitement and praise at this extraordinary rendition of something he associated with Argentinian avant-garde theatre. The pavlova-hatted woman was making dusting movements at her head, but she couldn't take her eyes off the riveting spectacle.

The lesbians wound their way onto the podium and obscured the overwhelmed committee. The Salvation Army man attempted to talk to the women but was told to sit down, and when he didn't, a spectre manoeuvred him towards the curtains where he stood with his hands twisting around each other. The tallest black-shrouded creature took the microphone from the terrified but compliant Dorothy Lewis.

It was the theatre of the absurd from beginning to end. Garth was utterly absorbed by it, the details, the brilliance; this was the most thrilling thing that had happened to him since he'd come back to New Zealand. Revolution in Latin America; it was here in front of him in his own country. He turned to Rex and hugged him. 'What fabulous lesbians,' he said.

'They're from Wellington,' Rex explained. 'You can rely on the girls to do what the boys can't muster, eh!'

'We must flog ourselves, and go to hell for this tragedy of being homosexuals,' the tall lesbian intoned eerily into the microphone. 'You are right, you normal people, we're evil and deserve no justice! Flog us! Kill us! Treat us like you did the Jews and the witches and the infidels!'

✳

Neddy Bouzikis had slept for almost twenty-four hours after his arrival in New Plymouth and felt invigorated by the cool sea breeze. He felt like walking swiftly, even running; everything that had been sluggish and debilitating had changed and he was amazed at how his spirits had lifted. From his hotel room he marvelled at the view of what he had learned was now called Mount Taranaki.

Striding along Devon Street, he recalled the stifling heat and filth of Beirut, and he breathed in deeply as he walked in the direction of where the ZYX Fruit Shop had once stood. After twenty years he could barely remember the lay-out of the city. He paused outside the Duchess Pantry, which he remembered for having sold excellent cakes and pastries. The same woman, he thought, serving the same provincial delicacies. The collection of wares in the window could have been the very ones from twenty years ago: fairy cakes smothered in hundreds and thousands, neenish tarts and lamingtons. There were even those jam things covered in desiccated coconut and glacé cherries. It was a window of culinary relics and he giggled at its cultural significance.

At the corner, he found himself standing next to a Maori man. 'Excuse me,' he said. 'Can you direct me to the intersection of Kowhy and Devon Streets?'

'Kowhai,' the man said, politely correcting Neddy's mispronunciation. 'Yeah, sure, mate, over there, just past the BNZ.'

Neddy crossed the road, his eyes on the Maori as he went up the street holding a child's hand and disappeared into a building. He couldn't help laughing at everything. It was so odd to have experienced so much, to have been so involved in the daily politics of life in these streets and to return two decades later as a tourist, stranger and Greek-Maori. A feeling of elation surged through him because the sun was shining and the breeze was pleasant. Life, he realised as he watched a blind man with a white stick nimbly manoeuvring down the street, had taught him to treat each event as calmly as possible and to appreciate the humour that might arise in any situation.

It was fitting that the fruit shop had been replaced by a modern building. Neddy was a man who believed in change and progress, and he didn't stop long to reminisce about what had been merely wood and concrete. His mother, his father... he still saw them as that... the Lebanese ones, shuffled about in his memory for a few moments before they petered out. He had a few vague thoughts of his Greek and Maori parents, but then he shrugged his shoulders and reminded himself that a man of his advanced years and long experience didn't need to weep and gnash his teeth about useless sentimentalities. His only serious wish was that Alex could have shared this invigorating and somewhat hilarious experience with him. And only for a moment did he think about Betty. 'Betty, Betty' he said to himself with some humour. A few years previously, a Sydney based Lebanese in Beirut had told him she'd raised seven children and had become a millionairess by founding a chain of boutiques throughout Australia called 'Elvira Eliveras'.

'So much for the ZYX Fruit Shop,' he said, and carried on down

Devon Street and turned left towards the library. He paused to avoid being hit by a boy on a bicycle, then he noticed a big hand-painted sign. 'My goodness,' he thought, 'the cakes haven't changed, but attitudes have.'

Three men sat behind a desk that had been set up on the footpath. One was a Maori about thirty years old, quite handsome, with gold earings reflecting in the sun. A Pakeha man was seated next to him. The third, a rather aged, suntanned man, stood up to adjust the sign, which proclaimed them to be gay men soliciting support for the Homosexual Law Reform Bill. Neddy's heart missed a beat. The man he was staring at was wearing a tight pair of shorts, despite being in his mid-sixties. And his tight T-shirt showed off his half-sagging titties. Neddy dredged his memory for several seconds before a vision emerged of his fruit van in the 1960s. A younger version of the man appeared, dressed in a drab outfit; a man who had hated himself but was so keen for a romp in the back of the van amongst the nectarines and bananas.

Neddy walked closer, the skin on his arms feeling chilly. His mind clicked, searched, went through the files of decades: 'Excuse me,' he asked. 'Are you George Crossett?'

*

It was about the fifth time that Rex and Garth had been in each others' company. It was a Wednesday night towards the middle of April and the first real chilliness of the changing seasons came in off Mount Taranaki. The group had been at a campaign strategy meeting all evening where they'd planned a march up Devon Street in support of the Homosexual Law Reform Bill.

'I'll drop you off at your place,' Garth said to Rex.

'Why don't you drop me at your place?'

'What?' Garth snapped.

'How did you get to be an intellectual if you can't hear properly?'

Rex asked. Garth was learning to enjoy that brutal Kiwi sense of humour. That sharp way of making a joke out of other people's foibles, but this time it did hurt.

'Get in,' Rex said. 'And drive to your place.'

They travelled in silence through the empty city streets, Garth's mind a mixture of anxiety and anger. 'You asked me the first time we met why I didn't stay in Mexico if it was so wonderful there, and I never told you,' Garth said eventually. 'Well, I'll tell you now since you seem so intent on being interested in me despite my being a prick to you. If I seem grumpy sometimes and distant, then it's because I feel fucked over. My child, his mother, Alfonso, Hamid my Egyptian lover, they all died of the disease. I killed them.'

'Oh, please. You killed them? Come on. I know all this and I'm sorry. George already told me. I'm really sorry. I really am. But this crap about killing them, come on.'

'The pain of losing them was so great that... that...'

'Look at me,' Rex said.

'I'm driving.'

'Then pull over, and look at me.'

Garth stopped the car, but left the engine idling.

'Don't you like me?' Rex asked.

For Garth, it was again one of those moments for truth, and on cue the stills from other important moments returned in full colour to remind him of the difficulty of this painful occasion. He looked at Rex but remained silent. The images of Monty, of Alfonso, of Hamid, of Janine, of his friend Thomas, of Enrique, of Franco, all of them; the list was longer than he'd realised and with that realisation was the thought that his life had been long enough to incorporate a whole litany of occasions in which truth had been made manifest at painful moments.

'You're an interesting and intelligent man. That's why I asked to go to your place,' Rex said. 'I'm really interested in you, in your company, in your body. Is it because I'm not well educated?' Garth laughed.

George Crossett had the same hang ups about never having been out of New Zealand, and he'd expressed that neurosis to Garth, squeezing it into their conversations, as if it were a major impediment to a successful friendship.

'Is it because I'm a Maori?'

'Oh, shut up, Rex. Didn't you hear me?' Garth said. 'I'm fucked up. I've had my life fucked up through Aids. Through losing literally everybody I loved in my life within five years. I've got the fucking virus myself. No, I am not a happy chappie!'

Rex took Garth's hand in his and stroked it. It was perhaps the first intimate touch Garth had had in the twelve months since Alfonso had died, and the tears formed behind his eyes.

'I'm saying that as much as I like you and am attracted to you, I don't want to get involved,' Garth said.

'This sounds like an American television show where they get all introverted and mushy about problems,' Rex said.

'Yes, it is. I have fears and emotions and sometimes those corny shows portray the reality of the way people think and react.'

'So what does that mean for us?'

'It means that I don't want to involve anyone in my disease and have them suffer what I went through with Alfonso and the others.'

'I could say exactly the same thing. You don't know what I went through in Sydney. You have never asked me what my history is because you are so concerned with your own, rightly so, but I have a history also.' A cat leapt onto the car bonnet and startled both men. The big yellow eyes peering into the windscreen like a witch's.

'You're right,' Garth said. 'I have become self absorbed and selfish. And I dare say I'll be like this for some time which is why I have come to this wilderness, this countryside, to think. To heal in my own way.'

The cat sat on the bonnet, looking in. 'A black cat,' Garth said.

'It's a cat. Black, white, yellow. Forget the introspection.'

'Introspection?' The images became stronger: Alfonso was silently weeping while Garth stood with unsteady hands filling the vial with heroin. The Egyptian said in his sexy accent that he was going to arrange for an accident that would knock out him and his diseased wife.

'So what do you do about it?' Rex said.

'Actually,' Garth said as the cat leapt off the bonnet, 'I don't think I am like that. I was just caught by circumstances. My life was fine until Aids. I had problems, but certainly no more than anybody else and I had wonderful happiness...' He paused because the first tears were flowing from the memories of a life which had once been filled with promise and expectations. 'But...' he continued. Alfonso was saying something in Spanish in Garth's mind.

'And so no more happiness for Garth Griffin, the handsome and intelligent man who had all the tragedies that no one else can ever possibly experience?'

'Don't knock me, Rex,' Garth said. Alfonso's words were staccato, incoherent.

'We're just talking. I think you're very fuckable.'

'Thanks. But I feel that part of my life might be over.' He looked at the night through the driver's window and shook his head to clear his dead lover's words.

'Bull shit. What's the old song? Pick yourself up, dust yourself off, and get on with it. I'm doing that. You can do it with me. Come on, please.'

'Yes, but... You see...' Garth remembered a student he'd taught who, no matter how gentle a remark about an essay's problems, would get absolutely defensive.

'Well,' Rex said. 'I know drama. I can be a drama queen myself, not that I would ever put that awful term on you. Yeah, you've suffered. Horrible things. But the sun does come out. I'm a trained nurse. I cared for my two best friends in Sydney, and when that all finished I was so exhausted I came back to New Zealand. I want to heal, and I'd like a nice man to do it with.'

The invitation was irresistible and for two or three moments it's warmth permeated Garth's mind before it soured. 'Which is what I mean. This disease is exhausting. It changes the parameters of love and sex and living and I can't find the wherewithal to go through with sex let alone relationships. It's too complicated and I just want to grow lettuces. To tend my garden.'

'So you want to be lonely?'

'If you want a fuck, I can drop you off at the Seaview Road toilets. You can find some suburban man who's told his wife he's going out for a drink with his mates.'

'Drive,' Rex said. 'To your place.'

Garth's mind echoed with Alfonso's words as he drove along the roads from New Plymouth to his farm house. The darkness was flecked with spasmodic patches of light from farm house windows.

'There is happiness,' Rex said.

'I know,' Garth replied. 'I've known so much happiness in my life. There is healing, I know. It's...'

'It's possible. Hey, I'll help you weed your garden.'

As they reached the lane to the farm house a white Holden with a red stripe emerged and sped away.

'I don't know that vehicle,' Garth said.

'Wrong road, probably,' Rex said.

'We can talk some more about what all this means, why I'm afraid,' Garth said as he parked outside the house. 'I have to know your history. I need to know what you have been through. I'm sorry... I... If...' He sighed with a mixture of anticipation and anxiety. Then Alfonso's words, the ones Garth hadn't been able to decipher just a few minutes previously, were there quite clearly in his mind. He saw Alfonso standing in their living room in Mexico City. Alfonso waved his arm at him playfully in a gesture which signified both goodwill and goodbye. Again Alfonso repeated his words and again he waved. Garth looked at Rex and smiled and took his hand.

'More talk?' Rex said. 'Is that really what you need? Or just some loving?'

They were on the verandah, about to go into the house. 'Come here,' Rex said. There was no moon, no lights. 'So. Where does this leave us, professor?' Rex whispered, brushing Garth's face with soft kisses. 'Come on, kiss me. I've been waiting for you since that first time when I ate you up with my eyes in the garden and you didn't respond.'

They went into the living room, Garth fumbling for the light switch because Rex was holding him tightly. Garth was giggling, searching for the light. His hand on the wall, his fingers touching something slimy.

'Fuck!' he said. 'What...?'

The light flooded the room and a sense of violence reared up. The room had been completely trashed. On the wall above the slashed sofa was daubed the words DIRTY AIDS FAGGOTS EAT SHIT and smeared over the walls were splashes of piss and shit.

✳

George was ecstatic that the party was going to be held in what he now referred to as his apartment. 'Flat' was definitely out as a term of reference to his abode now that he had such wonderful and sophisticated friends as Garth Griffin and Neddy Bouzikis. He looked around his living room, a haven of peace and loveliness, which would soon be the scene of the wild party he'd planned in honour of the passing of the Homosexual Law Reform Bill. *'All'erta! All'erta! Abb'etta zingara!'* he sang in a falsetto accompaniment to the opera blasting from his stereo. 'A new New Zealand.' He lifted the needle from the record and put it back a few grooves so that he could again hear the soprano rejoicing in his favourite refrain from Il Trovatore. *'All'erta! All'erta! Abb'etta zingara!'*

Food was displayed on the formica table in his kitchen. It looked glorious, the madeira cake and the stuffed mushrooms. But best of all was that fabulous Arabic concoction with the name he had the same difficulty in pronouncing as the frantic refrains from the opera.

'*All'erta!*' he sang as he sniffed Neddy's hommos.

God,' he said, 'it feels so good to be able to sing opera without thinking it might get me arrested. Us poor, poor queens, for so many centuries denied our pleasures!'

On the wall in front of him was a picture of Mount Taranaki, which he stared at as he reached into a cupboard for the bottle of sherry. The huge, handsome flanks of that monstrous mountain. So many decades of admiring it. So many tortures endured in its presence, each like the ice axes that climbers stuck in the flanks of that wily old mountain.

'And there you still are.' He saluted the mountain. 'And me too,' he said as he downed a mouthful of the deliciously sickly sherry. 'Still alert, still surviving.'

He bent over the table and stuck his finger in the delicious dip he'd come to adore since Neddy had first made it for him. 'Hmmmm, hmmiss, homos, oh something or other,' he said in a pickled hiss. He licked his finger with the creamy substance smeared over it and closed his eyes in satisfaction.